THE CRYSTAL ALCHEMIST

The Silver Order
Book 2

by Ella Leon

ARE YOU SIGNED UP FOR DRAGONBLADE'S BLOG?

You'll get the latest news and information on exclusive giveaways, exclusive excerpts, coming releases, sales, free books, cover reveals and more.

Check out our complete list of authors, too!

No spam, no junk. That's a promise!

Sign Up Here

www.dragonbladepublishing.com

Dearest Reader;

Thank you for your support of a small press. At Dragonblade Publishing, we strive to bring you the highest quality Historical Romance from some of the best authors in the business. Without your support, there is no 'us', so we sincerely hope you adore these stories and find some new favorite authors along the way.

Happy Reading!

CEO, Dragonblade Publishing

Additional Dragonblade books by Author Ella Leon

The Silver Order Series
The Sapphire Heiress (Book 1)
The Crystal Alchemist (Book 2)

PROLOGUE

November 1, 1891, Somewhere Among the Norwegian Mountains

THEO PIERCE LOADED his horse with weapons, every one he could think of. If that wasn't enough, he had a gun at his waist, as well as one strapped to his shoulders, and three throwing knives encircled his ankle.

His two guards had come prepared too. With them at his side, he felt unstoppable. They were his most capable guards and his closest friends. They'd die for Theo and Theo would die for them. He might very well have to. In London these days, they had more enemies than friends.

"Are you all right, sir?" Lawrence looked over his horse and pulled at his peppered beard. "Tell us what we can expect ahead."

"We just want to be prepared," Grice put in, sadness pulling his eyes. The strongest of all his men and with the battle scars to prove it, he never questioned their missions.

Theo went still in his work. He didn't know what was to come, who might die or who might live. Members of the Silver Order were sometimes privileged with that information. But not this time. Tonight, he only knew one thing: the steward of Whitestone Manor was dead. Not just that, he had been murdered.

"I can't tell you with any certainty, but bodies will no doubt line the path ahead." He didn't see a point in trying to minimize it. If they were going to take back Whitestone, they'd have to be prepared for the worst.

In these sort of fraught moments, he always turned mean and heated. He didn't want to admit to himself, but he was nervous for what was to come. What happened in the next few weeks and months would ripple far into the future. It had the power to shape the rest of his life and the next several generations ahead.

He could no longer be idle. How long could he pace these halls, trying to decipher who should succeed their steward? When all the while Whitestone Manor and all its secrets lay unguarded? The successor ought to be himself.

As soon as Lawrence had gotten word of what was to happen in London, they'd had no choice. He was only too happy to leave at once.

Almost immediately, he'd woken Grice and Charleston and demanded they take to arms. It didn't matter that it had been the middle of the night. He wasn't wasting any time. His enemies would be closing in on Whitestone soon. He was sure of that.

Though so far, he'd offered little explanation.

"We make for the train station. Then onward to London," Theo announced.

"Forgive me, but if we want to protect Whitestone, shouldn't we be heading—I don't know—there?" Charleston grumbled. In the horse stall ahead of him, all Theo could make out was his fiery-red hair.

Theo snorted. "They would be expecting that, wouldn't they?"

"You want to catch them while they're vulnerable," Grice guessed.

"Mortibel is conducting a meeting in London," Lawrence said. Several months ago, he'd had men successfully infiltrate Mortibel's faction. News before then had gotten too quiet. Yet Mortibel's supporters had been gaining ground, just as Theo had feared. "Days ago, I got word of the invitations."

"They're holding their own meetings now?" Charleston forced a laugh.

"Their own rituals too."

That was where they would stop them. Once and for all.

Theo gave the signal and they each kicked their horses, tearing out of the stable into a wide expanse of sparkling snow.

The early morning air was harsher than usual. The mountains were beautiful, as always, but Theo hoped he'd never have to set eyes on them again. If he could help it, he hoped never to return.

Guilt gnawed at him for leaving like this, with only a short note, but once his mother and father heard news of what had happened in London, they would understand. He considered looking back to see if there was light in her room, but he couldn't risk getting pulled back to the only place he'd ever felt truly and completely safe. Especially, when ahead, he only saw violence.

No matter how comforting or secure, what he was leaving behind wasn't home. Only Whitestone Manor was home. He didn't care how much his mother tried to convince him otherwise.

"Theodore, darling...our home is in the mountains now," she had said. *"We have everything we need."*

But their new home was hardly ideal. They were too far from the hustle and bustle of London. Here, they couldn't properly keep a tab on things, particularly their steward, Maximus Grey. News of his death still had yet to be officially announced. Quite on purpose—there was no doubting that.

Years ago, when Theo and his family had been forced to leave, they had planned to return. They always had. After his father's sacrifices, Theo was especially determined to. He almost didn't have a choice.

The panic of the evening was slowing down. His anger was building instead. He squeezed the reins harder and commanded his horse to run faster.

Whitestone would be his again, no matter what the cost. He didn't care how much blood he had to spill.

CHAPTER ONE

The Inheritance

One Month Later, London

"**T**HERE IS NOTHING like a well-planned party to secure one's place in society."

From her secluded spot in the ballroom, Hazel Grey sighed at her aunt's words. Of course, the older woman knew nothing of the pistols and daggers that could take one out of this world in a flash. Surely, there was nothing a "well-planned party" could do to prevent that.

Yes, the flower arrangements were robust, the conversations controlled, and gentlemen aplenty, but in London, Hazel never felt quite like herself. She wasn't meant for the social life that included dinner parties, garden soirees, and balls, where everyone's life and reputation depended upon the lips of gossipers or what they'd worn for an evening.

Here, her ability to see a wider spectrum of colors proved most bothersome. The colors and the patterns of each gown that were such a delight to others were so sharp and strong to her, they often stung her eyes.

She tried to wear a more subdued color herself, one that would not overcome her senses. But her aunt had insisted on a new gown, landing Hazel in a yellow as bright as the sun. It was nature she preferred. Only the natural world had ever gotten colors right, certainly not artificial dyes.

"Give us a smile," her Aunt Catherine reminded her. "Catching the eyes of a man from across the ballroom may be all it takes."

Hazel turned away, stifling a groan. It was a rare occasion that her aunt was out at all. She was usually too weak with a bad cough. She'd suffered them frequently since her fever four winters ago. But these last few weeks, her health had seemed to rally. That strangely warm autumn day, the weather had proven too nice for her to resist.

Her aunt wore her finest gown, which turned out to be quite elaborate with far too many trimmings. What really made her stand out was her layers upon layers of jewelry. She even had jewels in her auburn gray-streaked hair.

"Oh look, the Delaneys." Aunt Catherine clapped her hands, her cane swaying so wildly, she almost hit a passerby. "Go have a chat. I need some rest."

"Here." Hazel turned her to a cushioned settee. "Sit here."

"Make sure to mingle and do bring me a new introduction."

Hazel helped her down. The small seating area was low and surrounded by clusters of chattering debutantes. Thank God. Aunt Catherine wouldn't see her avoid Mrs. Delaney and her two daughters. She'd never liked them. The way they spoke about others, so nonchalantly cruel, made her wonder. When she wasn't listening, what did they say about *her*? The less she remained in their presence, the less her name might fall from their lips. Above all, she needed a moment of solitude, even if it was short-lived.

Out of the corner of her ever-watchful eyes, she caught the shifting shadow of someone making their approach. Perhaps an old acquaintance. A suitor?

She forced herself to turn around. Taking in the familiar figure, she tried not to grimace.

"What's this?" Mr. Marcus Mortibel threw his arms out, hat in hand. "Miss Grey all on her own? And no chaperone."

She cursed. She hated to meet him at a gathering like this. Here, she had to force herself to be someone else. Someone genteel and far chattier, when she preferred to be taciturn. Here, she was someone she hated. She was no longer the person he had come to know, who had once shunned society's ideals and expectations. For too long, she'd had to abide by its long list of rules. And for what? For a life that, while at least safe, was rather dull.

"I thought I'd have to fight off the suitors to get a word with you." He smiled his charming smile, his green eyes twinkling.

"They are occupied." Hazel turned her back on him and moved toward one of the many hors d'oeuvre and champagne tables. Though she had money enough, she had yet to attract a fortune hunter or any man of decent stature, really.

Her family might have been landed gentry with an ancient estate to boot, but her father's reputation was far from respectable. At best, people thought he was a recluse. At worst, utterly mad.

Hazel still wasn't sure she would ever really fit in. At least not so well as she had with Mr. Mortibel. Heir to the extensive estate neighboring her father's, he had been not only a family friend, but like a son to her father. The son he'd always wished he had.

Whether or not she wanted to admit it, she was glad to see him. His cheerful face was a welcome sight. It reminded her of better days.

"This really is quite the surprise." She still couldn't believe he was actually here.

How had he managed to sneak past the butler, especially without an invite? He never came to London to participate in any of the social rituals. But as a member of one of England's most clandestine societies, she supposed it was in his nature to enter places unseen. Just like her father, he could easily thwart anyone.

"How long has it been?" he asked.

"Two years and three months," Hazel said precisely. Nine months since two of her letters had gone unanswered. She should have seen it coming. He had seemed so strange and distant the last time she'd seen him—when he'd surprised her for her birthday. Still, she'd never expected he would disappear from her life entirely. Until late, they had been so close. Foolishly, she thought they had been something more than childhood friends. She had accepted the apparent rejection, but standing before him, anger swirled. She set her jaw and turned away.

"I wished you had written first." She grasped her hands together, not knowing what to do with them.

"I thought you'd be pleased to see me."

"Of course I am." Hazel put on a sweet face. But was she? She couldn't decide.

"How are you faring?" Hazel sought a change in subject. He certainly looked well. "Keeping yourself busy with the Order's affairs, I imagine."

"As always."

Mr. Mortibel might not have been a total recluse like her father. But he was just as obsessed and closed off about the Silver Order.

Hazel gathered her shirts and lowered herself onto a nearby bench. The memories he invoked swept over her like the ice-cold wind of a moor. The years he'd been away didn't matter. When he dropped next to her, she still shivered—a strange feeling he always evoked, no matter how many years had passed. She'd never forget their summers together as children, when Mr. Mortibel—then "Marcus" to her—had always been calling from the estate two miles off. No matter how her governess had chastised her for the lack of propriety, she'd returned the visits at least once a week.

Despite herself, she'd missed him a great deal.

"If these people knew who you were..." Mr. Mortibel clucked his tongue and looked about. "If they could have seen what your father was capable of..."

Something stuck out in her mind. Was *capable of*? Was?

Mr. Mortibel too must have realized his error. His smile fell. "I have news."

So this was why he had come to see her. Hazel snapped her eyes away, feeling the feather in her hair quiver with the movement. She didn't want Mr. Mortibel to see her pained expression. She wasn't supposed to feel this way. She wasn't supposed to care about any matter concerning her father.

Mr. Mortibel dropped down next to her. "Your father. He's moved on to the spirit—"

Hazel stopped him before he could continue with the usual nonsense. "Heaven, you mean."

But heaven or hell, what did it matter? She hadn't seen her father since she'd been twelve, since that night when she had witnessed the worst of the Silver Order. A whole decade ago. The very night she had run away to live with Aunt Catherine, her late mother's only sibling. Memories she didn't want to remember, that she still struggled to forget.

She barely knew who her father was anymore. When something in her throat caught, she attributed it to shock.

"He was sick for some time, I'm afraid."

"When?" She breathed out. "When did this happen?"

"A month ago. I came as soon as I could."

"'A *month*'?" Hazel exclaimed. "Why didn't you…Why didn't *someone* write me?"

A letter, however impersonal, would have been far more preferable to this, this meeting of false friendship. He hadn't wanted to see her. He'd only needed to deliver this hideous news. She should have known. Her unanswered letters spoke volumes. Not one, but two, had gone unanswered.

"Forgive me. There were other matters that needed attending. Please understand, I wanted to tell you in person." When he took up her hand, disregarding propriety, Hazel savored the small comfort, even if she hated herself for it.

It made sense, sadly. Even in death, her father still placed her second after the Order. Of course she was among the last to hear the news.

"You should know he left the estate to you."

"But why?" she wondered aloud. Her father had known well enough she'd wanted nothing to do with all the activities that went on there.

"I've been curious about that myself."

"Surely, he didn't think I might actually come to live in that horrid place. All the way in the Malvern Hills…"

"Do you even remember it? Your father's estate is far from horrible, I assure you." He spoke as if the manor were some prize. But Hazel knew better. She knew the true dangers that surrounded the Order.

"I don't care if it is gilded in gold." Hazel yanked her hand away, her sadness warping into bitter anger. She couldn't forget what her father had done. No matter how many years ago.

"I bid you. Come see the place for yourself. Without your father there, perhaps your feelings toward the manor will soften."

"You can't be serious." After all, it wasn't just her father who had kept her away. It was the Order and all its dreadful activities. Mr. Mortibel had to know her return was unlikely. "You know I want nothing to do with it."

She shivered beneath a sudden blast of cold. Someone somewhere must have opened a door onto the patio. "What if I sell? What will become of the Order then?" Without her father, their esteemed chairman, she hoped they would soon fade into nothing.

"Is that how you want things—after three hundred years—for the Order to simply end? To go out like the dimming of a lamp?" His voice ached.

"Everything reaches its end sooner or later. Better with fewer casualties than more." The words felt harsh on her tongue, but were no less true.

"You don't know. You never…" He hung his head.

"I know plenty." To call oneself a Silver Order member simply wasn't safe. And meeting like this wasn't safe, either. "For heaven's sake, haven't you been reading the papers?"

She cringed at the thought of the photos. In the last year, four seers, the most important among their members, had each been mutilated. They were dropping like bloody flies. Her guess was that someone had discovered their well-guarded identities. And now everyone was at risk.

"We can bring an end to it. *I* can bring an end to it." Mr. Mortibel looked out across the lawn and rolled his shoulders back. "There is no certainty the killers will stop simply because we've disbanded. We can't just surrender. We can't just give them what they want."

"You don't even know who *they* are." She sucked in a breath. She simply wanted to be done with this business. With the estate in her hands, she was in danger now. She worked a finger into her braids and yanked out one of the feathers. They'd been torturing her all evening.

"Yes, I know. But without leadership, without your father... I know there's no one who can take his place. I'm merely requesting...You see—" His brows pinched. "Those of us who remain— we've selected a new chairman."

"Already?" Hazel gasped. "Who?"

"Me." He leaned forward.

"*You?*"

He ignored her questioning stare.

"We're moving on. The Order still has a breath of life in it. We've accepted your family's role has come to an end, but not the Order itself."

"You can't do this," she let out quickly. Her gloved fingers began to twitch. "You'll get killed."

"Hush now." He risked a look behind him, bringing to Hazel's attention just how close they were sitting. People had begun to stare. The words "pleasing" and "improper" were on the lips of some women. She didn't need to read more to know which belonged to her.

She shifted back and cleared her throat.

"I'll never understand why the Order has taken over your life as it has—or my father's, for that matter."

But trying to convince him to leave the Order would have been a waste of effort. She had failed to do so when she'd first run away and would fail again.

"If you allowed me, I would help you understand."

"*No*," Hazel said fiercely. "If anyone in society found out what my father was involved in, I'd be cast out for good. And by connection, so would you."

"Forget society. The things we can do, they are worth the risk." He threw his hands out.

"No, they are *not*." For this reason and so many more, she preferred to distance herself as far as possible from her father and any other member associated with the Order. Given their early friendship, Mr. Mortibel was supposed to have been the exception. Unlike the others, she trusted him. But it was probably high time she distanced herself from him too. A fact that shouldn't have bothered her so much.

She couldn't deny that his visit had given her a spark of hope. Feelings once forgotten, Hazel remembered again. The intense way he looked at her. Was he glad to see her too?

If only he might endeavor to be like everyone else. Mr. Mortibel, however, couldn't stand normalcy.

She dropped her voice to a whisper. "Do what you will with what remains of the Order, Mr. Mortibel. But I insist you do so without me. I will be selling the estate and there is little you can say to persuade me otherwise."

She didn't care if they viewed it as the Order's meeting grounds. It was her entail, her dowry, even if it was never really her home. Before its notoriety reached London, she needed to sell the place fast. "I can assume I missed his funeral?"

"Afford me more honor than that. There is to be a memorial..."

"When?"

"Early morning the day after tomorrow. Three A.M., to be precise."

"I see the Order still keeps odd hours."

"The ceremony, or rather memorial, shall be held here in London… Will you come?"

"To say goodbye to my father." She swallowed. Her stomach turned. Part of her still wanted to stay away. But a goodbye was the least she could offer. Afterward, he'd be out of her life forever.

"Nothing more?"

When she had no response, he slipped her a piece of paper. Their hands touched long enough to bring back the memory of the Malvern Hills with fields of grass so tall, they could sit and talk unseen. The grasses swayed around them, the sweet taste of morning dew still in the air. But like that summer, the memory and all the good feelings that came with it had been fleeting too.

Before her stood a different man. And when their eyes met, she no longer caught something lusty and familiar, but a pointed stare, stiff and serious.

Despising it, she looked down at the card. When she read the meeting time and place outlined in simple, black ink, he took it from her grasp and lit it on fire with a match, crumpling the black bits in his hand.

"There will be a carriage waiting for you at that precise time and location." He paused. "Can you manage to sneak away for the night?"

"Just as well as you."

"Be sure to disguise yourself." He stood, ready to retreat, when her voice halted him.

"You're certain this will be safe?"

"Of course…" He blinked hard. "You doubt me?"

"I suppose I do." Hazel crossed her arms. Given what she knew about the Order, it had been a question worth asking.

"Needlessly."

With a nod and a pinched frown, he retreated back into the

crowd.

Alone again, she wasn't quite the same. For a long while, Hazel couldn't move. Her father was dead. She ought to have felt a deeper sense of sadness. More sadness than she currently felt. She hadn't even shed one tear.

Instead of mourning, her heart was filled with fear and trepidation of the memorial to come. This was her father, after all, her own flesh and blood, but was saying goodbye worth the risk of meeting with the Order? Mr. Mortibel could keep her safe, couldn't he?

He had done so on several other occasions. With that wild dog they had encountered in the woods and a second time when her horse had reared.

But against the dangers of the Order, she was less certain. And yet, to say goodbye to her father, to get the closure she needed, risking her safety and even her reputation was her only choice.

CHAPTER TWO

The Catacombs

HAZEL'S BOOTS SLOSHED through the puddles of the cobblestone street. Stagnant and slick though they may have been, it was far better than the horse manure that otherwise covered the stone.

Aunt Catherine had fallen asleep early that evening. So sneaking out in clothing borrowed from her lady's maid had almost been too easy. There was always the chance she'd wake up. In that case, a note that Hazel would be back before daybreak would have to do.

At nearly two in the morning, the usually bustling lane was unrecognizable. With black, lifeless windows, the neighboring townhouses appeared abandoned, if not haunted. Though the walk was a short one, she should not have been about alone, especially at this time of night. Aunt Catherine would be furious. A few wrong steps and she would find herself in the slums teeming with pickpockets, murderers, or worse. It didn't matter how late it was—those sort never slept.

The walk reminded her of the uneasiness she had felt upon her arrival. London had seemed romantic enough in novels, but in person, it hadn't quite lived up to her hopes. Its odors assaulted her and the black fog followed her home, staining her best dresses. And then there were the rules her aunt had recited to her. As if her reputation was worth more than her life.

None of this mattered, though. After what she had witnessed at her father's estate, she'd never wanted to return to the Malvern Hills. She tried to forget its beautiful gardens and that wonderful smell of the grass just after a rain. Now she knew only of the chimney smoke that turned the blue skies black, the sight of beggars that wrenched her heart, and drunken men who constantly had her on guard.

The grinding of wheels stole away her attention. A shadowed driver leaned back with the reins, bringing the clamoring horses to a halt. A few feet ahead, the gilded door flew open. Hazel gathered her skirts and entered. In the darkness, she worried for a moment that maybe she was in the wrong cab and that soon she could be in a whole slew of trouble, when a voice sounded.

"You were supposed to hire a hansom, not walk the streets alone at night." It was Mr. Mortibel's voice. Rough, yet full of the same tenderness he had held for her in childhood.

"The distance was nothing." Though perhaps she had judged wrong.

Her breathing seemed impossibly loud in that black silence. The journey thus far had already sapped her courage. "Are we alone?"

"Yes."

Her skin tingled unprovoked by the still air. Since he had been away, she had often thought of being alone with him like this—of what she might say, what she might do. She wanted to demand to know why he hadn't written and what precisely had kept him away. But none of the words came. The truth behind his silence would be too painful. She sat there frozen, glad to remain hidden in the darkness.

"I trust you were able to escape your aunt unseen?"

Hazel pushed back against the seat, wanting to keep her distance before her old feelings surfaced again. She didn't trust what she might do if they so much as brushed hands.

"Any noises she heard, she likely mistook for a spirit. You know how superstitious she is."

"At this hour? Oh, yes, the witching hour, is it?" He laughed in his short, raspy, and half-hidden way. "What nonsense."

Hazel narrowed her gaze. "The Order is not much different."

"I assure you, the two are worlds apart." He huffed.

"Please. Your lowest members may believe every farfetched claim, but not I."

For so long, they'd tried to get her to believe, but she had never obliged. She preferred a life that was both safe and practical, something that did not match well with her father's hermetic activities. So far, she was only privy to two: serums that sustained life no matter what ailments came over its user and an elixir that allowed them to glimpse days, months, years, and sometimes even decades into the future. The latter allowed them to sell what they called prescient advice. Naturally, it was their biggest call to power, gaining them political connections in Parliament and, most importantly, wealth. All of it impossible.

Mr. Mortibel just shook his head.

"How did she take the news?" he asked on a much more serious note.

"Well enough." Hazel shrugged. In fact, her aunt was relieved. She always had this fear that her well-connected brother-in-law would come one night demanding to take his daughter back. And yet he never had. He hadn't even asked for an explanation. He'd seemed to understand. Or perhaps he hadn't cared.

"I've already written to my father's solicitor. I told him to have the estate on the market by week's end."

"You waste little time."

"Will you and the others miss the place?" If not for his father's debts, he might have purchased it for himself. Everyone in London knew his father's gambling habits. Perhaps that was why Mr. Mortibel never showed his face. She felt sorry for it, almost.

"Some might. Matters little now. You really should have

hired a hansom. I wouldn't like to see you harmed. And neither would your father."

Hazel swallowed. She wasn't so sure her father had ever worried about her safety or if he'd thought of her at all. She pushed it from her mind.

"It was a short walk." Hazel tried to sound practical.

"You dressed properly, at least. No one would recognize you in that servant's garb."

As the carriage entered a better-lit street, Hazel caught his downcast expression. A haze of light illuminated his fidgeting fingers. He itched to escape the confinement of the carriage, just as Hazel did. The tense silence was almost more than she could bear.

Thankfully, after a few minutes, the carriage began to slow, the horses snorting as they came to a halt. Hazel leaned toward the door, but Mr. Mortibel caught her hand, freezing her in place.

A black, satin blindfold shone through the darkness. She shrunk back. Mr. Mortibel would no doubt try to keep her safe, but not being able to see while entering the unknown cast an unsettling feeling over her.

"Apologies." He brushed back a wayward piece of her dark hair then slipped the cold cloth over her eyes. "But since you won't be returning to us…" His fingers worked along the back of her head, careful not to ruin her braids. At this point, Hazel didn't mind her hair. She just prayed she didn't shiver at his touch. Her senses focused on the steady in and out of his breath. The unique musk of his skin mixed with the damp smell of London.

A warm, heavy hand squeezed hers and she followed him out of the carriage. Their footfalls clicked atop stone. A door opened; the continued silence meant they were someplace remote.

He wouldn't take her anywhere dangerous, would he?

"Here we are." Mr. Mortibel removed the oppressive cloth, revealing a set of stone stairs spiraling downward. Lanterns flanked the steps, the black, soot-covered glass suggesting frequent use. From some unknown source, dripping water echoed from every direction. It was chilling, to say the least.

The place was likely some old abandoned warehouse. But why make her go down stairs? She turned to Mr. Mortibel, but he simply nodded for her to go on.

"It's all right," he said. Hazel allowed that to comfort her for a moment. He seemed familiar enough with the place. How many times had he been here? She imagined this was where he gathered the members needed to attain her father's position. Lord knew what else the Order did here. She sighed, trying not to think of all that could go wrong. This memorial could not conclude fast enough.

She stepped down the stairs, noting the musky air and the gentle lapping of water.

Against the torchlight, the floor was sparkling. It wasn't until she came closer that she realized it was a pool of water, complete with a small cable ferry.

Hazel hesitated. "You know I cannot swim. Should this ancient boat topple over, I'll drown."

"Luckily, for you I can." He hobbled into the boat and reached out a hand. Wet skirts were inevitable now, but Hazel picked them up nonetheless. The boat wobbled as she stepped in, setting her heart to flutter.

She gripped his hand tightly, refusing to let go.

"We won't tip, not if you sit there." He pointed at the sliver of a bench.

Hazel dropped down, feeling the cold wood through her skirts.

With practiced deftness, Mr. Mortibel's arms tensed while he worked the cable, the boat slicing through water as still as the night sky. The torches well behind them, Hazel and her companion passed stone pillars in near darkness. Half-covered in mildew and crumbling in places, the architecture had to be centuries old. This whole underground system had most likely been built during much earlier Roman times.

Turning a corner, their boat approached a new set of gears

staked into the water. The more they gained, the louder the gears creaked against their weight. Mr. Mortibel changed his pace, pulling on the rope with more care. At any moment, Hazel expected it to snap, for them to become stranded with no choice but to swim. Lord knew what lingered in this black pool of water.

A new, unsavory smell grew stronger, a tinge of charred meat mixed with the usual rotting refuse that persisted throughout London. She couldn't place it until they hit the dock.

Packed into the walls, rows of coffins and loose bones stretched from the stone floor all the way up to an arched ceiling. The scent had been death. Some Londoners believed these gasses were strong enough to kill instantly. She raised her bare hand to her nose. She wished she could have worn her gloves. Satin ones would have really come in handy.

Though she almost preferred to stay on the boat, she let Mr. Mortibel help her atop the damp stone.

"Careful now."

"What sort of meeting place is this?" Hazel asked, already shaking with superstition. She had heard of the crowded graveyards the city had struggled to contain but never had she imagined this.

"A place long forgotten about. You need not worry. There aren't any plague pits. I made sure of that."

"As if *that* makes any difference." Hazel swallowed, clutching the small, silver crucifix at her neck. She tried not to think of the men and women, maybe even children, who had once claimed the skulls. With his foot, Mr. Mortibel slid one out of their path.

Three seers huddled between two columns. Hazel shivered. The room was arranged so much like the one that horrible night she'd witnessed at her father's estate, she almost turned back. For Mr. Mortibel's sake, she gathered some brass.

A chandelier flickered fiercely above, filling the small, stone enclosure with so much light, she squinted. They liked their altars bright, Hazel remembered with disgust. In the room's center was a small circle. Though this one was merely drawn in chalk instead of marble and smaller than the one she remembered too, it had the same strange markers. She had never cared to learn their meaning. In fact, she preferred to forget about them entirely.

She nodded at the seers, their eyes blinking beneath their silver masks. *Who is behind those masks?* she wondered. *Men, women?* Dressed in heavy white robes, they were disguised from head to toe.

Within the hierarchy of the Silver Order, the seers were the highest. Of the First Order, they knew the most about the Order's teachings. Furthermore, they alone—in addition to her father, the chairman—had the ability to use the infamous elixir. For those secrets alone, they had to protect their identities, even from their own members.

"We await a few others before we can proceed." Mr. Mortibel pulled out his pocket watch.

An uneasy feeling dropped through her. Surely, his men wouldn't be late for an occasion such as this. Tardiness in the Silver Order's eyes was a sign of great disrespect.

The empty boat lurched, slicing backward in the water. This time, moving fast.

"Here they are."

At the other pier, footfalls, a number of them, indicated people climbing into the boat. The rope creaked as it moved toward them. Hazel waited for the new people to round the corner and come into view. Mr. Mortibel watched too, stepping forward as if he were about to yell out, before reconsidering. His eyes narrowed. He even went so far as to push her behind him.

"What are you doing?" Hazel hissed.

"Something's amiss."

Hazel sensed it then. A feeling that weighed down on her like stone. Whoever was pulling the boat did not exhibit the same caution Mr. Mortibel had. The boat was moving too fast.

She froze. Again, she was stranded. Here, there was nowhere to go. Even the seers shifted uneasily.

The rope continued to turn faster, but the newcomers had

yet to make the corner. Waiting was its own kind of agony.

"I'm sorry." Mr. Mortibel tensed. By the time she looked over, he had produced a pistol, which was pointed at the approaching sound.

Whoever was closing in, would they have weapons too? If so, what were the chances they'd survive a gunfight?

She had the strange urge to laugh then. Of course the Order would be the death of her. She should have known better. No one, not even Mr. Mortibel, could protect her from the danger they posed. She glanced once more at her childhood friend, not liking the fear in his eyes. Since the day she had left her father's estate, she had wanted so badly to keep him from the Order and all of its dangers. If only he hadn't chosen this life, they might have had an entirely different fate. Perhaps even a life together. But he had always chosen the Order over her. Just like her father.

Before Hazel could think of anything to say, what might very well have been her last words, the boat appeared from around the corner. Moving fast, it was a faint outline in the blackness at first, but as it drew closer toward the candlelight, multiple figures appeared. Two, three, four, of them? Given their black cloaks, hoods, and masks, it was hard to tell.

"Identify yourselves!" Mr. Mortibel shouted, but the strangers didn't answer. In the next moment, their cloaks fluttered skyward. Metal glistened in light.

She didn't even have time to draw in a panicked breath. Gunshots broke out. Instinct threw Hazel to the cold, wet ground. Flecks of stone sprayed over her, coffin bits and bones too. She didn't dare look up to identify the men. She held every part of her, even her gaze, tight to the ground.

She needed to lie still like the dead around her. A series of violent thuds meant the men were on the stone landing now. She struggled to contain her shivering. Panic soared through her veins, urging her to run and at the same time freezing her in place.

Hazel squeezed her eyes shut, praying that when she opened

them, the sounds would dissipate and she'd be somewhere else entirely. But the chaos of indistinguishable noise continued. Her mind buzzed with fear, her heart screaming in her chest. She fully expected a bullet to hit her at any moment.

A shriek penetrated the air, filled with so much agony, her racing heart stilled from terror. She risked opening one eye. A man lay on his back, his silver mask pulled from his face. A wrinkled face she didn't recognize stared at her with dead eyes, blood blossoming around him. She pushed back as the red puddle inched closer, her movement interrupted by the crack of metal so loud, the walls seemed to vibrate with it.

More thuds echoed across the room, what could only be bodies hitting the floor. There was no way to tell if Mr. Mortibel was still alive.

She felt sick and almost retched when she heard a hoarse whisper.

"Escape whilst you can, miss. *Run.*"

She lifted her head. A man, bleeding from the back of his neck, stumbled onto the boat with his other companions. The light of a lantern flickered as they pulled away. There would be no catching the newcomers now. They had killed and gotten away with it.

Desperate to find Mr. Mortibel, Hazel sat up and circled the room. Three bodies, all of the seers, lay still on the floor. She pulled aside the silver masks of the other two, not recognizing either. With a horrible, vacant look in their eyes, death was all too obvious. She braced herself against the wall, resting her forehead against its grimy surface, struggling to catch her breath. She wasn't sure if she had the strength to call out for Mr. Mortibel. If he was dead, she didn't want to know. Not yet.

When a cough broke out, she almost didn't believe it. The sound echoed all around. She couldn't place it, either.

"Miss Grey…" The voice was wonderfully familiar.

At the other end of the room, Mr. Mortibel darted out from the shadow of one of the pillars, almost unrecognizable. The sight of him in the dim light stopped her in her tracks. He looked haggard. His face was slick with sweat and blood, his clothing torn in places.

"Are you all right?" Mr. Mortibel asked.

Despite the dread that seemed to collect like bricks in her stomach, she nodded. She wanted to embrace him, but something held her back. She couldn't forget the stranger's warning.

"Are you?"

"I'll be fine," he said, a weak smile breaking through his otherwise-tired features.

"Come."

Hunched over, he pulled at the rope, thankfully unbroken.

She itched to leave the place. All the death that lay behind her—she couldn't stomach it anymore. Only aboveground could they get the assistance they needed to take care of the bodies.

"Convenient this place is already a graveyard." Mr. Mortibel looked at the bodies behind him. Hazel shot him a look. She knew he wasn't serious, but she wasn't amused, either. The comment was rather cruel.

"I didn't like meeting here much, anyway," he said. "Nor in London at all, for that matter."

In the boat again, Hazel kept her eyes forward and waited for the landing to appear in case the men were still there.

"Don't worry. They're long gone," Mr. Mortibel confirmed.

Swallowing her fear, she followed him up the stairs. At the top, she stilled. Something was wrong. Next to her, Mr. Mortibel walked with a strange gait and his hand clung to his side. His coat darkened with blood. How had she not noticed it earlier?

"You're bleeding—"

He waved her off before she could come closer. "I'll be fine. It's only a flesh wound."

"You should let me tend to it."

"*No.*" Mr. Mortibel's roar froze her in place. "I've risked your safety long enough."

"Who were those men?"

"They hid their faces well. All four of them."

So it had been only four. With all the echoing, there had seemed more. Yet it had been enough men that Hazel wondered why they had left her alive. One of them had gotten so close, had *whispered* to her. She heard the words again: *"Escape whilst you can, miss. Run."* But from what? The stranger himself?

Mr. Mortibel called out. "This way."

They continued past the doorway they had originally entered into another brick tunnel.

"This will bring us back?"

They were headed in the opposite direction and the farther they went down the tunnel, the darker it became. The silence seemed a danger all its own, capable of breaking at any moment.

"My driver awaits at the other end of the catacombs, where it's more secluded."

"We need to go to a hospital."

"Those cesspools? A friend of mine lives not far from here."

"Mr. Mortibel—"

"Don't worry. My friend's a doctor."

They quickened their pace past several other tunnels, the catacombs transforming into an underground labyrinth. Mr. Mortibel's confidence didn't waver, though. The Order had to have been meeting here for more than just a few months. Maybe years.

Hazel wanted to pick up their pace. Mr. Mortibel's steps, however, began to slow. When she took his hand to steady him, the pain was clear in his tense grip. As soon as they reached safety, she would check the wound, whether he liked it or not.

Mr. Mortibel paused to draw in a ragged breath.

"Can you continue?" Hazel's heart ached with worry. She should have refused the meeting. She should have run the moment Mr. Mortibel had approached her at the ball. But if she hadn't attended this meeting, who would have helped him then?

"What of the others who were invited to attend?" Hazel struggled to make sense of the last half hour, possibly less.

Everything had happened so fast. "What do you imagine happened to them?"

"I don't know."

"But who even knew about the meeting?" Hazel could hear him gritting his teeth in the silence of the tunnel. "I'm sure only members…" She trailed off, a realization hitting her like a wall.

Mr. Mortibel clenched her hand tighter.

"My thoughts exactly," he said gravely. "We have a traitor amongst us."

MR. MORTIBEL'S CARRIAGE sped away. Amidst the precarious swaying, Hazel didn't so much as whisper a word of complaint. She was glad for the extra speed. It meant they would arrive at the home of his friend all the sooner. Darkness made Mr. Mortibel's face unreadable. Though she could sense his pain.

A new route, a shortcut, she hoped, brought them through the poorer parts of London. Despite the growing dawn, men deep in their cups still wandered the street. Some lay unconscious on the pavement—for all she knew, they were dead. And the puddles, the foul water that had been tossed out onto the street, pricked at her nostrils. Lord knew what her maid's petticoats had been covered in now. *Dash it all.* Instead of taking the Lord's name in vain, she needed to pray. Both for Mr. Mortibel and those raggedly-dressed children she had seen in the street. At this hour, they were likely starting another day at the workhouses.

She couldn't let them pain her now. Rather, she needed to focus on Mr. Mortibel.

"Let me see it."

He laughed. "I'd have to undress."

The lady she was supposed to be would have nodded and waited. Then again, a lady would not have been traveling alone with him in the first place.

She leaned forward. Her hair had fallen entirely out of its braids now, the curls swaying with the cab.

"Don't." He shrank back. Typical man—he thought the gore would upset her. It didn't matter that he could, in fact, be mortally wounded. She needed to know. If she could, she had to help.

Her fingers didn't wait for permission. They pried away his hands and his clothing. The fine patterned silk of his vest was blood-soaked and torn. She needed to stop the bleeding. Any half-educated woman knew that. Ripping fabric from the clean parts of her maid's petticoat, she packed it over the wound. He groaned.

"Press hard. You're going to be fine." Though she couldn't entirely be sure.

He straightened. "Don't sound so disappointed."

With the morning sun finally penetrating the fog, she could see him more clearly. His eyes were conveying his worry that her optimism might all have been a lie.

"Tell me you forgive me," he pleaded. "I have to know you still trust me."

"Of course I forgive you," she said, exasperated. She removed her cloak and wrapped it around him. "The home of this friend. Are we close?"

He peeled back the window curtain and looked out onto the street. "A few more minutes is all."

"And it is safe?"

"He's the only man I trust. Miss Grey, I…"

"No." She wouldn't listen to his apologies, even if he'd led her into this mess. They all seemed to indicate that he was worse off than she thought. There was still a large risk of infection.

"Perhaps the cabbie might hurry it up," she said.

"No"—he breathed in with effort—"use."

As the morning wore on, the streets came to life, not only slowing traffic, but surrounding them with a symphony of noise. More cabs crowded the streets, the clomping of their horses rising to a steady tenor, almost musical in nature.

Mr. Mortibel's eyes widened and she couldn't figure out why. Was the noise bothering him? It seemed to grow louder by the minute. Amidst the cacophony, she heard the fiddle of a street musician, followed by children's laughter. She placed a hand on his so he might focus on her and not the pain. A useless tactic. He only clenched his wound harder.

Just as the noise reached an oppressive peak, the hansom pulled to a stop.

Hazel stepped out first. She tried to steady Mr. Mortibel, but he shook his head, focusing his sights on the row of fashionable townhomes ahead. He clenched the coarse fabric of her skirts.

"That's the one." Mr. Mortibel gestured toward a white townhome with a black-iron fence and chestnut door.

Wasting no time now, he limped to the door and rapped loudly. Hazel didn't know how long he could keep to his feet.

By the time the door had opened, Hazel was struggling to keep him upright and he was gasping, incapable of speech. A step forward overwhelmed him, sending him straight into the arms of some woman.

CHAPTER THREE

Dr. Lagerfield

H AZEL SCREECHED OUT, finally releasing the anxiety she had held for an unbearable half hour. Mr. Mortibel had lost a lot of blood. When she looked out into the street, telling red drops led out to the curb.

Taking his unmoving face into her hands, Hazel cringed at his paleness and the black circles that swelled beneath his eyes. She moved her fingers to his wound, feeling the warm blood drip from his waistcoat.

When Hazel looked up for help, an older, large-bosomed woman stared wide-eyed. Dressed in an apron and mop cap, she could only have been one of the servants. Hazel sucked in a breath, a scream caught in her throat.

Footfalls clamored down the stairs. Hazel shrank back, half-expecting another gunman, but it was only a silver-haired gentleman. A man who would have been close to her father's age, had he been alive.

Hazel didn't move from her crouched position.

"Miss Grey." The man started. She was certain they had never crossed paths before. All the same, he rushed to her like an old friend. He grasped her bloody hands and steadied her. "Are you hurt?"

"*No*," she nearly shouted, tearing her hands away. She motioned toward Mr. Mortibel. "Please. *Him*! Help him!"

The housekeeper stared as if she couldn't look away. Hazel had the sudden urge to push her aside, useless that she was.

"Let me," the gentleman said. Despite his fine clothing, the stranger knelt down in the blood and lifted up the cloth that was stopping the blood. His eyes focused on the wound, unafraid, as if he knew exactly what to do. She hoped he did.

"It won't stop bleeding," Hazel cried.

A hand touched her arm. The housekeeper, Hazel assumed, was trying to get her away. Hazel ignored the efforts.

"We need a doctor—"

"Dr. Lagerfield *is* a doctor, miss." The woman pulled at her again. "Come, out of the cold."

Hazel paused. The sight of all the blood seemed more pronounced in the gold-gilded walls of the foyer. Such violence shouldn't have existed. This home seemed fit only for laughter and long, interesting conversations. Not the death they had dragged in from the catacombs.

"Perhaps I could be of some use… I've—"

"No, dear," Dr. Lagerfield answered her, both hands working to tie some piece of clothing around Mr. Mortibel's torso. "You had better go."

Dr. Lagerfield and this woman thought her hysterical. She just needed another moment, another breath. But they would never believe her and that left little room for argument.

Seeing that she was outnumbered, Hazel conceded. The housekeeper led her down the hall, patting her hand and whispering sweet reassurances she resented.

"We'll take care of him. Don't you worry." The housekeeper's voice was calmer, but her hands still shook.

The woman had to have been scared too. The servants of this neighborhood no doubt knew nothing of the horrors of gore. Hazel, on the other hand, knew it all too well.

A distant thump jolted her. She pictured Dr. Lagerfield and

some footman carrying Mr. Mortibel, still bleeding.

Blood splashed across her vision, weakening her knees.

"You're faint." The housekeeper hurried her steps. Hazel nodded. Weakness had come over her like a fog. Now that fog seemed to be thickening, darkening. She squeezed her eyes shut at the memory of blood. She wouldn't think of what had happened. She dare not.

"Even though you're dressed like that, you're no servant, are you?"

"No," Hazel admitted.

"Didn't sound like it. Not with the way you talk. Now come."

The housekeeper led her toward a chaise. Close to the fire, Hazel couldn't escape its lure. She dropped into the scent of down feathers. She'd relax just for a moment. In a couple of hours, she would defy the woman and search for Mr. Mortibel. For now, she would sit, feigning obedience.

"You wait right there. I'll bring you a washbasin."

"Thank you," Hazel said weakly.

When she returned, the housekeeper washed her jittery hands. Before she left Hazel to herself again, the woman said a little prayer, relieved that none of the blood belonged to Hazel.

Hazel closed her eyes. It was all she could do to remain still. And although it seemed only for a moment, when Hazel opened her eyes again, the fire had gone out completely.

It took her some time to recall the previous night. Soon, a pooling of blood filled her vision. The images wouldn't go away: the dying seers, Mr. Mortibel's bloodied face... She sprang upward, stumbling a bit before she could catch her balance on a bookshelf.

She drew back, mistaking the shadows that flickered across the books. It was just the dying embers of the fire. She was being foolish. *Breathe*, she told herself. She was safe now. She forced herself to believe it. There was no point thinking otherwise.

The room was ordinary enough—more than ordinary, in fact. She was in a library surrounded by more books than most might ever see in a lifetime. It wasn't one, but two stories with marble columns. Her father had told her once that there was much to tell about a person by the library they kept, whether they were just showing off or truly an intellectual. What about whether they were good or evil?

She read some of the titles. All alchemy related. Another enthusiast like her father and a member too, no doubt. She ran her hands along a few more spines, pulling her fingers back at the onset of voices.

"She doesn't know?" The housekeeper's voice was distinct.

"Blessed no, of course not. She need not. From what Mortibel told me, she would rather not."

Hazel's heart froze. Was Mr. Mortibel dead, then? Suppose he had died from his injuries while she had been asleep…

"How is he?" the housekeeper asked.

"Coping well enough. What of the girl? The blood on her hands… I have to say it distracted me at first."

"She was uninjured," the housekeeper responded. "The blood on her hands was not hers."

Hazel sank backward into the bookshelf. She almost didn't hear the other words. That Mr. Mortibel would live was all that mattered. Perhaps last night would be the last straw and he'd finally give up all this Silver Order nonsense.

"How did she seem?"

"A bit shaky, I'll say."

"The incident will no doubt encourage her to leave London. For that, I am glad. Perhaps it is better for it all to happen there."

Leaning toward the door, Hazel strained for more, but the voices had changed into whispers.

Hearing footfalls close in, Hazel rushed back to the chaise, her mind still spinning. Leave London? To get rid of the estate, she might not have a choice. She might have to—

Dr. Lagerfield entered, his peppered eyebrows lifted in surprise. "Awake, I see."

"Mr. Mortibel…"

"He lives."

Behind him, the housekeeper hurried in with tea and a tray of sugar biscuits. Dr. Lagerfield placed a hand on Hazel's shoulder. "You are safe." A teacup hovered over her face, steam filling her nostrils.

"Drink this," the housekeeper offered.

She took a sip to appease her host. It was only after she took a bite of sugar biscuit that the housekeeper seemed satisfied enough to leave. They both tasted normal enough. It was how she felt afterward that would be the true test.

"Poor girl. You have endured quite the ordeal," Dr. Lagerfield said.

"'Ordeal'? The word doesn't even begin to describe it." She leaned her head back against the cushion and shut her eyes, seeing the limp bodies on the floor of the catacombs yet again. She didn't think she would ever be able to forget it. The image would follow her the rest of her life.

"Please." He hovered a tray of biscuits in front of her. "You need your nourishment."

The man seemed to take her trust for granted. As a member, there was no knowing his intentions. Or if he was in fact the traitor.

"Forgive me." She placed her teacup back atop the tray. "But who, exactly, are you?"

"A friend, particularly of your father's. My condolences. I was very sorry about his passing."

Hazel looked down into her lap. The once-pristine muslin fabric was torn and blood-stained.

"Thank you." Looking back up into his gaze, she strained to find something familiar, wishing she had made better note of the Order's members when she'd been young.

"I know it will be difficult for you, but can you tell me what happened? Mortibel said the seers who attended… They're gone now. Was there anyone else?"

Hazel shook her head. "You were supposed to be there too,

weren't you? And the other members. What happened to them?"

Dr. Lagerfield didn't speak for some time. He must have known she'd want an explanation.

"The members have been growing fearful of our gatherings. I'm not proud to admit that so have I."

Hazel squeezed her fingers, trying to conceal her anger in Dr. Lagerfield's polite company. If Mr. Mortibel had been honest with her, if he had said any of the sort, she would have never attended.

"The men who attacked you. Did you recognize any of them?"

Again, Hazel shook her head. "They wore masks so we couldn't see their faces. The gunshots—I had never heard anything so loud. I couldn't watch; I closed my eyes. When I opened them—"

Dr. Lagerfield placed a hand on hers. She realized then she was shaking. She forced herself to take another sip of tea, trying to take comfort in its familiar taste and warmth. Last night, though terrifying and likely to haunt her for months, was over. She said it to herself again.

"Do you have any idea who those men were?"

"An inkling."

"Who?" Hazel demanded.

"They were members once. A long time ago." He blinked hard.

"'Members'?"

"Excommunicated members. Naturally, not everyone agrees with Mortibel's claim to your father's chair. It is the same with any organization that must name a new leader. But these dissenters are a minority, mind you."

"Just how small a minority?" she ventured.

"Our politics are complicated. Far too complex for you to concern yourself with."

The implication that she was just some ignorant girl made Hazel's blood simmer. For now, she pushed it aside.

"It's Mr. Mortibel I'm concerned about. Do you think he

could ever be convinced to leave the Order?"

"Mortibel will just have to be more careful. We will all have to be." Dr. Lagerfield took a sip of tea, as if there weren't the slightest possibility. Arguing would be no use. But she couldn't quite learn to accept that.

Once more, Dr. Lagerfield stretched out a tray of sugar biscuits, pulling it back at her refusal.

"He'll never be free of the Order's danger, will he?"

"Pardon my intrusion." The housekeeper appeared at the doorway again. "Mr. Mortibel has awoken, sir."

At the name, Hazel jolted upward.

Dr. Lagerfield's hand pressed her down ever so gently. "No, no, dear. I'd prefer you not to see him. Not yet."

"What? Why?" Hazel crossed her arms.

"He is in a much too fragile state to remain awake. Not even for the sake of one of your smiles."

Hazel blushed. "I just wanted—"

"You can't be ignorant of the effect you have on him."

This caught Hazel by surprise. After all this time, did Mr. Mortibel still harbor feelings for her? Had she been stupid to give up hope?

"There is much he and I have to discuss… In fact, it might be better if you went now. I'll have the carriage readied."

"No need." Hazel straightened her sleeves and brushed off a thin covering of soot, as if that might erase the night before. "I don't live far from here. Just a few blocks down."

"You're certain? An escort, then."

"I shan't trouble you. No one will notice me in this clothing." Furthermore, it was far too early for anyone of consequence to be out and about.

Her aunt would have already discovered she was missing. Hazel could only imagine the fits and vapors she was having. Hazel couldn't wait for an escort. She needed to get home now.

"Please give Mr. Mortibel my regards."

"Of course. We shall meet again soon. Of that, I am certain."

The statement sounded so oddly prophetic, Hazel paused before she rushed out into the street, crowded with pedestrians, carriages, and hackneys. She didn't care how much Dr. Lagerfield tried to push her away. She wouldn't give up. After what had happened, she was more determined than ever to convince Mr. Mortibel to leave the Order.

First, she had to collect any valuables at the estate and get rid of it. The best part was that she would get to see Mr. Mortibel again. He had only just come back into her life. She wouldn't see him disappear again, not this soon.

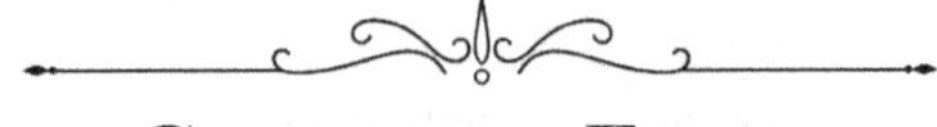

CHAPTER FOUR

A New Foe

THEO SQUARED HIS stance on the busy London street and peered into the windows of an empty carriage. The clear glass aligned perfectly on both sides so he could see right through to the home on the other side of the street. Right into Lagerfield's windows. The traitor had kept them wide open.

His eyelids grew heavy with exhaustion, but he forced himself to stand straighter. Long after he'd dismissed his men to a local inn, he'd insisted on pressing on. He'd needed to follow after the carriage.

The ostentatious thing was gilded on almost every surface. Shining brightly in the moonlight, it was almost too easy to keep track of. This—he laughed to himself—*this* was the man who was trying to take his family's place. A man who couldn't even stay hidden in the night. Mortibel had gained a surprisingly large number of supporters, far more than Theo had expected—he would give him that. But it still wouldn't be enough. Theo's men were building up his numbers too.

By rights, he should storm into that house and kill Mortibel and everyone who stood in his way. He'd cast out the rest of his supporters too. Revenge had a bitter bite and he could almost taste it. And yet something held him back. Or rather, *someone*.

Before he could act, he had to know who that mystery woman was and how in God's name she could possibly think Mortibel's life was worth saving. He wasn't happy that she had helped Mortibel. Not one bit. But sooner or later, she would discover her mistake.

He had tried to warn her. Clearly, she hadn't taken him seriously. If nothing else, he was going to find out who she was. Interrogate her, more like.

He didn't know how long he stood there, frozen in thought. It seemed a long time before the door finally opened.

At first, he almost mistook her for any other servant. But no typical servant would leave through the front door and he could never forget that hair. Still tied up but with several strands hanging loose, it was dark as night yet shiny as silk. No servant had hair so fine as that. He almost fancied he could smell the rosewater.

He'd realized the night before her servant's garb had been nothing more than a ruse so she could walk about unchaperoned. Even now, she had let herself become quite vulnerable.

His gaze settled next on her lips. Unpainted but still the color of raspberries. He couldn't see her eyes, but she had to be tired.

He'd thought she would be there all day. Surely, she needed rest after last night. She had to be tired. And yet, her steps were hurried.

Staying on the other side of the street, Theo took off after her, keeping in line with either the passing carriages or pedestrians. The late-morning traffic had picked up significantly. He almost lost her not once, but four times.

He considered taking her right there and then. He could take his knife and press it into her back and demand she tell him Mortibel's plans. But where would he take her for a little tête-à-tête? The inn wasn't suitable, nor was the alleyway. There were too many witnesses at this time of day. He was far better off waiting until she reached wherever she called home. At least then he'd know who in the blazes she was.

He expected her to get into a carriage. The lady he was sure she was had to prefer a cab to walking. In that case, Theo was already planning his next move. He could jump onto the back. He'd just have to be quick and light-footed.

But rather than signaling for a carriage, she kept walking. He crossed the street and closed in. Wasn't she tired? He certainly was. It was getting harder to maintain his determination. There was too much at stake for him and his family. The entire fate of the Order was in his hands alone.

He was catching up to her. Sidling behind a flower seller brandishing a bouquet of white lilies, he was almost inches away. Close enough to smell the gunpowder on her hair.

She looked behind her. It took him off guard, but he swooped into an alleyway just in time. He had stayed out of her peripheral vision. Was she a clairvoyant of sorts? Many in London claimed to be, though the real ones were few and far between.

She was not a member—he knew that much. But he was glad he had helped her. She could be very useful, indeed.

Again, she picked up her pace, almost to a run. She was no fool. Even if she hadn't seen him, she could feel the danger on her heels. After all she'd been through the night before, she'd no doubt be extra jumpy. That made it even a better time to strike. Her mounting fear would be enough to keep her docile.

He weaved between more pedestrians. The long trains of the ladies took up more of the street. The bright colors distracted him from his prize. She must have lived in the fashionable part of London. At any time, she'd be home. But it also meant that more eyes landed on him.

He tried to blend in, avoiding eye contact and giving casual nods when someone stared. It was little use. He looked as haggard as a vagrant. Not only was he covered in sweat with his hair askew, he couldn't be entirely sure if there was blood on him. His clothing was nowhere near as fine as that of the residents of this area, either. It was dirty and torn. He needed to get out of here, and fast.

Just as he feared someone might alert an officer, the woman hurried inside one of the townhomes.

He was about to force himself through the gate, when he noticed a familiar cypher. He backed away immediately. In less than three seconds, he disappeared into the street.

It had been Grey's cypher. He cursed. He knew very well the man had had a daughter. In fact, Theo had plans for her. Using fear was no longer an option. According to his sources, Whitestone Manor was in her hands and her hands alone. If he wanted it, he had to consider other tactics.

She was sure to return to the Malvern Hills to take stock of her new inheritance. So he'd be seeing her soon. Very soon. Not as a dangerous man of the streets, but as a gentleman. He could play both parts quite well.

CHAPTER FIVE

An Uncertain Journey

Five Days Later…

HAZEL HAD ALMOST forgotten the beauty of the Malverns. Not yet touched by snow, the grassy hills, a mix of green and gold, zigzagged along the horizon. The scent of hay and damp moss had replaced the scent of sewage miles ago.

The spires and turrets of great manors peeked out above the horizon. They were all occupied this time of year, at least until February, when their great masters left for the thrills and frills of the London Season. Still, Hazel had kept her plans quiet enough that she expected her time in the country to be solitary, by and large. If she had any luck, she'd sell the estate and the transaction would be carried through without rumors circulating.

She'd been off as soon as her aunt would allow.

When she'd discovered Hazel missing that morning after the memorial, Hazel's state of dress, her clothes torn and bloodied, had thrown her into an absolute fit. Naturally, Aunt Catherine had assumed some sort of tryst. She would believe no other tale. As for the blood, Hazel had said something about a dog fight. As innocuous as she'd tried to make it sound, it had taken a few days and nursing before her aunt was well enough and perhaps willing enough to let Hazel set off.

Entering a wood, the carriage shepherding her and her lady's maid, Delphine Emmerson, approached their destination. She wasn't quite as prepared as she'd have liked to have been. At the manor, she didn't know what to expect. A small staff of servants still maintained the home but under no supervision and only once a week.

When she arrived, Hazel hoped to make them full-time. She would probably have to hire a few extra from town too. Her father had never cared to have much help. He had always preferred his solitude. That had been the difficult part about him. He could be alone for days at a time and think nothing of it. After her mother had died, it had often meant a lonely childhood. And yet, when he had been around, his time with her had been actually quite impactful. Every conversation a lesson to be learned.

She turned her eyes to the window, hoping to see the great manor at any moment. What state would it be in? Without occupants for at least a month, it would be undoubtedly cold and dusty. Perhaps vermin had made their way in or a window had been left open, letting in all the elements and leaves.

Though she expected the worst, she allowed the bright-yellow elm trees to give her a moment of serenity. They were just as she remembered.

Many an afternoon, she had run up and down these woods, venturing far beyond where she ought to have. She'd return just after nightfall, her pockets full of odd rocks her father called "metamorphic." He had explained their unique properties and for once, she had actually listened.

She had found Marcus—Mr. Mortibel—the same way. Seven years old with violets bunched in his hand. The sun had been descending behind the trees and the forest air had been chilling fast. He hadn't been exploring, not anymore. He'd been lost and shaking like a leaf.

She'd offered him a way out and in exchange, he'd let her see inside Mortibel Manor, the great, gray palace perched on the hill.

They were minutes away now. From what seemed a distant dream, she remembered the trees grew denser here and the hills loomed higher, almost as a sort of protection. Few passersby would dare enter such deep, dark vegetation. In this terrain, there were any number of dangers: the carriage tossing a wheel, or vagabonds who sometimes camped out for the night, for example. Hazel, on the other hand, was much more fearful of the stately manor ahead, and whatever it was her father had left behind.

The carriage slowed along the drive where the trees had finally begun to thin out. She opened the window wide, half-expecting the place to be in shambles or perhaps charred from fire.

Nothing was visible save for the black, gnarled trees, their leaves a million different shades of gold and red. Her heightened sense of color had always been best suited for the country. Ever since she'd been a child, it had given her a particular penchant for nature and the changing of seasons. Something she had missed a great deal in London, where gray and black prevailed above all other colors.

"I do wish we had trees and woods like this in town," Hazel said.

Emmerson barely looked up from her knitting. Still sour about the visit, she had been silent for most of the trip. Her eyes narrowed at a barn. "I do hope you'll be mindful during your walks," she said. "Wearing my clothing might save you in London, but not here."

"I replaced them, didn't I?" Hazel protested when she felt a stab of guilt. "*And* I gave you a few of my cast-offs…"

"Just thought you might need the reminder."

Hazel groaned inwardly. It had been clear from the start that Emmerson would be keeping her usual watchful eye. In all likelihood, Aunt Catherine had instructed her to do so.

"I don't know what I shall do here with my spare time."

Emmerson pursed her lips. "I can't knit forever."

She'd no doubt miss their trips to the opera and theater the most. Only two years older than herself, Emmerson loved to be seen.

"Come now. I'm sure there are enough servants in the neighborhood with whom to share gossip."

"Not nearly so civilized as those in London, I daresay."

Hazel almost laughed. Emmerson cared more about status than those who had it. In the country, where every servant was beneath her, she certainly wouldn't have any friends.

Hazel felt bad about it, of course. But all she could do was promise to try to make her stay as pleasant as possible.

Despite Emmerson's pessimism, the unseasonably warm, sunny day seemed to brighten their prospects. A few days of warmth would give them time to air out the place before the cold followed them from London.

The horses began to slow, prompting Hazel to pop her head out the door. A tall, rusted, iron gate blocked their path. So heavily encrusted with dead brittle ivy, only snippets of a pale, green lawn peeked through. The rest of the white, brick fencing afforded no view at all.

Rattling the coach, the coachman alighted, dropping Hazel's and then Emmerson's trunks to the ground with a *thud*.

"Sir," Hazel said, stepping out before the coachman could come to assist her. "We have another several yards." Surely, he would drive them around front. Their trunks were much too heavy to carry.

"This is as far as I go, miss."

"You can't be serious." It was the rumors that scared him off. Hazel only wondered where he had heard them, though she guessed the inn the night before.

He grumbled something unintelligible. Before Hazel could protest, Emmerson stepped down. "Don't bother. We can take them one at a time."

Unlike Hazel, Emmerson didn't seem bothered by this prospect of being alone. The streets of London had hardened her resolve far more than it had Hazel's.

"Sorry, miss." The lanky coachman touched the tip of hat and hurried back to the reins. With a snap, the horses galloped away, leaving Hazel and Emmerson behind in a swirl of dust.

The bastard. Hazel had hoped to employ him for another trip to Mr. Mortibel's estate. Now she'd have to walk. Here, she had no horses, no food, no anything. Again, she was grateful for Emmerson's company. Her aunt certainly wouldn't have made the trip, not with her health.

"I cannot thank you enough, Emmerson."

"I'm just happy to be on steady ground."

Hoping to get a better look of the place, Hazel broke away a few of the branches bound to the gate. Instead, she revealed a crest of sorts. She might have recognized her own family crest had she ever actually seen it. But for as long as she had known, the ivy had covered the bars, keeping it hidden. With increased fervor, she tore into more ivy, revealing the engraving of a brilliant silver horse. The rest wouldn't budge. She panted, out of breath.

"I see the lock." Emmerson pulled aside more branches while Hazel took out the key her solicitor had provided. Would the place be as ghastly as she had come to believe or would it hold the same wonder she had seen in the place as a child? Several jiggles and a frustrated kick later, the rusted thing swung open. In that moment, Hazel forgot her aching limbs and the fact she'd have to carry her trunk some fifty yards.

The white, brick building barely stood out behind the overcast sky. Unlike the other Tudor manors in the area, the home had a much more intimidating medieval air.

Its flat façade was broken up by a series of Gothic archways and latticed windows, the black, marble columns and intricate ironwork adding a simple sort of grandeur. It was the kind of building that belonged to a higher class—one to which, growing up, Hazel had never felt as if she had quite belonged. With a set income, Hazel and her aunt had lived modestly in London. Certainly not like they had belonged here.

It almost pained her to sell a place so beautiful, particularly in autumn. The trees that dotted the lawn were alight with even more fiery shades of reds and purples. The shrubs and weeds were overgrown, of course, but manageable. *An adequately skilled gardener needs only to refill the flowerbeds and trim back the weeds*, she imagined telling a prospective buyer.

One might never guess the dark nature of the home. Hazel almost forgot it herself.

"I hadn't expected this." Emmerson stood wide-eyed.

With newfound excitement, they lifted first Emmerson's lighter trunk and proceeded to the front door. The next trunk, Hazel's, was a much more grueling effort, but at long last, they dragged it up the half-moon steps and set it down upon the marble floor of the foyer.

Hazel gazed up at the blade-like crystals of the chandelier. It mirrored a glistening vine mosaic built into the floor. This was the inheritance she had cared so little about, that she'd wished she could ignore. Already, the place had her under its spell. She had been away too long. With a hand to her chest and eyes wide, even Emmerson seemed proud to be standing in the place.

"For being short on staff, I thought there'd be more cleaning to be done," Emmerson said with a huff of relief. "All it needs is a bit of dusting and a few of the windows cleaned."

Hazel left the trunks at the door and made her way down a hall lined with windows and bathed thankfully in natural light. She had glimpses of the past still on her mind: running through the halls with freshly-picked flowers bunched in her hand and dirt trailing on the floor behind her. Collected over the centuries, tapestries and landscape paintings still crowded the walls.

She took in the painting of some woodland at dawn. She could almost smell moss and decaying leaves and feel the rays of light on her face. The same kind of magic she remembered as a child. Was everything here touched by it?

Emmerson's footfalls echoed behind her. "Should be worth a fortune." Her fingers trailed the frame.

Hazel nodded. She had underestimated the place. It was so quiet and peaceful. In London, she was used to a near-constant buzz of horse hooves.

"Shall I prepare our rooms?" For a brief second, Hazel had forgotten that Emmerson was a paid servant with whom she was exploring the house, not a friend.

"Yes, thank you…and thank you again for coming here with me."

Emmerson simply nodded and turned away.

For now, Hazel would have to explore alone. No matter how much that scared her.

In the library, she thrust aside heavy curtains, clouds of dust floating in the streams of light. The scent of dust had grown thicker in some places, the windows covered in a layer of grime.

More importantly, the books had remained, the sweet musk of them most welcome. Rising two stories, the shelves towered ten shelves high. She guessed there were several hundred books, each organized by topic, then by author name. Amongst numerous books about chemistry and botany, there were a variety of novels. She had a place to which to escape, then.

"Miss Hazel," Emmerson called out with some panic. Hazel dropped the book she had been reading and went into the hall.

"What is it?"

"Horse hooves!"

Hazel still hadn't located Emmerson, but she recognized the sound. The thuds and sprinkling of gravel were all too familiar. Hazel rushed to the door and opened it. A traveler approached with great speed, the air too clouded with gravel for her to see. A hand wave. A splash of dark black hair. Mr. Mortibel.

Hazel stepped out onto the drive.

"I thought I saw a carriage come through here. And when I saw the gate open…" Mr. Mortibel dropped down from his horse and sucked in a breath. "I thought you might have come. Dr.

Lagerfield too."

"Yes, well, there are certain matters that need attending to is all."

"I can't tell you how pleased I am," he went on, his eyes almost gleeful.

"You are?" What about the danger the Order posed?

"How is your aunt?" He looked behind her toward the hall. "She's not here with you, is she?"

"Her health would not allow it." Hazel had left behind several cough suppressants and relaxers she hoped would be enough.

"One day, she'll be well enough to join you here. I'm sure of it."

"She is happy in London. As was I." Did he actually think she would stay? How long could they keep up this false banter? "I don't mean to stay long, Mr. Mortibel. I just came back to collect some things."

"Don't be ridiculous." He closed in with a frown. "You've only just returned home."

"'Home'? This place is hardly my home."

At that, his face crumpled if only an inch. Did he actually think she should make a home for herself here, after all that had happened, all that she had seen? Here, danger seemed far too ripe.

"You need your rest. And food too, I imagine. How about dinner? Would you accept an invitation to supper? Grace should be out."

"Your sister's not in London? I thought she preferred winters there."

"You know how motherly she can be. She absolutely refused to leave me in my solitude."

Though he didn't say it, perhaps she too was concerned with his safety. Had he even told her about the catacombs? He likely hadn't wanted to worry her.

"What do you say?" Mr. Mortibel pressed.

"Very well." Hazel could hardly turn down a hot meal made by the Mortibels' famous cook. Plus, she and Mr. Mortibel could talk. "If it's all well with you, my lady's maid, Emmerson, will accompany me. I'd hate to leave her all alone in this big house."

"Wonderful. We'll make a place for her in the servants' hall."

His voice sounded as cheerful as ever, and his smile was gleaming. He really was pleased that she had returned. *Probably for the sake of nostalgia,* Hazel thought. Having dinner at his estate, it would be just like old times.

"Do you think you could be so kind as to spare a carriage too? Our coachman seems to have abandoned us and Emmerson has no way to get the necessary supplies."

"How's this: I will send over two, one to retrieve you and one so that Emmerson may go to town tomorrow. I'll even have our coachman, Nathan, leave you some horses in case of an emergency."

"That would be most appreciated." Hazel was not wholly unaffected by this sudden show of hospitality. After their long, arduous journey, it was nice to have a friend again. And he was right—she did need her rest. Every muscle ached from all the thrashing in the carriage.

"Your timing couldn't be better, really." His smile widened. "I have something of the utmost importance to discuss with you."

"As do I," Hazel said weakly. Mr. Mortibel's news, whatever it was, would have everything to do with the Order. Hazel was certain of that much.

CHAPTER SIX

The New Chairman

AT THE PALACE on the hill, Hazel had never been more pleased to be sitting before a blazing fire, hot cup of tea in hand. Though perhaps she would much rather be alone. Not long after Mr. Mortibel had left her to attend to some business, footfalls approached. Miss Grace Mortibel swept in. As her cloak was still on, she'd clearly been out. With downcast eyes, a freckled lady's maid gathered the emerald velvet from Miss Mortibel's shoulders. The artificial dye was so concentrated, that to Hazel's color-focused eyes, it was practically glowing. For those who had less acuity to colors, it likely appeared a pleasant shade, but to her, it was quite garish.

Miss Mortibel, who had sharp, aquiline features like her brother, smiled wanly, holding Hazel under her typical scrutiny. A look Hazel remembered well. She had disapproved of Hazel's close friendship with Mr. Mortibel from the start. Even at a young age, Miss Mortibel had been as much aware of her high reputation as she had been of Hazel's father's poor one. But as hard as she tried, Miss Mortibel's efforts to separate her brother from Hazel's acquaintance had never succeeded. If Mr. Mortibel's parents hadn't been so busy with their own affairs, they might have tried too.

Among the dozens of gilded landscapes and distinguished portraits, Hazel felt out of place enough. She had managed to change out of her traveling clothes but had elected to don her warmest, albeit plainest, grayish-green gown. Miss Mortibel's dress, however, was a glossy sheen of lavender silk with striking silver trim along the neckline.

"I thought I heard word of your arrival. You look well."

Despite the pleasant words, something in Miss Mortibel's voice didn't quite ring true. They hadn't seen each other in years, but Hazel had not forgotten her difficult manners, particularly the other lady's often rude remarks about her father.

"Your journey proved uneventful?" Miss Mortibel prodded.

"Quite, if not somewhat treacherous. I half-expected to toss a wheel and be forced to walk."

"The roads were that bad?"

"Compared to London."

"Oh, *London*. Don't remind me. I loathe to think of all the engagements I cannot attend."

"Your presence is equally missed, I'm sure."

A painful silence fell over them with only the crackling fire to break the somber atmosphere. They simply were nothing alike, had nothing in common.

Even the way Miss Mortibel sat down and smoothed out her skirts seemed a cut above. Somehow, it had been easy to forget that one day, Mr. Mortibel would be a baronet. He hadn't outranked her within the Order, at least. So they had gotten along easily. With Miss Mortibel, on the other hand, Hazel didn't feel this at all.

"I was surprised to hear you had elected to stay in the country," Hazel finally managed.

"The estate won't manage itself. With all of Marcus's distractions, it is incumbent upon me to take over the necessary duties." She waved a hand through the air. "I won't stand for his deviations much longer, though. I mean to return to London very soon."

Hazel almost forgot how much Miss Mortibel hated the Order. She supposed they had that in common. "I don't mean to stay here long myself."

"Oh." Miss Mortibel raised a knowing brow. "Then you must not be aware of his intentions."

"I'm not sure what you mean."

"He means to ask for your hand, of course."

"He *what?*" Hazel laughed, half in shock. "That's ridiculous. And impossible."

He wasn't supposed to have any feelings for her. She wasn't supposed to either, not after all his months of silence.

"I quite agree. Unfortunately..." Miss Mortibel cusped her hands together with careful grace. "I don't much approve of the match. Connecting the two estates would be advantageous, yes, but there is our name to consider. It would ruin me and any hope I have for a respectable marriage."

The blunt words caught Hazel off guard for a moment.

"W-What? Why?" she stammered. "Yes, most are aware of my father's strangeness but not his exact...activities. And it's been years since I last saw him." Some—at least a few—could see past her father's oddness, couldn't they? Proposal aside, this was her reputation Miss Mortibel was questioning now. She couldn't let her get away with insulting her thus.

"Have you received any other offers?"

"No—but—"

Was Miss Mortibel implying there had been a reason she'd gotten no other offers for her hand? Had she and her aunt naively believed the past could be forgotten?

"I'm afraid I must insist you decline. Aside from the damage it would do to me, Marcus *is* to inherit our father's seat in the House of Lords."

"There will be nothing to decline. All we have to discuss is his departure from the Order. I feel the same as you on the matter. It isn't safe."

"Because of your father."

"Who is dead." Even in the grave, resentment continued to follow him, and worst of all her as well.

Miss Mortibel showed no pity. Dark thoughts concerning death were unwelcome in this tea room with its bright floral arrangements and lofty windows. Wooden floors and wallpaper would have been insufficient here. There could be nothing less than intricate, mosaic tile and fresco wall paintings. Just like Miss Mortibel, it was all pretentiousness.

"Promise me," Miss Mortibel demanded.

Hazel stood up with plans of escape when Mr. Mortibel strode in. He caught his breath at the sight of them but recovered quickly. "Why isn't this a lovely sight," he said, the distress clear in his eyes. "Just like old times."

"I am famished." Hazel remained on her feet. "Is dinner prepared?"

"Quite. I had Cook make something special for your homecoming." He turned to his sister. "Unfortunately, I had hoped for a private audience. You'll forgive me, won't you, sister?"

Miss Mortibel glanced frantically between the two.

"Grace?" her brother asked again.

The woman didn't bother to argue. With a huff, she swept out of the room, her skirts shaking with each annoyed step.

Mr. Mortibel's smile broke at the sight of his sister's retreat, his brow furrowed.

"She hasn't changed much." Hazel tried her best to laugh it off, but it only ended up sounding more nervous. She didn't think she had ever been more nervous in her life. Mr. Mortibel wasn't going to propose. There was no chance.

Then why was she so nervous? She couldn't simply ask him about it. If it wasn't true, it would only serve to both anger and embarrass him. If it was true… Hazel didn't know what to think.

"The odious woman. She still hasn't learned to accept my plans. I doubt she ever will. Whatever she said to you, it is best to ignore."

Hazel swallowed, barely hearing any of his words. All that

stood out to her was the word: plans. What exactly was he planning?

"One day, I shall be rid of her." He went on with a roll of his eyes.

Hazel understood now. Miss Mortibel's presence meant he was constantly being watched. He could hardly go about any Order business now. Yet another roadblock to Mr. Mortibel's efforts.

Rather than just stare, Hazel forced herself to say something. "You think she'll marry soon?"

A butler stepped in and rang a bell, jolting Hazel in her already frantic state. "Dinner is served."

"For her sake, I hope so," Mr. Mortibel answered. The veiled threat in combination with a hand on the small of her back sent a shiver down to her bones. Though he smiled, anger still lingered in his eyes. "Forget about her. Dinner awaits."

In the short distance to the dining room, she had grown increasingly nervous. Something in his quiet demeanor told her Miss Mortibel was not far from the mark in thinking an offer was imminent. It had to be the news he had spoken about earlier.

Hazel should have felt elated. A few years ago, she might have been, but a dark thought passed her mind. What if it wasn't herself he wanted? What if it was the estate and all the strange Order-related things it held within? In lieu of a cash offer, marriage was really the only way he could get it.

A footman pulled out a chair for her closest to the fire. Her hands went from shaky to clammy. Suddenly, the heat of the fire seemed oppressive.

"The place hasn't changed much, has it?" Mr. Mortibel commented, innocent enough.

"Not at all." She took in the familiar way the chandelier glittered across the latticed windows that stretched from floor to ceiling. In the daytime, the room boasted an impressive view of endless green and golden hills. But at this time of night, there was only blackness.

The footmen came in then, placing down their first course of consommé. In her ravenous state, Hazel could have gulped it straight from the bowl. Amongst such extravagant place settings, propriety only allowed her to swallow a mere spoonful.

Somewhere in the below stairs, Emmerson was with the rest of the servants. At the moment, they'd be readying dinner for the family and their guest. But in an hour or so, she hoped Emmerson would be able to enjoy a meal with meat. She'd likely sit with at least a half dozen servants. So at least she'd have company.

Mr. Mortibel cleared his throat, as if not quite sure how to continue. "Have you had much time to go through your father's things?"

"Not yet, no."

"When you do, I feel I should warn you…your father's home still holds some…*strange* items. Should you come across them—"

"I'm no idiot, Mr. Mortibel."

She was smart enough to keep out of the laboratory. It was the part of the manor Mr. Mortibel wanted most of all. Once the place sold, she would have to have it cleared out.

"Have you yourself seen anything of late?" she asked.

"What do you mean?" He tilted his head.

"Have you already searched the place? With it sitting abandoned, I assumed…"

"I wouldn't dare betray your trust like that. Nor your father's." He released a huff of breath.

Quite frankly, Hazel didn't see what was stopping him. Being so close to the estate, knowing it had long since become abandoned, it had to have been tempting, though apparently, he had too much honor.

"Your father once trusted me with his life, Miss Grey. And you treat me like…like I'm some adversary. Do you not remember that we were once friends?"

"Of course." Didn't he know that she had once wanted so much more? It was still possible for them. If only he could leave the Order behind.

"It is because of our friendship that I don't want this for you," she said. "After what happened in the catacombs, you can't take my father's place, Mr. Mortibel. You just can't."

Somehow, sitting here before him, the words felt so futile. With his gentle smile, any hope of convincing him seemed to wash away. She had been a fool to think she could.

"Your father would not have wanted me to abandon the Order like this. Nor would he want to see your home abandoned as it is. Or sold. *If* it can indeed be sold, mind."

"You don't think the place will sell?" She swallowed. If that was the case, she'd be in a world of trouble. She'd have to hire a manager for the estate and that would cost money… She couldn't possibly live here. Not a chance.

"It has a reputation is all. Everything your father touched does."

Hazel raised her chin. "I still mean to try."

"Would it be so bad to stay? The lands make a healthy income."

Hazel shrugged.

"I know what you and your aunt need. You'll not get it in London, no matter how many Seasons you endure."

"That seems to be a popular opinion lately." The words stung. Even more than when Miss Mortibel had said them. Was she really right?

"You must be aware of your reputation. Everyone knows about your father. Why else do you think you are invited to so many gatherings? You're little more than an intrigue to them."

The words were almost too cruel to bear, but that was the truth of London society. She should not be surprised in the least. She knew Aunt Catherine had been too optimistic.

"You're a curiosity to them, but I'm afraid you can't expect to have any offers. But one, that is… Miss Grey. That is, Hazel—"

"Please." Her heart began to thump louder in her ears, as if trying to be heard. Her heart wanted her to say *yes*. But in her mind, there was more than a hint of caution, there was panic.

Even though Miss Mortibel had prepared her, she was still taken aback.

"We could be happy together." His hand reached out for hers, but she didn't grasp it.

She tried to remain calm.

She didn't want to say it. As if saying it would make it true. But she had to. "Your offer has nothing to do with my father's estate? *My* estate?"

"It will be easy linking the two estates," he admitted. "You have much to gain, you know. A title someday, for one. You would do well to consider it."

"'A title'?" Hazel shot up from her seat, her struggle for composure gone. "Of all the things, Mr. Mortibel. You think *that's* what I want?"

Where were his declarations of his endless, undying love? They didn't always accompany proposals in London, she knew that, but that was what she wanted nonetheless. Had that not even occurred to him?

She considered leaving, but her feet wouldn't allow her. Part of her was still holding out for him to tell her otherwise.

"Hazel, please." He stood up and stretched out a hand. When she didn't take it, he shook his head. He'd never admit the truth.

"Is my offer so ridiculous to you?" Though his words were calm, there was no disguising the fury in his eyes. "Even your father once had the notion we might do well together."

So had she. Her old feelings didn't make her wistful, though. Rather, they had the opposite effect. They reminded her of his months of silence that had been nothing short of painful. In the last *nine* months, not once had he written, not even a short note.

A silence that had ended only because of her father's death. It was too convenient. She didn't need him to confirm the obvious truth: his offer had everything to do with the estate and little with love. She should have seen the offer coming the moment she'd heard her father had died.

"Why didn't you—" The question was coming out just as

pathetic as she'd feared. For the sake of the footmen standing nearby, she lowered her voice. "You didn't even bother to write."

"I—" His voice was starting to shake—from fear or anger, she couldn't tell.

Footfalls sounded, a footman delivering yet another course. It smelled of fish, but Hazel wouldn't let her gaze stray from Mr. Mortibel for a second. She wanted to gauge every twitch for any hint of a lie.

Mr. Mortibel waved the servant away. "Out please." He raised his voice. "All of you."

He waited until they had all padded away before coming around the table toward her. "I told you how ill your father was. I was occupied with caring for him. Had I thought you'd have wanted to help… Yes, maybe I would have written."

Hazel dropped her gaze to the pristine, white tablecloth. She had been a terrible daughter. There was no denying that. But her father had never been a great parent, either.

"I think he thought that if he left you the estate, you'd change your mind about us. That you'd stop denying everything you are. You're not made for London, Hazel. You're made for the beautiful Malvern Hills. For the Order."

"London may not be my proper place, but neither is the Order." As much as the child in her wanted to say *yes* to his offer, marrying him would mean marrying the Order too and staying here forever. She couldn't have that.

"Then your father's a fool for leaving the place to you." His nostrils flared. The words were the cruelest he had ever said to her.

Hazel kept her stare on the table. The tears that gleaned over her eyes shouldn't have surprised her, but they did. In his will, her father's intentions had been clear. Even after all her years of denying the Order, he'd still held out hope that she would one day love the Order as much as he had.

She took a calming breath. She had managed almost a week without a single tear and now she couldn't seem to control herself. As much as she had tried to bury the feeling, she could no longer shake this sense that she should have been there for him in his final days. No matter how distant he had been, it was her duty as a daughter.

"He should have known better than to leave it to me."

"He did so because you are family, because you share the same blood." Mr. Mortibel's voice turned gentle again. "There are few who would have done differently."

Hazel swallowed. She could only imagine Mr. Mortibel's resentment that she had been given the estate instead of him. Much more than she had been a daughter, Mr. Mortibel had been like a son to her father. From childhood on, he had wanted to follow in her father's footsteps, preferring it, in fact, to his own inheritance.

"You used to love this place, helping your father gather special plants and herbs… Why, you even helped grind the necessary bases for his formulas and experimentations."

"That was just a few times."

"But you had an interest in his work once. You inherited his gift, remember?"

Mr. Mortibel was talking about her propensity for colors, her ability to see a thousand more than the average person. Most useful in distinguishing the powders and chemicals used in alchemy, but particularly useless otherwise.

"I was entirely ignorant. He never told me what he was really doing." Her father had only promised to tell her once she was older. "The truth, I had to see for myself."

"If you could just tell me what you saw that night." He leaned in, his eyes shining.

Hazel shook her head. She had only ever shared the details of the event with her aunt. All Mr. Mortibel needed to know was what it had led her to do. She had never done anything more brazen. That night, she hadn't even waited for morning to come. She'd packed a carpet bag of her things and taken her horse to town. The next day, she'd sold her horse for a train ticket and made her way to London to the safety of her aunt's. She hadn't spoken a single word to her father since.

In letters, Hazel would only tell Mr. Mortibel that she had seen something horrible, truly horrible, and nothing else. But it was likely he knew exactly what she had seen, a fact that should have warned her against him.

"Would you consider leasing the place?" he asked. "I could pay you in due time. You and your aunt would be quite comfortable for years to come."

The words stunned her for a moment. He was still trying to take hold of the place. He would never stop.

"Perhaps you should heed your sister's advice. You're far better suited for the House of Lords."

Mr. Mortibel crossed his arms. "All Grace cares for is tea parties and the highest title in the room."

"But not you. You care nothing for power."

"Not that kind, no. Not in the least. But the kind you could have had…I would never squander that away. What would our members care that you were a woman? We're not like the rest of the world, are we? We're more cultured than that. Ours is an ancient wisdom going back not hundreds, but thousands—*tens of thousands*—of years. A society that was greater than the ancient Romans, even. But the position is beneath you, somehow. You care only for the guineas the estate will fetch. I never thought you so greedy."

The insult dug its claws in deep. "You are proving to be as cruel and immoral as the Order."

"You were born to be one of us." Mr. Mortibel's jaw tightened.

"What binds you to this cause? Just because you followed my father around like a dog doesn't make you his son."

Mr. Mortibel leaned in and squeezed a fist, scaring her for moment. "If you'd seen the things I have… There are circumstances you wouldn't understand." Mr. Mortibel spoke half under his breath. As usual, he refused to explain precious Order business. All her life, he, like her father, had been determined to keep secrets from her.

"Is safety your primary concern? Is that why you want to leave us behind?" he asked—almost *begged*. "You need not worry about safety here. Not with me."

Hazel considered this a moment. The pure irony of the question after his little outburst. "I hardly feel safe at all."

"Please consider your options. You haven't many. There isn't a single gentleman in London who would make you an offer. Not amidst all the rumors swirling. Do you have the slightest idea the kind of words that have been spoken about you? Witchcraft, potions, daughter of a sorcerer. Things of that sort."

Hazel almost screamed out at the terrible words. She could not imagine anyone saying these things about her, much less Mr. Mortibel. The words seemed to echo across the dining room. For how long had they been circulating? She didn't want to know.

She'd always feared her father might ruin her chances. She'd hoped she might be safe behind her aunt's name. In reality, society's morbid interest in her father was all that kept them from being cast out entirely.

"Forgive me. Before you make any rash decisions, I just thought you should know your true position in society."

As hungry as she still was, she couldn't stand to remain here a moment longer. She backed away from him, shaking her head.

"At least take the evening to think it over," he said. "You know how much I have cared for you over the years. I have all your life."

Hazel wanted to believe him. Hell, she wanted to say *yes*. But not with all the doubt lingering in the back of her mind. Unless she discovered otherwise, she would always wonder if she was just a solution to his problems. A way to gain a stronger foothold within the Order.

There was only one way she could be certain. She gave it one last shot.

"I will accept, if you abandon the Order," she said. "Leave the

Order and I will do anything you ask of me." She held her breath, waiting for an answer. She had laid it all out, stripped herself of everything that might have guarded her from rejection, and she almost couldn't bear it. "We could leave the Malvern Hills. We could go anywhere. I don't care where."

He stilled. "Why would you want such a thing? This is your home. My home."

"You know precisely why."

"Perhaps one day I shall."

But that was really code for *never*. "It has to be straightaway."

"You know I can't do that. I can't just leave. I need time."

"Then I can't stay. I have no choice but to sell."

"You've chosen to remain obstinate." He threw his head back.

"Practical, rather."

"I'd call it *rash*. You're selling all your family's possessions and you're not even in debt," he barked.

"There is little point in this." Hazel turned for the door. They were at an impasse. As much as she wanted to convince Mr. Mortibel to leave, all he had wanted was to convince her to stay.

She paused at the doorway. "If you don't mind, I'll need to borrow your driver—"

"Of course." Mr. Mortibel stood. "No hard feelings. The offer stands."

Hazel retreated down the hall, searching for a servant to summon Emmerson. A scullery maid was kneeing before the seating room's largest fireplace.

"Call for Emmerson in the servant's hall, will you?" Hazel said tersely, still angry from the previous exchange. "I'll be waiting in the carriage."

The maid rushed off and Hazel proceeded to the foyer. She hated how well she remembered the place from childhood. Little had changed, indeed. The same pale-blue drapes lined the windows. The front door still had the same lion head doorknob, tarnished in all the same places.

There was a time Mr. Mortibel—*Marcus* to her then—would have followed her through the hall and begged her to stay. They had gotten into their little childhood squabbles before. Hazel hardly remembered those days any more. He had changed and all for the worse.

She didn't want to stay a moment longer in this house, much less continue to live next door. She was determined more than ever to sell her estate now. She didn't belong in these vast, elaborate manors any more than she had belonged in the Order. London at least felt like home. Mr. Mortibel's home in particular, with its gold-gilded walls and halls of mirrors, could never be.

CHAPTER SEVEN

The Buyer

EARLY THE NEXT morning, Hazel had given up on any hope of sleep. In her dreams, she saw the ritual again, the very one that had sent her running to London. Somehow, the manor had made the memories even stronger.

Her father was kneeling down on a circle of marble. She didn't understand why, but he was bleeding down his chest. And willingly. He was cutting the blade into his own skin. Razor-thin cuts zigzagged along his body. And the seers were closing in, lapping it up like dogs...

She rubbed her eyes as if to scrub the image away. At some point in the night, the fire had gone out, leaving only a few crackling embers. A chill ghosted through her. Was it just the cold or something more than that? Most of the locals wouldn't dare set foot on the property, let alone stay the night. She couldn't blame them.

When a knock came, she half-expected a ghost.

"There you are!" Emmerson burst in between the curtain of Hazel's four-poster bed, her face unusually bright. "You have a visitor. A Mr. Pierce. He says it's about the estate. He says he is interested in buying it!"

For a moment, Hazel wasn't sure she had heard her right. She leaped out of bed. "He actually said that?"

"Hear for yourself." Emmerson began undressing her. "May I suggest the light-blue chiffon?"

It was a little formal, especially with all the lace trim and that gigantic, silk rose at the waist, but Hazel shrugged. "If you think it will improve our chances."

"I know it will." Emmerson began braiding her hair too. She took longer than normal to ensure it was piled perfectly atop her head. Almost as if she were headed for some London ball, Emmerson fussed far more than usual.

When Hazel stepped out into the drawing room, she realized why. The gentleman was a great deal younger than she had expected. Likely just a few years older than she. Men of his age were off touring the Continent, not buying estates. He was something of a catch too, his eyes dark and piercing with the kind of face that was either genuinely or deceptively kind.

"Miss Grey." He extended his hand. "I'm so glad I've finally found you."

"You are?"

"I've been interested in your estate for some time now. I've talked with your solicitor, but it appears you haven't been answering his letters."

At this, Hazel felt a twinge of guilt. "That's because he doesn't know I've left London yet. My aunt must not have gotten around to forwarding his letters."

"It is lucky that you are here, then. I was hoping you might be."

"You must sit down and have some tea…" Hazel motioned him to the damask-patterned settee. Emmerson disappeared to prepare a tray.

"I presume my solicitor gave you the price…Mr. Pierce, is it?" She bid he sit nearest to the fire.

"Yes."

Pierce. Piercing, just like his eyes, Hazel couldn't help but think. She swept back a piece of wayward hair, suddenly self-conscious in his presence. She was sure she was blushing too, like an absolute fool.

"And yes, he in fact did."

"Well? I do hope we can come to some agreement."

"I'd prefer to take a look around the place first. That would be fair, wouldn't it?"

"Why, yes, of course." By then, her head was already spinning with hopes of selling the place. She might have agreed to anything. She ignored the nagging feeling that the man's interest seemed too soon, too easy. But she was more consumed by the idea that the manor might finally be out of her hands. With any luck, she would only have to stay in the home a few more weeks. Any longer than that and who knew what she might encounter? The memory of the catacombs was still fresh on her mind. She didn't quite understand the politics behind the killings, but she knew well enough that the dangers surrounding the Order could not be underestimated—nor were they over.

His sudden arrival was fate, simple as that.

"Do sit down," Hazel tried to instruct him to take a seat again, but Mr. Pierce began pacing the room, studying it with scrutinizing eyes. He even took up the most delicate vase. As if the place already belonged to him.

"Please be careful with that."

"Fourth-century Italian, I believe." He moved to the next antiquity, some tiny marble carving of a stag. Instead of chastising him again, Hazel realized she needed to be congenial.

"Forgive the dust. I've only just arrived yesterday. And the home hasn't been occupied for over a month." *Ever since your father died*, a dark voice reminded her.

"You reside primarily in London, then."

"For much of my life, yes." The slightest hint of alarm ran up her neck. Where was Emmerson with the tea? He was still a man, after all. And they were quite alone.

Hazel followed him as he continued about the room and took in every detail. She supposed the room *was* rather splendid. Beneath wide, stone arches, the stained-glass windows were something out of a fairy tale. The light cast in through red and purple glass gave the room a rosy glow. How long had it stayed like this, unchanged through the centuries?

"May I ask what sparked your interest in the place?"

He looked at her quizzically. "You don't know, do you? I thought with my name..."

"I can't say I've heard of you, no." Was he some high-ranking nobleman? A duke? He hadn't corrected her use of "mister" with his surname, though.

"Then suffice it to say, the home, Whitestone, as we've always call it, holds special meaning to me. Every brick."

Beyond that, he would not elaborate. The man was strange, indeed. Hazel was at a loss for words, when thankfully, Emmerson arrived with the tea service. She placed it down, then with hands clasped almost piously, stood in the corner of the room.

"May I offer you something?" Hazel tried to get him to sit again. "I know how tiring the roads can be."

Mr. Pierce obliged this time and she handed him a cup, the delicate china looking a thousand times smaller in his large hands.

Though she couldn't quite place it, there was something familiar about him. His eyes were warm and kind. And yet, he presented something of a mystery too. How in the world could her father's estate hold "special meaning" to this man? Had he previously been here? When? All she knew about him was that he was interested in the estate and that given his age, he was most probably a bachelor too.

She just hoped he had nothing to do with the Order. But there was really no delicate way to ask. She could employ their special handshake, she supposed. Mr. Mortibel had taught it to her once. The handshake was like any other, save for a few points of pressure. That way, no one else in the room might notice. The thumb pressed inside the person's palm, a pressure that would be returned two-fold. Secrecy was integral to everything they did. It was necessary to protect the things they studied, and also those who studied them. Centuries ago, studying their subjects of interest hadn't just meant social exile, but persecution—maybe even execution.

"Where do you presently reside?" Hazel took up a teacup, desperate to keep up the conversation.

"For some years, I have lived up north."

"In Scotland, then," she said with some relief. He couldn't have had anything to do with the Order.

"Farther than that, unfortunately. A place that's bitter cold. Thankfully, the mountains make up for it."

"And what brings you to want to live here?"

Mr. Pierce shifted in his seat, clearly uncomfortable.

"Forgive me. I shouldn't be questioning you like this." None of this should have mattered. So long as he bought the home, what difference did it make if he was affiliated with the Order in some way? And yet she couldn't deny her building curiosity. There were those small, familiar bits about him she couldn't quite figure out.

When he didn't reply, Hazel stood up, remembering her objective. "It's no matter. Shall we take a look around?"

Mr. Pierce escaped the room before she could. Emmerson shifted to follow, but Hazel held up her hand. "It will only be a second."

She didn't care if she wrote her aunt about it—she was almost free of this place.

Picking up her skirts, Hazel chased after him. Oddly, he knew just where he was going. He didn't stop at any of the rooms, though they had walked past several impressive ones. Hazel tried and failed to attract his attention. He was too determined.

He made a turn into one of the arterial hallways that ran through the northern half of the home then into a narrower hallway that led to the east stairway. Only the servants and herself had ever used it. Certainly not guests.

"Don't you want to see the other rooms?" They had passed several.

"I already know them." He went up the stairs and stopped

briefly to admire the spiraled post at the top of the landing. "You shall see why in a moment."

After passing half a dozen guestrooms, she wished he would just tell her where they were going. What he possibly had to show her in her own home, she had no idea.

Finally, they stopped at a door. This one was not particularly familiar to her. Then again, there had been many rooms in the great manor that she'd dared not explore, no matter how strong her childhood curiosity. She hadn't been stupid. She'd had a healthy fear of the Order even then.

Mr. Pierce twisted the knob. "That's odd. It's locked." As if he were in a position to know whether or not this door should have been or shouldn't have been locked.

"Apologies, Mr. Pierce. I haven't the slightest idea where the key might be."

"What about a skeleton key?"

"I can ask Emmerson if she's found one." Hazel was about to turn back.

"No, forget it. You don't mind if I try…?" he asked with a gleam in his eyes.

Hazel shook her head. The last thing she expected was for him to thrust his shoulder into the door.

"Wait!" she shouted too late. The wood splintered instantly. With one more shove, what little was left of the door swung open.

She winced. "I don't suppose you'll be reimbursing me for that."

"Perhaps I shall include it with the price of the home."

Hazel waved it off, trying to be congenial yet again. For the moment, the broken door didn't matter. She was more curious about what lay inside. Despite the brightness of the day, the room was almost pitch black. Somehow, Mr. Pierce knew to throw open the drapes. Dust swirled in the new light. The room wasn't a room at all, but a long gallery.

Ten or so portraits lined the hall on either side. In fact, she had been in this room before, but only once.

It had been years ago. Her father must have heard her foot-falls from the floor below. When he'd come up, he'd taken her by the hand and locked the door behind him.

"Who are all those men in these paintings?" she had asked.

He had only shaken his head. *"You are never to come into this room again, you understand?"*

She still remembered their faces. Their dark eyes had remind-ed her of a cat's mischievous glare. Mr. Pierce had the very same. There was no denying the likeness.

"They are your relatives," Hazel said meekly. It was silly that she had ever thought they might have been hers. Her father had looked nothing like these men. But as a child, she had never considered this. Born here, she'd merely assumed the home had been in her family for years. Her father had never told her that, but she had never asked, either. She'd never even considered that her father might have purchased the home.

She studied Mr. Pierce's face once more against the portraits. Along with the eyes, he had an identical curve of the chin. Even the thickness of his brows was similar. Seeing him beside the portraits, she might have guessed he had walked out of one.

Of course, these men weren't Greys. They had nothing to do with her in the least. Rather, the home had been in the Pierce family for centuries. Standing there amidst all the portraits, she was still struggling to grasp that.

"We had no choice but to sell," Mr. Pierce said. "My father made one too many poor investments and well…we needed the money. Your father, with his funds, helped restore its honor. The estate's, at least."

"How terrible that must have been."

"I was only a child then. I didn't fully understand the gravity of what we'd lost."

Hazel counted twelve portraits. "After so many years in the family too."

"It's not all that uncommon. Great houses change names all

the time. It was kind of your father to purchase the place from us."

"He's gone now…"

"I know… I'm sorry. You are, of course, his daughter?"

She nodded, wondering if he was truly sorry. Her father's death was rather fortuitous for him, she should think. It was the only reason he had the opportunity to get the place back in the family again. She was fortunate too. Living so far north, he was completely unaware of what her father had done to the place. She felt guilty, almost, keeping it a secret.

"So you see the resemblance." Mr. Pierce stood tall beside one of the portraits. Even the most ancient of the men bore a resemblance.

"There's no denying it."

"You must see one more thing."

He said this as if she weren't entirely convinced. Hazel wished he would desist. She was quite done with the topic. She would much rather move on to the matter of money. It didn't matter to whom the house had once belonged. In fact, his connection to it should make selling it much easier.

But the man could not be deterred. Whether she followed or not, he did not slow his fervent steps. Before she could stop him, he rang the bell and asked Emmerson for their cloaks. Hazel could not believe the audacity. But she played along, relieved by the fact that he would almost certainly purchase the home.

With leaves swirling at her feet, Hazel was forced to follow him through the brisk air. "Is this truly necessary?"

"I want to see if it's still here." His face turned hard as stone. Was he mad?

Loose strands of her hair whipped across her cheeks. She clenched her arms, absolutely chilled. But soon, she wasn't thinking about the cold at all. Mr. Pierce was at the front gate, ripping away at the vines on both sides. Three—almost five layers through. His arms struggled at the weight of some.

The ivy had been decades in the making. The greenery had

once been part of the gate's charm. But slowly, the crest that she had seen in part upon her arrival began to surface. Between patches of black tarnish, silver shone proudly, sparkling beneath an overcast sky.

Two horses flanked a shield with a large, detailed rose on it. Above that, the name *Pierce* was written in big, block letters, impossible to deny.

"You've made your point," Hazel said, out of breath from the whole ordeal. It was really her identity that he had ripped away, not this vegetation. Everything she had thought she'd known about herself now left in shambles. Even if she had hated everything about her background. At least she'd had one. Now she had nothing.

"It is cold, Mr. Pierce. Shall we return inside now?"

"Better yet, I'll name my price."

Hazel straightened. Finally.

"This was all I needed to see. It's enough to convince me to give you the asking price and half."

"'And half?'" Her heart squeezed. He couldn't have been serious.

"We both know your solicitor placed it under market value. It's only fair."

Did he pity her? Was that why he offered this kindness now?

"I'll give you a quarter now to secure it. The rest I'll have in no more and no less than three weeks."

"Very well." Hazel thought it best not to argue. At that price, the man was clearly too mad to be reasoned with. "You've restored your family fortune, I see."

"And then some," he said rather smugly, smiling like a fool at the tarnished fence. After the papers the solicitor had provided were signed, it was settled.

He left just as abruptly as he had come. He'd refused dinner, preferring a packed meal instead. She felt guilty watching him ride off on horseback. He had been so honest about his father losing their fortune. How could she keep so much from him?

How could she leave him to discover the horrible things her father had done here?

She need only look at the bank notes to remember. Whether Mr. Mortibel liked it or not, it was done.

CHAPTER EIGHT

The Pawn

I T TOOK A day before she had the courage to tell Mr. Mortibel the news. When Emmerson insisted upon coming along, Hazel didn't argue. In fact, she was glad for it. She hadn't liked his temper the other day.

In his solarium that morning, he seemed approachable enough. Alone, he stared down at a chess board mid-game.

"Need a partner?"

He barely turned his head. "Playing alone keeps me sharp."

She couldn't hold back any longer. "I've sold it. It's done."

He stilled for some moments, then, rising from his chair, went to the liquor cart. Odd. She never knew him to be a drinker, especially at such an early hour. It must have been a habit he had picked up recently. Though she might otherwise scold him for it, she bit her tongue. They had much more important matters to discuss.

"Do you remember the old days, Hazel? How often I came to visit? It wasn't just to see your father, you know."

Something deep within her sighed when he called her by her Christian name. It was just like they were children again. An intimacy he hadn't used with her in years. Only now it was for all the wrong reasons. She wished her father's work hadn't been so deeply intriguing to him that it would one day take over Mr. Mortibel's life.

"I miss the old days too," she admitted. "More than anything."

"Why can't we have them again? I was hoping your presence here—with your lady's maid—meant you had reconsidered my offer."

She wondered how much of the tall, half-empty decanter he'd already had.

Hazel tore the liquor from his hands, the golden liquid splashing onto the silk rug. "They were never my family's possessions." Her rage bubbled over. "The estate never belonged to my family. Just my father. But no one ever told me. Not even you."

Mr. Mortibel hardly looked surprised at all. As Hazel had guessed, he'd already known. "So you've met the charming Theodore Pierce. I thought he might be your buyer. As it is, I haven't seen him in years. Was he to your liking? Dashing?"

Hazel turned away, tired of this crude line of questioning.

"I thought as much. Charming as a devil, isn't he? Your father hated him, you know. They were great enemies, those two. Almost as much as the elder Mr. Pierce."

"He seemed a decent enough man to me."

"I'm sure. And handsome, wouldn't you say? Let me warn you that the man will say and do anything to get the Order back in his grip."

Just as Hazel had feared. "I might have guessed he had something to do with the Order."

Somehow, Mr. Pierce hadn't seemed the type. Or perhaps she was just naïve in all this. Perhaps he was exactly the type.

"If you think your father's practices were awful, the Pierces are far worse. They have yet to pay homage to your father and after all he did to carry the Order forward."

"That matters little to me."

"You can't sell the place to him."

"Of course I must." Hazel turned back at him with a glare.

"Who else will take it off my hands? You certainly don't have the funds. And with my ill reputation, which you so kindly reminded me of…who will have me?"

"If you knew who the man was…" He took a breath.

"Why didn't you tell me about the estate and its true owners?"

"There was much your father and I kept from you."

She understood that very well now. Her father, a man she had thought she had known at least in some respects, had become a complete enigma. "I know nothing about him, do I? It's all a complete and utter lie."

"I didn't know you cared." He rubbed the back of his neck.

"I just want to know the truth."

Mortibel frowned, perhaps pitying her for a moment. "If you must know…his beginnings were not very glamorous."

Did he think she would be disappointed? Rather, she'd celebrate any legacy that didn't involve the occult. She might finally understand why she hadn't fit into her father's plans, why she didn't have the same passions that she'd once thought had been passed down for generations. She wasn't the strange outcast. Her father had been.

"Tell me," Hazel pleaded. Leaning back with his arms crossed, Mr. Mortibel seemed to enjoy this slight advantage he had over her. Having this bit of knowledge she didn't must have seemed a small victory against someone, who by inheriting her father's estate, he perceived to have everything.

"Your father didn't like to talk about his beginnings. He wasn't born into greatness like so many of our other members. Rather, greatness chose him."

Hazel was reminded again of the reverence Mr. Mortibel seemed to hold for her father. It lingered in his eyes and on every word. She had never understood it. Ever since the night she'd fled, any respect she'd held for her father had vanished.

"He didn't want to become the poor farmer your grandfather was. No, he was meant for something much more. He realized it in the early days of his life. He was little more than a boy when he made his way to London."

"He ran away?" Hazel breathed out. Just as she had done. Was that why he'd never sought to get her back? He had understood her decision better than she had thought.

"Fate stepped in then. He needed to make a living and a popular apothecary—the best in London, in fact—needed a broom sweep. Their window displays caught his attention first. Against the dreary grays of London, the vibrant green, blue, and red liquids suspended in glass must have seemed like pure sorcery."

Hazel knew about these show globes. They had no practical purpose. They were merely marks of the creator's talent. They were how her father had discovered his talent for colors.

"It wasn't sorcery your father soon learned, but alchemy: a few chemicals at the precise measurements that, when mixed together, could achieve a desired color."

"Yes, I've seen them before."

"He borrowed—or stole, most likely—the necessary books, ingredients, and tools. Though soon he was creating much more practical concoctions. That's when your father got his chance. When one of the owners of the apothecary fell ill, your father cured him with one of his very own remedies."

Over the years, how many different remedies did my father create? she wondered. *Hundreds, thousands, perhaps?*

"In a matter of just a few years, your father rose from broom sweep to apprentice. He was quite the talented alchemist."

Hazel didn't need Mr. Mortibel to tell her that. She had witnessed her father's work firsthand as a child. She had delivered herbs so he could draw out their oils, heating and mixing them together. Hazel had liked the eccentric variety of vials, a myriad of shapes and colors, their properties numerous and unknown. Her father had warned her against them, telling her the substances inside had been powerful and needed to be treated with great respect. Though she had been curious, they had always been kept just out of reach. At least until she was older, her father had promised. By then, she hadn't wanted to know. Not now, not ever.

So many other daughters inherited jewels and furs. She still craved that sort of mundane simplicity. Life at least would have been safe.

"Your father couldn't hide his talents for long. Word of his special remedies spread throughout London like fire. It was this talent that attracted the Pierces. They lured him with the promise of unique materials. Plants and botanicals with special properties, the type that he could never hope to attain, no matter how far he traveled. For that opportunity alone, your father would have done anything. Naturally, he proved to be quite useful to the Order, enhancing their elixirs and serums, by rate of absorption, concentration, purity, etcetera. Sharing knowledge with each other, they were friends at first…though not for long."

During their meeting, Mr. Pierce had failed to mention this short-lived friendship. He had made it seem as though her father's purchase had been a simple real estate transaction. He had lied by omission. Clearly, it had been something more. "And yet, the estate still fell into my father's hands?"

"That's where the quarrels began. The Pierces had no choice. After a hundred years in their rule, the Pierces ran the Order into such tremendous debts, only your father's newfound wealth could save them. He owned an apothecary and a few others by then. To buy the estate, he needed to sell them all."

"That's quite the price."

"It wasn't just the estate that had changed hands, but the entire Order itself. Your father built it up again, gained new members, tripled the necessary fees to gain our teachings and above all, our prescient advice."

Mr. Mortibel, of course, didn't mention their dark habits, the ritual Hazel wished she hadn't seen. The one that had made Hazel want a simpler life, free of the Order's dangers.

"That's why they want it back," Mr. Mortibel continued. Your father achieved what they had wanted him to and more.

And it cost him much more than his apothecaries. It cost him his life."

"How?

"They killed him, Hazel." Mr. Mortibel sniffed.

Hazel checked his eyes for tears, but they didn't even hold a gleam. Instead, Mr. Mortibel stared unblinking, clearly adamant in his theory. Like so many other truths about her father, she was only hearing it now.

"And perhaps our other seers too. I believe the Pierces are responsible for it all."

Her stomach twisted. The idea that she had hosted a murderer.

"I didn't want to tell you," Mr. Mortibel said. "I wanted you to have some peace."

"You said my father was ill."

"But how did he become so? They made him ill. With poison, most likely."

"You might have warned me they'd return. Especially after my father's death."

"What good would it do? Hell, you'd likely seek them out yourself. They are lucky Grey had a daughter like you. Someone who doesn't believe, who might so easily be convinced to sell. Though they're sure to run the place into the ground again. Perhaps all I need do is wait."

Mr. Mortibel's face reddened like it always did when he was frustrated. He took back the bottle and poured what was left in the decanter into a short glass. "The Pierces don't mean well—I can tell you that much. They certainly can't be trusted. They've wanted your father dead for years. For no other reason than the manor itself. Lord knows what else they might do to obtain it."

Everything centered around the manor. Perhaps something hidden in its walls. Behind some secret passage she had yet to discover. She wasn't sure she wanted to.

"You should not meet with him again."

Hazel was inclined to agree. But there was the manor to

consider. How badly she wanted it off her hands. The contract she had signed... She wasn't sure about all the legalities, but at the very least, there could be monetary ramifications.

Mr. Mortibel clasped her hands. "Just think it over," he begged. "You have not one offer, but two."

Foolishly, perhaps, she promised.

CHAPTER NINE

The Duel

THEO DISMOUNTED HIS horse, boots crunching down onto the gravel path. Mortibel was but a small figure down the drive.

He must have seen him coming. The bastard had had warning. And there was only one person who could have told Mortibel of his arrival. Theo should have known Mortibel was familiar with Grey's daughter. He had seen how close they'd walked together when they had first arrived at the meeting in London. There was something like affection between them. But how much? Just how far was the bastard willing to go to claim Whitestone? Enough to try to marry her?

"Don't tell me she turned you down," Theo said when Mortibel closed in. It was all he needed to say. Even from five feet away, Mortibel's features twisted quite clearly.

"Rejection can't be easy." Theo kept taunting. "Especially from someone so fetching, if I do say so myself."

He had to admit she had been a vision in that blue gown of hers, so striking that he had begun to wonder if it had all been a clever manipulation to get him to buy the house at a higher price.

Theo turned serious. "As it is, it's too late."

"She's already told me. Best keep in mind the deal isn't final yet."

"Miss Grey is merely awaiting a transfer of funds."

"But has she accepted it? She has my offer to consider too."

So he *had* proposed. As Theo had guessed, Mortibel would go to any lengths to obtain Whitestone, and, in turn, the Silver Order.

"Legally—" he started, ready to show the contract, but he stopped himself, remembering the look Miss Grey had given him all too well. It hadn't been the look of a woman recently engaged or even about to be.

"Still waiting for an answer, I see," Theo said. "She accepted my offer right away."

To Theo, it was almost a point of pride. He'd like to think he had charmed her. Far more than Mortibel had, anyway.

Mortibel crossed his arms, his face still sour. "She's become so lost since her father's death. She just needs time."

"When were you going to tell me of his death?" Theo's tone suddenly turned as hard as stone. "The day after you were appointed chair? Do you really think you could have gotten that far?"

"My allies believed as much. They think you've forgotten us."

"Just because I was forced to live up north doesn't mean..." He squeezed a fist. "The Order remains of the utmost importance to me." They were his life, his entirety.

"It is the very reason you are forced to live up north that have many doubting your family's ability to lead again. Your father I hear, is very weak."

"Make no mention of my father. With Grey gone, the chairmanship is mine now. Just as the Whitestone shall soon be."

"I think you'll find there is some opposition amongst us."

"You mean that little faction you met with quite inappropriately in the London catacombs? Meetings outside the proper purview of our Council, over which *I* still sit as chair, is punishable by death—or did you forget?"

"I appreciated the reminder."

"Even if I counted your now-dead supporters, you don't have

the numbers for a coup. You never did. Never will." He didn't know what, exactly, Mortibel had been carrying out down there, particularly with Miss Grey, but his spies would soon find out. Just as they'd found out about Mr. Grey's demise and the meeting itself.

"I will have the numbers soon." Mortibel took a step, widening his stance and crossing his arms. "I will."

"You were lucky to survive London. You won't be so lucky a second time."

"That so?"

"Abandon your plans," Theo bit out. He wasn't liking Mortibel's continued defiance. His body was already tensing for a fight.

"Never."

"Then I release you from your oath."

"On what grounds?" Mortibel huffed. "Just for a little meeting?"

"Deception, if I'm being specific. You also meant to keep Grey's death *and* the fate of Whitestone from me."

"You can't do this." Mortibel shook his head, softly laughing.

"From henceforth, you are banned from all contact, from any and all of our premises, meetings, and possessions. Above and beyond all other considerations, you are banned from releasing our teachings."

"You can't," Mortibel grit through his teeth, "do this."

Theo only spoke louder.

"The Order has a duty to its secrets, I'm afraid. We must enforce these terms. Unfortunately, that means death."

Something in Mortibel's expression seemed to crack. Then he pounced, reaching his arms back high and swinging down. Theo had prepared for violence. There was no way Mortibel was going down without a fight. It was why he had insisted on meeting Mortibel alone. He wanted to fight him one-on-one and kill him himself. He didn't need to outnumber him with his guards. He could take him on blindfolded.

Theo threw out a rigid arm to block the blow. The edge of

his bicep screamed in pain. Apparently, this was a knife fight. Of course Mortibel did not have the honor to announce weapons or ensure his opponent was equally armed.

Theo was nonetheless. He bent down and grabbed one of the knives around his ankle. He flung one, sending it deep into Mortibel's left shoulder. The blow sent the bastard back a step. They were on equal footing again. Should Mortibel make this a gunfight, Theo had come prepared for that too. Theo took advantage of Mortibel's momentary setback to deliver two blows to his jaw. He could have easily come at him with his second knife. But Theo wanted to savor this. Those blows were something he'd envisioned the whole way here. *God, did it feel good.*

He threw another punch. This one so hard, it sent Mortibel straight to the ground.

Theo's knuckles were aching with pain and desperate for a break, but Mortibel was already struggling to his feet. He took two more feeble swipes with the blade. Theo kept blocking them. It was almost too easy. Still. He told himself not to let his guard down.

His several years of training accumulated to this one moment. It all came down to this.

Theo arched backward, missing yet another blow. "Perhaps you should have spent less time in the laboratory and more time training," he hissed.

Before Mortibel could reply, Theo swung again, hitting him in the chest. It took the breath from him, just as he had hoped. Theo was sure the fight was over.

It would be to the death, then. Theo had already come to terms with that after that night in the catacombs. Holding a meeting without the consent of the reigning chair was not a matter to be taken lightly. He had given Mortibel a chance to abandon his plans with dignity. Falling short of that, he was in his rights to dispatch him.

Theo tossed his knife into his dominant hand, bloodied as it was from the blows. Mortibel sputtered for breath. Blood covered half his face. But now was not the time for mercy.

Theo tossed the blade into the air and caught it again. Perhaps he was relishing this too much. He almost felt dizzy from it. More than dizzy, actually. The ground tilted. He stumbled.

Mortibel's sputtering turned into gurgling laughter.

The world spun more violently. Theo dropped the blade and gripped his bicep, still bleeding. Mixed in with blood, he felt something else. Instead of just slickness, he felt something gooey and thick. He stumbled again.

Mortibel had poisoned him. Theo had been prepared for Mortibel to fight dishonorably, but not *this* dishonorably and certainly not this prepared. How long had it been since the cut? Only minutes and the stuff was already taking effect. By now, Theo had taken it deep into his veins.

"You bastard," he croaked, his voice sounding odd and unfamiliar. "Do you have any idea what they'll do to you for this? They'll come for you. I promise you."

"They've already come for me and failed, remember? No doubt they'll fail again." Mortibel smirked. "Moreover…you feel that chill in the air? Weather's taking a turn this evening. That's what's going to kill you. Not I."

Theo yelled out. For a moment, the pain was all he could think about. Then it brought to him a strange sort of clarity. Mortibel had too much confidence to believe he could take the membership by persuasion alone. No, he had something that he believed would sway them all. There was only one thing that could. As Theo shifted in and out of consciousness, the crunch of gravel echoed in his ears, growing softer and softer into the distance.

By the time Theo opened his eyes, darkness had taken hold. His vision was too blurry to see much, anyway. He couldn't just lie here. He had to get up, only his limbs wouldn't cooperate. He wanted to scream too, only his mouth wouldn't let him. He breathed out. At the very least, he could do that. *Start small*, he told himself. *Fight through the fog.*

He moved his fingers. First his index, then his middle finger, then the next, until all five of them worked enough to grip the ground beneath him. Then he moved his other hand, then his knee. It wasn't much and each movement felt agonizing, but he was moving. If only inch by inch from the estate.

From where he had fallen, he knew exactly how to get back to Whitestone. It didn't matter how long it had been—he knew every inch of land between Mortibel's estate and his own. He just had to cross it.

The gravel dug into his arms like acid, leaving a wake of blood. It took over a dozen pulls to get himself onto the grass, crisp with frost. At least it worked to numb his wounds. Each of them burned with fire. Then it started to rain. Big, fat drops that hit his skin like ice. As the temperature continued to drop, his skin seemed to harden. Soon, he'd be too frozen to move. He needed to move faster. Even though he couldn't see it, he continued to picture the route in his mind. For a little while, he was even able to get to his knees and crawl. He still didn't think he'd make it. But he had to. Theo promised himself he'd find a way to survive, if only to get even.

☾

Hazel wrote to her aunt before bed. She wasn't sure how much she should share about her discoveries. The last thing she wanted was her aunt to think she was in any sort of danger.

Concerning her father's past, it would only serve to fuel her aunt's anger. Catherine hadn't trusted him from the start. She had begged Hazel's mother not to marry the man. There had been something not right about his lack of relations, Catherine had said. She had been right. Her father had kept too many secrets to count. In many cases, he had downright lied.

Hazel would never know how much her mother had known.

The sickness had taken her long before Hazel could ask her these things. She had seemed happy once. But those memories were too vague to offer any certainty.

Hazel turned back to her letter. Deciding to keep it optimistic, she wrote instead about Mr. Pierce's offer. It meant she would soon return home. Even if it was to a place where her name was forever sullied and she'd likely end up a spinster. Whitestone would be out of their hands. That was all that mattered.

In no more than a fortnight, it would all be over. She doubted she could last that long. Opulent though it may have been, the manor served as a constant reminder of the night that haunted her. In her mind, the image of blood dripping down skin was as clear as ever.

Her only comfort was the order under which Emmerson had enfolded the estate. For the time being, she had hired a modest staff that would serve their purposes well, taking over as Whitestone's de facto housekeeper, at least for now. But the place still felt empty and as lonely as ever.

Hazel had no visitors. Save for one.

"It appears you'll have to return to your social obligations sooner than we thought." Emmerson threw open her curtains the next morning. "Early this morning, you had a caller. A Mrs. Coldstone. But since it was outside your calling hours, I refused her."

She placed her usual tray of tea and pastries on a low table.

"Emmerson!" Hazel sat up. "You should have woken me."

Emmerson's mouth dropped. "You would have been in no state!"

"Things aren't the same here as in London. What if it had to do with my father? Where is her card?"

"She hadn't one," Emmerson flicked her eyes upward. "Nor much manners. She didn't even ask for your 'at home' day." She shook her head, continuing her disapproval, though Hazel herself had never specified a day. "Just said she had something of your father's to give you and that you ought to see her."

"What?"

"She didn't tell me."

"Did she leave it?"

"No. She preferred to meet with you first."

"How strange." A sort of gift beyond the grave, she considered, her body chilling at the thought.

"Perhaps it's not something you'll even want."

Mrs. Coldstone, Hazel repeated in her head. She vaguely remembered the name. Perhaps from local gossip. Just as well. If her father had had an acquaintance with the family, she could hardly refuse them a simple visit.

"It would be rude not to return her call." And what else had she to occupy herself?

CHAPTER TEN

The Storm

HAZEL WAITED FOR some time in her coat and feathered hat before the borrowed carriage pulled up the drive. With gold trim on black, lacquered doors, it was much finer than she needed for her purposes. But she could hardly ask Mr. Mortibel for a more modest one. At least Mr. Mortibel's borrowed driver seemed competent enough.

"Nathan, is it?"

"Yes, miss." He held open the door.

"You know where this Mrs. Coldstone lives, correct?"

"Oh, yes, best hurry along. The sky is lookin' ripe for a storm."

Indeed, the air had become a great deal colder these last few days. A mass of dark clouds had already drained the landscape of its brilliant autumn colors.

Somehow, it seemed like a bad omen.

Nonetheless, Hazel was glad she had gotten out. She wanted to refresh her memory of the nearby properties. Mr. Mortibel's home was by far the largest. Curving around a hill, they passed the shining tall and stately manor. Then to their left, Morton Manor, home to a wealthy industrialist, if Hazel remembered correctly. She had a feeling they despised her family. Not once had they ever visited. But then, neither had Mrs. Coldstone.

Topping a few more hills, they arrived. The stone cottage, wholly unfamiliar, appeared abandoned, if not for the flickering lights that hinted at a fire. It was modest at best and not well kept. Though the iron windows and winding stone path had some charm, moss had started to grow on the roof. Ivy mingled with the chipping bricks. The fact that her father had had anything to do with the woman who lived here was odd, indeed.

She pushed open the iron gate and winced at its sharp groan. She considered turning back. At the same time, she was too curious to be driven away even as a whistle of leaves swirled along the hems of her skirts. The day really had proven cold. She didn't care how derelict the home was so long as it was warm.

She lifted a fist to knock on the door. The response was almost instantaneous.

"Come in," someone shouted.

Hesitantly, Hazel obeyed. Through the small foyer, she entered the parlor, a rather dusty one that probably hadn't been used in years. There wasn't much but a few pieces of furniture and a large, stone fireplace set to a healthy blaze.

"Hello?"

Warming her hands, she wondered if Mrs. Coldstone matched her home, the woman looking weathered and worn with age too. She fully expected to meet someone old and hard of hearing. But that wasn't the case at all.

Rather, a woman closer to her age came into the parlor. Her hair hung loose about her shoulders in thick, black waves as dark as her eyes. She was quite beautiful, really.

"You're Mrs. Coldstone?"

"Well, Miss Coldstone, to be precise."

"I expected…" Somehow, Emmerson had gotten it wrong.

"You can call me 'Lenora.' Sit."

Hazel sat down onto a small armchair, the cushion squeaking and sending out a poof of dust. How could her father have known a woman so young and low in station? Since she had given Hazel her Christian name, maybe she had been a servant in their household. She didn't quite have the courage to ask. Instead, Hazel fought for some pleasant conversation.

"Have you lived here all your life?" Hazel asked.

"This is home, yes." Lenora plopped down on the settee, releasing a sigh that sounded wistful.

"I wonder how it is we never met." Though Hazel knew precisely. They ran in different circles. Her mother, at the time, would have never allowed it. But she needed to say something, anything. Above all else, she wanted to get to the point of the conversation.

"I understand you have something for me."

Lenora merely smiled as Hazel trembled with suspense. It would not have been polite to press, though Hazel ached to.

"It was the oddest thing when your father arrived at my doorstep some two years ago. We'd only ever spoken a handful of times. He seemed...off. Worried, perhaps? I expected that he wanted to see my mother, but he seemed to know she was ill in bed. I often think he had the foresight that she would soon pass."

Hazel straightened at the words. *That's impossible*, she wanted to burst out. *All of the Order's claims are impossible.*

"He didn't have much to say. He merely gave me a small parcel and asked that I give it to you when you returned to the manor. He seemed to know you were destined to return."

"I had to. He left me the estate."

"Makes sense, I suppose. He did say you were destined to spend the rest of your days here. I thought you quite lucky. Your home is beautiful, you know."

Hazel nodded her thanks. The word *destined* gave her pause. Something told her it had been more than just a hope. Had it been a vision?

"There were times when I thought I should just have someone deliver it to you. But he strictly advised I hand it over in person. And, well, I suppose I wanted to meet you." Lenora eyed her, almost like a curious child. "It's not often I get to meet with a lady with such immense fortune."

Hazel had a feeling she wasn't referring to luck.

Lenora sucked in a breath and stood up a little taller.

"Well," Hazel swallowed, not quite sure how to respond. "I assure you, I'm no one of consequence but I am pleased to make your acquaintance…"

Lenora bowed her head awkwardly.

"My father must have trusted you," Hazel said, though she couldn't understand why. Why couldn't her father have left it for her in a private bank?

"He trusted my mother."

"Nonetheless. Thank you for watching over it." She perched forward on her seat, her eagerness building.

"I have it here. Follow me."

Hazel was glad to leave the dreariness of the parlor for the other parts of the home that seemed much more lived in. A myriad of smells intensified as they entered the kitchen. Something stewed on the hearth that smelled rich in plant matter, no better than fresh-picked weeds from a garden. Whatever it was, it could not have been food. Several books, their pages stained with water, lay open on a long, wooden table. Behind it, glass doors opened up to the greenhouse.

Planters were finely labeled along with the several tiny drawers of a rather large cabinet. There had to have been hundreds of different herbs here. Hazel read the names, some too exotic to pronounce.

Lenora caught Hazel's gaze. "That's one of my remedies you smell. I'm a midwife for some of the farmers' wives. The only one for miles."

Hazel nodded, but she still wasn't convinced that what went on here was entirely innocent.

Lenora straightened out her apron, which was hopelessly wrinkled. "Not the kind of profession where one bothers wearing fine clothes like yours."

Was that jealousy in her voice?

"I do like your gown, though. What a pretty shade of purple."

"Thank you." The dark-maroon dress had actually been one of her plainest.

"I've always admired fine gowns. From afar, of course." Lenora led Hazel deeper into a greenhouse, a room made entirely of glass and iron. In addition to rows of greenery, plants hung down from the ceiling in various stages of drying. Hazel could only identify the bunches of roses, their beauty sucked away with the moisture.

Hazel had heard about Lenora's kind. People who clung to the more ancient traditions of the Malverns, the part that still held true to pagan pastimes that had once dominated the area for centuries. Lenora's work might have intrigued her once. As children, they might have even gotten along.

Perhaps they weren't all that different. Ever since Mr. Mortibel had told her the truth about her father, she'd wondered what her life might have been like had her father never moved here, if the Pierces had never introduced him to the occult. Life would have been simple. She might have been no more than an apothecary's daughter who had grown up to know her father quite well. He might have still been alive. And she might never have been born… She sighed. Being cast into the dark and strange Silver Order was simply her lot in life.

Lenora opened a nearby cabinet, filled entirely with glass jars save for a small, white box held together with string. When Lenora turned around with it, something cold washed over Hazel's skin. She didn't know what it was. Maybe it was just the general aura of the room all around. In the right doses, some herbs Hazel knew to be poisonous. Her father had trusted this woman, but could Hazel trust *him*?

She took the box, wondering if Lenora already knew its contents. Perhaps it would prove entirely worthless.

"No need to open it here. I understand it may be of a personal nature."

"Thank you." It was strange, though. Her father had never

sent her things. He had never even written.

"It was my pleasure. Your father was a good man." She paused. "You didn't know him very well, did you?"

Hazel shook her head.

"There is little my mother would not do for him."

A friendship Hazel had never known existed.

"She died just last year."

"I'm sorry to hear." Hazel frowned. "Was she sick for very long?"

"A few months. She always had her bouts."

"My aunt has her share of illnesses, as well."

"What does she suffer from?"

"It's the London air, I suspect. She has a terrible cough that weakens her."

"Perhaps I can recommend a remedy."

Just then, rain began to trickle across the windows. The sky darkened to black. Nathan, the driver, had been right about the storm. The time for polite conversation was over.

"This winter will be a harsh and peculiar one." Lenora sighed. "I can already feel it in my bones."

"I should go." Hazel was relieved to have such an easy exit. This woman, her house, and her herbs were too strange for comfort.

"So soon?" Lenora moved from the counter to block her exit.

"Tonight, the rain could freeze one to death."

"I just… Well, there's something you should know before you open that parcel…about your father. But if you must go, you must." And yet Lenora didn't budge.

"What, exactly?"

"That night he dropped that off, there was something wrong with him."

"I heard he was ill." That was what Mr. Mortibel had told her anyway.

"In a way." Lenora turned back into the greenhouse.

"If there's something you know, say it at once." Hazel

grasped Lenora's arm, surprising even herself.

Lenora's face darkened for a moment before returning to her smooth demeanor. "It's true he was ill in the weeks leading up to his death, but not like my mother or your aunt. He was mad. I'm afraid it isn't pleasant the way they had to restrain him in the end. Or so I heard."

"He was mad?" Yet another truth Mr. Mortibel had omitted.

"I thought you should know before you opened that." Her eyes landed on the parcel.

Hazel looked down at the seemingly innocuous box, her heart tensing.

"I'm sorry," said Lenora. "I debated whether or not to tell you. I—"

"No, I'm glad you did. It explains so much." Hazel tried to sound calm.

"There are other rumors too. Much different than what they reported in the newspapers." For the first time, Lenora's face crumpled, betraying some sympathy.

"Please…"

"I'm afraid they're rather gruesome."

Lenora hesitated, but Hazel nodded for her to continue.

"The madness had done him in. And well, he killed himself, they say. Stabbed himself to death."

Hazel felt her stomach turn. She wasn't sure what was worse: suicide or murder. Of the two, she didn't know which to believe. Did it even matter? In less than a few weeks, she would be gone from here. Her father's death just another painful memory.

"Thank you for the parcel." Hazel showed herself to the door, Lenora's footfalls following closely behind.

"Please understand—I didn't mean to cause you pain."

"You said my father knew your mother well?" Hazel turned back.

Bewildered, Lenora nodded. "Quite. He liked her remedies very much."

"Then you probably saw more of him than I did. We didn't

talk, not for years. I've felt little pain since his passing. In fact, I haven't shed a single tear."

Hazel didn't wait for Lenora's response. She rushed into the carriage and barked at Nathan to drive on. She needed to get away from here. Weather be damned, she wanted to leave for London at once. Those things about her father, she hadn't cared to know.

There was no stopping her morbid imagination. The darkness of the carriage seemed to intensify the images: her father's hands restrained with rope, the knife in his hands that went in and out of his chest, covered each time with more blood. The pain she'd told Lenora she had never felt had been a lie, the tears too. They slid down her face faster than her shaky gloves could catch them. She tried to focus on the passing hills, but within the building storm, everything had gone black.

The carriage stopped, the iron gates whining open and shut behind them in a rattle that sounded more like prison bars. She heard something in the wind too. Nathan was shouting. Hazel opened the door, letting in great sheets of rain. "Nathan? What is it?"

"There!" He pulled the carriage to a halt. "Stay back."

A mass lay hunched over the front steps. A man. It had to have been. Hazel exited the carriage and moved closer, disregarding Nathan's shouts of caution. This man, whoever he was, was clearly incapacitated.

"Come over with the light!" Hazel shouted. Her clothing was soaked through, the rain dropping like pebbles across her cheeks.

Nathan huffed over, the lantern flickering over them.

Only the side of the man's face was visible, but she still recognized him, the unique curve of his chin, the broad build of his frame. *Mr. Pierce*, she mouthed to herself in shock. He had made a more lasting impression than she'd cared to admit. From their last meeting, she'd almost had his features memorized.

With her gloved hands, she brushed away some wayward strands of hair. His eyes were shut in what seemed a peaceful sleep, if not for the deep gash across his arm. The blood seeped out, still fresh.

"Who is he, miss?"

Ignoring the question, she moved her hands along Mr. Pierce's throat. Though he felt like ice, he managed to maintain a heart rhythm, albeit a weak one.

"We'll send for a doctor in the morning. We'll not get one tonight, not in this weather. Help me bring him out of the cold."

The driver cautiously stepped forward. But first, she pulled off her cloak, wrapping the material around his wounded arm. Her dress might as well have been paper thin. She could only wonder how Mr. Pierce had managed. Had he been here another hour, he would not have been alive.

The driver heaved him up by his arms while Hazel took up his feet. He was a heavy one. Holding just half his weight, she could only make it a few feet.

The moment they crossed the threshold, Hazel shouted for Emmerson, for anyone who might listen. A footman and a maid, both of whom she had met only once upon their first day of hire, came rushing forward. Emmerson trailed behind.

"What on earth?" Emmerson yelped.

"This man needs our assistance." Hazel let the two men carry him upstairs. "Put him in the blue room." Hazel followed after them.

"The blue room?" Emmerson knew it was one of their best. "What in—"

"Quiet now," Hazel demanded. "I don't want you alerting the other servants."

"Everyone within a hundred miles will know come morning," Emmerson said. "You!" Emmerson pointed at the young woman looking bewildered at the bottom of the stair. "Get us several clean cloths and some hot water."

"Can you make a proper bandage?" Hazel struggled between breaths.

"I'll manage something. Don't you worry."

Hazel followed the men through the dark, drafty hall. Luckily, they hadn't far to go. "The second door on your right," Hazel directed.

They entered the room in complete darkness. Emmerson, the only one with a candle, worked feverishly to light the lamps. Though it was plenty bright, it would be a long while still before the room warmed.

"Get a fire going. Fetch some water and coals, will you, Nathan?"

When the two men left, Emmerson pulled back the cloak.

"It's that man!" Emmerson gasped. "Did Mrs. Coldstone have anything to do with this?"

"We found him on the doorstep. What do you think happened to him? Didn't you hear anything?"

"Not in this rain." Emmerson examined his head injuries, though Hazel could distinguish little with all the blood. "Looks to me he got in an awful bad fight. How does a man like him have such cruel enemies? He seemed a true gentleman and so kind."

Hazel knew one. Within such close proximity, it wasn't possible, was it? Could Mr. Mortibel have been responsible? Could he really want the estate so badly? If only Mr. Pierce could confirm this. She had to be sure one day he could.

Hazel pressed hard on the wound. "Where is that girl? We'll have to dress this wound."

"I'll grab some whiskey..." Emmerson stepped back with hands on her hips. "What is he doing here, you think? He didn't change his mind, did he? About buying the house?"

"Just go. And get some rope too."

She wasn't quite sure how much she believed Mortibel, who claimed Mr. Pierce was dangerous, but she'd be cautious nonetheless.

"Be mindful what you're getting into now." With an exasperated look, Emmerson ran out.

Hazel sighed, suddenly exhausted. She was trying to save his life, for heaven's sake. But it was good advice. Thus the need for rope. She turned up the lamp, throwing flickers of flame across the pale-blue wallpaper.

She couldn't recall the last time she had even been in this room. When she had been a child, most likely. This had been her mother's room. Also, the bed in which she had died. No wonder there had been so much gloom in the air. She shouldn't have brought him here. She didn't want him to have the same fate.

She pushed back the cloak and placed her hand on his bare shoulder. His skin was still ice cold. They needed a fire and fast. For now, she would keep him covered and use her sense of touch to find any other wounds.

He'd wake up at any moment, no doubt, her hands on him like this. Already, her cheeks were reddening. She moved quickly over his stomach, chest and other arm, all taut skin and hard muscle. Her hand moved down to his thigh next. There were bruises and several cuts, but none deep enough to cause concern. *Thank God.*

She looked up at his face, half-expecting his eyes to open. Flat on his back now, he seemed so still, so vulnerable. He didn't deserve to die. There was still something about him beyond the familiarity of the portraits, something that had drawn her toward him from the start. He had to survive this. New questions ate at her, begging for answers.

How could Mr. Mortibel have done this to him?

CHAPTER ELEVEN

Rumors

THEO AWOKE IN a panic. He tried to move his arms, but something tight encircled his wrists. The bedposts creaked and cracked under the weight of his pulling. He stilled, silencing his movement.

There was no knowing who could have done this to him and he didn't want to alert them. Then he caught sight of a woman, Miss Grey. He couldn't see her face, but he could see the black braids of her hair. Its exact shade, he could recognize anywhere. He had rather enjoyed how it looked against the pale blue of her dress the other day. In the morning light, there was a sheen that made it seem soft as silk. He wished he could see it loose around her shoulders and bury his face in it.

She stirred. As if she had heard his thoughts.

Perhaps it was wise she'd tied him up like this. Even though she was inches away, he couldn't so much as touch her.

And yet, for someone they feared enough to tie up, he'd been taken care of rather well. The bed was soft, his wound well bandaged. The room even, was a nice one.

He cleared his throat, loud enough to wake her in a flutter. She groaned. Her back must have been aching almost as bad as his.

He tugged on the ropes once more, surprised at the strength of the knots. He'd have to remain a prisoner, then, and she his guard. He sighed. He thought he'd been convincing as a proper English gentleman.

Miss Grey brushed down her hair and collected herself.

"Miss Grey," he said, as sweet as he could muster. "Will you kindly inform me as to why I am being restrained?"

He tried to stretch his aching legs, but the pain was too great. He had to have had a thousand little scrapes from pulling himself up the gravel drive. At least the poison had seemed to wear off. Though he still had a searing headache.

"I've called for a doctor. He should be here before noon." She checked the makeshift bandage across his arm. "I'm afraid you were poisoned."

"How could you tell?" He quirked a brow. She was rather clever, apparently.

"There was a residue in your wound. A very distinct green."

"Surely, these restraints are unnecessary."

"Before the doctor arrives, you'll need to explain yourself." Miss Grey stepped an inch closer. "How did you get here bloodied as you were? Who poisoned you?"

"I had nowhere else to go." Theo looked up at the ceiling.

"Who did this to you?" she demanded.

"A coward of a man. Perhaps you know him. Marcus Mortibel."

She stared at him blankly, though he could sense the storm behind her eyes. "We are neighbors."

But they were more than that. Theo was sure of it. Even if she had said *no* to Mortibel's offer. He couldn't help but wonder. Nor could he help an odd pang of jealousy. He did his best to ignore it.

He'd had plenty of time to indulge lust up north, plenty of dalliances that he had been all too aware couldn't last. They'd helped pass the time, at least until destiny had come calling. Now it was time to take back what was his. He didn't have time for that sort of thing. Not any longer.

He yanked on the ropes again. "Do you mean to kill me too? Gut me with that hot poker?" A tad delirious, he glanced at the iron rods next to the blazing fireplace. "Had you changed your mind about the sale, a simple *no* to my offer would have sufficed."

"I haven't changed my mind." She stepped closer to him. It surprised him that she wasn't afraid. "Don't be morbid. I would never encourage violence, unless of course…"

"Unless of course what?"

"Unless…you were the one who killed my father." The words came out surprisingly nonchalant. Words she must have heard from Mortibel. It was an outright lie, but he couldn't blame her for testing the waters. "I've been hearing all sorts of things, you know."

"Mortibel is the dishonorable one between us. Not I. He was the one who poisoned me instead of facing me fair and square."

"Why would he do such a thing?" Hazel placed a hand to her lips.

But Theo guessed she knew exactly why. If she didn't think Mortibel were capable of violence, she knew now. For Christ's sake, wasn't it obvious enough that he had been left for dead?

"I take it he's heard of my offer?" Theo quirked a brow. Maybe it was a mistake to come here. She'd never trust him over Mortibel. But he needed her to. If he wanted to survive not just last night, but the coming days, she needed to choose him.

"I've never harmed your father, Miss Grey. Now please undo these restraints. I can't be like this when the doctor comes."

Unable to pull herself from his gaze, Miss Grey was already bending to his will. He hoped if he made her feel something, it was far from fear. Otherwise, she'd never would have untied him so willingly.

Miss Grey began undoing the knots, her fingers shaking as they slid over his wrists. Silence fell over the room, reminding him how alone they were. In a home as big as his, the servants were probably far off in the kitchen.

"I needed to be sure you wouldn't cause me harm is all." Her cheeks blazed red.

"I take no offense." He laid his head back down, his arm slung across his forehead. Of course he had no intention of hurting her. He simply needed help. He was glad she had found him. Even though he didn't want to admit it, he had hoped for that.

☾

"YOU MIGHT FEEL a bit dizzy over the next few days. By all rights, that poison probably should have killed you."

"It didn't go in deep enough," Hazel explained. She had also wiped away what she could.

"It must not have… You're lucky you don't have frostbite or any broken bones, either," the doctor intoned. "Duels are unlawful these days, you know. It's in your best interest to avoid them."

The doctor packed away his stethoscope. "He'll be fine, miss, but he needs a couple days more rest before he can travel. I'd advise you to keep him as far as possible from Mr. Mortibel in the meantime."

"You might want to see him next," Mr. Pierce said.

The doctor gave Hazel a weak smile. As if these two were no more than a couple of feuding school boys. As if they hadn't been trying to kill each other.

"Thank you, doctor. Emmerson here will show you out."

Hazel waited to hear their steps descend the stairs before walking closer to the bed. Mr. Pierce sat up, his bandaged arm resting across his chest. Unlike the man she had met a day ago, he was no longer determined and imposing, but downtrodden and foreboding.

"Looks like I'll be here a few days. Not the greatest news, is it?" Mr. Pierce said.

"At least you'll live."

"Yes, well, I'll heal with as much haste as I can. You need not care for me. I know you'd much rather leave."

"Not until the details of the purchase are worked out..." Almost as soon as she'd said the words, she cringed at their harshness. "After you've offered to buy the estate, it's the least I could do."

The words were shaky, though. Even she wasn't entirely convinced by them. How could she be after Mortibel's accusation? She didn't know what to believe anymore, nor what to think. When Mr. Pierce had told her he hadn't killed her father, she had believed him. Maybe she couldn't trust Mr. Mortibel. Maybe she shouldn't trust either of them.

"Other than tying me up earlier," he said, licking his lips, "you have been a most gracious host."

"I'd have to be a monster to do nothing."

Hazel looked out at the strange world beyond the window. The rain had transformed to snow. Great swaths of it had formed across an otherwise-flat lawn, the snow whisking away like sand. Half a night in this weather and Mr. Pierce most certainly would have died. It would be murder then. She still couldn't believe that Mr. Mortibel would resort to such measures. But he must have changed since she'd seen him last before all of this. Or maybe he had always been that way. He was as obsessed as ever with the Order. He was that determined to take her father's place.

"Do you require anything?" Hazel asked.

"Not at the moment, no."

"Follow the doctor's wishes and get some rest, then." She needed some herself.

Hazel twisted to the door. Should she say she'd check on him soon? Or mention the next time he'd see her? Their situation was an odd one. She didn't quite know how to handle it. She only knew that it made her uneasy to have this stranger in her home. He had made a charming first impression, but she still had her reservations. He was more than just a potential buyer. He was quite possibly her father's killer. Just as Mr. Mortibel could be, she reminded herself. She couldn't be sure of anything anymore.

Hazel shut the door behind her. Mr. Mortibel would have wanted her to lock it. But her guest was too weak and injured to be a real threat. It certainly wouldn't help keep the rumors at bay.

More than rumors, Hazel was concerned about Mr. Mortibel. What might he do if he found out Mr. Pierce was here? She couldn't allow him to hurt Mr. Pierce again. Not when she believed even a little in his innocence.

She couldn't help it—she was curious about him too. He wasn't like the other men in London. He wasn't a man of leisure; he was a man of action on some kind of crusade. Though what kind of crusade, she had no idea.

As the day went on, the mystery surrounding him and home only deepened. She saw his family's mark everywhere now. The crest, a pair of horses and the rose shield, was carved into the bricks of the fireplaces and the wood railing of every staircase. They had been out in the open for so long and yet she had never noticed them. What else within the manor might he open her eyes to?

She still held out the hope that she might find something good in the place. Something that would help her to forget some of the bad she had seen as a child. And that one night she still had yet to unsee.

LATER THAT AFTERNOON, Hazel sipped her tea in the kitchen, where it was warmest these days.

A letter from Aunt Catherine had finally arrived. It would likely be several days before she got another. She sat at the window watching the snow drift down and collect across the front lawn. Its consistency that day was light and soft, like clumps of dust. And it was falling fast. There'd likely be at least a foot, making the roads impassable, particularly for a man recovering from injury.

Ill or not, he was stuck here. Emmerson didn't like it one bit. Having an unwed gentleman in the house was uncouth. They couldn't expect to control the rumors that would develop. Hazel, on the other hand, had yet to care. So long as Mr. Pierce came through with his offer, spinsterhood didn't mean starvation, just loneliness.

She winced at the thought and looked down at her aunt's letter, disappointingly brief, but optimistic, just as her previous letter had been. Soon, they would be done with the place. If only things were turning out to be that simple.

"I don't care how much you want the guineas—I don't like him staying here. He's a stranger. And he's got violent tendencies." Topping off the teapot, Emmerson placed the kettle back over the hearth.

Hazel had told Emmerson as little as she could about the matter, knowing full well every detail shared would make it home to her aunt. So far, Emmerson believed that Mr. Mortibel and Mr. Pierce were nothing more than old rivals from their days away at school.

"Mr. Mortibel's actions may well have been justified," Emmerson said.

"We don't know that for certain."

And they could hardly throw him out now. The wind had begun to pound against the windows. Despite the steady warmth of the hearth, a chill still resonated from the stone walls. Winter was well on its way. The first storm of the season already here.

"You can't expect to hide him. What will we tell the other servants?" Emmerson asked with hands on her hips.

"I don't see why we have to tell them anything." She blew out a noisy breath.

"If we don't give them a story, they'll make up their own."

Hazel sighed. Emmerson was right. Most servants, especially those she knew in London, had a penchant for not only spreading, but *creating* truly hideous tales. She thought for a moment.

They needed an explanation scandalous enough that it might be convincing. "Tell them he's a troubled relative who indulges in too much drink."

"Very well." Emmerson poured more tea. "Just promise me you won't be alone with him again."

"You can't expect to chaperone every meeting." It would have been silly. Hazel hadn't a reputation to uphold, not anymore. And for once, she didn't want Emmerson intruding upon her affairs. Whatever Mr. Pierce revealed, she didn't want Emmerson writing to her aunt about it, either. Aunt Catherine still didn't know their estate's original owners and Hazel meant to keep it that way, at least for now.

"You're not worried about his intentions?"

The thought sent a tingle up her spine. *That isn't why I want to be alone with him*, she told herself. She merely wanted the opportunity to ask him questions, delicate ones about her father. Frankly, it was none of Emmerson's affair.

"As far as I know, his only intention is to buy the estate."

"If he's a gentleman, he will understand the need for a chaperone."

"There's no need for it."

Emmerson clucked her tongue. "It would only be right…"

"No. As I've said, you need not be present at our every meeting." Why was she being so insistent?

"But this man—"

"You are to do as I say." Frustrated with this whole business, Hazel was losing her patience. "In this, you should know your place."

Hazel strode out the door and into the gloom of the hallway. She hadn't yet reached her room and already, she regretted the words.

Emmerson had every reason to be concerned. They hadn't just one, but two men in close vicinity they needed to be cautious of: Mr. Pierce and Mr. Mortibel both. And here, alone in this estate with only a handful of servants, they were quite vulnerable.

Hazel could feel it in the empty air of the estate, building to crescendo.

If only Emmerson would trust her mistress's judgment. For all she knew, Mr. Mortibel was the one who killed her father and Mr. Pierce was the innocent man.

CHAPTER TWELVE

The Vision

HAZEL ENTERED THE silence of her room and locked the door behind her. The fire was still going, but barely. She added some fresh kindling, poking at the logs until they reignited. The smell reminded her of Lenora's home, particularly of the parcel Lenora had handed her.

Hazel still had yet to open it. She wasn't sure if she wanted to, especially if Lenora was right about her father's madness or illness. There was no knowing what was inside. She considered tossing it into the flames. After what had happened in the catacombs and more recently to Mr. Pierce, she had seen enough of the danger brought by her father.

And yet she found herself pulling at the strings, the box collapsing open. In the center of the simple package was a lump of velvet cloth.

Hazel picked it up, feeling the weight of something inside. Pulling away the folds, she recognized the crystal-clear vial at once. She had seen it only on the rarest of occasions. The delicate vial with its raised, swirling design was beautiful, yet nothing compared to what lay inside. This kind of beauty could only belong to the elixir. Like liquid pearls, it was viscous and glossy, flickering like fire.

It was supposed to be the Order's greatest claim to power. The liquid gave its user the ability to see glimpses into the future—what Hazel had always thought was no more than hallucination, no different than those brought on by absinth.

Of all things he could have given her, why had her father left *this* to her?

Simply being in the presence of the elixir was known to bring on strange effects. For once, the rumors might have been correct. Before her eyes, it seemed to have an indescribable pull, begging her to take a sip.

She couldn't believe she was considering it. She was supposed to be escaping this place, not immersing herself, dragging herself further in. Stranger still, why hadn't her father trusted Mr. Mortibel to give this to her? Why couldn't he have left a note?

Perhaps it was because her father hadn't needed to. It was too obvious what the so-called gift meant. Her father had wanted her to take it. Just as he had wanted her to join them all those years, he'd wanted her to drink the special infusion of Lord-knew-what and change her mind about them.

What had he envisioned? That she would become a believer and take his place? Hazel still didn't understand why her father wanted this. Was it as Mr. Mortibel had said? Simply because they'd shared the same blood?

Nothing could change her mind about the Order, not in a thousand years. She didn't want to endure their way of life. She'd known that from the moment she had run away as a child.

She considered another possibility. What if he'd meant for her to discover something? Hazel had heard enough about the elixir to know how it worked. One saw glimpses into the future and while one couldn't change the outcome, it could help one prepare, to know who could be trusted…

Was that not precisely what she needed? She still couldn't be completely certain if either Mr. Mortibel or Mr. Pierce could be trusted. Could the elixir tell her? Could it explain her father's death?

No. The elixir doesn't work, she reminded herself. It was all a trick of the mind. A hallucination at best. Too many foolish Londoners had been captured by the new craze involving all things supernatural. Not her. She had long ago closed her mind to it.

But there'd been a time when things had been different.

Alongside everything else, the manor seemed to awaken these long-forgotten memories, when Hazel had been more wild like Lenora: not caring if her hair was pulled back and braided or if she was sweaty from running in the fields.

She'd had a foolish, unabashed curiosity then. The laboratory had been a place of exciting discovery, not fear. She'd witnessed her father's so-called experimentations, what had been the precise measuring and heating of ingredients that had often resulted in a draft of a beautifully specific hue—a color that couldn't be off by the slightest.

Now that she looked back at it, their creations had been too fantastical to be real: this fortunetelling elixir, among others that could heal, invoke delirium, and even force someone to speak the truth. No matter how much she'd begged, her father had never let her try them for herself.

Until now.

She turned the elixir over in her hands, uninhibited. The same childlike curiosity fell over her again. A taste wouldn't hurt. She lifted up the vial, a thousand silver specks dancing. She had never known before, but perhaps this was how the Silver Order had derived its name.

She breathed out, a rush of excitement filling her lungs on her next breath. So this was what it was like to be one of them, not knowing what might happen once she took a sip and swallowed.

There was but one outcome of which she could be certain. She would finally know whether or not her father had been a charlatan. Perhaps only then could she move on to a life of much-needed normalcy.

Hazel pulled out the cork and sniffed. Oddly, it didn't smell much like anything. What had it been made of? More than smell, she worried about taste. Would it burn down her throat like liquor? She would have to swallow quickly.

Without further thought, she put it to her lips and tilted her head back. Not knowing the correct dosage, she dared only to finish a quarter or so. After all, she could always take more. It tasted sweet, almost, but also crisp, refreshing, and warm, like fresh spearmint picked under a hot, midday sun.

At any moment, the stuff would take effect.

She braced herself in an armchair. From there, she had her favorite view of the gardens. Even if the flowers were dead, with the sun going down, the crystallized snow reflected a thousand colors. There was no vision, however. No change in anything just yet.

Was it really all a bunch of lies? She had guessed as much. She'd at least thought there would have been a hallucination of sorts. Some imagery she wouldn't be able to comprehend.

She paced the room for almost an hour. Darkness had descended and a ripening moon slid out from a patch of clouds, illuminating the room into a colorless white. She wondered if she was supposed to have taken more.

Just as she was about to sit down again, Hazel fumbled, gripping the back of the chair. But it was little use—she was slipping toward the floor. Her vision had tunneled and there was only blackness. She had lost all sense of her surroundings. No longer could she feel the hard floor below her. She stretched out her hand, searching for the curtains, for anything to ground herself back in this world. But everything was impossibly and jarringly out of reach.

Then the light returned again, impossibly bright.

The sensations happened all at once, rocking her to her core. She was lying in her bed, amidst a swirl of blankets, sprawled out and fully nude. She was gasping as if thrown into a tub of cold water. Though oddly, she was impossibly warm, her insides hot and molten. An arched, stone ceiling took shape above her. Her hands gripped the smoothest silk. Whatever she lay on was soft. A face came into view. Mr. Pierce's. Inches away. Then impossibly close. A deep passion in his eyes. She knew exactly what he was doing to her now. Things that she had never done, that in her talks with her aunt, she had almost come to fear. It wasn't as she had expected, however. And she didn't fight it. Rather, she felt herself surrendering to it.

☾

HAZEL PACED THE room. Outside the window, it was early morning.

The experience had taken all night, though she felt as if she hadn't slept a wink. Rising out of it, she struggled to catch her breath. She was still heaving. What she'd seen, what she'd felt, had been nothing short of mesmerizing. She understood now her father's fascination. Mr. Mortibel's too. It was as if she had been there, as if it had actually happened. She couldn't believe it. Her all-too-logical mind didn't allow it.

More troubling was the vision itself. She barely knew the man.

Perhaps that could soon change. She shook her head, digging her hands through her hair.

Everything about the Order and the elixir was supposed to have been a lie and yet…the vision had been so real, every sensation, she could still recall the feel of him across her skin. There had been many details. The exact crinkle of his brow, her memory of it so vivid.

No. It was impossible. It had to have been an illusion of some sort. She refused to believe what she'd seen could someday take place like the Order so adamantly believed. She was sure it wouldn't.

The idea was too distasteful, not to mention improper and wrong. She wasn't the type of woman to engage in such salacious behavior. These sorts of thoughts never even crossed her mind—well, rarely at least. She wasn't a nun who needed to deny herself those things. But, still, it seemed the actions of another woman, not her.

Perhaps the elixir was simply a trick, a way to make people believe they would do things they normally would not, all because they believed it was inevitable. It was sick, really. And she would not fall for it.

My father and the seers were charlatans, she told herself firmly. When Mr. Pierce was gone out of her life without so much as grazing hands, that would finally prove it. She need only wait.

And yet, despite all her skepticism, she itched to take more. In case the rest of the vial wasn't enough, she might even dare to go down into her father's laboratory and search for more. To see, to feel again what she had just experienced, a longing that stirred within her so intensely, it worried her.

Was the elixir addicting, like the laudanum that plagued even the brightest minds in London?

Hazel took up the vial, the liquid still shimmering even in the darkness of early morning. The images from the night before made her shiver. How deceiving the elixir's silvery beauty was. She didn't trust it. Rather, it was something to be feared. Lord knew what other visions it might reveal to her, what other things it might force her to make come true.

If the elixir really was addicting, she didn't want to risk it.

Still grasping the vial, Hazel swept down the hall. She didn't care that she was still in her nightdress and there was a strong chill in the air.

The house seemed quieter than usual. The frost of the last few days had silenced the birds and insects. There was only the creaking of dry leaves and the shuddering of windowpanes.

Each room she entered seemed to drop in temperature. Without any fires lit yet, the parlor and sunroom were absolutely chilling. She half-expected walls tipped with frost.

Through the back doors, the pale-faced moon was setting

against a dark-blue sky. Even in the grimmest of moments, the beauty of the estate was impossible to ignore. It was striking, the way moonlight filtered through a web of tree branches. And yet there was nothing beautiful about the things that went on here. The twisted scene she had experienced confirmed this. She should have known better. Once again, the Order had lured her into a trap. Before she endured any more harm, she best be rid of it now.

She threw away the stopper and poured the rest of the contents onto the cold, black soil. She wouldn't let it mesmerize her again, even as it fell in a stream of a thousand diamonds. But this did little to rid her of the vision. It was still so fresh in her mind. She didn't just see it. Rather, she *felt* it. She felt warm skin against skin. How wonderful it was. The sensations, unlike anything she had ever experienced before, had left her breathless and, despite herself, wanting more.

She thought of Mr. Pierce lying in the bed upstairs, unawares. His features pleasant and still as he thankfully slept for several hours more. She wasn't sure she could face him. Not with the constant blush that warmed her cheeks. Every time she looked at him, she was sure she'd see the vision again. Would she ever be able to forget it? The images were all so shameful, yet so vivid.

Hazel turned back up the paved path and slammed the glass doors shut behind her. As soon as he got better, he'd be off and the sale of the estate would be finalized. It should only be a matter of weeks. Could she endure being in such close quarters with Mr. Pierce until then? The realness of the image struck her again. But it couldn't have been real. Impossible.

Walking the halls, she could not help hearing her father's words. *"No vision, once seen, can be undone,"* he had told her. That was the burden the Order's seers must bear. A fate they could never erase. She would have to at least try.

Hazel's eyes flicked up from the wooden flooring. Steps echoed at the end of the hall. Emmerson was carrying a breakfast tray.

Hazel forced her eyes back down.

"Up already?" Emmerson asked. "I was just about to deliver breakfast to our guest. Care to see how he is faring?"

"Not today." Hazel hurried past, her cheeks ablaze.

CHAPTER THIRTEEN

Open Secrets

THEO SHIFTED IN and out of sleep. Each time the room got hotter. It didn't make any sense. He knew what time of year it was. He had felt the cold rain pelting down on him, what couldn't have been more than a few days ago. But if were honest with himself, he couldn't entirely have been sure.

Finally, somewhere in all this daze, he managed to open his eyes a sliver before shutting them again, just long enough to see large chunks of snow flitting across the window. He had confirmed it, then. He was running a fever. One of his wounds, his arm, most likely, had gotten infected. He knew from experience that infections could turn deadly fast.

He tried to rally himself. He needed to give the servants orders on how to treat it. But the fog that drifted over him was too heavy. He could barely lift his head. Just opening his eyes earlier had seemed to drain half his energy.

When he heard steps, he couldn't have been more grateful. It was possible it was just a hallucination. Then a voice confirmed it. Before he could even try to speak, Emmerson was calling for Miss Grey. Emmerson placed a cool hand on his forehead.

"Oh, dear." She shuddered.

More steps entered the room.

"His condition has worsened," Emmerson said.

For all he knew, he might very well die. He struggled to open his eyes again, if only to see Miss Grey. If she was going to be the last thing he ever saw, at least it would be her beauty that saw him out of this world. He would get to hear her voice again too.

Emmerson pulled back his bandage, tugging against his skin. Warm blood trickled down his forearm.

"The wound has opened again," Emmerson said.

To Theo's despair, Miss Grey was gravely quiet. Then at last, she spoke. "In this storm, there's no hope for calling a doctor."

He tensed. He needed to tell them what to do.

"Is he going to die, Miss Grey?"

"No. I promise. Gather some snow and press it against the wound while I prepare a poultice."

"Snow, Miss Hazel?"

"It will encourage the blood to retreat. Not much, but I shall be working quickly."

Theo relaxed a little. Perhaps Miss Grey knew what to do, after all.

"Have the kitchens been well-stocked?"

"Indeed," Emmerson said.

"We have garlic, then. Star anise for astringent qualities and cinnamon to speed healing." Miss Grey's words faded as the two disappeared down the stairs. They put Theo at great ease. Like her father, she knew her herbs and botanicals. Before she'd left this place, her father must have taught her well. He thanked God for a moment. Maybe he'd survive, after all.

Theo wasn't sure how long she was gone. He woke again at the sound of footsteps. The promised poultice lay over his arm. Though it throbbed, it felt better. All because of her. If he could have managed it, he'd have been thanking her profusely. As it was, he could barely lift his head to see her.

She froze. "You're awake. I'm sorry. I thought you were…"

"Dead?" He lay back down, wincing slightly at the motion. "Perhaps I should be."

Beneath the crinkled brow he remembered so well, he caught her eyes and swam in them for a moment. She visibly gulped, her cheeks reddening. Why was she so nervous all of a sudden? Weak and covered in a layer of sweat, he couldn't have been more vulnerable. If it weren't for her, he was certain he'd have been dead.

"I came to change your poultice." She raised the folded cloth in her hand. "I'm afraid this will have to do until the roads clear and a doctor can see you."

Theo groaned as he sat up. Every little movement hurt. His body, after all, was covered in cuts and bruises. Had it really been just rocks he had pulled himself over or had it been knives?

"Please." He offered her his arm.

Miss Grey got close again.

"I applied this one while you were asleep." She lifted up the old, blood-soaked rag and placed it carefully on the nightstand. "You were quite feverish."

"I had the oddest dreams."

"As have I. Something about this house, I think."

Theo knew what she meant. It was the obvious thing hanging between them that neither cared to mention. The Silver Order. How much, precisely, did she know?

"I remember hearing your voice," Theo said, still slightly out of it. "You promised I wouldn't die. You sounded so certain."

"I don't think that was me."

But she had done other things. He distinctly recalled fingers running along the muscles of his arms and down his thighs. He wanted to press her further on it. But he remembered he was still playing the part of the gentleman.

She was still so nervous too, her hands shaking slightly as she examined the wound.

"Only a small amount of fresh blood accumulated," she said.

That was a comfort. Using the rag in the basin, she cleared away the blood. The water revealed more of the wound: streaks of deep red and pools of pus.

"Garlic, is it?"

"Yes." Miss Grey smiled. "Its scent is strong, but it will stop any chance of infection. Now be still."

She scooped the paste onto his skin and pressed it down hard. In her concentration, they remained silent for some time. In the country, there was no escaping it, especially in winter.

"I see the snow has ceased," Theo said. Out the window, the day seemed bright and clear.

"Finally. Last night's storm left a half foot of snow in its wake."

From the window, it looked like a white blanket wrapped tightly over the lawn.

"As a consequence, the servants who live in the village failed to make it in."

"Is that why you're treating my wound? Not some servant?"

"I know best how to apply it," she said softly, her eyes deep in concentration.

Silence fell over them once again. He had to say something, anything that would get her talking. He needed the reprieve. And there was something soothing about her voice and how it filled the quiet. The soft and gentle way she spoke to him.

"Did someone teach you these remedies?" he asked.

"My father. He always said if one knew how to use the right plants, mashing them up was akin to creating miracles."

"Your father was a passionate man."

"He took it too far, if you ask me." She wrinkled her nose. "He collected basket after basket of just one plant, concentrating the oils and compounds, heating them, separating them, doing things that weren't natural, making them flammable and even toxic to breathe."

"That's what he liked to do. Push the limits." While it was something Theo praised him for, Miss Grey clearly looked down upon it.

"What about your mother? Is she here with you?"

Miss Grey flinched, tugging on his skin. A flash of pain reverberated through him, but he tried not to show it. Even as she pressed hard and deep into the wound.

"She died when I was just a child."

"What happened?" Theo asked, eager still to keep her talking. The words were not just a comfort—they also distracted from the pain.

"During a winter far harsher than this one, she became ill."

"What ailed her?"

"My father called it pneumonia."

"Is that how you came to live in London?" After her mother's death, perhaps she'd needed a change of scenery.

"I didn't come to live with my aunt until a few years later."

"Why?"

Miss Grey sighed. "Can't you guess?"

For the life of him, Theo couldn't. He wanted more than anything to know. Everything he could.

"There's no point in hiding it," she said, but still, she hesitated. "I'm referring to the Silver Order."

"You know about the Order and still, you want to sell?" Despite her connection to Mortibel, she didn't seem to care if he ended up with Whitestone or not. Or perhaps she was playing both sides. He'd thought he would be able to read her so easily, but she was just as much a mystery to him than ever. It needled him.

"Of course."

"To *me*, no less."

"So long as you have the funds, yes. Then I'll be on my way."

"Once the snow clears."

"Yes."

She had to know the power of this place. She wasn't the least bit fascinated by it? Or interested in learning more?

As a child, the intrigue that had gripped him about everything, particularly the plants here, the sheer power he could feel in his fingertips when he touched them… It had never left. When he'd returned, he'd felt it come alive in him once more. This was where he truly belonged. He was surprised she didn't want to belong too.

"How long have you known Mortibel?"

"Since childhood."

"And still you didn't want to sell to him?

"I never wanted to sell to him," she bit out. "I wanted too badly to protect him."

"You think the place is dangerous."

"If I had it my way," she said, pressing down a little harder into the wound, "he'd be finished with the Order."

Theo laughed. "We have that in common. As it happens, I want him out too."

"Unfortunately, I've recently come to the conclusion that it can't be done. He's changed. The Mr. Mortibel I know would have never done the things he did to you."

Theo sniffed. "Do you think he knows I'm here?"

She kept looking out the window, as if expecting to see him.

Hazel nodded. "His driver, Nathan, would have told him, yes. But he left that same night, so for all he knows, you're dead."

"That will have to do, I suppose."

"But it won't stop Mortibel from visiting once the snow clears, will it?

"You could lie for me. Tell him I'm dead."

She didn't confirm either way.

Theo clenched his jaw. He never wanted Mortibel to see her again. *You're better off without him*, he wanted to say. She was too good for someone like Mortibel—he knew that much.

Miss Grey shut the drapes. Undeterred by the estate's old, brick walls, the wind still whistled through every crack.

"Anyway, I've already accepted your deposit. Soon, there will be other papers to sign, but that sort of business can wait until you are properly healed. You need more rest."

"Then you'll hold it for me?"

That was all he should have been concerned about. Not the downcast eyes that dimmed her expression. He'd won the house.

She had accepted *his* offer and yet he was still a little jealous. Because of all things, she still held on to some affection for Mortibel, even though she wouldn't sell him the house. She had wanted to protect him. She probably still did.

He couldn't think of anything more ridiculous. She didn't understand Mortibel. She didn't understand the Order or the house. Before she left, he wanted her to see it all much more clearly.

"Miss Hazel." Emmerson peeked her head into the room. "There's something you need to see."

CHAPTER FOURTEEN
The Vines

A S SHE TRAVELED through the halls, Hazel wished she had brought her shawl. With the fires still unlit, the servants' absence meant the home was little warmer than an icebox.

"What is it I need to see?" Her voice came out more irritated than she had meant it to.

"Patience, Miss Hazel. It's rather difficult to explain." Emmerson hurried ahead.

Hazel was just chilly and perhaps irritated with the conversation concerning Mr. Mortibel. Even though she'd said otherwise, she didn't want to give up on him yet. Years ago, she would have never dreamt it possible. But he had changed. He wasn't the boy she had grown up with. Nor the young man to whom she had talked for hours within the privacy of the tall grasses. During those hot, summer afternoons, her feelings had begun to take a turn. Feelings she'd thought had finally dissolved months ago. Not even close. His proposal had been too painful. Despite her hopes, it had had nothing to do with love. It had been about securing his place as chairman.

When had he become so ambitious? The moment her father had died? In the years following her move to London? To resort to such violence, Mr. Mortibel—her childhood friend Marcus—

could not have gotten this way overnight.

In a way, she was glad he stayed away. What would he think if he knew she had taken the infamous elixir? He would be delighted. He would try once more to persuade her to stay. Then he would want to know what she had seen. Hazel cringed at the thought. No, she could never tell him. She could never tell anyone.

Worse than that, what would he think of her taking care of his attacker? Maybe she didn't care. How could she not? With his still and perfect features so similar to those dignified portraits, Mr. Pierce wasn't just some vagabond. He was a gentleman. To her, he'd been nothing but kind. His injuries alone had softened her. Not unlike herself, he too was vulnerable here. Wasn't he? Perhaps when the house warmed a bit, she'd be able to think more clearly.

At the moment, pockets of cold lingered throughout the hall. If Hazel were superstitious, she might have thought them ghosts. The howls that echoed through the home were even worse. They were all coming from the morning room.

The glass door into the courtyard had been left wide open. The air rushed over her with an ice-cold intensity that stilled her heart.

Across the courtyard, vines of brilliant green crawled across every inch of open ground. Long cords as thick as a person's arm mingled with smaller twigs as thin as hair. Emmerson stood in the center of it, a dusting of snow whipped up by the wind around her.

Nothing should have been able to grow in this cold. Certainly not overnight. It hadn't been here the day before, not when she had disposed of the elixir.

"Impossible," she whispered as she stepped deeper into the courtyard. Hazel was using the word so often, it was beginning to lose its meaning. Sooner or later, she would have to accept that everything, no matter how unlikely, was possible here.

"What do you think it is?" Emmerson followed closely behind.

A blessing or a curse, Hazel couldn't have been sure. The plant, a thick cord of emerald with white-speckled leaves, was beautiful, after all. Though Emmerson probably couldn't see it, the leaves had a hint of purple to them too.

"I'd not touch it, whatever it is," Emmerson said.

Given its invasive quality, the plant was likely to be poisonous.

In the open air, the slightest spasm traveled over the back of Hazel's neck. The thing defied all logic. But for all intents and purposes, it was weed. As such, there was only one thing to do with it.

"Just have it chopped up and burned straightaway," Hazel said.

"This is a job for more than one man," Emmerson said. "It'll have to wait."

"Then first thing tomorrow. No later."

Emmerson went inside. But not before she gave her a look that said, "I told you so" and "Of course this place is cursed."

Cursed was right. Hazel walked along one of the vines. They all had the same point of origin. The growth had started at a single point, the point in which she had poured the elixir.

Hazel touched the black soil, icy and nearly solid to the touch. No normal plant could have grown like this at this time of year. This was the work of the Silver Order and the result of an elixir that could not so easily be tossed away.

The servants, who already had their hesitations about the estate, would be beside themselves with superstition. Some might even take it as a bad omen and abandon their posts. She wouldn't blame them. She wanted to leave herself.

If not for the man sleeping upstairs, she might have. She needed him to get well and finish this business of selling the estate. Only then could she escape the dangerous workings that surrounded her.

CHAPTER FIFTEEN
The Antidote

THE THING COULD not be restrained. Still without servants the following morning, Hazel and Emmerson had struggled to clear away the vines that now sprawled over the walls and every surface of the courtyard. With shears proving not quite sharp enough, they had since resorted to axes.

Hazel hacked away until her face grew hot and damp with sweat. But try as they might, the vines would not die away. The vines kept coming back and each time with more force, until eventually, Hazel resolved to let them grow unfettered. Within the week, it had already begun to grow upon the manor. Although its leaves were covered in frost, somehow, it was still alive. The vines inched up over the windows too, the vibrant greens and purples threatening to consume the place, if not all of England, by the end of the year.

The things worried her. Had she released something horrible onto the small plot of her garden? She had tried various remedies to stop their growth. But neither vinegar or salt had prevailed. At least not in the amounts they had available to them.

The weather would not let up, either. Another storm had swept through that morning. She was glad it continued to keep the servants away. It was a blessing to have the vines buried too, but Hazel feared they'd only grow taller. A harsh and peculiar winter it was turning out to be, Emmerson had said. Just like Lenora had. If nothing else, it was proving to be a miserable one.

For Hazel, winters were always less than pleasant. It was her least favorite season. She preferred the warmth of summer, which allowed for picking the best and brightest fruits at market. With her talent for seeing colors, she had a good eye for picking the ripest. But in winter, it was all too easy to get lost in a world covered in plain, white snow.

Pacing back and forth in the library, Hazel considered telling Mr. Pierce about the vines. Knowing the home as well as he did, he might know what to do. But it also meant she'd have to mention the elixir. Her palms went clammy and her heart raced at the mere prospect of telling him what she'd seen. But perhaps the strange vines weren't related to the elixir at all. Perhaps they were some kind of rare plant her father had cultivated. A type that just happened to reveal itself in winter?

She still held out hope. Convinced she would find answers, she spent the whole of the morning in the library, flipping through all the books she could find on botany, focusing on evergreens. She was sure she'd come across a vine similar to the type in the courtyard. While she paged through hundreds of drawings, she couldn't find the vines' likeness. The closest in appearance were tropical vines from the farthest reaches of the world, yet they thrived only in the most humid and hottest of climates. If a winter in the Malvern Hills couldn't kill this plant, what else could?

She took up a green and gold botany book, surprised when it opened to a dry cluster of mitten-shaped leaves, brittle to the touch. The memory was so clear in her mind, she didn't know how she had forgotten it. She had been out collecting specimens for her father, weaving in and out of trees. The orange and pink of sunset had meant she hadn't long until nightfall. In the distance, her father had called for her. Eager to make her return, Hazel had made a quick grab of the plant and run off.

It hadn't been until later that night that her hands had begun to burn and itch from the plant's poisons. Her mother and father had shared harsh words with her. While her mother had been furious, Hazel had been rather intrigued by the plant. Using her father's tweezers, Hazel ventured to keep it for later study.

That had been long ago, before she'd known the truth of her father's studies. Before she had been forced to learn them firsthand. As the snow had intensified, so had the image of that horrid ritual. It had been snowing then too. Big clumps that had caught in her hair and eyelashes. Melting then freezing solid so she couldn't stop shivering.

The memory of it, so clear in her mind, thankfully vanished at the sound of the door.

"Your father spent a lot of time in here too." Mr. Pierce displayed a calm and steady grin.

Though his arm was still bandaged, it was if he had never been hurt at all. When he stepped forward, however, he stumbled slightly. Hazel rushed to his aid. The touch all too familiar. After her vision, she had grown to know it so well. Too well.

"Come sit down at once." Hazel took some of his massive weight on her shoulder and led him to the settee. If only to escape the sudden, unexpected contact, she went to the fire and propped up another log.

"Are you sure you don't need more rest?" she asked.

"I've slept long enough."

Hazel stared at the flames. She had done her best to avoid him after the vision, but these last few days, she had begun to crave company. Any company. Even Emmerson had been too busy caring for him and the estate to offer much.

He was the only companion she was going to get out here. But even she had to admit he wasn't all that bad.

She rather liked the mystery about him. The foreign place he had come from, his secret past. She could learn more about him without immersing herself further with the Order, couldn't she? He was simply a much-needed diversion in the quiet loneliness of the estate. Nothing more.

Despite the bandage on his arm and his messy hair, he looked well. Better than well, really.

"What a poor host I am." She jolted upright, suddenly self-conscious in his presence. "You must be famished."

Hazel rang the bell and Emmerson arrived at a moment's notice, no doubt listening in on them from afar.

"Would you kindly prepare a breakfast tray, please?" Hazel asked.

"You wouldn't like me to set a table?" She glanced at Mr. Pierce.

Emmerson had only wanted an excuse to wait on them and chaperone. To stand idle in the corner while she listened to their every word.

"I'd rather not."

"It would only be proper..." she mumbled under her breath as she left the room. At this, Mr. Pierce smiled.

"Ignore her." Hazel shook her head. "She doesn't understand that things are different in the country than in Town."

Mr. Pierce leaned back in the seat, propping his feet up on the ottoman, rather at home. "There are certainly fewer eyes."

The words filled Hazel with a hint of caution. "There *are* servants, of course, who talk. They should be in tomorrow, if the roads have cleared."

"No wonder it's been so quiet. It's unusual to have so much snow here, isn't it? Snow and cold, I'm used to up north, but you don't like it much, do you?"

"Difficult to say." She didn't particularly like that it trapped her here with him. Saying as much would have proved rude. She didn't want him to think she was afraid, either.

After all, Mr. Pierce and his languid, at-ease posture didn't seem particularly dangerous. But in time, would that change? She needed to understand what really had happened that night in the freezing rain.

"Now that you are feeling better..." Hazel focused her gaze

back upon his eyes—they didn't seem tired at all, but actually quite vigilant. "Is there anything else you can remember about that night? You said Mr. Mortibel did this to you. What started it all?"

"He still hasn't come to pay a visit, has he?"

"The storms. They have not let up." Rather than pass through, they seemed to hover over the place.

Unexpectedly, he laughed. "I brought it all on myself, you might say. I was a fool to think someone like Marcus Mortibel would be willing to fight fair. He's acquired more ambition than I gave him credit for and far too much pride."

"*You* were the one who challenged *him*?"

"I was hardly the one to cast the first stone. He did the moment he tried to take the chairmanship. There's no denying that I am first in line to lead. Before your father, we Pierces always have."

"But you could have spoken to him instead. You—"

"I came with the hopes of a fair fight. That is noble, is it not?"

"No," Hazel said boldly. "It is not what I would consider noble at all. Violence should always be avoided. If it can be."

"In this case, it could not."

Hazel wasn't so sure. Had Mr. Mortibel not poisoned him, would Mr. Mortibel himself have survived? Hazel doubted it. Mr. Pierce was taller and far bigger in build. She had felt his arms herself. He had no shortage of strength.

Emmerson arrived then. She placed the tray on a low table and with a look, promptly left.

"Please." Hazel invited him to eat.

Mr. Pierce obliged, not hesitating to scoop up a mound of eggs with a corner of toast.

Hazel let him take a few bites before continuing.

"Do you think Mr. Mortibel sustained any injuries?" she asked.

"If he did, he deserves them. He left me for dead." Mr. Pierce clenched his teeth. "He didn't even have the courage to deliver the death blow. Mortibel is the true scoundrel, Miss Grey. Not I."

Hazel held her tongue for a moment. It was clear Mr. Pierce didn't much like recalling the memory. She couldn't forget that, beneath his clothing, he had many other bruises and cuts, however minor. In this weather, the doctor had been right. He was lucky to be alive. Most would not have gotten far.

"How did you get past the gates? I know there's no break in the fencing."

"The gate key. I have one," Mr. Pierce said between mouthfuls.

"But how?"

"Your father never changed the lock."

"But you hadn't a key to the front door…"

"Your father was wise enough to change those." Mr. Pierce swallowed a gulp of coffee. "I considered breaking in. But then…I suppose I fell unconscious."

He ate the rest of his plate and she allowed him to finish hers too. She watched him in a sort of fascination. Just three nights before, he had been like stone, his face a pasty white, his lips blue. She would have been forgiven thinking him dead. Now, of course, he was quite alive. He almost looked better than he had that first day she'd met him. A little disheveled, but filled with a new kind of energy.

"Can I get you anything else, Mr. Pierce?"

"Please, we're acquainted well enough. No need for this 'Mr.' business." He stilled in his eating and held her gaze.

"That's rather presumptuous. I hardly think I know you at all." Hazel narrowed her eyes at him.

"You've saved my life. Doesn't that make us friends?"

She crossed her arms. "Ladies and gentlemen can only use each other's Christian names under the most specific of circumstances. You know this."

She wasn't sure she'd ever get used to his loose manners. In London, no gentleman would dare cease the use of a lady's title without an engagement first. Nor proclaim them "well acquainted" after a few short meetings. But he wasn't like the men of London. He was much less reserved, much less particular with his choice of words. He said what he wanted to say and didn't care if he offended. Even if she was unaccustomed to it, she supposed it was at least honest.

"I've been a guest here for nearly a week, you know."

"*Asleep*," Hazel clarified. Was he serious? They had barely gotten to know each other at all. Nor did he need to force her to explain such things. It felt all the more improper spoken aloud.

"Perhaps you prefer it that way. Don't tell me you're still afraid." He leaned forward. He was toying with her, trying to make her shrink back. Hazel held her place, even as he got close, too close. He should have known she wasn't afraid at all.

"Say Mr. Mortibel had a good reason to kill you—" Hazel felt foolish keeping her eyes on the door. As if she would have any hope of escape had he attempted something.

"You don't entirely trust him, either. Do you?"

Hazel froze. After all these years, she should trust Mr. Mortibel or at least she should *know* if she could trust him. Perhaps she'd never known who he was. She feared that most of all.

"Because I'm here, aren't I?" Mr. Pierce went on.

"And there is the matter of the estate."

He laughed. "Whatever my past, it doesn't diminish my generous offer, does it?"

"Precisely. It's purely business, Mr. Pierce. Emmerson and I will be gone the moment the snow clears and your payment is complete, just as I've said."

"You are so quick to sell the place. *Too* quick. You didn't much like the things your father did here, did you? Or *him*, for that matter."

"The Order and everything they do is horrid," Hazel spit. "How you or anyone else can bear it continues to astound me."

"'Bear it'?" He sat back and nodded slowly. "Do you really find us so terrible?"

He didn't know the things she had seen, though perhaps he

could have guessed.

"If you took the time to understand and learn, perhaps you'd feel differently. I can tell where you've spent your time. Not here, but in London. Specifically, dancing halls, dining halls, halls of that sort."

What was he saying? That she was some silly debutante? She was far from it.

"This place is much more than a home to me." Mr. Pierce snapped to his feet. "If you but knew its secrets… Hell, there are a few in this very library. Rather out in the open, I'd say."

Teacup still in hand, he walked over to the set of three shelves, the only ones secured with doors of swirling iron. He lifted the lock and let it clatter back down. "These bookcases, do you have any idea what they contain?"

Hazel had studied the ornate wrought-ironwork before. The design was clearly the work of the same artist who had designed the front gate. Between the gaps, she could make out brown and leather books, their spines title-less. She assumed the books were rare antiques. She hadn't ever bothered to try to unlock it.

"Really, Mr. Pierce, there's no need—"

"They contain the Order's teachings. The three shelves mark each sect of the Order. The first, second, and third."

She rolled her eyes. Of course they were books relating to the Order's so-called teachings. What else?

"The first shelf seems fuller than the others."

"It belongs to the First Order. For the other chapters, I'm afraid information they are allowed is much sparser."

"And they don't mind?"

"This may be the age of science, but that doesn't mean it's not limited to the privileged. Those who want our knowledge must pay dearly."

To Hazel, it seemed more the age of secrets. Especially if knowledge was limited to those with money and connections—as it usually was, she supposed.

"And here's another secret." He pushed the top, righthand

corner of the bookshelf. Simultaneously, the locked shelf popped out from the wall like a makeshift door. Despite herself, Hazel peered in, seeing only darkness.

"Priest holes are common in old houses like this one. They were meant to protect priests from persecution. But in more recent history, I find it's the perfect place to overhear privileged conversations."

"How charming."

"But hardly the Order's greatest secret," Mr. Pierce said.

"I know well enough what that is." She had hoped he wouldn't bring it up. Before she could stop herself, part of the vision flashed before her eyes. "In fact, I think you've said enough."

"But I've said so little."

"I left this place behind me when I was no more than a child, Mr. Pierce. And for good reason."

Hazel thought back to that ritual she had seen. The horrible pooling of blood. Her heart began to race, just as it always did. She took a deep breath, barely managing to calm herself before Mr. Pierce could notice her sudden shift to panic.

"I see. Saw something you weren't meant to? No wonder you care so little for the place. Amusing, isn't it, how a single event can alter one's life forever?" Mr. Pierce didn't ask for specifics. He simply stared down into his empty teacup. "And what happened to your father? You don't care to find that out, either."

Hazel straightened. She had hardly expected him to broach the topic. Now that he had, she stumbled for words. "I've heard a few theories. There are some who even suspect *you*." It was obvious who. Mr. Pierce had the wounds to show for it.

"And you don't mind selling your father's home to his murderer?" Somehow, the accusation, even if it was the second time she had made it, didn't fluster him one bit.

"You don't deny it? Come now. You have your own theory. You've been so adamant."

"Enough to make fast enemies." He smiled, though it didn't

quite reach his eyes. "But whoever did it matters little. What really matters is *why*."

"You're that certain he was murdered." Perhaps she didn't care. Her father had caused her enough trouble in life. She couldn't allow it to continue in death. "You don't know, do you?" he said, quite amazed. "For years, your father was looking for something, an antidote to a powerful poison. Its discovery would have been significant to the Order. My guess is that he found it."

She had been wrong. Of course talking to Mr. Pierce would entangle herself deeper in the Order's affairs. But she had a feeling that as long as she stayed here at the estate, she hadn't much hope otherwise.

"You believe my father was murdered for this antidote? An antidote for what?" More than that, Hazel wondered why Mr. Pierce was sharing this with her. Perhaps he had simply come prepared. "If this is all a ploy, Mr. Pierce, you needn't bother. As I said, so long as you have the funds, the manor is yours."

"This is no ploy." He leaned in, his eyes shining.

"Then why bother telling me this at all?"

"How could I not? This man was your father."

At this, Hazel felt a pinch of guilt.

"As I've told you," he continued, "my father and your father, they were great friends once."

Once. Just as Mr. Mortibel had said. "And yet something changed."

"We tried to keep the connection over the years, but your father became aloof. That doesn't mean we wished him ill. When I heard about his death, I had to return. To fill his post, yes, but I needed to find out what happened to him too."

He dragged a hand through his hair. "You're not the least bit curious about what may have happened within these walls or down in the laboratory?"

"All the Order has ever brought me has been danger and pain, Mr. Pierce. If I've learned anything of my experiences, it's that indulging my curiosity can only lead to trouble. I'll thank you for keeping me out of it."

"This is different. This is your father. The question of his death could haunt you for the rest of your days."

"Either that or the truth will. What difference does it make?" Her heart began to race. She was starting to think her father's death would haunt her no matter what. It had already led to so much.

"Nonsense. I'm convinced the truth can set one free."

Hazel couldn't help but warm beneath his determined gaze. He was not only unabashed, but passionate.

It might have been true, after all. She couldn't deny how her father's death had been nagging at her. Ever since Mr. Mortibel had shared her father's truths, it was only natural to want a conclusion. Perhaps then she would be able to let go of the resentment she still held for her father in her heart.

Trapped in this merciless, wintry landscape, she certainly had the time. Since she had listened to the other theories, it was only fair to hear his. She would listen to Mr. Pierce's theory at least for a little while.

"This antidote, then. Tell me, what was it for?" Hazel walked back over to the low table and reached for her coffee, cold by now. She had forgotten it entirely.

Mr. Pierce grabbed her hand over the bell, stilling her before she could summon Emmerson for more.

"How about I show you? Your father's laboratory—"

"The lab?" She almost jumped.

He released her, letting her draw her hand back. She pressed both hands between the folds of her skirts.

"I won't. I absolutely refuse." Hazel wanted to laugh at herself for sounding so much like a child, but it was true nonetheless.

"The lab, I'm afraid, is at the center of everything."

Hazel gripped and pulled at her skirts, considering this.

"Tell me, is that servant of yours to be trusted?"

"Emmerson? She's been with me for years."

"Good, then it will be no trouble at all. I've been aching to look at your father's notes since I've arrived."

"But…" It didn't seem right that he knew about the lab. It was her father's most private space. There was no knowing what they might find, which was part of the reason why she had refused to go down there in the first place. Not to mention, it would be dark and dank, just like the catacombs, a memory that still tightened her heart.

Somehow, Mr. Pierce's excitement was contagious. It brought back a familiar childhood curiosity. Once it grabbed on to her, it refused to let go.

CHAPTER SIXTEEN
The Laboratory

THEO WAITED ON pins and needles for Miss Grey—or Hazel—to answer. *Hazel*, he repeated fondly in his mind. She might have demurred the informality, but what they had been through transcended all this "Miss" and "Mr." business.

The moment she gave him a nod, he burst out of his seat with alacrity.

"Are you sure you should be running around like this?" She trailed after him. "You should take some time to digest."

"We need to make up for time lost." He grabbed one of the oil lamps.

As excited as he was, Theo could sense her trepidation. So, in the hall, he slowed, ensuring they walked side by side.

"I won't allow any harm to come to you, you realize. At least not till you hand over the deed."

She laughed and the hall itself seemed to brighten. They needed a bit of joy and laughter. Even the uncovered windows didn't let in much light, as they were too covered in frost. Outside, great wisps of snow blew across a bleak landscape. He could hardly believe that it could ever be summer here.

Closer to the windows, it grew colder too. Hazel clutched her arms to her chest. Instinctively, she seemed to step closer to him and his radiating heat. Theo couldn't help smiling to himself. The basement level, where her father's laboratory was located, would only be worse. Down there, she'd have to move into him even closer.

They stopped at a tapestry. Theo remembered it well from what seemed like centuries ago. Most of the image had long faded, but he could still identify the ruby stitches that had formed a rose and the silver threads of dew drops.

Anyone would think this was a dead end, but they both knew otherwise. Theo pulled the tapestry aside. There wasn't a door, per se, just another panel of wood.

"Let us see…" Theo pushed in a part of the wall and a clicking sound erupted. The paneled wall swung open. "Just as I remember."

"My father used to disappear down this hallway." Hazel leaned forward to look down past him. "Sometimes for days."

Theo had his memories too. When the heat of the summer had made the stench of the harsh chemicals strong. He could almost smell them now, as distinct as every other memory that seemed to seep from the home. Moments he hadn't thought of in years.

In the doorway, a cold icier than the winter wind leached out. The first few steps of the stairs were cast in shadow. It didn't help that they were steep.

"Don't be afraid." Theo held out a hand and helped Hazel down the steps.

The stairs continued to spiral until they reached the stone landing. He had a vague memory of the place, but over the years, he was sure it had changed.

Theo brandished the lamp across the room. It should have been predictable, really, the tangle of tubes and the stacks of specimen jars and ceramic canisters. An inch of dust covered everything. Yet in some places, the glass still gleamed.

The chaos lured them both forward. Hazel's steps crunched over glass.

"Careful." Theo blocked her path forward. He shined the light on the floor, revealing a shiny pool of water and a lump of some dark mass a few feet away.

"It's not human." He put a hand on her shoulder before she could react. "Just another one of your father's jarred specimens. It must have fallen."

He stepped around the pool, lighting two other oil lamps.

Pieces of glass were spewed everywhere across both the tables and on the floor. This hadn't been a mere accident. No, someone had been here. He just couldn't tell when.

"You're sure you've never ventured down here? Not any of the servants, either?" Theo asked.

"No, no one."

Theo moved along the walls and began lighting sconces. Each of them illuminated an arched ceiling.

In such deep darkness, Hazel had hoped for electricity, but this wasn't London, where electricity was becoming increasingly common, especially in the homes of high society.

Nonetheless, against the reflective, white tile, the gas lamps gave the room a decently bright glow. All the clutter shone.

"I can see how my father lost track of time here," Hazel said. "There are no windows. It would have been easy to confuse day and night."

Laid out on various tables, off-kilter scales and other metal apparatuses he didn't recognize collected dust. Shelves and glass cabinets organized with hundreds of tiny name plates stretched to the ceiling.

Hazel crossed the room and he followed after her, keeping close.

A familiar smell grew stronger. It was an earthy musk that brought back memories of her father weighing various chemical powders.

"I used to hammer herbs over here." Hazel pointed.

"Your father made improvements."

He thumped open a leather-bound book filled with various

alchemy symbols and formulas.

Hazel hovered near his shoulder so close, he could breathe her in. He cursed. The circles and lines blurred. Now he couldn't concentrate.

"Do you recognize any of the symbols?" he asked. Part of him didn't believe she was completely ignorant.

"Not one."

Hazel tilted a scale back and forth. She looked at him through a glass silo of pale purple. Her face distorted.

He laughed. "A nice shade. Not easy to accomplish."

"My father made me that particular shade and a thousand others." Hazel tapped on the glass of the show globe beside it. "I prefer this one."

"That's the same."

"Not quite. Only you can't tell."

"But you can?" Theo eyed her suspiciously.

"It's called tetrachromacy. It means I can see a much wider spectrum of colors. I was born with it."

"Just as your father was," he recalled. "A useful gift for alchemists."

"When I was a child, my father took full advantage. He had me gathering plant specimens, sorting powders…"

"It's a pity you have no interest in the ancient art."

"I have yet to see any good come from it. At least from the sort my father practiced."

"Come now." Theo climbed up one of the ladders along a wall of shelves. He fumbled through several vials before bringing down a bright-blue glass. "This one I've always found particularly benevolent."

"What does it do?" Hazel took the dusty glass from his hand. "It's thick. Like honey."

"It would be much better for you to see." At a nearby table, Theo shifted through the metal and glass, taking up a small blade.

Hazel stepped back. "You don't mean to…"

But he did. Ignoring her protests about the dirtiness of the blade and possible infection, he laid the blade carefully against his palm and pressed down until blood blossomed. He held out a hand. "The vial. Hand it here."

Hazel watched carefully as he smoothed the thick, cloudy, white serum over his finger. He held his hand up closer to the gas lamps.

The skin began to close in until it sealed, leaving behind a smooth and even surface. Hazel gasped and grabbed his wrist. She smeared away the remaining remnants of blood. Any hint of a wound completely gone. In its wake, there was only clear and perfect skin.

"Works like a charm on wounds."

"And your arm?"

"Oh, yes, almost forgot." He sniffed, feeling a little silly for needlessly cutting himself. She brought that out of him: the need to show off, at the same making him so nervous. "It's healing so well."

She helped him peel off the layers of bandage.

"May I?" Before touching him, she looked up at him for approval. When he nodded, she smeared some of the serum onto his wounds.

She shivered at the contact. Theo could feel it ghost through her fingers. He had to steel himself not to do the same. Even though she'd dressed his wounds before, the contact was suddenly intimate between them. It was the closest he had been to anyone in what seemed like years. Was it the same for her? He suspected it was. It would be foolish to deprive themselves of more.

He almost reached out for her other hand, to do what, he wasn't quite sure. He just wanted her touch to last a while longer. But it didn't. She pulled her fingers back in the next instant. The serum didn't even sting. Like the one on his palm, the wounds disappeared in moments.

"And other ailments like a sore throat? A cold or fever?"

"It's only good for wounds, unfortunately, but there is no

limit to the severity."

"Tell me how it works. There has to be some sort of scientific explanation for it. If my father taught me anything, there always is."

"That's where my family disagrees. There are things in our possession far more confounding than this. Not everything is meant to be understood, you know."

"Including this?"

"This serum has been in our possession for some time, but your father made improvements." Theo smiled fondly. "It contains high concentrations of saturated fats and a special bacterium that works to bind the skin. It's all very scientific, just as your father liked it."

"At any rate, you might have told me about it. Your life was at stake."

"I had no idea if there was any in stock. At any rate, I thought your poultice very effective."

"I almost feel foolish making it. The thing was nothing compared to this. Or..." She looked about the room once more. "Perhaps you didn't want me to know the manor holds such treasures."

"Must you always be so distrusting? Here. Take it," he offered. "It's yours."

"I wouldn't dare." She placed it on a nearby counter. "What of my father's antidote?"

"I haven't forgotten."

He opened a drawer and pulled out a large jar, full of a silver liquid that shimmered in the artificial light.

She reached out but stopped herself. "The elixir...the one that gives foresight...supposedly, anyway."

"You know it?"

"Vaguely..." She looked down and shrugged. "Just that it's the Order's biggest claim to power."

It was a lie, he could sense it. But why lie?

"That isn't the antidote, is it?" she asked.

"No, this is what requires the antidote." Still craving her

touch, he came toward her again, testing for her reaction.

"You don't mean..." She remained perfectly still.

"Over time, it kills, I'm afraid. A rather tragic side effect, hmm? Every gift has its price, I suppose. The gift of foresight most of all." He released a breath. "You'd think no one would want to do it. But there is no shortage of *seers*, as we call them. They consider it a small price. *A noble sacrifice*, my father once called it."

Hazel stared into the depths of the purple show globe, her eyes searching.

"It's a slow poison that takes months. A madness slowly creeps over you in the final days. You don't know what's real. Past, present, and future all begin to blur..."

Hazel's breathing doubled. "He was mad," she mumbled to herself. "Lenora said my father was mad... Mr. Mortibel told me he was ill...Why didn't someone tell me sooner?"

"What's wrong?" He finally found the courage to grasp her hand. She didn't shrink away like he feared. At least not instantly.

"Just tell me what happens," she blurted out. "Tell me what the poison does."

"Madness is indeed one of the symptoms. Physically, there are changes too," Theo continued cautiously. "You begin to bloat, sores begin to form—"

"It can't be true. How can you talk this way?" She covered her face with her hands. "To tell such lies... I should have never agreed to come down here with you."

"It's true. If you would just consider it..."

"There's nothing to consider. It can't be."

⸺

SUDDENLY, THE QUIET of the basement, the jars of suspended organs, and the building stench were all too much to bear. Hazel felt the room tilt and her body almost went with it.

The elixir he had presented, there was no mistaking it. The

liquid had the same glimmer and shade of silver. She had poisoned herself.

Mr. Pierce—or *Pierce* if he wanted her to drop her manners—rushed to her aid. She tried to brush him away. They weren't intimate enough friends to allow for that kind of touching, even if he was just trying to be comforting. And not in a thousand years would they ever be so intimate as to go by given names.

If she was being honest, keeping him back was about so much more than manners, though. She couldn't endure the touch that sparked a million sensations and a memory that shouldn't have existed. Even the slightest graze brought back that scene. She could never un-feel it. She remembered every sensation, even the way his mouth had tasted. She swallowed, suddenly sick with the taste of him, with a want of him. A feeling so sudden, it would not abate. She needed some fresh air.

"Have your fill of this depraved place, but leave me out of it." She raced back up the stairs, heaving, desperate for the fresh, cool air of winter. She wished she could return to the normalcy of London, where things like logic and practicality still reigned, not this supernatural nonsense.

Pierce's claim couldn't be true. If he wasn't lying to her, the man had clearly been misinformed. Why would her father and the seers take the stuff if it would only kill them? Could they be mad enough to believe it was a noble sacrifice, like Pierce had said? In the quest for the ultimate knowledge, how could they really think death was a fair trade?

She stopped at the window at the end of the hall, staring out into the whiteness. It might as well have been an ocean separating them from the world. Still at least a foot deep by the looks of it. Given the thick, dark overcast sky, there seemed no end of coming storms. After his lies, Hazel wanted to throw Pierce out. But it would be a death sentence and where would she be? Right back where she'd started with a disreputable estate on her hands and no one to buy it.

Hate him as she might, he deserved the cursed place.

CHAPTER SEVENTEEN
The Red Death

HAZEL SWEPT ROUND at Pierce's encroaching steps, cautious of him more than ever. Of course Pierce hadn't brought her any answers. He had merely complicated things further.

"I'll hear nothing more. Not another word." There was a shakiness to her voice that she could not still. She had learned enough disturbing facts about her father.

"No more," she begged with hands over her ears.

"But it is true. Among its many properties, the elixir is a slow poison," he said. "First comes the confusion, paranoia, then—"

Hazel stumbled backward against the ice-cold surface of the window. Pierce reacted fast, pulling her into him before the glass could break under her weight. His face stilled, his mouth agape. He seemed to understand now.

"Don't tell me…you haven't…" He stared, blinking wildly.

Her stomach continued to churn. She ran out of his arms and into the library. Certain she was going to vomit, she leaned out one of the windows. She felt only a morsel of relief when a gust of winter wind hit. Finally, some good had come of the cold. Her whole body shook, racked with fear. Her face was so hot and clammy; the icy air was nothing.

She just needed to breathe. She practiced slow and easy

breaths, trying her best not to think.

Pierce didn't matter, and her future with him didn't, either, because she hadn't much of one, not if she was destined to die.

Whatever fear and danger she had faced before was nothing compared to this.

"How long ago?" Pierce asked behind her.

"It was only the tiniest amount. A thimbleful, really, but that matters little, does it not?"

Pierce said nothing, throwing something over her shoulders. The warm fur of a cloak graced her cheek.

"Come inside. I beg you." His hand fell onto her shoulder, both firm and cautious.

The brief moment of nausea seemed to have passed. Hazel grabbed a bit of the snow from the sill and dabbed it over her forehead. She didn't care if she froze to death. It didn't matter.

"I'll drag you out if I must. You'll freeze." His tone suggested he would not leave her. No matter how long she ignored him.

Nodding, she pulled herself back into the library beside the roaring fire.

"Drink this." Pierce handed her a glass of some amber liquor, filled up halfway. "It'll relax you."

The stuff—cognac, she guessed—was atrocious. She nearly choked on it, forcing herself to swallow.

"There is hope, you know."

"How?" Hazel demanded, tears building in her eyes again. How could he seem so confident when the situation was clearly so bleak?

"I told you, I think your father found the antidote."

"He couldn't have found it. He was mad," Hazel said. If that was a symptom of the elixir, then it had killed him. Just as it would kill her.

"'Mad'? Who told you this?"

"What does it matter? Don't you see? He wasn't murdered. It was the elixir."

"But you saw the laboratory," Pierce countered. "All the

broken glassware, shattered across the floor. Someone broke in and searched the place. They likely took the antidote when he still needed it most, to save his own life."

"He could have made that mess himself."

"*Or* there was a struggle. What if it happened down there?" Pierce said. "His *murder*..."

Hazel winced at the word. Perhaps the rumors Lenora had heard were wrong. Perhaps her father had been murdered for this antidote.

"But wouldn't there be blood?" Hazel asked. "I didn't see a drop."

"Not all deaths involve blood."

Hazel bit her lip, fear oozing over her like slime. Her father could have been poisoned with some noxious gas, like Mortibel thought, or strangled.

She couldn't think about any of that at the moment.

"Tell me," she demanded, her voice rough from the liquor. "How long do I have?"

"No one can know exactly. It takes months for the first symptoms to appear."

"How many?"

"Most likely three." Pierce cast his gaze upon the carpet, as if he didn't want to face the truth, either.

"How can such a thing exist?"

"It wouldn't if I had it my way. At least not without an antidote."

"But that didn't stop my father from having others..."

"You might guess that's where some of our disagreements began. I've had them with many members, even my own father."

"But..." Hazel took another quick sip of the liquor as she struggled to make sense of it. "In the last year, seers were still dying. Four in total. It was even reported in the papers."

What she had assumed had been murders had been, in fact, suicides.

Pierce rubbed his chin. He didn't have answers, either.

"I can see why they wear masks now." She remembered the ones from the catacombs. "To hide their constantly changing identities, even to their own members.

How many seers must her father have gone through? How many people had died?

"How does it happen?" she asked softly. "Is it a painful death?"

"I already told you."

"Tell me again," Hazel demanded, her voice harder than she had ever heard it.

"We call it 'the Red Death.' It eats away at you…quite literally…" Again, his gaze shifted back and forth across the floor, unable to look at her. "It damages your skin first, then your organs. Your brain… The sight, unfortunately, is quite unseemly."

Hazel felt her stomach tighten but willed herself not to be sick. "And the symptoms, do they begin gradually?"

"The mind goes first." He nodded. "I'm sorry, I shouldn't—"

"No, please. Do not apologize for telling me the truth."

She had been denied it for too long, particularly by Mr. Mortibel. He had only ever told her half-truths. He'd told her how the Order was full of wonder and fascinating discoveries, praised her for the position she could have had in the Order, but he had never told her anything that mattered, like the truth about the elixir. Hazel paced the room, too angry for words.

When the room swayed and vomit threatened again, she tried to focus on a single object. That one snag on the rug. She couldn't become ill again. She refused.

Hazel bit down harder on her lips, focusing on the pain, anything but the nausea passing over her. All she had wanted was to leave this wretched place. But as much as she had tried to stay away, the manor pulled her back in, reigniting memories she had long wanted to forget.

She couldn't breathe. The air was too heavy, too thick.

"We still have time, Hazel."

Hazel stared up at him. She should demand he call her "Miss Grey" again. But the sweet sincerity on his face was too great. Despite herself, she even liked the way her name sounded on his lips. It was an intimacy, indeed. Dear Lord, she might even have been blushing. Instead of mentioning it, she just sighed.

"The antidote is down there, Hazel. You must let me try to find it."

"Of course." Hazel nodded. "That would be a kindness."

Her father certainly hadn't had any. He had meant for this to happen. He had left her the elixir for a reason. He had known what it would do. She had never hated him and the estate more. More so even than the day she had seen that horrible ritual.

Even in death, he'd only left behind misery. There was the inheritance of the estate and now this.

Pierce woke her from her daze, laying a gentle hand over hers. "The rest of the elixir—is it safe?"

Hazel struggled against the door. The vines had grown over it, so only small bits of sunlight peeked through the remaining glass.

Pierce motioned her aside and gave the door a hard thrust. A million brittle vines snapped and the door sprang open.

Just as she'd predicted, the vines had taken over the entire courtyard. But they weren't that magnificent emerald color of the days before. They were dead, brown and withered almost to dust.

"I don't understand. They were alive just a day ago. The most beautiful green I'd ever seen. Could they have finally succumbed to the cold?"

"Doubtful." Pierce took a vine between his fingers and snapped it in half. "It's the way of the elixir. A euphoric, albeit temporary, gift."

The sight was dreadful, the brown and gray leaves dulled and faded. And yet, despite the days it would take to clear away, her relief was immense. She wouldn't have to come up with some excuse for the servants.

"It's a mercy no one was killed." Halfway through the courtyard, Pierce tapped his foot on a bundle of vines. Beneath tightly-packed tendrils, Hazel saw the pale-gray wood of an old bench. It was as though the plant had tried to strangle it.

She was grateful the snow had kept the servants away now. Could this have happened to one of them? To herself?

It was just another way the Order might take her life. Yet one more to add to the list.

"One would think I'd be used to it by now."

Pierce raised a brow.

"This is hardly my first brush with danger thanks to the Order," she explained.

"Given your earlier precautions with me, I suspected as much. You tied me up, remember?"

She smiled but could not forget the fear she had felt when she had first discovered him. Even though he'd barely known her, he'd seemed to trust her first. He hadn't just told her about the antidote, he'd told her about the books in the library, had taken her down into the laboratory…

Still, she couldn't erase the doubt Mortibel had planted in her mind. Was she a fool to continue to be alone with him like this? She liked to think she had known danger well enough to sense when it was upon her.

"Was there something else that happened?" he asked.

"Two weeks ago." She still had yet to fully process it, let alone speak of it with anyone. "I should have seen it coming. Everything about that night seemed to warn me. The meeting being held in the depths of London and in the dark of night…the worst was bound to happen."

Pierce had stilled in his study of the vine, staring at her intently.

"Heavily armed men tore through the place." Hazel blinked,

catching a glimpse of stone and dust spraying across the room. She swallowed a chasm of emotion building in her throat.

"It was a miracle I wasn't hurt. Mr. Mortibel was not so lucky. He was wounded. Badly. I saw the wound myself. It could have killed him." She set her focus back on Pierce. "We never found out who the attackers were."

Pierce crossed his arms.

A harsh wind blew past, a cloud of dust rising in its path. Hazel turned against it. She was starting to shiver and perhaps the point was moot. "We should return inside."

Pierce blocked her exit. "So let me understand. They harmed Mortibel, but they spared you. Don't you ever wonder why?"

Hazel recalled the words whispered to her: *"Escape whilst you can. Run."*

It had been a prophecy of sorts and good advice. There seemed no end to the dangers of her father's manor. And now, it was too late.

"Perhaps Mortibel deserved what he got," Pierce said. "Maybe it was fate."

"What do you mean…'fate'?" She wasn't sure she wanted to know her fate. When she had taken the elixir, she'd just wanted to see if it worked. She hadn't even thought it would.

Just like that night, she was breathing heavily, fighting for air. Would she ever return home? Would she ever see her aunt again?

"Whether you accept it or not, I think you have some role to play in the Order. There are forces keeping you here for a reason."

Unlike Mr. Mortibel, who was always trying to convince her she belonged, she believed Pierce. Mr. Mortibel had something to gain. Pierce did not. He had more to gain if she left entirely.

"I was so convinced I'd be back in London by now."

"These are terrible circumstances, but I'm glad you're not."

The less skeptical part of her was glad he was here too. His confidence navigating the manor and the way he'd studied the vine, he had a reassuring presence amidst all of the Order's horrors. But why should he want her to remain here? Was it because of this so-called role she was to play or something else? Perhaps something of a much more personal nature? Before she could ask precisely what he meant, she caught Emmerson staring through the window glass, watching them. For how long, she didn't know.

Catching Hazel's line of sight, Pierce turned too.

"I didn't want to interrupt." Emmerson stepped through the open doorway, all red-faced. "A note came from Mrs. Coldstone."

"You mean *Miss* Coldstone."

"Whatever her name, here it is." Emmerson handed over the folded piece of paper that had apparently been delivered without an envelope. For this lapse in decorum, Emmerson made no comment, likely due to Pierce's presence.

"She was able to make it in this weather?"

"What weather, Miss Hazel? The storms have let up at last. I imagine the other servants will be returning first thing come morning."

"That's great news," Hazel turned to Pierce. Or was it? They'd have people watching them now. Perhaps she had liked their solitude. Minus Emmerson, as it was.

"Now I've prepared two place settings in the grand dining room," Emmerson went on with some indignation. "And I'll have you know it's already twenty past eight."

"You're acquainted with Miss Coldstone?" Pierce asked the moment Emmerson had left them.

Hazel nodded, reading the list of herbs in the cough remedy the woman had promised.

"She's the one who gave me the elixir."

CHAPTER EIGHTEEN
The Coup

THROUGH THE MULLIONED windows of the dining room, Theo glimpsed a glittering of stars for the first time since the storms had calmed that morning.

Somehow, he hadn't noticed that the sun had been out all day, finally allowing for the roads to clear. It would only be a matter of time before Mortibel showed up on his doorstep now. He steeled himself for another confrontation, a fight that might very well be more violent than the first. He had other concerns too.

"Tell me, how precisely did this woman—Miss Coldstone, is it?—come to possess something of such immeasurable value?"

"My father. She said he left it for me." Hazel drank her wine more deeply. "Terrible, isn't it?"

"He must have had his reasons."

Hazel picked at her plate of chicken. Ever since she had discovered her fate, she had become so listless. He couldn't blame her, of course. Rather, his heart ached for her. More than he thought possible.

She dabbed her mouth daintily with her napkin. "I can think of no reason aside from his terrible character."

Theo wanted to speak out in her father's defense but held his tongue. He didn't want his loyalty for her father to renew her suspicions. Although they seemed on friendly terms, Hazel had yet to fully lower her guard.

"Is that another reason you came here?" Hazel lifted her gaze. "For more bottles of elixir?"

Theo cleared his throat, taken aback by her sudden insight. "I was hopeful your father had found the antidote too…" He took a big gulp of wine.

"I see."

Even he had to admit, the ability to use such a gift without consequences would mean true power, indeed.

"I always planned to return at some point." It had been his family's home for centuries. Who was he to change that?

"Once your family rebuilt its fortune."

"Yes. Precisely."

"You must think I'm quite foolish, don't you?" She chewed her lip. "You must think I'll believe anything."

"'Foolish'? I could never think you foolish. Not with who your father was."

"We had little in common, save for our blood."

"What about this beautiful estate and its gleaming wood-work? Don't tell me you don't favor it."

"The woodwork appeals neither to me nor to you," Hazel said. "No, you want the estate for other reasons. Particularly to become the Order's next chairman. With the elixir and its antidote, you could rule the Order and so much more."

She was right. Why shouldn't those two things give him that sort of power?

He couldn't help but smile. "Perhaps."

"So you admit it."

From her glare, he could tell she was onto him. But would that really be so bad? He was tired of the lies. The moment she'd brought up the catacombs had torn at him. It felt like such a deception.

"You're no different than Mr. Mortibel," she said. "You want this place and the Order for yourself too."

Theo hated the comparison. But in some ways, maybe he *was* like Mortibel. He even wanted Hazel, like he did. At first it had been a way to get his revenge upon the man, but that had been weeks ago. It was more than that now.

He tried to laugh it off.

"You have to admit I fit in well here. I even match the drapes."

Hazel flicked her eyes to the ceiling, not amused. "You don't just have plans to become chairman, though. You plan to start a coup."

"Do you really find it so necessary to label it?"

She shrank back as if he were suddenly dangerous. Just when he'd thought she'd been starting to open up, even if only slightly.

That didn't change that she still needed him. He was starting to relish this need, just like the fact that he owed him her life since that night of the rain storm. It was all beginning to bind them together. He also wanted more than anything to repay her.

"Mortibel's death was supposed to be the easiest solution," he said.

"But what about his allies? What if they retaliate?"

"I have my supporters too. The numbers have always been on my side."

"Are you so certain? After being away up north so long—"

"Would you prefer there be a vote? I haven't time for such things."

"You make it sound so easy. As if you aren't starting a civil war. You're going to try and kill him again, aren't you?" Hazel visibly shivered at the idea.

"When the timing is right. Within the Order, there's a proper time for everything."

"Not unlike my father's death. With your fortune renewed, you had much to gain from it."

Whatever bond he had worked to create between them was quickly unraveling. In an attempt to rescue it, Theo placed down his fork. "I had nothing to do with your father's death. Despite your low opinion of me, I respected your father and his accomplishments, most especially his commitment to the Order."

"Accomplishments are not what makes a good father or even a decent one...." Hazel stared at her plate.

He'd known she'd disapproved of her father's passions—he'd even thought she might have disliked him. But Theo had had no idea how deeply she hated her father, especially since receiving his little gift.

"His discovery of the antidote is the only logical explanation for why he used the elixir and I mean to find it. When I do, you would owe me a favor then, wouldn't you?"

Hazel wrinkled her nose. "Is that all you know? Political ambition?"

He almost liked this spirited side of her. It gave her a certain glow. Despite her disgust with the Order, if she allowed herself, she could fit in here. He had a sense for these things, an intuition. Fate had brought them together for a reason.

He wanted more than anything to test the theory, to be her guide and show her everything the place had to offer. If only she would let him. Maybe then she would understand her father's passions. She wouldn't hate him. The poor man didn't deserve it.

"Is that how you regained your fortune?" she asked. "Political favors? Smuggling or gambling? Which is it?

Now she was just being cruel. Nonetheless, he wanted to be honest with her. He wanted to rebuild the trust between them. She didn't actually believe he killed her father. To be sitting here across from him, she had to trust him at least marginally. But he wanted so much more than her trust. First, he needed to give her some peace of mind, especially if he was going to stay here and search through her father's things for the antidote.

Theo sighed. "To tell the truth, there was no fortune to regain. We never lost it in the first place. That's just what we told everyone."

"That was a lie, then." Hazel hardly seemed surprised.

"I'm afraid there were other circumstances that led to our departure. It's a rather long story, but if you would like, I will share it."

Hazel crossed her arms, evidently still suspicious. "You think your story might change my opinion of you? You've already lied to me once."

"You have to at least let me try. Either way, I'm not going anywhere."

Hazel opened and closed her mouth. "You vow no lies or half-truths?"

He placed a hand on his heart. "Cross my heart and hope to die."

Hazel nodded her agreement. "Very well."

"Over brandy, then," he said.

That evening, he was too consumed by her sudden distrust to eat much of anything, either. Drinking, however, seemed a far better option.

CHAPTER NINETEEN
Pierce's Story

A S IF THE home were his already, Pierce directed Hazel to a chair. Behind her, he shut the double doors, keeping away both the cold and Emmerson's prying eyes.

"Your father was always gifted the finest brandy. Too bad he never drank the stuff." At the liquor cabinet, Pierce took two full gulps whilst Hazel swallowed the smallest sip of the glass he offered her. She wanted to keep her wits about her, to ask the right questions and be sure she remembered every detail. She wanted to watch his face for any hint of a lie.

"The real reason your father ended up with the estate is rather complicated." He added an extra log to the fire, intensifying its roar. "It was my fault, really. I was reckless…" He shook his head, laughing at himself. "And an idiot, to be fair."

"I imagine you were very young."

"Not more than six and already so confident of myself. I'd grown up with a silver spoon, as they say."

In an estate like this one, that was obvious enough.

"Much was expected of me. I had the best tutors, the best books, and plans to go away to one of the finest schools in England. I was being groomed, you could say." In his pacing, he paused at the fireplace. "Just as my father and all those before him in the family line.

"Many men of great prominence knew our name. But after centuries of no deviation, one evening changed it all. We all make mistakes, don't we? Some you can't so easily walk away from."

Was it death? Hazel wondered. *It had to be some great tragedy, given the look in his eyes.*

"That evening is half the reason I despise London. You're familiar with its downsides…"

Hazel nodded. "There are too many to list."

"My unsociable father didn't much appreciate Town, either. But there were some social obligations not even he could escape. Alas, at the insistence of an old friend, we were made to stay with him for a fortnight or two. My father's friend tried to make up for what would prove to be a boring few weeks alone with the nanny. He gave me writings after writings of what I would later learn were the Order's darkest secrets. I was just a child. I didn't know what I had—I swear it. Not until I almost ruined us."

Pierce stared into the fire.

"One morning after several days inside, my father took me out for a walk around one of London's finest parks. To pass the time during our carriage ride, I brought one of the notebooks I had been given. One of the most controversial with descriptions of experimentations of a more sordid nature."

He broke eye contact with Hazel, staring off as if watching the scene play out from afar. "It wasn't until late afternoon the following day when I realized the notebook had been missing. I need not have looked for it long. The cab driver the day before quickly approached my father with it. He'd said he'd read it and that he'd expose our secrets if we didn't pay him a fee."

"You were blackmailed?"

"Yes. And by the lowest of men. We didn't dare refuse. You know how quickly word spreads in London. The damage to my father's reputation as Chair would have been irreparable. Keeping the Order's teachings a secret is considered one of our utmost duties. So we paid the man, even though my father knew his silence wouldn't last. He was right. The devil returned, even with safeguards in case we tried to have him murdered." Pierce sniffed.

"Did your father actually consider it?"

"Years later after all that happened sank in, I know *I* did." Pierce's face grew grim.

To Hazel's dismay, he looked almost wistful at the thought. Hazel hadn't known he was so predisposed to violence. Clearly, it wasn't the first time he had considered it.

"But that would have been fruitless. Other men knew our secrets, he said. And they'd been given instructions to go to the press in case he died suddenly. The cabbie had us cornered. Naturally, he demanded more money and then more money until finally… we could risk our fortune no longer. We had to leave it all behind us."

"And give the place to my father?"

"We had no choice but to hand him the deed. We needed to ensure the sale made the papers too. It was the only way to convince the blackmailer that we were gone for good."

"But why my father?"

"We trusted him, I suppose. And he was close to an antidote. At least that's what he told us."

All of this before her father had met her mother. Before Hazel had even been born.

"We didn't know how he would change things or that our letters might one day go unanswered. It took our spies years to discover he that he had others utilizing the elixir despite its dangers. We thought your father must have grown frustrated."

"He might have never developed it. You can't know that for certain."

In answering this, he hesitated. He rubbed his face, more uncomfortable than she had ever seen him. "It wasn't just the broken glass in the laboratory that convinced me," Pierce finally said. "My father witnessed it—your father's death."

"He actually…"

"It wasn't in person. It was a vision. He saw the murderer

too... Well, somewhat. Enough to know he had killed your father. No doubt to take the antidote. At least that's what I suspect."

"He saw who did it?"

"Unfortunately, the man's face was in shadow. He wore a black cloak with no other identifying marks."

Hazel didn't want to believe it. But if this vision was real, then so was her own.

"Your father didn't deserve to die that way," Pierce said. "He was a decent man. A good man."

"He was?" Like Mr. Mortibel, Pierce spoke highly of her father. It still baffled her. She had spent too long resenting him for her mind to see him any other way.

"But using the elixir like he did. Letting people slowly kill themselves for the sake of visions..." These were heavy crimes.

"The seers were well aware of what they were doing. They sign their own death warrants, just as my father did."

Hazel didn't get it. How could anyone think death was worth just a glimpse, a taste, of foresight? Hazel's heart stilled. There was Pierce's father. He'd known well enough.

"So then your father...Is he dead?"

"If I don't find the antidote, he will be."

So he didn't just want to find the antidote in hopes of gaining power. Even if it was true in part, it was awful that she had ever accused him thus.

"Lord knows I didn't want him to do it, but we needed someone to. We needed something. We couldn't go on not knowing, not just our fate, but the fate of the Order. We had to put an end to so much. My father's most prized activities, mainly: our expeditions to search for all things supernatural beyond the sea."

"You tried to warn my father, didn't you?" Hazel didn't know why, but tears began burning behind her eyes. Perhaps because she already knew. By then, before Pierce had been able to send the warning, it had been too late.

"Once my father saw it, he sent out messengers, two in case one got delayed. But it takes weeks to reach the estate and by then…they reported back that your father was gone.

"We should have returned sooner. We should have stopped the use of such a dangerous tool. We knew what was going on. But my father refused to risk our fortune or our good name. The Pierce name and fortune didn't just belong to us, he told me, rather to all who came before us and all who will follow."

"But you had to return sometime."

"It was reckless of me to do so. But I was hopeful the black-mailer had moved on or at the very least wouldn't recognize me. Our plan was always to wait long enough for the blackmailer to either perish or give up his search. One day, I will make certain either way."

Hazel nodded. The idea that the blackmailer was still out there, waiting to try and exhort more money out of Pierce, made her blood simmer.

"Our family, we don't think in terms of ten years or even a hundred years, but several generations ahead. In order to be certain of our success, my father made a sacrifice. He used the elixir. All for my mistake."

"You were only a child. What about the man who handed you such secrets?"

He shrugged. "Either way. I doubt my father will ever forgive me. I barely can forgive myself…not until I set things right."

He rested his forehand against the mantel of the fireplace, hiding his pain. *But he needn't do that*, Hazel wanted to tell him. She understood his guilt. She had been carrying it since learning of her father's death, wondering if she should have paid him at least one last visit. Every time Pierce spoke so highly of him, she wondered if she should have given her father another chance.

These past several weeks must have been so hard on Pierce. "You've been holding on to guilt ever since that day at the park." Hazel came up close behind him and placed a hesitant hand on his back. "You have to let it go." Just like she needed to let go of the guilt since her father's death.

"Don't you see?" He turned over his shoulder at her. "This is my punishment."

"A punishment you put on yourself. I'm sure your father doesn't wish to punish you."

"For so long, my life has been consumed with nothing but thoughts of the Order, reclaiming my spot, bringing it back to life. Everything else was merely a passing fancy until…" He hesitated. Then so quick, she almost gasped, he took her hand. For a brief moment, Hazel felt fear, danger even. A feeling that drained away when she looked into his eager eyes.

"That night I collapsed on your doorstep, my face pressed against the jagged stone…I was so certain of death. So certain that I had ended everything my family had worked for. The dread and guilt that swallowed me whole… Then I saw you in that armchair." He smiled simply. "It's the first time I wanted anything other than redemption."

Hazel almost missed his meaning. Then she saw it, written so clearly in his eyes.

"I wanted you."

She was frozen, speechless.

"You loved him, didn't you?" he asked. "Mortibel. He's more than just a neighbor or friend."

How did he know? Was it that evident in the way she spoke about him?

"He proposed," she said before she could stop herself. Hazel hadn't shared this with anyone, not even Emmerson.

"And you rejected him. Why?"

"He wants the estate and nothing more." It was a harsh truth she had come to accept. "He cares more about the Order than he ever has for me. It's an obsession for him."

"It can become that way for some."

"For you as well?" she asked meekly, knowing what the question would imply.

They were near enough she need only whisper. After he had

pulled her into him, she hadn't pulled back. They inched toward each other closer than that night she had applied the poultice, close enough to garner whispers at any London gathering.

"Do you think you'd ever leave this place?" she had to ask.

Pierce raked a hand through his hair.

"Perhaps one day, you'll see the mystifying sort of beauty that surrounds us here. And you'll be begging me to stay."

Slowly, Hazel was already starting to. That was what separated him from Mr. Mortibel. Somehow, Pierce made her want to believe.

"I had plans, you know. A vision, you could call it. First things first, I was going to stop use of the elixir right away. We'd focus on the other plant life that surrounds the estate. This foresight, it's not worth the risk."

"'*Had* plans'?" she questioned.

"All I care about is finding the antidote now. Damn my other plans."

Hazel blinked hard. Maybe it was the curse word, but something woke her from his spell.

"It's getting late." She glanced at the clock. It was almost witching hour. Was that where this strange sensation was coming from? This need to pull him closer, like some wanton debutante? It went against everything she had ever been taught. It was disgraceful. And yet…

If she knew what was best for her, she would retire to bed at once.

"May I escort you to your room?"

Hazel swallowed.

Was he really suggesting…? Maybe it was just the liquor talking. The fire danced in his especially glossy eyes. He was drunk. That was why he was saying these things. They didn't mean anything.

"Emmerson might still be awake," Hazel protested, if only slightly.

"And what will she think?" he breathed.

The vision certainly crossed Hazel's mind, stealing her breath and warming her skin.

"Is she known for starting rumors?" Rather than interrupt her thoughts, his voice only seemed to fuel them.

"All servants are."

"If there are to be rumors," Pierce said, "perhaps we best actually earn them."

That night wasn't tonight, she told herself. *I still have power over my own fate.*

Though it almost pained her, Hazel pulled away.

"Good night, Mr. Pierce."

CHAPTER TWENTY

The Green Cloak

HAZEL WOKE TO a room much brighter than usual. The blue sky had returned. The roads must have cleared too. She could hear the bustle of servants below stairs. She could only pray that they had stayed out of the west wing.

A knock at the door startled her. Emmerson seemed to have an innate ability to tell the exact moment when Hazel had woken. Something about the bed or floor creaking must have cued her in.

She peeked her head in at first then brought in the water pitcher for her basin. "He's not in here, is he?"

"Now, Emmerson…"

"Well, where is he, then?" Emmerson pressed her lips into a hard line.

"In bed, I imagine."

"Not that I found."

Hazel paused. He was in the laboratory, then. She had no doubt of that. Hazel threw the covers aside with some annoyance. She'd have to warn him about wandering around amongst the servants. It would be much better if they thought he was still hurt.

"You really need to be careful. Last night—"

"I know." Hazel splashed some water over her face. She didn't care about her reputation anymore. She had bigger problems to deal with. Mr. Mortibel, for one. How long did they have before he returned for Pierce, especially now that the snow had cleared? She didn't want to give him another chance to hurt Pierce. It was all she could think about. She might already be doomed, but Pierce could still be saved.

"Why doesn't he leave already?" Emmerson asked. "Sign the papers and be done with it."

"These financial matters are not so simple."

"You've taken a liking to him, haven't you? I saw it the first moment you met. You had that glitter in your eye." Emmerson fluttered her eyelashes in a crude imitation.

Hazel said nothing. She could hardly admit her own feelings to herself. They had been building so quickly.

"It's not like that at all," she lied. There was so much she wanted to tell Emmerson, but it meant she would soon have to tell her aunt. For that, Hazel had neither the time nor the patience. It didn't seem a fair burden to lay upon them, either.

For now, she would have Pierce alone with whom to share her secrets. But this new isolation worried Hazel. The more time she spent with him, the more Emmerson seemed to grow distant. Ever since he had arrived, really. Hazel didn't know how to fix it. More than ever, she needed her lady's maid's support.

"Shall I tell the servants, then? What was the lie again?" Emmerson implored. "That he is your cousin?"

"Not yet. Just help me dress. And quickly."

"Anything special you'd like to put on?"

"Don't be ridiculous."

Emmerson went through the usual motions, tugging tight on the strings of her stays.

"No," Hazel said when Emmerson took up her hair. "Not all the way. Just half. With most of it down, if you please. Something her aunt would have never allowed. The hairstyle was, to her, far too close to having her hair down all the way.

Emmerson obeyed, but given her silence, she did not approve. Hazel was just relieved she had given up on arguing. And even more relieved when Emmerson left with the slamming of the door.

Hazel examined herself more closely in the mirror. She almost didn't recognize herself. She was a different person here. She certainly wasn't the same opportunistic social climber as she was in London. She hadn't changed, though. She'd simply returned to the person she'd once been, however long ago. Something in the cool, winter air surrounding the estate had brought it out of her.

Descending into the laboratory, Hazel was taken aback. Somehow, the place was messier than before. Papers were strewn about, and the beakers and other glassware lay sideways and stacked in corners. More than the usual smells lingered, ones she couldn't decipher.

She found Pierce hunched over one of the worktables, his eyes running along a notepad. His determination warmed her—even if he had only greeted her with a grunt.

Despite herself, she was glad to see him. The night before had stirred something inside her. She wondered now if she should have said *yes*. Would fulfilling her vision have been so terrible? It seemed a decent consolation to an impending death, even if it was reckless.

"I assume you took care not to be noticed?" Hazel asked.

"Are you truly that concerned about what the servants think?"

"That's not what I mean. I don't want Mortibel to discover that you are better...and ready to fight again."

That was enough to silence him.

"Now that the servants have returned, you mustn't be seen," she said again. There was no knowing who could pass on the news that Pierce was still alive.

"Then I'll stay here until they leave for the day. So they won't talk."

"That won't be till evening."

"All the better." He turned back to the notepad.

She fumbled for words. "Have you discovered anything?"

"Not much," he said, flipping pages. "Not much at all."

So things weren't going so well. Hazel might have guessed.

"Unfortunately, your father's writings up until his death are becoming more and more illegible."

Hazel looked over his shoulder at the scrawl. She knew her father's handwriting well enough. It had been fine and delicately written, never like this.

"That would prove my father wasn't completely himself at the end. He was mad."

"I don't believe it." Pierce shook his head. "If that's true, it throws all of his most recent writings into doubt."

Pierce ran a hand through his hair, clearly troubled by this fact. He punched down on the wooden table. A thousand glass beakers rattled.

She could see in his face how hopeless matters had become. Hazel didn't want to believe it, either. Of all things, she didn't want the Order to be the end of her. She wanted Pierce to find the antidote so she could escape all this. The manor, the Order. Mr. Mortibel.

"We still have time," she reminded him. "Your search has only begun."

"You mistake me. I've not given up. Not at all."

But he needed help. They both did.

"Lenora Coldstone," Hazel said. "She knows more about what happened to my father. I'm sure of it." That evening they'd met, she hadn't the time to properly question and discover all Lenora had known. The rain and strange atmosphere of the home had distracted her. "We should go see her at once."

"Perhaps. The family has lived in the neighborhood almost as long as mine. They seem kind. Even if their practices are a little rudimentary."

"At any rate, she seems harmless."

"Ah, yes. A quality I aspire to myself." He smiled sardonically. "In your eyes, at least."

Hazel laughed. "I daresay you might have attained it."

"Maybe one day, you'll prove it to me."

But it's true, she wanted to argue. She trusted him far more than Mr. Mortibel now. Despite herself, the story Pierce had told her over brandy had indeed persuaded her. He had laid so much bare. Mr. Mortibel, on the other hand, had never told her anything that had been half so personal, let alone disgraceful. Somehow, she felt she knew Pierce just as well. They hadn't just a few afternoons together, but entire days.

"We should see Miss Coldstone soon then. While the roads are clear."

"But how? Nathan hasn't bothered to show up this morning." Suddenly, she realized. "Do you think it means anything? Maybe Mr. Mortibel wants to make sure you can't escape."

"He can't know I'm better. That will give me some advantage. What about horses?"

"Yes, Nathan did leave a few horses in the stables."

"I had no idea."

"Emmerson has been a great help in keeping them. Of course, Nathan was kind enough to leave us plenty of feed. Do you think we could manage on horseback?"

"Hardly preferable." His brows pulled in. "Have you checked the coach house at all? There must be an old carriage in there. It won't be much compared to Mortibel's, but it'll do."

"Who will drive it?"

"Myself, of course." Pierce smirked, as if it were nothing.

Hazel brushed a hand through her free locks of hair. "Very well."

"But first, I have a request." He hesitated, as if he didn't know how to say it. "I'd like to draw some of your blood."

All Hazel heard was *blood*. She pictured the blood she had seen during that one terrible ritual. The bright-red blood that had haunted her always.

"Why?"

"To run some tests. Your father makes mention of your blood on a few pages and I have reason to believe it holds some significance. It may lend some credibility to his notes. It'll take some time, but I think—"

"Just tell me how you intend to take it."

Pierce turned round and rummaged through a collection of beakers, metal tongs, burners, and the like. When he turned back, he held up a long syringe, its needle glistening under the artificial light.

"But you're not a doctor. You haven't ever drawn blood before…have you?"

"No, but I've read about it and it's simple enough. Please understand, I wouldn't be asking unless it were absolutely necessary. Come. Will you at least try to trust me? Just this once?"

She nodded. "Just this once."

Pierce directed her to a stool and instructed her to place her arm palm up onto the table. "Now squeeze your fist."

She brought her uneasy gaze back to him, unable to control the hammer of her heart in her chest. She wasn't sure why she was afraid. There was something about the coldness of the basement and the glass and the tubes that surrounded her.

When the needle penetrated her skin with a pinch, she flinched. She could feel the slight tug under her skin. Tainted with the elixir, she half-expected her blood to be black, but it filled the glass tube with the usual deep crimson.

"You said my father made mention of my blood? What did he write?"

"It was on the labels of some samples and on his notes to obtain more. He provides no other explanation."

Samples? When had he collected them? While she had been asleep? She shivered at the thought. More importantly, what strange things had he done with them?

Pierce took out the serum from before and dabbed it over her wound. Like the needle, she felt a slight pull on her skin and even a little tingle but nothing else as it healed in a miraculous instant.

"Shall we?" he asked casually enough. "I think a bit of fresh air would do us both good."

Before he could step forward, Hazel held him back, her hand on his arm. He froze, looking down at the point of contact.

"The servants, remember? They can't know you're well." Hazel half-whispered. "Please. You can't be so forgetful."

"Damn Mortibel." Pierce squeezed a fist. "We have much more to concern ourselves with."

"I'll go see about that carriage. You're certain you can drive it?"

"Of course."

"Good. In the meantime, stay here. When I'm sure all the servants are occupied, I will get you then."

Pierce worked his jaw, then grudgingly nodded.

IN THE OLD-FASHIONED carriage, Hazel insisted on sitting in the driver's seat alongside Pierce rather than inside. She didn't care how tight the space. She just wanted to feel the sunshine.

The clear sky had held, allowing her some optimism for the ride ahead. But she couldn't forget where she was going. It reminded her once more of what her father had done. How he had cruelly left her a gift that would one day lead to her death.

Who knew what else Lenora might reveal about her father. She cringed to think of it.

"It's horrible, isn't it?"

Pierce cleared his throat. "What is?"

"That my father gave the elixir to me quite on purpose."

"He might have been mad. You can't forget that."

"Or perhaps he was willing to go to any lengths to have me believe."

"And do you? Believe, that is?"

"I'd prefer not to." The vision, however, was still strong in her memory. Just like the healing serum, it had been too real. In it, she had seen and felt things that had carried over into her present: a certain look in Pierce's eyes she could not have imagined in a mere dream. The same look that burned into her in the days following, particularly late that night over brandy. It was the real reason she, at times, thought she knew him so well. A familiarity she had felt in the vision, she felt now too.

"That doesn't answer my question."

He had never asked, but Hazel knew what he wanted in the silence that followed. She didn't think she'd ever tell him the truth. Even if she had grown to accept the vision. More than that, she wanted it to happen. What hope had she of a normal life, anyway? There was no point in fighting it any longer.

In the steady stream of sunlight, she caught that familiar expression again. A certain glint in his eye followed by the faintest of smiles. Waiting, she decided, was like torture.

Pierce sighed. "Whatever your father intended, I think Miss Coldstone is hardly innocent in all this."

"She seems little more than the messenger."

"I think she knew what she was giving you. Your father was too close with her to think otherwise. I know the type. A person of her class only has one reason to become so-called friends with your father. She has ambitions, Hazel."

"She says it was her mother who knew my father."

"A lie, perhaps."

"You think she's a fortune hunter?"

He nodded.

"You think she opened my father's parcel and resealed it?"

"She would at least want to see if it was worth money. I don't think she was the woman your father thought she was. It pains me he would ever trust such a woman with something so valuable, particularly a non-member." Pierce groaned.

"It is only a matter of time until we know more," Hazel said. "I'm sure of it."

She was ready than ever to confront the woman and ask more demanding questions.

"After that, the council would determine her fate," Pierce said.

Hazel had heard of the council before. Made up of her father and the First Order, they alone determined who could join and apparently who to punish.

Pierce pulled on the reins to slow the horses. There was a wagon on the road. "I think that driver's waving us down."

Had the driver tossed a wheel? The horses slowed until they came to a gentle stop just a few inches from the man. Without the aching of the wheels and crunching of the snow, silence closed in around them. The icy air graced her cheek. There was nothing here, nothing but hills and hills of white snow.

"Beware!" a gruff voice yelled. The man was a farmer most likely, given his sun-beaten face and patched-up cloak. "'Tis not a sight for your eyes, miss."

"What's the matter here?" Pierce demanded.

"There's no unseeing it." The farmer pointed behind him.

Hazel got to her feet and gazed farther down the road, squinting.

Across the quarter mile or so of flat, white plain, several carriages lined the lane. They'd been too distracted by the farmer and his wagon to notice them.

The law in their black, shiny hats lingered throughout. She heard their concerned voices but could not distinguish the words.

More than that, a deep-red smearing of blood caught her attention, the brilliant color strewn across the snow. There was a deep impression in the snow too. Her imagination soared. Clearly, a bleeding body had been taken away.

It had to be Lenora.

Hazel sucked in a gasp. Though it was faint, she still recognized the smell of that strange brew over the fire. As if nothing were amiss, the gray, stone chimney still puffed out smoke.

Her gaze caught another brilliant color in the white canvas of the landscape. A deep emerald green. Hovering near the scene, a woman had just turned the green hood up against the wind. Hadn't Miss Grace Mortibel worn a cloak that exact shade last she saw her? Nearby, Hazel recognized Grace's lady's maid too. What were they doing here?

"What's happened?" Hazel asked the farmer.

"Murder, by the looks of it. Lucky to be discovered so quickly, I say. In this weather, it might have been weeks."

"Quick, indeed. The chimney is still smoking," Pierce observed. "And in this cold, no fire could survive longer than a night or two. Who discovered her?"

"The owner of that fine carriage is my guess." The farmer pointed to the white-lacquered carriage that blended in with the landscape. Hazel could barely make out the black outline of the Mortibel crest on the carriage door. The woman in the green cloak had to have been Miss Mortibel. What was she doing in this part of the neighborhood? The road didn't lead to town or any of the nearby estates. No, the home was quite out of the way.

Hazel shivered. She didn't like the danger that seemed to carry on the wind. Neither did Pierce, it seemed.

"Let's turn round," Pierce gave Hazel a gentle pull on the arm. "We can inquire more tomorrow."

Hazel dropped back down into her seat. Shivering in the wind, she didn't mind the tight confines any longer. She was glad to have him near. "I can't believe it. I spoke with her no more than a week ago."

Hazel gripped her arms tight across her chest, trying to still her spinning mind. "The woman in the green cloak," she said. "That was Miss Mortibel."

"Who?"

"Mr. Mortibel's sister."

"You don't think she's involved somehow, do you?" Pierce asked.

"She can't be a friend of Lenora's. And she has no reason to come out this way."

She couldn't help picturing Miss Mortibel's face twisted with anger, shooting off a pistol, or lifting her arms high and bringing down a glistening knife. Her imagination was too wild for her own good. But why would she have done such a thing? It didn't make any sense.

Hazel pushed the thought out of her mind. For the moment, she needed to focus on getting Pierce back into the house unseen. There was only so much loyalty her wages could buy.

Perhaps the danger she sensed in the air was more death on the horizon. She couldn't bear any more violence. More so, the thought of Pierce being injured again. And not just because she needed him.

She turned to warn him when the carriage suddenly seemed to narrow. Dots of gold flashed before her. Everything was spinning, an array of bright and dull colors. Just before the blackness settled in, Pierce shouted her name.

CHAPTER TWENTY-ONE
Discovery

THEO DROPPED HAZEL down upon the chaise, her hair falling like a sheet of black silk over the headrest.

She flinched as though waking up from a nightmare. Theo leaned closer, desperate to do something, anything, that might help. There were so many things that could have gone wrong. He couldn't be sure if she had fainted from shock, the serum, or his blood draw. The only thing he knew was that her heart was still beating and her bosom still rose and fell from her breath. He bit back any crude thoughts. He couldn't allow any distractions, not when she was like this. Over the last few days, he'd had enough of them.

He gave her hand a squeeze. "Hazel?"

When her eyes flashed open, she flinched. He placed his hands on her shoulders, trying best to calm her. This shouldn't have happened. He should have whisked her away from the scene at once. This was all his fault.

She gripped his arm. Although he felt her nails pinch his skin, he didn't move away.

"Am I…?" She hesitated. "I'm dying, aren't I?"

"Of course not." He tried to reassure her. "You fainted. Nothing more." He tried to say the words confidently, although he couldn't be completely sure.

"Were you seen?"

"Don't concern yourself with that now." In truth, there was no doubting they were seen. Everyone had seen. When he'd swept into the house with her in his arms, her skirts billowing over his shoulders, the reactions, naturally, had been varied. Most had gasped, while others, mostly the younger servants, had giggled. He could only imagine the stories they were coming up with in their whispered exclamations down the hall. It was likely the best entertainment they'd had had for weeks.

Hazel looked around the calm of the library and took a breath. They didn't have to worry about prying eyes here. The privacy made him want to lean in even closer. *If not now, then when?* he asked himself. They were running out of time. The serum that was in her veins was spreading, likely to her organs by now. More than anything, he needed to find a way to save her. But if he didn't, he had to seize what few moments they had left, didn't he?

He had never been one to hesitate. He just didn't want to start something that he feared would end too quickly. He didn't want this to be a dalliance like all the others and yet it was the only one that was very well destined to be—all for reasons beyond his own doing. Wasn't that always the way of things? He wanted to kick something. It wasn't fair. He didn't want her temporarily. But it was that or nothing at all. If she died, and he never got a taste… Hell, he couldn't be sure he could go on either way.

"What happened?" she asked.

"I imagine it was my blood draw that did you in. I should not have taken so much."

"But I thought with the serum…"

"It can't replenish the blood I took."

"Well, I suppose you needed it. In your search."

"I needed it to save your life." He put a hand to her face. "That's all that matters to me now. Nothing more. You know this, don't you?"

When she'd fainted, he'd feared the worst. As he drove back to the manor, all he could think about was that she might never know his true feelings. How he might never get the chance for a proper kiss.

She swallowed. He doubted anyone had ever spoken to her like this. Gentlemen who courted in London were anything but direct. Least of all men like Mortibel. Though he was hardly competition.

"How long do you think I have?" she asked, surprisingly brave, given the question.

It was only fair to be honest.

"My father believes it could be several months. Sometimes as long as a year or two in most cases."

"I see." Her face dropped. All he wanted to do was lift her back up again.

"But you didn't answer my question. You don't know it, do you?"

She stared back. "Know what?"

He exhaled. It bore repeating. "You're all that matters to me now. You're all I think about. Particularly how I might soon lose you." At her silence, pain flashed hot over him.

Hazel opened her mouth, but she hesitated.

He shook his head. "We're not in some ballroom, you know. There's no need to be polite. If you don't mind, I'd very much prefer it if you spoke freely."

"As if that wouldn't be undoing years of my aunt's training." She laughed nervously.

"If I have to pry out your thoughts and desires, I will. In fact, I intend to. Unless you decide to give them away…"

Hazel stood up, distancing herself from him. A fact that tugged at him. He could still feel the warmth of her on his skin. He couldn't let that be the last time she gripped him like that.

"I had no idea you thought…this. It never occurred to me." She brushed her hair quickly over her shoulder. She wasn't used to wearing it like this, he could tell. Nonetheless, it suited her far more than all the braids, anyway.

"You have your mask on so tight, even you can't see past it."

"What mask?"

"The one you wear in London. To keep up 'appearances.' You're all silence and propriety, when I know you are hiding so much more."

"Unfortunately, it's required. I would not have survived society without it." She grasped her hands tightly. "You haven't spent much time in London, have you?"

He shrugged. "I was forced to stay away."

"If you want to be accepted, there are certain molds you have to fit. I'm supposed to be the perfect, demure debutante. Always. Unattainable yet within reach, a goddess yet modest. Shy yet confident. Never chatty. Otherwise…you're cast out. And there's no chance of catching an advantageous match."

"Would that be so bad? What are you so fearful of?"

Hazel closed her eyes for a second then flinched. He knew that look. He'd seen it on the seers many times before. What had she seen? He was desperate to know. Again, she remained closed off.

"What point is there?" Hazel said. "I have only months left."

"You don't need to say it aloud." Theo stepped close. "I know exactly what you're afraid of." Society had trained her to believe it was something she wasn't supposed to want, that she ought to regard it with trepidation.

He leaned in an inch closer, waiting for her to protest. "What you should really fear is never knowing it."

He pressed his lips to hers. He kept them there for as long as she would allow, his hands tightening around her waist until she pulled away. At the very least, she was smiling.

"You're not destined for an early death," Theo said boldly. "You're meant to stay here, together, with me."

She shook her head. "Strangely, Lenora said my father believed the same thing. That I was destined to spend the rest of my days here…"

"You don't believe in destiny, but you should. I beg you. You know you have a knack for color. That matters in the world of alchemy. Beyond that, you're well-studied and bright like your father. You have a purpose here. It's how I know I'm going to find the antidote. Because I know. I just know."

Before she could reply, footfalls echoed down the hall.

He leaned away to a more acceptable distance.

"Don't." Hazel pulled him back.

As much as he wanted to close in again, Theo thought better of it. They had other harsher realities to face. At the end of the hall, Emmerson was already shooing away servants.

"They saw me carry you in," Theo admitted.

And they were already wild with gossip, from the sounds of it. Given the look on Emmerson's face when she appeared at the door, there was something else too.

With some reverence, Emmerson dropped down a tea service.

"Mr. Mortibel awaits you in the drawing room, Miss Hazel."

HAZEL FROZE, CERTAIN her whole body was flush with red. "How long has Mr. Mortibel been waiting?"

"Some time now. You can't expect me to hold him back much longer."

Pierce placed a hand on Hazel's back. The warm, heavy weight was comforting for a short moment before he said, "Send him here, then."

Emmerson nodded and turned away. Typically, she wouldn't have dreamt of allowing visitors if Hazel or her aunt felt the least bit ill. And yet, Emmerson hadn't even asked how Hazel was faring. She was gone out of the room before Hazel could stop her. When had she become so cruel? When had Pierce?

"What are you planning?" She turned to him. "I'll not have violence, Mr. Pierce. Not in my home."

"Of course not. Remember the priest hole I showed you?"

Hazel nodded, a thousand thoughts rushing through her mind. Pierce was likely sick of waiting too, not knowing when Mr. Mortibel would arrive, if at all.

"I won't be far," he promised. "Perhaps *he* has the antidote… Find out. We have no more time to waste." With that, Pierce disappeared behind the bookcase mere seconds before Mr. Mortibel appeared at the doorway.

Rising from the seat, she didn't know why she was so nervous. She'd known this day had been coming. She'd already thought of what she might say when confronted about Pierce. She only hoped it would work.

Mr. Mortibel didn't say anything at first. He simply stared, his gaze unblinking. Then, slowly, he began to trail the rows and rows of endless books. Hazel's heart pounded harder when he crossed the priest hole. Was he aware of its location? She wondered if her father had known of it. Unless he had been told, how could he have?

Rather than press that particular button, he turned to face her, a storm already raging in his eyes.

"Where is he?" Mr. Mortibel demanded. "I had to see him for myself. I couldn't actually believe you'd be so foolish."

Nathan, as she'd suspected, had told him everything that had happened that night of the storm. "I am hardly being foolish."

"Foolish, no, but prone to error, yes." He paced across the room and looked down the hallway. She might even think him a jealous lover with that scowl on his face. "There are dangerous people in this world and much more so to you and me."

"I would never host someone whom I considered dangerous, if that's what you're insinuating."

"You can't listen to his lies, Hazel."

Even though they were alone, she still didn't like Mr. Mortibel's casual drop of her title. It implied too much, more than she had agreed to.

"I'm quite accustomed to lies. I've been lied to my whole life."

"Don't start on that. You've never wanted any part of this. Why should we tell you any of our secrets?"

Hazel bit her tongue. She needed to keep her indignation under control.

"After all your time here, you still don't believe, do you?"

He seemed shocked by her silence.

She couldn't deny the serum, the things she had seen in the vision. Not when she wanted it to come true now. More than anything. "To think my father wasn't a charlatan, after all."

"So you do believe. And you still plan to sell to that bastard?" Mr. Mortibel thrust out an angry arm.

"Not sure there'd be much of a point. He's hardly in the proper disposition," Hazel lied.

"What do you mean?"

"He's dying." Another lie. A much bigger one. She'd said it exactly as she had planned in her head days ago. It was the only way she could think to protect Pierce before the papers were signed. But now saving him was about so much more than money, but a chance at love—for however long. She straightened, trying to show confidence in her words. "The least I could do was give him a bed and not cast him out into this cold."

"Is he conscious?"

"Hardly. I'd be surprised if he survives another week."

Mr. Mortibel dropped down onto the settee, rubbing his face. "I did what I had to."

"Poison him, did you? I saw the size of him."

"You should be glad. If you knew who he really was..." He looked around the room. "You should be glad he's dying."

Hazel swallowed. Was this the same Mr. Mortibel— Marcus—she had known as a child? The same she had tried to remain close to even after she'd left for London?

"Haven't there been enough deaths?" Hazel sat down across

from him, desperate to see some sort of remorse for Pierce, perhaps even Lenora. If his sister had somehow been involved in Lenora's death, perhaps so had he.

"If Mr. Pierce dies, his death will fall to you. It would make you no better than a murderer."

"I couldn't control myself," Mr. Mortibel said in a low voice. "I had reason to believe...the man killed your father. And I'm sure he's one of the men who attacked us in the catacombs."

This, Hazel hadn't expected. Mr. Mortibel had held back truths, yes, but she didn't think him capable of telling such an outlandish lie.

"Didn't you recognize him?"

Hazel heard the harsh whisper in her head again: *"Escape whilst you can. Run."*

But a whisper could too easily disguise any man's voice. Could it really have been him? Had he really killed all those men? That night had turned so bloody and violent, like a nightmare. Was he the reason for it? Suddenly, everything she'd thought she'd known was cast into question. He ought to have told her this himself. If he cared for her, he'd at least be honest.

But she couldn't dwell on that now. This was her chance. Perhaps her only hope before the elixir claimed her. She swallowed her breath.

"What do you know about my father searching for some antidote?"

Mr. Mortibel perked up. "What has Pierce told you?"

"That's why he came. To find it and exploit it," Hazel reminded herself out loud. He hadn't come for her and he certainly wasn't searching for the antidote *just* for her. But for his father. For the Order.

Mr. Mortibel snorted. "Then he came on a fool's errand. Your father never even came close. In his state, Pierce must be delusional. Have you considered that?"

Hazel felt herself deflate, not knowing if she should disclose her fate. Perhaps Pierce really was delusional thinking he could find it. In all his hours of searching, he had come up with nothing. Only the mere mention of her blood in her father's notes.

"Don't trouble yourself listening to him," Mr. Mortibel said. "Soon he'll be dead. Tell me what will you do then?"

"There will be other buyers…"

"I have an inclination it will be some time before it sells. A bit of foresight, you could call it."

The word *foresight* gave her pause. Who could say Mr. Mortibel hadn't consulted with one of the seers? Who could say he hadn't found the antidote, taken the elixir himself, and seen all her treachery to come? What clues could a face hold? She searched his expression for a man capable of her father's murder and saw nothing, only the same face she had known for years. But it *was* different, somehow. There were days she'd thought maybe, just maybe, he would choose her over the Order. Once she'd realized he had chosen the Order, he had changed to her. And he was never changing back.

Mr. Mortibel stepped toward her, his eyes full of meaning. "Join me for dinner soon, won't you? We have this and so much more to celebrate…should you let me renew my wishes." He took her hand, his lips lingering on her knuckles. It was bad enough that he assumed enough familiarity to call her by her first name, but now this? Taking her hand without permission?

"Your wishes have not changed?" she asked, surprised.

"Not for a moment."

Nor had his ambitions.

"And your feelings on the matter?" he asked.

"I will have to reconsider them, I suppose."

Mr. Mortibel sighed. "How long?"

"Just another day or two."

Hazel walked him out in silence, watching him get into his carriage. Only when he was far enough down the drive did she feel safe returning to Pierce. In the halls, she soaked in the new quiet. The overcast sky had swathed the estate in gray again. The library seemed particularly drab.

When she entered, Pierce was already seated. His eyes were no longer warm, but cold and unreadable. She knew what had irked him. Mr. Mortibel's accusation about the catacombs. Perhaps even his renewed sentiments.

"I venture you heard most of our dialogue. How did I fare?"

"Very well. Although I think he's lying."

"Regarding what, precisely?" Her skin went cold at the thought of Pierce's role in the catacombs. When Mr. Mortibel had first brought it up, she hadn't said anything in the panic of the moment. She had been silent when she should have been defending Pierce, especially when she knew he could hear.

It was possible, though, Hazel had to admit. She wrapped her shawl tighter around her shoulders. Despite all that had happened, she still didn't know whom to trust.

"The antidote. I think he has it. I heard it in his voice."

Of this, Hazel couldn't have been sure. "Perhaps I should tell him what I've done."

"Something tells me he already knows."

When the room fell silent again, she could hardly stand it. If he had heard Mr. Mortibel's accusation about the catacombs, he made no mention of it. Nor did he say a word about Mr. Mortibel's renewed sentiments. He likely didn't give a farthing about either. In the end, it didn't matter if she believed Mr. Mortibel or not. She needed Pierce for a myriad of reasons and he knew it.

She studied his face, imagining it hidden behind a black mask like those of the men in the catacombs. She had seen the mask often enough in her dreams. They were the reason she had grown so wary of dark rooms, the reason every little noise woke her at night.

"We'll find the antidote," Pierce said, his optimism evidently returning. "I promise."

He stood up without a word. There was no question where he was going. In the laboratory, he'd likely spend the rest of the night.

CHAPTER TWENTY-TWO

The Stones

IT TOOK HAZEL some time before she finally gathered the courage to go down. It wasn't until the following afternoon, when she was finally determined to do so. There was no knowing what she'd encounter or just how Pierce would be using the blood sample he had taken earlier. But she couldn't stand the silence a moment longer, nor did a solitary dinner appeal to her.

When she descended the stairs, she was relieved to see Pierce reading from her father's notebook.

"Oh, good." Pierce looked up from the pages. "I could use a moment's distraction."

Hazel glanced at the still-open pages, the lettering even more foreign to her than before. There were no letters or numbers, just symbols. "What does it mean?"

He laughed. "I'm not entirely sure. It's written in code. I have yet to find a key."

Again, there was that growing possibility they were a step behind. That the antidote already lay in someone else's hands.

Pierce tossed the book aside. "We'll discover nothing in his notes."

And there seemed little else they could do about it. They had few other alternatives.

"You must have found something of note."

"Only this." Pierce grabbed the book and opened it to a page. "This symbol has my interest."

In black ink, her father had drawn a sun peeking below the horizon. A simple half-circle and line.

"And you know this symbol's meaning?" Hazel asked.

"The winter solstice, an annual celebration on the longest night of the year. And it's just two days away. It's significant somehow."

"It's just pagan nonsense." Hazel said. "Ancient beliefs that have fallen out of favor to everyone in England save for the Order. I doubt it's significant at all."

"But it's everywhere. The only pattern I've been able to find thus far."

"Celebrating darkness?" Hazel guessed. "That can't be good." Nothing about the Order was.

"It's far more than that. And it's not about darkness at all, rather the return of light. Remember the nights shorten afterward. The days grow longer. The ancients believe it held a sort of power. The way the world and the stars align that night. The Order considers it an ancient wisdom. We believe the stones are more powerful then."

"This is what the Order believes?"

"There are more people who hold true to these traditions than you think. Particularly in the Malvern Hills."

"Lenora, for one," Hazel mumbled.

"You have to admit the manor has a certain influence, particularly in winter."

"I've never been fond of winter here." The season held too many bad memories.

"Do you find the cold too oppressive?"

Hazel shrugged, not wanting him to dig deeper on the matter. "I suppose there's a certain peace and quiet to the place."

"I'd like to show you something." He stood up.

"What?"

"Some more of that pagan nonsense." He raised a brow. "We'll need to gather our cloaks. And quickly, before the sun goes down."

"You want to venture outdoors at this hour? It will be absolutely frigid."

"You'll find it diverting, I promise."

She supposed she needed the distraction, anything to forget the fate that closed in upon her. So with a sigh, she conceded.

"Let me get our cloaks." She stopped him before he could get up.

In her own house, she tiptoed through the halls. After the servants had seen Pierce carrying her that morning, they had been wild enough with rumors. They certainly would have noticed Pierce's state of health. It would only be a matter of time now until that fact made it into Mortibel Manor.

On top of his health, her untoward behavior might be discussed too. At this hour, it would seem strange going out into the dead of night with not one, but two cloaks.

In the cloakroom, she pulled Pierce's cloak from the hook. Even if it was torn in places with stains of dried blood, it would still keep him warm.

She hurried back. Entirely unseen, she hoped.

Despite her warnings, Pierce waited in the hall, swathed in a beacon of light. Lamp raised high, he had it aimed at one of the landscape paintings. The same Malvern Hills that extended just outside the window was alive in vibrant shades of green, a painting that made her long for summer. Instead of being trapped inside, they could have been eating on the lawn, taking horse rides through the valley, or walking in the garden. All the things one ought to do in the country.

"Now, where are you taking me?"

"Follow me." Pierce threw on his cloak and assisted Hazel with her own. "We'll have to climb a few stairs is all. Up the tower."

Hazel guessed which one he was talking about. The tallest,

most secluded. She'd thought it only served as decoration. She'd never actually considered climbing it.

"We haven't much time before it gets dark." Pierce led her forward.

The doorway was hidden away, much like the laboratory, in the wood paneling of the wall. As if a simple locked door would not have sufficed. But here, everything was a little strange.

She had a feeling whatever he was about to show her had everything to do with the Silver Order. For once, Hazel didn't mind. Pierce and the Silver Order were practically synonymous. But not like Mr. Mortibel was, never like Mr. Mortibel. To them, the Order meant different things. For Pierce, the Order was his family's hard-earned legacy, an idyllic mission to foster and guard knowledge, a mission he sought to protect with every part of his soul. For Mr. Mortibel, it had only to do with power.

The stairs spiraled endlessly for what Hazel guessed had to be four, even five stories. The space was tight, though at least they were traveling upward, not downward like the catacombs. Instead of wet, moldy stone, in this ascent, Hazel breathed in the crisp wind of winter. The space was so open to the elements, frost had begun to accumulate on the stone around them.

"Careful." Pierce came in close and grasped her hand. "If you don't mind, it's safer this way."

Hazel made no argument. The contact brought her warmth. His body radiated so much, she almost forgot the cold. When the stairs opened to the sky, the wind pushed her into him. She looked up into his eyes, uneasy.

"Are you all right?" he asked.

Hazel pulled away and tightened her cloak around her shoulders. "Of course."

The sun had just begun to go down, casting a haze of blues and purples onto the blank canvas of snow.

"I daresay it's worth the climb," Pierce said, coming even closer, likely so she could hear him over the roar of the wind. Suddenly, she didn't mind that her eyes were watering from it.

Even the view was nothing. Her focus fell entirely on him.

"Look down," Pierce instructed, prompting Hazel to snap her gaze away, her cheeks flushing despite the cold.

Beyond the courtyard, where the vines had taken over, she turned her gaze to the open, snow-covered field. There seemed nothing unusual about it at first.

"Along the edges." Pierce pointed at tall, pillar-like shrubs. They had been planted to form a perfect circle, the brown, brittle masses dusted with snow. She didn't know how she had never noticed that before.

In the growing darkness, Hazel blinked to focus. They weren't snow-covered shrubs at all. The sleeping vines were hiding something else. A whiteness sharper than the snow peeked through.

"They're pillars of some kind," Hazel whispered. "All arranged in a circle." Hazel had heard of these formations. Discovered in various parts of England, they were leftovers of a world today's society no longer understood. No one except for the Order, that is.

"What are they doing here?"

"I'm not sure anyone knows that. But we protect them nonetheless. We use them during our rituals, naturally. Particularly, the winter solstice."

"An important day, I'm beginning to understand." She just didn't know why.

"Your father never cared much for the rituals, either. He was much more concerned about the science of it all, about finding some sort of explanation. He believed there was something special about this particular location. The way various magnetic fields lined up, further enhanced by the stones. They give this place a sort of palpable power. You can feel it, can't you?"

Hazel nodded. It seemed to come over her all at once. Faint, but still there, as if she had walked into early-morning fog.

"Your father had a penchant for blurring the lines between science and sorcery. I happen to believe they are one and the same."

Mesmerized by the crystals, she almost didn't hear him. It was as if they had appeared spontaneously. She had walked by them on many occasions, assuming they'd been tall shrubs and nothing more. She'd never realized they were part of some formation. Hazel leaned forward, as if a closer look might change her perception.

"Careful now." Pierce pulled her back.

In the moonlight, the white stone sparkled beneath the brown vegetation.

"There's a glimmer to them." She turned into Pierce, so close, she could see the speckles in his steel-blue eyes.

"Well, they're more than mere stones. Care to see them up close?"

"It won't be too dark?"

"You won't need much light to see them."

They practiced more caution going down, his grasp tighter, his body tenser. The chill of the wind swept over her in waves, invigorating her. She didn't want to tread through the snow to see these stones any longer. She wanted to stop right there in the stone tower and pull Pierce even closer.

But all too quickly, they had reached the bottom. Even though she was safe now, her hand stayed in his. Damn what the servants said or thought. She wouldn't part from him, not even when they exited the manor into the quieter courtyard. A fresh layer of snow covered almost every inch of the vines. All evidence of their existence was nearly gone now.

Pierce picked up their pace as they moved onward past the gate. The field was a wild place, a tangled mess of shrubs without flowers, even in the summer. In her childhood, Hazel had lamented that they hadn't transformed the field into a proper garden with rhododendrons, roses, and the like. But clearly, there had been a reason for this.

Hazel stopped at the first stone. She spun around, her cloak dragging in the snow as she took in all the others. She could see it: a sort of perfect neglect keeping the stones hidden from view. Plain as day. How could she have been so unaware of it before?

Pierce reached up and yanked at the brittle vines until they snapped. He broke the vines away more violently until a large pile had accumulated.

The great, stone slab beneath sparkled more intensely than it had before. *Stone covered in frost,* she'd thought at first. But there was something else that made it shine not like ice or frost, but like marble. She put her hand against its icy surface. "This isn't mere stone, is it?"

"Quartz, actually." Pierce smiled proudly, as if he had presented her with some invaluable jewelry. "We've protected them for centuries."

Hazel looked around again before the darkness closed in. Not just the stones, but the whole courtyard around them seemed to shimmer. The cold had turned everything to crystal. The manor with its beautifully capped roofs and crystalline windows seemed meant for this sort of weather. Even the trees, though dead and lifeless, gained new life with the snow settled on their branches. No longer blending into the night sky, they stood out, a stark, complicated web against the stars.

A view that hadn't changed in a thousand years. The stones seemed just as old. She could tell by the dinginess that had accumulated over the glass-like structure and the natural divots that had formed after years of hard weather.

No wonder Mr. Mortibel was so determined to own the place. The Order could not simply move their practices elsewhere. They could never abandon these stones.

"What happens here?" As beautiful as it was, she had a deep, foreboding sense that dark activities had taken place in this location. "The stones hold some sort of power, don't they? That aura you were talking about." She couldn't believe she was asking.

Pierce hesitated.

"They give power to the flora all around us. Power enough to create our serums and elixirs. There are some who believe that the blood gives them power too."

"'Blood'?" She winced.

"From sacrifices. Only animals, of course." He eyed her, weighing her reaction.

Hazel understood now. "How medieval."

"Is it any different from the roast you eat for supper? Just ritualistically. It is simply the way of the ancient world."

"And this is done every year?" she asked.

"Save for this winter. It will be the first time one hasn't taken place in centuries."

"Are you sure this event is limited to animals?"

"I know it is."

Hazel didn't want to think about it.

He pulled off more of the vegetation, ripping it into shreds. Atop the crystal, someone had etched the symbol she had seen in her father's notebook. Hazel felt along a unique engraving, smoothed over with age. A tendril of caution ran through her. The solstice was mere days away.

"I still remember when I first saw them as a child," Pierce began. "One of our members had spent all morning stripping away the vegetation. They must have poured water over them, making them glisten like diamonds. Like statues, men in silver masks and white cloaks filled in the gaps between each slab. Their chants echoed against the stone. The smell of the incense intense—"

"As lovely as that sounds, how does it all relate to the antidote?"

"I don't understand it myself. I wish I did."

So did Hazel. More than half a week had passed already. There was no knowing how much time she had left. She might only have a month or two, maybe even as long as a year before she went mad—maybe less.

"Perhaps it's no use. The antidote is either there in my father's notes or it isn't. And you've already read plenty of his notebooks."

"Some of them many times over," he admitted. "But I'm not going to stop trying, I promise you."

Hazel pulled her hand away from the stone, warming it beneath her cloak.

"You're never going to tell me, are you?" Pierce asked, the harsh, roaring wind seemingly giving him an excuse to get close again. "About your vision."

Hazel looked away, struggling for an excuse that would make him drop this subject at once. "It's too…personal."

"They often are."

Hazel blushed, the feelings too close. Foolishly, she feared he could read her mind and see all the raw images that flashed before her eyes: just lips, skin, and tightening grips.

"Are you also of the opinion that they can't be changed?" she asked.

"These glimpses, they're pictures of a future that has, in a sense, already occurred."

Did that mean they had some kind of future together? If they did, undoubtedly, that meant a life here amongst the Order. She couldn't imagine Pierce leaving behind his birthright.

She closed her eyes for a breathless minute. She couldn't believe she was actually considering a future here. Nor could she believe she actually *believed*. But just as she had told Mr. Mortibel, it was true.

Pierce had changed that about her. He made her see all the wonders the Order kept hidden from view. For at least a little while, he'd made her believe that he could protect her from all the dangers too. That was before Mr. Mortibel had told her the truth about his role in the catacombs. She hadn't forgotten. She just didn't want to believe it. No matter how much it made sense. She still wanted what the vision had shown her. Not just one night of it either, but more.

"My." He stepped forward. "Is it that awful?"

Hazel felt her cheeks flush hot again.

"Visions are a heavy burden you need not carry on your own," Pierce said, pressing her again.

"It is not so much a burden… Not at all. In fact, part of me has come to look forward to it." It was a better fate to look forward to than death.

"I grow more curious by the minute. You'll be the end of me." He tapped his finger to his chin. "How about a trade? Some other secret, perhaps. I deal best in secrets."

"There's more?" As little as she had cared at first, she was suddenly quite curious.

"Much," he said. "For one, I never told you how my forefathers created it. The elixir, that is."

"Pierce—"

"An infusion that you think would be quite complex utilizing multiple plant extracts only requires one. A special plant found in this very valley where the manor is situated. We've merely built around it. The manor, you might not be able to tell, is built upon the side of a hill."

Hazel looked back at the manor. As a child, she hadn't noticed it.

"It grows nowhere else. The stones give it power, you see. It's quite beautiful too, like all roses are."

"A rose…" Hazel remembered the symbol. It had been on the gate, that tapestry that led into the laboratory, even in her father's notebooks. Its stark beauty stood out among all the other symbols.

"But we've hardly confined ourselves inside the estate's fences. On our expeditions, back when we had them, we found other objects with powerful properties like our rose. If you can believe it, there are even stones that can help us live decades beyond what our modern medicine allows. Centuries, even."

She shook her head. She wanted to deny such a fantastical claim. But she had no choice in the matter anymore. Her feelings for Pierce proved it. She did more than believe. She hoped for the vision to prove true.

"Where did you find them, exactly? You can't just have stumbled upon them."

"These things always have some basis in myth and legend. Especially if one has the funds to look into them deeply enough."

"What about that healing serum?"

"Oh, that comes from a special kind of vine found right here at the estate."

"And the stone?"

"Deep inside some crater, rumor has it. Perhaps from another world entirely or someplace where time has less meaning. One day when the Order is back, well, in order again, we can continue those kinds of expeditions. Shall I go on?"

"Don't bother. I have no intention of telling you anything." But Hazel wasn't sure she could keep the vision in much longer. Under his gaze, she was helpless.

"I thought things were different now. I thought you could trust me."

Hazel hesitated. He was right, after all. Things *were* different. He had revealed so much about the Order, himself, his family...but he was still holding on to secrets. He still hadn't told her the truth about that night in the catacombs, that all those deaths had been his doing.

"I've felt a duty to watch over you since the moment I saw the home listed for sale," he went on. "I owed your father that. Even if you didn't notice it, I was keeping an eye out for you around the manor, listening for your steps in the morning and in the hall, examining everything that seemed the least bit suspicious. At first, it was for your father. But now it's for you and only you."

She felt it again, the fated energy that existed between them. It had all seemed to accumulate so subtly that she hadn't noticed it until it had been there. Like innocent snowflakes that seemed to disappear into the ground then accumulate into a thick covering of snow the next morning, trapping her with no escape.

"I should've known... I just didn't want to believe it. I didn't think it was right," she said.

"'Right'? What could be more right than—"

"Because you've fallen for a dead woman," Hazel said quickly. It may not be today or tomorrow, but soon, she'd be dead and he'd be nothing but hurt.

"I don't care."

He pressed his lips into hers. They were standing so close, he needed to only move an inch. It was inevitable, really: her back pressed up against the slab and every inch of him. The crystal didn't even feel cold. The wind by then had dissipated and she had grown accustomed. She felt only warmth outside and within. Every sensation, sudden and fleeting, was over too soon.

For once, she could feel the power the estate had over her. The darkness alone seemed to invoke a sort of frenzied impatience. The naïve, young woman who had arrived here from London that first day would never have done this. Since then, she had changed. She wanted things she shouldn't. The utter seclusion of the place made it so easy to forget the world beyond.

Dash her reputation. What was there to ruin? She was dead, anyway. If he didn't care, then neither did she.

At long last she had given in.

It didn't matter the way Pierce had simply appeared at her doorstep. His motives. The details about his life that she still didn't know. All that mattered was what was happening between them at that precise moment. Just like it had in the vision.

"It was this." She pulled away and confessed. "I saw this."

He laughed, digging his hand deeper into her hair. Somehow, he had known from the start that this had been fated. Deep down, so had she.

It felt so natural to be with him. The sudden sensation of skin against skin that she had never known made perfect sense. A new normal. She could never go back to a time before.

CHAPTER TWENTY-THREE

The Scars

THEO LOOSENED HIS grip around Hazel's waist and exhaled deeply. He couldn't remember a time he had felt so present. It wasn't just this much-needed release. It was every moment of these last several days, every time he'd been with her.

His life before had been consumed with either regrets of the past or plans and fears for the future. Never the present. Until now.

He actually stopped to notice the little things, like how her hair glistened in the dark or how she smelled of freshly-cut apples when he breathed her in. Moments he wanted to sink into forever.

When she pulled herself into him, his insides tightened again. His worries and fears about the Order melted away like ice thawing in the spring. All he could think about was his need for her.

He'd expected to find blood and death here at the manor, yes. But never her. Never this impossible love, of all things.

A bliss he knew all too well would be too temporary. While he could block out thoughts of the Order, he couldn't block out thoughts of her. How, until he found an antidote, she was still doomed.

Was that why she had finally bedded him? Had her coming death sentence made her that reckless? He wanted it to mean far more. Just as it had for him.

He might have gauged her thoughts had he the courage. He didn't think he could bear anything but confirmation that her feelings and his were one and the same.

Next to him, she ran a finger along his collarbone.

"Mapping out your territory?" he asked with a grin. He wanted her to know, if nothing else, that he was entirely hers now.

It was only a matter of time until her fingers encountered the scars that ran over the top of his shoulders, around his neck, and down his back.

The ones on his neck were the freshest. Just barely healed shrapnel wounds from that night in the catacombs. How could he explain them away? He couldn't. All he could do was pray she wouldn't recognize them.

He wanted to admit the truth about the catacombs, if only to tell her that night had been a mistake. Not the attack, per se, but the fact that he hadn't done more. He should have warned her more clearly about Mortibel. He should have pulled her away from all the terror. Lord knew what Mortibel had planned for her—hell, *still* had planned for her.

He was too worried she'd hate him for it. She'd think he was nothing better than a violent, murderous monster.

He winced with guilt. That day he'd followed her down that London street, he'd had no idea she was Grey's daughter dressed in servants' clothing.

If she knew he had been stalking her for information about Mortibel, what might she do? It wasn't like he had planned to hurt her—or any woman, for God's sake.

Still, she'd think he was mad, that he was willing to do anything and everything for the Order. Once upon a time, maybe he had been. Only now, she meant more to him than the Order. He wasn't sure there was anything he wouldn't be willing to do for her.

He had tried his damndest to charm her into giving him the estate. It wasn't a farce anymore. It was for another reason entirely.

He should just confess. Tell her the truth. But how could he explain in a way that didn't completely destroy her trust? He was still a villain. At least he felt like it. He'd almost killed her that night in the catacombs. He'd certainly killed those other men. It was pure luck that Mortibel and, maybe even Hazel, had survived. How could he ever hope to come back from what he'd done?

When Hazel's fingers reached the back of his neck, she froze.

"What's this?" she whispered.

He swallowed. "I've spent my whole life preparing for the day I'd return to Whitestone. Unfortunately, all that training came with scars."

"'Training'?"

"I've trained in every form of combat you could imagine. Ever since the day my family and I left England."

He shouldn't have been surprised about what had happened in the catacombs and his failures to better protect Hazel. He was nothing more than a killer. He had been trained to be.

"Because you expected to fight someone like Mr. Mortibel?"

"Any time there's this much power at stake, there's almost always someone waiting on the sidelines to snatch the reins."

"The wounds are still pink," Hazel remarked.

She was no dummy—he'd *liked* that about her. Lying to her wouldn't be easy. But he didn't want to lose her for the mistakes of the past. She was too virtuous herself to love anyone less than noble, let alone someone who had murdered people, guilty or not. He hated himself for what he'd had to do. More guilt swirled at the bottom of his stomach. He wasn't sure he'd ever be rid of it.

"I wear them as a badge of honor," he said, trying to distract her. "Some men fill their wounds with horsehair to gain these kinds of scars, particularly fencers."

"That's not what you did here, is it?"

"No. I actually do enjoy fencing, though. Sparring too. Believe it or not."

"Actually, I would." She stared up at him, her eyes holding him in place.

"You think you know me so well, do you?" He grasped her hand and pulled it away from his neck and onto his heart.

She sighed, her eyes searching his face. "I'd like to think you came here not for the Order, but for me."

"I'm here for you now nonetheless." He placed a hand on her neck. Just as she knew all the spots on his body that made him swoon, he knew hers.

She leaned into him. He had successfully distracted her yet again. And he hated himself for it.

"Good," she breathed.

He leaned in slowly, cautiously, not sure she'd give in, as if the night before hadn't really happened.

Hazel let him have her again. He had something to prove this time. So he brought her in an inch tighter. She wrapped her hands around his neck. She must have felt it again, those strange ridges. But he was too lost within her to care. Nor did she say anything more. She simply dug her fingernails into him. He doubted she had the strength to do anything else.

WITH THE FIRE out, the room grew colder. Under the blankets, so did Hazel. But rather than build the fire anew, she needed to be alone. She needed to think. She thought again about those scars on Theodore—was that what she called him now? They weren't engaged, like usual decorum called for, but they had certainly become intimate enough. She rather liked calling him by that name, surprisingly, even if so much was being called into question again.

Was it possible that Mr. Mortibel had been right? Had Theodore been among the men who had attacked them in the catacombs? That night of the storm, when Mr. Mortibel had poisoned Theodore, had he merely been trying to protect her?

The scars seemed to prove it.

While Theodore slept, Hazel fumbled out of bed. She found her dress, corset, and chemise strewn across the floor. She started putting her underthings back on, realizing that at some point, Theodore had torn the sleeve of her dress completely. Perfect.

"Are you cold?" Theodore took in a gust of air. The bed creaked beneath his weight. It reminded her yet again of the full feel and prowess of him last night. It had been something unexpected the vision had not provided. That and so many other sensations. They had proved so much stronger.

But she wasn't ashamed of what she'd done like she'd feared she might be. Not in the least. Rather, she was sad that a second night was not as certain as the first. She was beginning to see why.

"I could start a fire." Theodore yawned.

"I need to replace my dress first." Hazel escaped out into the hall, closing the door behind her.

It was abrupt, yes, but she couldn't risk any questions, especially about when she might return. She was more worried the servants might see her in this condition. She could not think of any proper excuse at the moment. It didn't help that her room was on the other side of the manor.

Pausing at an intersection of corridors, she blinked hard against a sudden burst of light streaming in from a window. The air was warmer here. It didn't have the same bite as it had before. The harsh winds of winter were finally letting up.

In the new quiet, she listened for footfalls and voices. Anything that might indicate a servant. She had been lucky after all. The only servants she heard were on the first floor. At the start of a warmer day, their conversations sounded more cheerful.

Across the remaining distance, Hazel kept her footsteps light and quick. And yet it was all for naught. When Hazel entered her room, Emmerson had been waiting.

"I dare not even ask where you've been," she said, wide-eyed.

"You're not my mother, after all." Though her aunt would soon hear of it, Hazel was sure. And she would be just as livid as Emmerson.

"Something has changed within you. Ever since we entered this damn house." Emmerson walked toward her. "I'm starting to believe you've been put under some sort of spell."

It was possible, Hazel admitted to herself. A spell that had been cast by this very home seemed quite possible indeed.

"Are you even listening to me? You've been hopelessly distracted for weeks." Emmerson took up her torn sleeve and crossed her arms.

"Just help me dress, will you?"

Emmerson gave her one more exasperated look before moving to the armoire. Hazel tried to remember where they had last left things. Emmerson had been furious about Theodore's lingering presence. The snow had let up yesterday and he was still here. Hazel had yet to announce any upcoming departure, much less offer an explanation. If only she could now. Then Emmerson might have understood everything.

"This one?" Emmerson held out a dress. Hazel nodded. It was forest green and silky with buttons down the front.

"None of the other servants saw you?"

Hazel splashed water onto her face from the basin. "Save for you, no one." But was Emmerson so unlike the others? Could she actually be trusted? Hazel didn't know why the question had come to mind. And yet it had been lingering there for days now.

Emmerson's behavior had been all too strange lately. It was odd, for instance, that she was here in her room at such an early hour. Emmerson knew Hazel preferred to sleep most mornings until 9:30 or 10 A.M.

Rather than just help her to dress, Emmerson really wanted to pry. She worked slower than usual, removing the old dress and replacing it with the new one, seemingly inch by inch.

"How is he feeling? Everything all right?"

Hazel ignored the question. "What time is it?"

"Eight A.M." Emmerson stiffened. "I was going to wake you. I have terrible news, I'm afraid. About that woman Lenora."

Lenora? Hazel questioned. First, Emmerson hadn't known whether the woman was Miss or Mrs. and now this? It was a strange and rather sudden sort of familiarity.

"I already know." Hazel's heart began to race nonetheless.

Emmerson looked concerned, worried that perhaps they'd be next. "It has nothing to do with us." Hazel tried to reassure her. "Nothing at all."

Emmerson turned away, not meeting her gaze. She didn't believe her—Hazel could tell that much.

"Though perhaps I should be certain... Retrieve my cloak, will you? And have the new groom—Samuel, is it?—prepare one of the borrowed horses."

She wasn't much of a horsewoman these days, but she'd have to manage.

"At this hour?"

Hazel insisted. If she got to Mr. Mortibel in time, she might catch him before his usual morning ride.

Those strange scars on Theodore's skin—she couldn't release them from her mind. Although those men in the catacombs hadn't harmed her, what about the three other seers who had been killed? Mr. Mortibel had almost been among them.

No more lies. Today she would tell Mr. Mortibel the truth. Perhaps he might even be willing to share the antidote, should he have it.

She could only hope.

CHAPTER TWENTY-FOUR

Betrayal

T HEO PULLED BACK the window curtain, his hand still holding the bundle of sheets around his waist. He didn't have to stand there for long before he saw Hazel and her borrowed horse trot across the snow.

He cursed to himself. She had seen the scars. Of course she had realized they were fresh. He should have tried to explain. Now she was headed straight into the arms of danger itself.

He threw away the sheet and began to dress at once. After all their time together, he'd thought she'd trusted him. But trusting the man who had killed others and almost herself? Maybe that was too much to ask. He wasn't like the other London gentlemen with whom she had probably pictured herself in love. How could she reconcile falling for someone so vastly different? Even if her heart demanded it, perhaps she was too practical to let in someone so dangerous.

As he buttoned his shirt, he was already formulating a plan to get her back. He just needed a moment to explain was all.

He needed to get back in touch with his men. No doubt they were still in London helping to gather his supporters. But he needed them for what was to come next.

Good thing they'd be eager for blood. The only problem was

that he had no one he could trust in this household and therefore, no one who could deliver the message. He'd have to steal a horse and head over there himself. But he didn't have that sort of time. He only had one hope, then. After an entire week without word, they *might* already be on their way to see what had become of him. Especially since they knew all he had intended to do.

He wasn't sure he was that lucky, though.

His thoughts turned back to Hazel. She was probably already on Mortibel's front lawn. The thought of her speaking to Mortibel heated and cooled his blood at the same time.

Every muscle tensed, urging him to go after her. He bit down, so angry, he could scream if it wouldn't scare all the servants.

Go ahead, he thought to himself. Once and for all, he wanted her to find the truth about Mortibel and come running back to him. Maybe then she'd stop doubting him and everything he felt for her.

He was also mind-numbingly terrified of what Mortibel would do to her. It was time to end him once and for all. He moved to the door, ready to race after her, then paced back into the room, full of indecision.

But would he hurt her? Mortibel hadn't touched her that day in the library, when Theo had been hidden away and waiting, eager to pounce.

There was a reason for it. To him, she was too valuable. He suddenly knew why. Hit hard with the sudden revelation, he ran out of the room and down the stairs.

Hazel is quite safe, he told the part of himself eager to shed blood. He knew why. He just needed to prove it in the laboratory.

☾

IT WAS A moment of weakness, what she was about to do. But

staying alone at Whitestone with Theodore wasn't the wisest thing, either. She had trusted him too easily with her life.

That morning, she had begun to feel the edges of regret. Last night had come at a high cost. The fulfillment of the vision had forced her to face the truth about both her father and the Order. For as long as she could, she had pushed it aside. Not any longer. It was all real. The impossible possible. She had no choice but to accept it, no matter how much it pained her.

She took solace in the fact that some good had come of last night. She had a new sense of freedom. Out in the warming wind, she breathed in deeply. The vision had finally been fulfilled. She was no longer bound to Theodore like she had once believed. She could choose for herself and decide, once and for all, if she could trust him.

She kicked the horse faster along the lane. Above a thin lining of trees, she could already make out the pale-gray stone of Mortibel Manor. It had been perched almost condescendingly on the hilltop, as if to claim all the land beneath, including her own, or rather Theodore's soon enough. How profitable their marriage would have been to him. How easily they could have connected their estates. Perhaps that had been her father's thinking, that she would marry Mr. Mortibel so he could connect their two estates and take the reins of the Order. Her father hadn't known how difficult she would prove. Nor perhaps that he himself would soon die, however it had happened.

She squinted at the horizon, seeing the faint outline of a rider. It had to have been Mr. Mortibel. Hazel closed in on the man, growing more certain of it. She shouted his name and his horse reared, kicking at the sky. She let out a breath of relief as he came her way.

"What in the world are you doing out here? You'll freeze," he said, as if he himself were somehow better equipped.

"The ride has warmed me well enough," she said between breaths.

"Is something the matter?"

"You were right," she said. "About Mr. Pierce. He was one of the men who attacked us. I'm sure of it. Just this morning, he—"

"He's still alive?"

She nodded.

"That would explain the rumors, then."

"What rumors?" Even if she had tried to be careful, after the servants had seen Theo carrying her inside, they had no doubt filled in the blanks themselves. Lord knew what was being said.

Mr. Mortibel leaned back, a hand on his hip and sighed. "Horrible rumors, I'm afraid."

"They've become quite twisted, I'm sure."

"I thought he'd be dead by now." He lifted his chin.

"He has more strength than I thought." Hazel looked down, regretting the previous lie.

"What's happened? What has he done to you?"

"Nothing. It's just..." She couldn't bring herself to say the words.

"I can remedy this. There's something we can give him. It'll be peaceful, I promise, and also justified."

Hazel shivered. "You mean something poisonous." Probably the same thing he'd given him during their fight.

"I'll have to double the dose this time."

Yet again, more violence. To even consider murder! Were Mr. Mortibel and Theodore both mad? She was beginning to think the Order had made them so.

"To what purpose is all this death?" she demanded. "I don't understand it. I don't know why..."

"Don't be so naïve. It could not be more simple. It's the same reason Pierce wants to buy your estate. It's about the Order, Hazel. Nothing more... If we let him live, Pierce could very well have it."

Before he could gallop toward her estate, Hazel blocked his path. "You are too hasty." She couldn't bear the thought of harming Theodore, no matter what he was guilty of. "We have other concerns."

The cold began to embrace her again, causing the usual shivers.

"Come, your lips are turning blue." He tilted his head and frowned. "We shall talk by the fire."

He turned back to his estate, which was much closer. As Hazel rode toward it, the air seemed to grow colder. Her instincts told her to go back, but still, she pressed on.

When they arrived at the front steps, a groom was already waiting to grab both horses. Within a matter of moments, Hazel was defrosting before the fire, but she was hardly at ease enough to sit down. Where was Miss Mortibel? No doubt she'd want to chaperone and play host. Or more likely try and come up with some excuse that would force Hazel to leave.

Footfalls sounded, but instead of Miss Mortibel, the housekeeper came in with the tea and poured her a steaming cup before exiting.

"Now what is it that concerns you?" Somehow, Mr. Mortibel seemed unaffected by the cold, used to it, almost, while Hazel still shivered. Perhaps it wasn't from the cold, but something else entirely.

She struggled to get the much-needed words out. It wasn't like it used to be. Nothing about being here alone with him felt right. The horrible feeling burned in her gut, telling her to run, to return to the safety of her estate.

"I still cannot begin to understand why you won't stay. Or why you ever left at all," he said.

How different her life would have been. She might already have been dead instead of soon-to-be dead.

"The truth is your rejection of the Order was really a rejection of me." He stared her down, his jaw tight.

Hazel set her tea on the mantel, unsipped. "I was trying to protect myself. You know I saw something."

"But never, not once, did you ever divulge the truth to me. Have not you expressed anger with me for the same kind of secrecy?"

"You know very well what goes on there."

"We have any number of rituals," he said softly. Quite quickly, he took up both her hands. "I would never let you come to harm. If you resigned to stay, I'd remain near to you always. I'd protect you."

Hazel swallowed. He was renewing his intentions. She needed to stop this now.

"I took it—the elixir." She spit it out all at once. There was so much she was forced to keep in. So much she wanted to spew his way. Right now, this alone would have to suffice.

He turned to stare at the fire, the flames dancing in his eyes. An actual smile crept over his face. "I knew it would change your mind. Not just about the estate, but the Order."

"You don't understand. It will kill me. It's *poison.*"

"Who told you this? Pierce?"

"My father's notebooks prove it. He was looking for a cure."

Mr. Mortibel straightened, his face darkening as he came toward her. "Now how could you have possibly found that out?"

"Mr. Pierce told me." She shrugged, trying to appear unbothered when all the while, she trembled on the inside. Could it all have been lies? "He told me my father was working on an antidote. The laboratory was a mess and with my father dead. Well, it seems…"

"Don't tell me you suspect I have the antidote? Is that why you've come over here? To accuse me?"

"So it's true, then. The elixir is dangerous." Her heart sank.

"For some."

Hazel's gaze swept around as footfalls echoed through the halls. Mr. Mortibel cursed.

A feminine voice rang through the air. "We have a visitor."

Hazel caught the brilliant-blue dress and white frills first. She had expected Miss Mortibel's false smile. Little could have prepared her.

"Lenora?" Hazel stepped back. Though her hair had been pulled back instead of around her shoulders, there was no mistaking her black locks.

She gave a raucous laugh. "I'm supposed to be dead, I know." There could be no doubt. The woman was a witch. "But it seems that I am otherwise."

Mr. Mortibel simply shook his head with disapproval. "You should have let us be, Lenora."

"But how?" Hazel demanded an explanation still. "I saw a body... The police..."

"Lenora Coldstone *did* die that evening. Only Miss Grace Mortibel took my place." She turned to Mr. Mortibel. "How rude of you not to tell her."

"What about..." Hazel remembered back to the day she saw blood. "Her lady's maid... She's somehow agreed to this farce too?"

Was the world full of that many horrible people?

"She never much liked Miss Mortibel, did she?" Lenora giggled. "One can only threaten to fire someone without references so many times. After that, a pay raise would be awfully enticing. A rather significant one, though it was nothing to us."

"Miss Grey didn't need to know yet," Mr. Mortibel bit out. "She'll not take it well."

"She seems fine to me. Tell us, Miss Grey, how *are* you taking it?"

"I don't understand," Hazel managed, her breaths more rapid. Each exhale came out shaky.

"What's not to understand?" Lenora paced the room, her lush skirts swaying wildly with each movement. "I, Marcus's cousin from London, got lost in the country and discovered her. Marcus, of course, identified the body."

"That was you in Miss Mortibel's emerald cloak?"

"It looked nice on me."

"You killed her?" Hazel turned to Mr. Mortibel—to Mortibel, rather. The man deserved no title, no respect, not after what he'd done. "Your own sister?"

"She felt no pain," Mortibel crossed his arms defensively.

"Not with the draft her lady's maid prepared for her."

"And all the blood?"

"That wasn't spilled until after her death. We had to make it appear as if some passing vagabond were responsible."

"What did you do?" Hazel's voice strained. "Did you cut her…with a knife?" She didn't think he was capable of something so dreadful.

Mortibel frowned, but his eyes quickly narrowed with anger. "She would have betrayed me. You know she never wanted me to be part of the Order, not from the first. She was already doing everything in her power to ruin my plans. She could be quite calculating. My father might be a baronet, but he's feeble-minded and only too willing to do what she demanded. She wanted him to bar me from the Order entirely."

"She was trying to protect you." Just like Hazel had once tried. "She is—*was*—your sister… How could you?" The room began to turn. Hazel saw the blood, bright-red streaks cut across the snow. There had been so much of it.

"Listen to me. She was going to tell everyone of consequence about my affairs. All of society. I couldn't let her do that. She would have compromised more than myself—but every member of the Order. It was practically my responsibility to dispatch her."

"And the clothes do suit me." Lenora sucked in a breath and smoothed out her skirts.

"People will notice," Hazel said, her voice shaking. "They will question you."

If there was any justice in the world, they couldn't get away with this.

"Why? I've already told everyone that I've shipped her off to marry a wealthy landowner in India. I even convinced my father to write the letter of consent. Like I said, he is rather feeble-minded. Frankly, I doubt anyone will miss her."

Hazel turned to Lenora. "People will recognize you, though."

"Maybe. But in these clothes? With my new hair? Among my new circle of society?" She graced a hand over her perfect curls.

"Not likely. People see what they want to."

"Trust me, Hazel. Few in the county are daring enough to accuse a lady of being a peasant," he huffed. "It would be no better than calling her a dog."

Lenora's smile cracked at the comment, then she fixed her face into a scowl aimed directly at Hazel. Lenora was a fool to trust Mortibel, just as Hazel had been.

"You're murderers…" Hazel hissed. She should have never doubted it. She should have known it ever since Theodore had shown up at her front step.

"My father never left me the elixir, did he?" Rather, Lenora had given Hazel the elixir. She was sure of this. Hazel grasped at her throat as if she could feel the burn of the poison.

"I didn't want to do it," Mortibel said. "I know how frail your nerves can be. But it was the only way I could be sure you'd believe, that you'd stay."

Hazel hated that it had worked. He had been planning all this far longer than she'd thought.

"My father was never mad like Lenora claimed, was he? You just wanted me to believe he was sick."

"It's interesting what a few badly scribbled notes would have you believe."

"You put those there." Her mouth fell open. "You *planted* them."

Mortibel shrugged. "I couldn't have you believing any of his other notes. There was no knowing what he'd revealed. I thought of burning them, but that would have been too obvious, eh?"

"Why would you disgrace him so? He was like a father to you." More so than he had been her own.

"Much like Grace, he didn't approve of my plans."

"What plans?"

"You'll see for yourself. On the night of the winter solstice."

The symbols Theodore had seen.

"No!" Hazel almost roared. "It is *my* home. I don't care what you're planning. I forbid it."

"Is it your home or Pierce's now? Either way, I'm afraid it's quite out of your hands. You'll be there no matter how hard you try to escape."

"You can't possibly know that…" Hazel inched away, backing herself toward the door, testing to see if they'd stop her. With cruel smiles, they remained in their places, watching as she headed, more determined, toward the door. They let her go, probably because it no longer mattered, because her future had somehow already been foretold. She just didn't have the courage to ask how. She already knew.

CHAPTER TWENTY-FIVE

Blood

HAZEL COULDN'T SHAKE the horrible image of the blood. Mortibel's hands stained with it. This man she had once called a friend, this man to whom she had once wanted to surrender her hand, he was a murderer. All for this antidote. She was sure of it.

Only some people were badly affected by the elixir, he had said. Because they didn't have the antidote. Because he did.

The night of the solstice, if she wasn't already dead, he was going to kill her. But why wait? He'd had so many opportunities. If he wanted Whitestone so badly, he wouldn't want to wait long enough for Pierce to sign the necessary contracts.

She had the horrible feeling she was falling right into a trap. Already, it was too late. Whatever he had planned at the solstice, fate had already determined it. She feared there would be nothing she could do to stop them. Mortibel had said it was out of her hands. She remembered what Lenora had said too: her father had believed she was destined to spend the rest of her days here. Had they been visions? Or more lies?

Lenora and Mortibel were partners. More than that, they were lovers. The way Lenora had looked at Mortibel and the bitterness Lenora had displayed toward Hazel—there was no doubting it. Sure enough, they wanted her gone. But was there any escaping what they'd claimed they had already *seen*?

In the wind, tears froze halfway down her cheeks. She didn't know what to feel when she saw Theodore waiting for her in the stables.

The relief that poured into her just then told her all she needed to know. Even though Theodore had been a stranger to her not so long ago, he was the one she should have trusted all along. Those seers he had killed down in the catacombs had been as good as dead, anyway. He had spared her, hadn't he? He had even warned her.

She could understand why he hadn't told her all this time. It was because her trust in him had been so fragile. Not anymore. As she closed in on the stables, she wanted to leap into his arms, to again feel the warmth of his skin, to hear his familiar, rough voice.

Earlier when she had gone to Mortibel, she had just been so overwhelmed. She wished she hadn't gone at all.

She dismounted and handed the horse off to the groom, Samuel.

There was no time to catch her breath. Pierce already knew where she had gone. He was pacing the stables, barely able to look at her.

"You went to him?" His voice was hard. When he did look at her, his eyes were soft with pain. More pain than she had ever seen. More so than when she had found him on her doorstep or when she had been redressing his wound. That sort of pain he had seemed used to. Not this. She could tell it was a type of pain entirely new to him.

"What game are you playing with me?" he asked. "Or are you trifling with the both of us?"

When she didn't answer, Theodore grabbed her by the arm. "Are you in league with him now? What is it you had planned for me? To kill me in my sleep?"

Hazel ripped her arm free. "I'm in league with no one."

Theodore stepped back, his eyes shining. "You still don't trust me."

"No, I do…" She heaved. "But, I, admittedly, had my doubts. Can't you understand why? You're no different than Mortibel. You act as if you're more noble, more righteous, but you both want the same things. And you're both willing to kill for it."

Theodore turned to the other end of the stable, where Samuel was talking to one of the horses.

His voice dropped to a whisper. "We shouldn't be talking about this here. We should go inside."

She saw no point in waiting. "Just admit it. It was you that night in the catacombs."

For a moment, he stared in disbelief.

"Do you deny it?"

"I do not." Theodore sighed, defeated. "But I can explain. *Inside*. Out of this cold and beside the fire."

Hazel didn't feel any of the cold. All she could feel was the hot fury behind her eyes. Why hadn't he just told her? Keeping things from her, it was the same thing Mortibel would have done, that her father had done. All the men in her life had done.

Alas, she had no choice but to follow him inside into the library. She didn't care who saw them together now. Like Mortibel had said, rumors were already in circulation.

Theodore closed the library doors. He didn't need to say a word. His pained eyes already admitted his guilt. He made no effort to hide it.

When he spoke he held her gaze. "It was the only way to stop him."

"You could have told me from the start."

"Truly? Would you have done what we did…knowing I…"

"You mean last night?"

He nodded, his face aglow.

She heard the shots again, felt the bits of stone rain down over her. The lives of the seers had been taken so fast. A few quick moments that had troubled her ever since.

"How did you even know where to find us?"

"Mortibel has spies. So do I."

She swallowed her building emotions, a mix of anger and fear.

"I can't even say I regret it. Because I may be the only reason you're still alive… I've thought about it for days now. Consider it. In the catacombs, late at night when no one knew where you were. As if hiding your body would have been much trouble at all. Mortibel meant to kill you that very night."

Hazel stared off; her heart began to race.

"The estate would be up for grabs."

"It was supposed to be a simple farewell…" she whispered, too overwhelmed to think.

"And where was everyone else? All of the attendees of your father's so-called farewell?"

Hazel's mouth gaped open, searching for words.

"My only regret is not doing more. Not taking you away from all that madness at once."

She remembered his whispered warning. The words had been his. Once more, they sent the same shivers down her spine.

"I saved you," he said. "Nothing less."

Hazel nodded. He had. She almost felt like she should thank him.

"Rest assured, Mortibel will try again. Haven't you guessed when? During the solstice. It all has to do with the solstice."

Hazel looked down into the fire. The power of the stones was real. Just like her vision. Everything the Order claimed was.

"They've already poisoned me with the elixir. If they want me dead, why wait at all? He killed Miss Mortibel without a moment's thought." Turning it over in her head, she struggled to make sense of Mortibel's plan.

"He did what?" Theo's face stilled in horror.

"He killed his sister." She shivered in the silence that felt colder than the air. "He killed her." It all came out in a deluge, everything that had happened. She told him how Lenora had never died. They had been tricked.

"There's a reason they let you leave." Theodore's face stilled in renewed horror. Hazel nodded. A reason Hazel didn't want to admit.

"It's like I suspected. He's waiting."

"For the solstice, you mentioned?"

"That's when the magnetic fields are at their strongest, when we try and enhance the flora though ritual." His face hardened. "Not to mention, Mortibel has always been fond of ceremony. The ostentatious bastard. Mortibel doesn't just want you dead. I think he wants much more than that. Something worse."

"Oh?" Her lip trembled.

"I'm going to take care of everything." Theodore came in and grasped her face. His grip was firm but gentle. She turned away from his gaze but didn't step away. "It's going to be fine."

"How do you know that?"

"I found something in your father's laboratory."

At the words, Hazel's spinning thoughts slowed. "I thought… You told me you discovered nothing."

"Listen to me." His voice tensed. There were tears in his eyes, a glossiness that made them shimmer in the firelight. "I've done tests. There's no doubting it now."

"Doubting what?" Hazel demanded in a hard voice.

"I found the antidote."

CHAPTER TWENTY-SIX
The Plans

HAZEL WOULD LIVE. After all her bouts of panic and fear, she finally had some certainty to grasp on to. At least for a little while.

Theodore led her down into the laboratory, which was now covered in a mess of papers. In fact, it no longer looked like a laboratory, but some sort of archive. Papers were stacked everywhere. On the worktables, the beakers and other equipment had been cleared away to make space.

"How is it administered?" For a moment, Hazel forgot all of the betrayals, both Theodore's and Mortibel's, and ran to the work table, thumbing through her father's papers. As if she could read any of it.

"You need not do anything," Theodore said. "You're immune. And so was your father."

Hazel breathed out slowly, allowing this welcome information to sink in, to relieve some of the tension and anxiety that had torn through her these last few days. Of course it didn't completely go away, not with what they had done the night before. Her cheeks warmed at the thought.

Her inevitable fate had been her excuse. Perhaps even Theodore's too. Now this news changed everything. That night was no longer free of consequence and she no longer felt as shameless. She had ruined herself. In truth and in the rumors already in circulation. And yet she would never give back the things she had felt, not for anything.

"You're certain? How can you know?"

"I was looking at the wrong papers. On a hunch, I started farther back in your father's documents." He opened the cabinet, containing stacks and stacks of notebooks. "Dating back before you were even born. Your father kept detailed notes. Unfortunately, that made my search longer, but this morning, I found it. The antidote. He'd been immune for some time. Only, he didn't tell my father as I'd expected he would have."

Hazel paged through the journals—dense and detailed with meticulous handwriting, these were the kind she remembered from childhood. They were nothing like the sloppy notes Mortibel had planted. She should have never fallen for those forgeries.

"Here, I'll show you." Theodore walked over to two plant specimens, each suspended in water. In one jar, the plant was like those turning to dust in the courtyard: gray, brittle, and void of all life. In the other jar, its leaves were a brilliant green, still very much alive. "This live one was beginning to shrivel, but it only took a drop of your blood to reverse its death. Whatever experimentations your father had done to himself, you must have inherited it."

"Is that why he never tried to bring me back from London? But to leave me the estate…"

"Don't assume the worst. There's no knowing what your father knew or *saw*."

He was talking about a vision. Quite possibly about the coming night of the solstice. A vision that included her and what else? Was she really destined to spend the rest of her days out here like he believed? Or had it been just another one of Lenora's lies?

"Why didn't he warn me?"

"I'm sure he made an attempt. At some point, he might have

even tried to run, but Mortibel perhaps caught up with him, maybe even imprisoned him and then…"

Hazel shivered. How he must have suffered.

"He stopped," Hazel said, barely above a whisper. "For a time, he must have refused to be let."

"What makes you think that?" Theodore asked.

"Because of those seers, those ones I read about in the papers. In the last year, four died. That would explain it, wouldn't it?" She swallowed, trying to assuage a sudden building panic. "Maybe that was when Mortibel decided to murder him."

"I'm sorry," Theodore said weakly. "Once I learned who you were, that Grey was your father…"

"What?" Hazel snapped up.

He cleared his throat. "You should know that after the catacombs, I followed you. I had to know who you were. It was a feeling, I guess. I just needed to talk to you. Ask you a few questions."

"But you didn't. Why?"

"I discovered who your father was. That the estate was in your hands. I still wanted to talk. Just differently."

"Did you set out to seduce me?"

"No." Then he caught himself. "Maybe. At first. But I didn't need to. You sold me the estate at once. Then I seduced you, anyway." He smirked cautiously.

Even if it had been him in the catacombs, it didn't change the look in his eyes, the sincere tenderness she had seen first in the vision.

Hazel flipped mindlessly through the papers on one of the lab tables.

"Things are different now, aren't they? After last night… Given the news, I feel I should tell you…" she began. "I don't want you to feel as though I've trapped you and that you're obliged to me in any way. The circumstances were different last night. In fact, it would be quite fine for you to forget about it entirely."

"Do you have any idea how hard it was not to go after you? I had to fight every instinct. I had to keep reminding myself that he wouldn't hurt you. But my heart didn't want to listen to logic."

Guilt washed over her. The fear he must have felt that morning when she'd left to see Mortibel. He must have been terrified for her. He'd had every reason to be.

"Why didn't you?" Had he meant to wash his hands of her? She might have deserved it for what she'd done.

"Because I knew he wouldn't hurt you. Not yet. Just like he hadn't in the library. I had a revelation. And I had…" He gulped. "I had to prove that last night wouldn't be our last."

He brought her in close, forcing her to face him. The way his lips touched hers, no longer a memory from a vision, but a possession all her own, one that she didn't want to release from her grasp. Damn the dangers. In spite of what he had done in the catacombs, she didn't want to leave him. Not at all.

Hazel pulled back, the revelations and guilt of what they'd done weighing her down. All at once, it was coming together. Her blood. Her father's blood. The night of the solstice.

"I know now what Mortibel intends to do," she whispered. Perhaps he had even meant to do it in the catacombs. The flickering torches, the cloaked seers—it had seemed ceremonious then too.

"Tell me at once."

"Their plans for the solstice. I've seen it before. As a child. It was the reason I left this place."

Theodore's brows pinched. Perhaps he already knew the horrid tale that was to come. She wondered briefly if he had ever played a part in it or anything of the sort. An idea that chilled her.

His hand on hers offered her a modicum of comfort. She hoped somehow it would stay there always, that he might never let her stray, even if she had no other choice.

"I might have recognized those giant crystals you showed me," she said. "If it hadn't been so dark and there had been a moon, I might have seen them glistening. I might have even hidden behind one as I watched. But I focused on something else. I couldn't tear my eyes from it, no matter how gruesome the scene became."

Unable to bear the knowing look in his eyes, she closed her eyes and saw it again. It wasn't hard to conjure the image that seemed to follow her everywhere. "I should have stayed in bed, but the voices kept me up. The steady chanting like a hammer to my brain. The manor then was always filled with strange noises at night. I never could sleep through it." If only her fear of the dark had lasted another night.

"It was winter then, just as it is now. The ground was packed with three days of snow. The sky a black abyss entirely without stars. My eyes were drawn to the torches. The hazy circle of light barely bright enough to see the seers draped in their usual cloaks. They stood in a half-circle behind my father. And my father…"

She took in a breath, surprised at the emotion caught in her throat. She had never spoken of it, not for years, not since she had told her aunt. Since then, neither of them had mentioned it again. London didn't seem the right place for such talk and there had been so much else to distract them. They hadn't needed to be reminded of such things. For once, they had been happy. At least briefly.

"What did you see?" Theodore pressed her, his voice shaky.

"It was a glimmer of silver at first. But soon, I realized they were blades. Each seer had one and they were bringing them down, dragging them slowly across my father's skin. I thought they were killing him. I was so afraid, I couldn't move. I was frozen.

"For some reason, my father wasn't resisting. I think that was what scared me the most. Even as they began collecting the blood that surged down his back. The seers—they filled vial after vial with it. They let it spill down into the snow. Then they moved closer. They turned into beasts, licking at him, their faces coming up smeared with his blood."

Theodore had gone pale and she was sure she had too.

"I don't think my father wanted you to know about me and what runs in my veins," she said. "I don't think he wanted anyone to know."

She had been wrong. Her father hadn't been a murderer for allowing the seers to use the elixir. No, he had been a martyr of sorts, sacrificing himself for this so-called gift. But he wouldn't live forever. Mortibel had known that. Somehow, he had found out about her too.

Hazel and Theodore stared at each other, the horrible truth hanging between them that neither wanted to admit. She couldn't stay. Not with the antidote running in her blood.

The only question was how far she would get. Mortibel's words buzzed in her head. *It's quite out of your hands.* Even her father had seemed to know her fate. Perhaps that was why he had left her the estate. There was no escaping it. But she could hardly admit that to herself, much less tell Theodore. She wanted him to believe there was still hope. It would make things easier, wouldn't it?

Theodore crossed the room and proceeded up the steps.

"What are you doing?" Hazel followed after him. He was too fast. She was unable to stop him before he entered the sitting room and rang the bell.

"What are you doing?"

"Having Emmerson prepare your things. I'll drive you to London myself if I must."

"Yes?" Emmerson appeared at the end of the hall, irritated, as she usually was these days. No doubt she had been waiting to hear their footsteps, eager to spy.

"Miss Grey would like you to begin packing her things and a meal too," Theodore commanded, his tone leaving no room for argument. "Have the groom ready the horses and the old carriage. You two depart for London at once."

With a subtle grin, Emmerson bowed her consent and turned on her heel. Of course she made no argument. She was gone before Hazel could contradict the order.

"The night of the solstice, Mortibel is going to drain you to save his seers. More than that, I think Mortibel believes you will help enhance the flora too. They likely did the same with your father." Theodore peered out the open window toward Mortibel's estate. The same field he had crossed before he'd collapsed at her door.

They both knew what Mortibel was capable of. And yet Hazel still wasn't quite ready to leave. It felt too much like she was running away. Most of all, she didn't want to leave Theodore to endure Mortibel alone, not after all the former had done for her.

"We can stop him. You said it yourself. I'm meant to stay here." She repeated the words, hoping they would have as equal an impact on him as they did her. "Together. With you. Remember?"

He bowed his head, evidently defeated by his own words. "What I wish to happen doesn't always come to be. No matter how badly I want it."

"You can't know that for certain. If I stay—"

"He knows what's in your veins, Hazel, and I have no doubt he means to take it from you. Every drop. And that is the best scenario. In another, he could very well keep you alive and make you no less a prisoner than your father likely was."

Hazel squeezed her eyes shut at the sudden image. Whether or not her father had been willing or for how long, they would never know.

"Mortibel might not even have the decency to take it from you without pain," Theodore said.

Hazel wanted to deny these horrible truths. But it explained so much, why Mortibel had suddenly shown interest in her again in that London ballroom. Why he had wanted her hand.

Out of his coat, Theodore produced several banknotes. Far more than any man had the right to carry. "Toward my bid for the estate. Sign it over to me and you'll have the rest soon enough."

All Hazel could do was stare.

"You could live off these funds before the bank transfer, could you not? And this." Theodore unclasped the chain of his fine pocket watch. "Any other jewelry in the house worth taking?"

"It's all in the bank. Theodore, listen to me," she said. His hastiness was beginning to frighten her. She didn't care any more about the catacombs. He had only been trying to stop Mortibel and his wicked allies. That was all Theodore had ever wanted.

"Come now. You'll have enough funds. I'll even give you more. I can have it waiting for you the moment you arrive in London."

More money. That was what she'd wanted when she'd first come here. Not anymore. Not in the least. There was a frantic nature to his voice that gave her some hope that it was not all he wanted for her, either.

"You don't have to do this. I can handle myself fine." Hazel pushed the crumpled notes back toward him.

"You must take it. The money is nothing. I would trade it all. I should have made an offer before you listed it. Then perhaps you would never have had to leave London in the first place."

Somehow, that hurt her more. The idea that they never would have met. That they would never have spent this impossibly cold winter together struck her hot and hard across the face.

"Promise me you'll leave tonight," he said.

"And leave you here alone?" She didn't think she could bear it. "It's not safe for you, either."

"But it's different for me. I have a duty to stay."

"For your family name, is that it?" Hazel hadn't forgotten his story, that part of his past he couldn't let go, that he was desperate to rise above.

"You're more than just a name. You're more than just the Silver Order. You deserve an actual life and all that one entails. You know that." She grasped his arm. "Tell me."

"I know that." He smiled gently. "But it's not the Order I'm giving my life for. It's you. You have to leave. You must."

Hazel cursed herself. She had forced aside her feelings for too long. Now, amidst this unmistakable heat that flared up between them, she was powerless to do anything. In the last hour, it had only seemed to build. The things that they had shared. It couldn't all have been for nothing. *Just one more night,* she repeated to herself. One last time she would get to pull him close. Experience all those lusty feelings that had become so horribly fleeting.

But the danger of the estate was right on her heels. Staying wasn't logical. It was foolish and naïve. She would likely end up dead. And yet, to be with Theodore, she considered it.

"I'll guard your carriage in secret. All the way to town. All right?" He squeezed her hand. "While I'm there, I'll send word to my men."

"You'll be careful?"

"If Mortibel wants to fight again, it will be a fair one. I'll take care of things."

"Your father too. With my blood, you could save him."

"I know." He smiled, though it didn't last.

"Do you need more of my…my blood?"

He shook his head. "I still have your sample. It should do."

"Just in case, I should give you more."

"No." His voice turned as hard as iron. "Just tell me you'll leave."

For him, there was no other choice. And there was nothing she could do to convince him otherwise.

She nodded, her heart icing over. Slowly, her lips reached up to his. Only under its spell could everything bad be forgotten. She needed this. Everything that he had made her feel. There was no fooling herself. This was more than just a momentary affair. She could feel it in the pressure of his touch, the quick intake of his breath. It didn't matter if she left—whatever had existed between them would still be here. They had been fated from the beginning. And at the same time fated to part.

Fate really was a cruel thing.

CHAPTER TWENTY-SEVEN

Goodbye

THEO HANDED HAZEL the pen. With Emmerson serving as witness, she signed the deed to him.

"I shall see to our trunks." Emmerson gave a slight bow and hurried off.

Theo couldn't have been more relieved. Never mind the deed—he was just glad they were alone again. He shut the door and glanced back at Hazel, standing at the desk. Her eyes were full of worry. He didn't know what to say, only what he wanted to do. He wasn't wasting any more time. He couldn't cross the room fast enough. The moment he reached her, he pulled her in tightly.

He only had so much time left. And there was so much he wished to do. He shouldn't have been so reserved. Damn society's dictates.

They didn't seem to bother her, either. At least not anymore. She leaned back into him and breathed him in. When he dropped his lips onto hers, she didn't hold back. She clenched on to him tighter than ever before.

"I want to stay." She released him by an inch. "I could help you."

"Please." He kissed her again. "We have such little time."

She stepped back, gripping his hands instead. "You think it would be a fool's errand. But don't you see? Taking off in this carriage is the real fool's errand. Fate will pull me back. Just as Mortibel alluded to. Just as my father predicted."

"I don't know for certain if it will save you, no. But you have to at least let me try."

Knowing she might return to the manor was not the comfort it should have been. He didn't dare let himself think of all the things that might happen to her. Theo swallowed. He forced himself to ignore that panic building in his stomach. If *he* was this worried, he couldn't imagine what she must have been feeling. He needed to get her away from here and make sure she never turned back. It was all he could think about. No matter how much it pained him. Or her. Somehow, being close like this only made it worse.

"Come." Theo forced himself to step away. "Tea might do us some good."

The familiar ritual always worked to calm her. It was one detail he had learned during their time together—that and so much more. The little quips that made her smile, the words that made her cross and how everything in the last few moments had made her scared.

Adopting the staff with the house, Theo gave them the orders now, directing one of the maids to prepare tea and some food. Like any gracious host, he even directed Hazel to the breakfast room. Through the tall, wide windows, the sun beamed in gentle warmth. Best of all, it was private. He knew all too well these were their last moments alone. He didn't care who walked in or what they saw. And yet it felt so useless. His cup shook no matter how hard he gripped it.

"Eat more please. You'll need your strength," he encouraged her. They both did.

Between sips and small bites of day-old biscuits, a tense silence lingered.

She could say nothing that could convince him she should

stay. But there was one other possibility he dare not even entertain: He could leave with her. Leave this manor and everything related to the Order behind. Damn Mortibel and fate itself. Damn his so-called duty as a Pierce.

The suggestion was on the tip of his tongue, but in the end, he couldn't gather the strength.

"I could write," Hazel suddenly offered. "There's no reason we need to be cut off from each other completely."

After these last few weeks together, he didn't think he could endure that, either. Even death would seem a release.

"We aren't supposed to end things like this," she continued. "We're destined for so much more. Like you said. I can feel it now. But no matter how badly I want it, my future isn't mine to decide, is it?"

As much as he wanted it to be, Theo's future wasn't his own, either.

Not since he'd been born a Pierce. There had always been others he had to think about. The seers and other members, not to mention his ancestors and future descendants. She had no idea how much this fact weighed on him. He might have admitted it, but he had caused her enough pain.

Even his kiss earlier. It had only made her more adamant in her feelings and him in his. So perhaps this distance between them was for the best.

Theodore poked at the flames of the hearth, unable to look at her. "You should forget about this place," he said as meanly as he could manage. "Just as you've always wanted to."

If he was cruel, maybe that would make her departure less painful.

"What you really mean is 'forget about me,'" she accused him.

Theo stared down at the floor. "Do you have any idea what it would do to me to see you hurt or even killed? Knowing I could have done something to prevent it? Do you?" He demanded with sudden fervor.

Stricken, Hazel didn't reply. She didn't need to.

"Miss Hazel." Emmerson burst in; she must have worked hard to keep her steps silent. She seemed surprised to see them so far apart, disappointed, even. Did she actually think she would catch them in the act? "Everything is prepared."

HAZEL REMAINED FROZEN in her chair. There had to be something she could do. Something in these final moments that might convince him to depart to London with her. Was all lost?

"We'll be right there." Hazel signaled Emmerson to leave. The moment the French doors clicked closed, Hazel forced herself to meet Theodore's gaze.

"What if something happens on the road?" she said, anything that might enable her to stay.

"I'll be right there to help you."

"But Mortibel, he—"

"I know."

He held out his arm and took her out of the warm comfort of the room. Perhaps he knew she couldn't do it entirely on her own. Clenching his arm, she was prepared to hold on forever.

Outside on the drive, she couldn't even look him in the eye. Deep down in her bones, a tense shivering had started that had little to do with the cold. She bit her lip, forcing herself to gather some courage. She rallied what little she had left and pressed her lips carefully on his cheek.

"I'll set off in a moment," he whispered. "I shan't be far."

"Will you say goodbye when we stop in town?"

He bit down. "It could draw attention."

"Then…just be careful of his tricks this time, will you?"

Theodore nodded and squeezed her hand, as if to convey both the hatred he had for Mortibel and the love he held for her. When he released her, she turned and entered the borrowed carriage. She kept her gaze on him the whole time, even as he went off to the stables.

Behind her, Emmerson's heavy breathing signaled her presence.

"Whose tricks?" Emmerson asked. Of course she had been listening.

Hazel shrugged.

"Nevertheless…I'm glad you are finally seeing clearly. You're quite right in wanting to return to London. Well before the start of the Season too."

"Then what?" Hazel said, more to herself as she watched the trees flicker by.

"You'll have plenty of money for a decent enough dowry. Word of that will spread quickly enough."

"I won't waste a second more with society."

"Don't be silly."

"I'm serious. And it's none of your concern." Hazel looked forward to seeing to her aunt and checking on her health. Nothing more.

"I knew this place would only bring us trouble."

But it isn't my fault, Hazel responded inwardly. It was fate. Her father had set the path years ago with his decision to join the Order. At the very least, he had left her with a means with which to support herself.

Hazel turned to the back window. Just as he promised, Theodore followed close behind. Even though he never came close enough to make out his face, she kept turning back to see his figure growing smaller in the distance.

Emmerson sighed. "I'm just glad that Mr. Pierce gentleman convinced you to leave. You don't want to get involved in their mess. I tried to tell you."

Hazel turned back from the window. "How do you know it was Mr. Pierce who convinced me to leave?" Had Emmerson overheard their conversations? Emmerson must have heard some bits, but how much?

"Please. You were adamant about staying." Emmerson shrugged, nonplussed.

Something about her was off. There was no knowing all that she knew. All that she might tell her aunt. Hazel ached at the idea of having to explain.

"I suspect your calendar should fill quickly when we return," Emmerson said.

Hazel rolled her eyes. "Actually, once Aunt Catherine is well again, I'd like to travel," Hazel said. "Perhaps head north. I've heard it's beautiful there."

People often traveled in the hope that society might forget their scandals. Why couldn't she in the hope of forgetting Theodore? She could fantasize about the possibility at least for a moment. Even if she knew escape was not within the realm of possibility.

But every mile, they seemed to pick up speed. Perhaps Mortibel's threat had no merit and they'd make it to London safely after all. For Theodore, his safety was less certain. Part of him knew it too. His eyes had turned dead with the knowledge of it. The moments before she'd turned to enter the carriage, she had never seen them so empty.

But these weren't the memories she wished to invoke. Rather, she wanted to remember the way he had looked at her when she'd first stepped into the drawing room. The way he had stared when he'd told her about the notebook he had lost in London. The trust that had developed so quickly.

"It's snowing," Emmerson whispered as she pulled back the curtain again. It seemed a bad omen upon them both, especially when the snow turned to sleet and eventually, rain. Already, the cold, winter air penetrated the carriage with the wind knocking at both sides. Hazel clenched at her cloak wincing at the thought of Theodore out there in all this. She turned around to the back window, but he had disappeared behind a veil of ice.

In the Malverns, the weather was so strange. Stones, not droplets, seemed to fall on the roof above. Hazel wondered how long it might hold. How far they might have to journey before they reached town. Though it was still mid-afternoon, the carriage had fallen into complete darkness. Aside from the glistening of Emmerson's eyes, Hazel could make out little else.

Next came lightning. Great, rumbling booms of it that shook her to her core and lit up the entire carriage. The horses snorted, the wheels rocking back and forth on uneven terrain. Mud splattered across the window. Once more, the carriage swayed, throwing her into Emmerson. The carriage would toss at any moment—Hazel was sure of it. With her luck, they were cliffside too. She kept her eyes on the window until the next burst of lightning. A tight forest of evergreens lined the road, blocking out the stars.

"Ho there!" the driver called out. The horses whinnied, slowing to a complete stop. The sudden stillness was such a sharp contrast to the swaying of before, Hazel had to remind herself to breathe.

"Nothing more than a fallen tree limb, I'm sure." Emmerson waved a flippant hand.

But in the next flash of lightning, Emmerson's eyes went wide.

Again, the driver called out, almost as if he had seen someone. After a few moments, horse hooves rang out, what had to be Theo's horse. Hazel couldn't wait any longer. She shifted to get up. What if he needed help?

Emmerson grabbed at her. "Are you *mad*?"

"If something is amiss, we are no safer in this cage," Hazel snapped.

She pulled away and pushed the door open against the rain. A deep rumble of thunder greeted her, the storm drenching her at once.

Her eyes squinted against the falling droplets. She could see little beyond a dense lining of trees. She thought she heard something, but in the roar of rain, she couldn't have been sure.

At last came a flash of lightning. Up ahead, there was one

figure—no, two. And they were fighting.

Lightning flashed, seemingly inches away. A glimpse was all she needed. She recognized Theodore's frame at once. But with whom was he struggling? Another burst revealed Mortibel. She could have guessed. They were both bloodied, their faces contorted with a rage Hazel had never seen. She repressed her rapture at the idea of Theodore handing Mortibel death. It was too dark to tell who was winning. Amidst another burst of lightning, Theodore must have seen her too. Against the pounding rain, she could barely make out his yell.

"Run!" he said.

In the shadows of the night, three other men closed in on her. Behind her, the carriage door had been left wide open, banging against the carriage with each coming wind. Emmerson must have thought her life was in danger and already escaped into the darkness. At least she hoped. Either that or she had already been captured.

Having no better plan, Hazel set off into the forest, tripping over twigs and foliage she prayed weren't thorny. In the darkness, she couldn't tell how much distance she covered. She could barely see the trees in front of her. She could only see far enough ahead to avoid them.

Though the rain slowed, the cold winds persisted. She could die out here in her soaked skirts. An intense shivering she couldn't control had already begun. If they had captured Emmerson, she hoped she was at least dry. They wouldn't hurt her, would they? It was Hazel they wanted, after all.

She was tiring fast. Weighed down by her soaked skirts, she stumbled and fell onto a pile of rocks. No doubt she had bruised her knees. They might even have been bleeding. She didn't bother to check them, though. She was too exhausted. With her final reserves of strength, she pulled herself onto a large rock and pressed her cheek against its smooth, hard surface.

She struggled to catch her breath against her chattering teeth. Never before had she felt such bitter cold. The icy air bit at her skin, the slightest stirring of wind making her wince.

She must have closed her eyes and fallen unconscious. When she opened them, a new jarring quiet surrounded her. She had almost forgotten the violent rain of before, save for the droplets that quivered down from the trees. Even the wind slowed enough so she could hear the first signs of danger. A sudden crunch of feet over branches.

She was too dazed to move, not knowing what good it would do her, anyway. She had not an inkling where she was or if the safety of a town awaited nearby. She worried most for Emmerson. She prayed that she had made off. With luck, the poor woman might stumble upon a cottage and get help. Hazel refused to believe otherwise. She had put Emmerson in so much danger, she couldn't bear if she actually got hurt. Or worse, killed. Theodore too.

The danger was nothing now. She didn't care about the pneumonia that might soon set in. She was already doomed. The steps that sounded off in the distance confirmed it. They closed in cautiously, as if she would bother to try to stop them. Of course she wouldn't. She didn't even make a sound of protest when a hand gripped her arm and thrust her upward.

CHAPTER TWENTY-EIGHT
The Winter Solstice

HAZEL SWAM IN and out of consciousness. The line between reality and her dreams was no longer distinct. She had no concept of time. In one moment, she heard laughter. In another she was weeping. Then she was running again in the woods. Far out in the distance, Theodore appeared, apparition-like. But the closer she approached him, the realer he seemed to become. A few feet away, Mortibel suddenly took his place. He was grinning, but something was off. He had blood in his teeth and, oddly, a knife in his hand. He was coming after her, forcing her to turn back in the opposite direction. She screamed, but no sound came.

Her hands twitched atop the bed. Though she couldn't yet see, feeling returned to her limbs, grounding her once more in the present. Sensations that she knew had to be real: the heaviness of her eyelids and the ache against the bottom of her skull. In a brief moment of clarity, she felt a pinch in her skin, no different than when Theodore had taken some of her blood.

Something rushed through her veins. Slowly, she continued to pull herself upward, out of what seemed a deep, watery abyss. Above her, she could see light. She kept fighting, kicking her feet harder against the heavy, all-encompassing water, until at last she broke the surface.

Hazel snapped up in bed. She heard the voices first, the terse words of an argument. But the room was empty. She was back at Whitestone, in her own room. She recognized the faintest scent of Theodore still lingering on the covers around her.

Had he been the one to bring her back? She could scarcely hope. How much she longed to see his face and hear his voice. How much time had passed since she had been forced to leave him behind? It felt like weeks.

Throwing aside the blanket, her toes touched ice. Immediately, she was reminded of the terrible cold that stormy night and her failure to escape. She braced herself on the mantelpiece, savoring the warmth and her dry clothes. Gray and thin, it appeared to be some servant's gown. But at least it did not stick to her skin like her wet ones had.

She shuddered away the sensation. She played that night over in her mind again, running in the rain, stumbling upon the rock, then being dragged from the forest and into a carriage. As much as she had hoped, the hands that had seized her had been too rough to be Theodore's. And yet somehow, she was still alive, her blood still in her veins. For now.

She ran to the door, desperate to find Theodore. The hall was the same as it had always been, yet different somehow, filled with a new kind of energy.

She wasn't alone. A crowd of voices echoed toward her from the grand staircase, beckoning her forward. Looking over the banister, she recognized none of them, but unlike the ones she had heard in her sleep, they were cheerful. Some woman even burst out in laughter.

How many people were here in her home? Fifty? A hundred? The foyer was absolutely buzzing with the crush of strangers. They were dressed in their finest silks and lace. The amount of jewelry that graced their necks was a thief's dream. She hadn't seen a sight like this since her mother had still been alive. But unlike at her father's gatherings, these people were not welcome.

They were all trespassers, every one of them. She was about

to shout at them and demand they leave at once, when a hand closed like talons upon her shoulder.

"The injection worked." The voice confirmed the horrible truth. Mortibel breathed behind her, pulling her back into the shadows. "I shall have to pay my regards to Dr. Lagerfield."

She twisted around. Like the other guests, he was dressed in formal evening attire.

"What's this? No hug, no kiss?" He seemed puzzled. "You should be thanking me."

"*Thanking* you?" Lord knew what Theodore's fate had been at Mortibel's hands. He couldn't have died. Not for her sake. But she didn't have the courage to confirm it.

"For rescuing you. You were minutes from death." He looked behind him. There was an edge to his voice, a certain kind of concern. What for? It seemed he had everything he wanted.

Mortibel swiped a hand across his brow, his whole forehead glistening.

"Best you give up your delusions about Pierce. He ran at the first opportunity."

'*Ran*'? Hazel shook her head. Theodore would not run off and leave all this behind. He would return. He would come back. If not for her, then for the Order.

Yet Mortibel's tone had a certain finality to it that frightened her.

"And Emmerson?" Hazel shivered to ask.

"You mean my loyal spy? I imagine she's on her way to London now that I've finished with her."

"Your spy?"

He nodded brusquely.

"We've talked often since the catacombs. Our alliance wasn't an instant one, but with time, I convinced her to see my side of things."

"But, but…why?"

"I had to keep an eye on you somehow. Or would you rather I tell you she is dead?"

Hazel stepped backward bracing herself against the wall.

"Rest assured she heard and told me *everything*. Like most servants, she has a penchant for gossip and listening through doors. I knew every lie. And you, my dear, told many."

Hazel didn't want to believe it. They had been growing distant these last couple of weeks, but enough to betray her thus?

"That day you told me Pierce was dying? Emmerson told me the truth before I left. I was biding my time, you see… But this time, my plans shan't go awry like the time in London."

"She wouldn't." Hazel still tried to deny it.

"I think you underestimated her ambitions. Once I promised her a place as a lady's maid for a countess—one of the most loyal supporters within the Order, in fact—she didn't hesitate."

Hazel had also underestimated Emmerson's hatred of the countryside. Perhaps she should have done more to keep her happy.

"I was surprised how much you confided in her. Particularly your feelings for me."

"Old feelings of a distant past." Hazel narrowed her eyes.

"She was convinced I was the best choice for you. After all, you would become a baronetess. She really had your best interests in mind. I fear sometimes that not even you know them."

Emmerson had never understood how titles and money could mean so little to Hazel, not when it came to love.

Perhaps Hazel could believe this betrayal. Perhaps it all made sense.

"We trusted her. I trusted her…" Now that the shock of it had passed, her anger took over.

"Quiet now. We have guests, remember? And a great many esteemed ones too."

Hazel's fogged mind figured it out. The winter solstice had finally arrived, filling the house with his faction of allies, people who would do little to help her. But she could not let that temper her will to escape. Staying here was no longer an option. She didn't care if it was what her fate was supposed to be.

"Be sure to behave, my dear." Mortibel brushed aside a lock of her hair. "There are men down there who could do much worse to you than I. Whether you like it or not, this is your home. You best treat it as such."

Hazel had been prepared to spew some insult, but the words had caught her off guard. Whatever was to happen during the ritual tonight wouldn't kill her, as she had feared. No, that would end their supply too quickly. They much preferred to keep her a prisoner.

Mortibel grabbed her arm, pulling her forward. "It is not my wish to force you. Alas, it is out of my control. There are others, you understand."

Whoever they were, perhaps she should at least try appealing to them. She was wasting her time with him. Regardless of his supposed title as chairman, there were others who held power too, perhaps more.

"You have a wonderful gift. I can protect it—better yet, I can protect *you*. Reconsider my offer." He practically begged. "You could have everything you want. Money and position. All without having to step foot into a London ballroom ever again."

It seemed a safe enough choice. What would the Order do otherwise? If she proved difficult, would they chain her up inside her own home? Either way, they would drain her, just as they had her father. Accepting Mortibel would only mean that he might trust her. He might even give her the freedom she needed to escape. It would be a loveless marriage, yes, but one from which she could run away at the first opportunity.

Saying *yes* was the logical choice and yet she couldn't shake this feeling that she was betraying Theodore. But how sure could she be that he would return? She never imagined he would have run in the first place.

"You'll see it is the better option." Mortibel took her silence as acceptance enough. "We'll make a spectacle of it. I'll announce my intentions tonight."

He picked up his pace toward her bedroom, dragging her away more excitedly. "You shall get dressed at once. I have the perfect gown for the occasion."

Hazel couldn't believe she was being so agreeable when all she wanted to do was hit him hard across the head and run. How far might she get in this icy cold? If it weren't raining, she might make it to the nearest estate that wasn't Mortibel's. But without a cloak, she couldn't be certain.

Mortibel opened her armoire. Just as he had promised, a dress she didn't recognize hung inside, the deep-ruby-red silk stealing her attention, if only for a moment.

He pulled it out so she could admire its details: ruffles of black, eyelash lace, a deep-scoop neckline and cap sleeves. What proved most impressive was the rich sheen of the fabric. Ruining any chance of escape, it was certain to make her stand out in the crowd.

"I'd say it's fit enough for a queen. After tonight, you will be one of sorts."

He would be chairman, after all. Tonight, it would be official. Though she had never wanted this, she would be forced to stay. Just as he had hoped.

"Borrowed again from your sister?" Hazel asked.

Mortibel's face darkened. Did he think she might actually forget what he had done? That he, this man who was soon to be her husband, had killed his own sister.

"Only lowly servants wear the clothing of their betters." Servants like Lenora, he meant. But why this sudden disdain toward her? The other day, they had practically been entwined. Had he already done away with her? "I'll have you know that I purchased it for you in the days leading up to my proposal. Remember it?"

Mortibel threw the dress over the bed. "I'm not proud of what I've had to do, but I *had* to do it. For the Order. You must understand that. The sooner you do, the easier life will be for the both of us."

"And Lenora?" Hazel said. "Was that affair also a necessity?"

"A passing amusement, if you must know. A means to an end."

Like herself, Lenora was just another tool, one whom he used to kill his own flesh and blood. He would never entertain marrying her. Even if he didn't care much for titles, she was much too beneath him.

"We won't have to wait long once I've announced my intentions." He approached her, a dark smile spreading across his face.

"Until then." Hazel raised her chin, her breath catching. "I think it rather uncouth having you here with me in my bedroom."

It seemed she had no end of things to fear. Waiting for him to leave, she wondered how far the drop would be from her window and how hard the brick drive.

"You know what I want." Mortibel turned at the door. "I promise, if you grant me it, I'll never keep anything from you again. There would be no need to and in time, you'll grow quite fond of the Order. I'm sure of it."

Though Hazel didn't want to admit it she had already become partial to the Order—ever since she had tasted the elixir, ever since the vision had been fulfilled and she had seen Theodore's wound heal in a matter of moments and then the stones— all of it had fascinated her. She couldn't deny that she wanted to know more, danger be damned. It followed regardless of what she did.

"Let us enjoy the evening. There will be much to celebrate." He inched closer. "And know your cooperation will mean a much more pleasurable experience."

Hazel remained silent. Again, Mortibel took this as welcome obedience.

"I'll send someone to help you dress and fix your hair." Mortibel straightened his tie and brushed back his hair before exiting. "I'll send a few guards up to watch your room too...for protection, of course."

Hazel jolted at the slam of the door and the click of the lock. Unless she wanted to jump to her death from her second-story window, she'd have to wait for another opportunity. If one ever came.

CHAPTER TWENTY-NINE

Escape

THEO OPENED HIS eyes to blackness. It was so deep and complete, he couldn't be sure he was actually conscious. That was before he felt the pain in his shoulders, across his back, and down his legs. Everywhere, really. On the surface of his skin and deep within his bones.

The floor beneath him, what felt like pure ice, was his only relief. His only hope to numb any of the pain.

Yet again, Mortibel had refused to fight him fairly. He shouldn't have been surprised. The bastard. Mortibel might not have poisoned him this time, but Theo had been greatly outnumbered. It was just as Theo had feared. He'd had a feeling Hazel's carriage would be intercepted. But he'd had to at least try to send her safety. What else was there for him to do?

He wasn't about to give up. Not yet. Saving the Order was second to him now. As long as he had Hazel, it always would be. He never should have doubted that.

He shifted to his side, numbing what had to be a deep-rooted bruise. He expected to see some source of light, but still, there was nothing. It was as dark as hell itself. Was he buried alive? What else but a coffin could be so dark? There was enough space around him for him to move, though.

Then again, the pain was so great, he couldn't move much. The floor was so smooth, it had to have been tile, so he couldn't be in a cave. All he knew was that it was dark.

He couldn't completely rule out that Mortibel hadn't poisoned him again. His mind was already fading. A wave of exhaustion poured over him, dragging him down. He couldn't fight it for long.

Where were his men? Without a single message since he'd set out a week and a half ago, they had to know he was in trouble by now.

More importantly, where was Hazel? He cursed himself. He was the one who was supposed to save her. But here he was in some hole he couldn't dig himself out of. Only his right arm could stretch out enough to gauge his surroundings. Every which way he turned his head, he faced darkness. Even the underground lab had short windows.

He bit down on his lip. It was the only thing that could distract from the pain and approaching death.

Then he realized. If he was close to death, there was only one place it made perfect sense to put him. He even recognized the glossy tiles. He had to be in the family mausoleum, surrounded by all his dead ancestors and statues of their likenesses. Each of them well armed with stone pistols and knives…

If they came back for him, at least, he wouldn't be unarmed.

Stiff and cold with cold, he reached out until he felt the cold, hard surface of a sarcophagus. He pulled himself up with one arm, just like he had pulled himself across that field. He reached the base of some statue. He didn't know whose.

Cursing the cold, he crawled up the statue inch by inch until he felt a stone arm and then a hand and a…barrel. *Blast.* He'd been hoping for a knife.

He dropped down and worked his way to the next statue, trying to remember the layout of the place from memory. The last time he'd been here was as a child during his grandfather's funeral.

There were a lot of caskets, more than he could count, all lined up perpendicular to the wall with an aisle down the center.

The older statues farther back in the tomb always had knives, but in complete darkness, he had no way of knowing which way was which. He wasn't sure how long he'd be able to stay conscious, either. But upon the third statue he tried, he felt it: a blade. Made of stone, it wasn't sharp, but it was pointed and that was all he needed.

The trouble was breaking it off. He didn't need the whole thing, just a good deal of the pointed tip. This statue held two stone blades, one pointed toward the ceiling and another pointed to the wall in an L shape. He pulled on the one pointing to the wall. It wouldn't budge, not so much as a crack. It was thin stone, though, so it had to be fragile.

"Come on, fellow Pierce," he begged. "Release it."

He lifted his body higher and hung his full weight on it until finally, it snapped, throwing him to the floor.

For a long while, he lay there, the breath knocked out of him. But he didn't care about that and all the other places that were aching and no doubt bleeding again. He smiled, even.

He was armed again.

Just one more chance. What he wouldn't do for another opportunity to face Mortibel. What he wouldn't do to free Hazel from their grasp. If only he could change their fates and have the happily ever after he wanted so badly. Not this. This couldn't have been their destiny. His anger burst into flames. Forget the pain. This was so much worse.

It made him want to lash out. But after all the exertion he had put into getting the stone blade, he was too weak. His mind continued to fade, deeper and deeper into a blackness he didn't think could get any darker. He tried to fight it, but it was so much easier to give in. In his last moments of consciousness, he thought of one subject: Hazel.

As Mortibel had promised, two maids came within moments to prepare her. They stepped inside, one of their heads bowed. When she lifted her head, Hazel stepped backward.

It was Miss Mortibel's lady's maid. The maid who had been willing to poison her own mistress. For what? To serve as a maid to a baronetess rather than merely the daughter of one?

She had the decency at least to look ashamed. She didn't dare look at Hazel in the eye, no matter how close they got when they slipped on her underthings.

The two maids worked quickly too. Somehow, Hazel's hair had already been washed. Though she expected to see splotches of mud, her skin was clean too.

She winced when they tightened and tied the strings of her corset. All she needed to do now was step into her gown, a puddle of red fabric on the floor. They lifted it over her shoulders and smoothed down the buttery satin. The maids did her hair last, combing then piling her hair atop her head. The braids this time felt tighter than ever.

They tried to start a conversation, gushing about being maids to a future baronetess, but Hazel didn't say a word. She didn't think she could speak if she wanted to. At any moment, she feared she would burst into tears. She preferred to offend rather than appear weak. And there was no knowing what they might tell Mortibel. She wouldn't dare risk it, not with what had happened with Emmerson, and knowing what one of them had done to Miss Mortibel. The mere thought set her teeth on edge.

Too soon, Mortibel announced himself at the door.

"Ready to come down, my dear?" he asked.

Their work done, the two young women rushed out of the room. Hazel was left to stare at herself in the mirror, alone again with Mortibel. Before he could get any closer, she snapped around to face him. No matter how angry she was at Emmerson or how forlorn she felt about the future, she kept her face indifferent. She wouldn't let him see the pain he'd caused her. At least not yet. For now, she had to appear indifferent.

He paused in his steps.

"You look...beautiful." Mortibel took the back of her hand and traced a careful line from her wrist to her knuckle.

He seemed to know how difficult this was for her. And yet he did not doubt her acquiescence. He needed her too badly. Something told her his chairmanship depended on her. For tonight at least, this fact gave her a moment of security. He would protect her so long as she remained a means to that end.

"They are impatient to see you." He grasped her hand.

Whoever *they* were, Hazel had no idea. Perhaps the same people who would force her to stay like Mortibel had warned. Dangerous people, then. People whom she would be expected to please.

She stepped down the hallway, craning her neck. Her home was no longer familiar to her. An evergreen garland she hadn't noticed before wrapped around the railing and she could smell roses, bringing to mind some vague, distant memory of her childhood.

"How...?" Hazel struggled to understand how they had prepared her home so quickly.

"I had my staff do some much needed improvements," Mortibel said. "A great deal."

Emmerson would have been so proud. More than herself, she always appreciated a properly decorated ball. Hazel still didn't fully accept the betrayal. All she could think of was the times they'd talked of her feelings for Mortibel. Emmerson had always encouraged her, saying how advantageous it would be to marry a future baronet.

Hazel bemoaned the idea now. But there was a day when Hazel had indeed hoped for it, even prayed. Maybe Emmerson really did believe she was helping her. Hazel bit her lip, wishing she had been more honest with Emmerson. She shouldn't have tried to keep so much a secret.

Hazel continued reluctantly down the stairs. The place had been completely transformed. It was no longer dark and cold with curtains tightly drawn. Several candelabras gave the room a brilliant glow. The floors had been polished too. A hall fit for their queen.

They certainly looked at her like one. A dozen or so faces followed her path down the stairs. The crowd was so large, it spilled from the drawing room into the foyer. And through the tall windows, she could see more carriages pulling up along the drive. Finely dressed servants she didn't recognize littered the place, refilling glasses of champagne or standing there like decoration against the walls, ready to wait on their every whim.

But not even the beauty of her surroundings or the magnificently bejeweled ladies could erase her sense of caution. Mortibel's supporters were all trespassers and villains. Every smile was a grimace of sharp teeth. Every laugh mocked her.

Like in London, she was a mere spectacle to them. Only now she could finally see it clear in their faces.

Hazel entered the drawing room. More garland hung down from the chandeliers. She could smell the cider and mutton. As they stepped farther into the room, the crowd parted in their wake. Every face was on her. With no need for an introduction, they even gave her gentle, subdued applause. She was a prize to them. Someone Mortibel had won and was graciously sharing with them all.

Mortibel nodded and shook hands with someone while she stood there, practically shaking. She wondered how much these members knew. In addition to those among his supporters, these could be the ignorant ones too. Members of the second or third less involved chapters who gave their fortunes in exchange for a few of the Order's secrets. She recognized some of them: famous scholars, aristocrats close to the Crown, and even a famous poet. She wondered what it would take to turn them to Theo's side. All she needed to tell them was the truth.

Together, she and Mortibel closed in on one man with vibrant, white hair. She almost didn't recognize him. It took her a moment to remember so far back.

"Dr. Lagerfield?"

With a smile, he handed her and Mortibel each a glass of champagne. "She's arrived at last. And looking very well, indeed."

"I've kept her quite intact," Mortibel said, though he seemed distracted. His eyes darted to the other side of the room.

"I have no doubt. She is finally here once and for all, yes?"

"As promised," Mortibel said. As if she weren't even there, he did not let her answer for herself.

"The dress suits you." Dr. Lagerfield acknowledged the low neckline of Hazel's gown.

Hazel bit down on her lip. She had never wished she could hit someone more in her life. Summoning much effort, she restrained herself.

"With any luck, you're going to be just as powerful as you are beautiful," he said.

But it all came with a price. While her role appeared to be one of privilege, it would all be a lie. Just as Mortibel appeared a gentleman, when he was really no more than a traitor to them all. *Theodore is your true leader*, she wanted to shout to them all. In response, Hazel imagined Mortibel just laughing it off and saying she'd had too much to drink.

This was the man who meant to drain her that night in the catacombs. Completely? She couldn't know for sure. All she knew was that death was better.

It just wasn't her destiny. He was the reason her father had known she'd have to live out her days here. As much as she didn't want to accept it, she was to be Mortibel's prisoner.

How often would they bleed her, she wondered. What if he took too much? So much, she could no longer stand? Or she lost all sensation? She remembered her father, the way he had been on his knees. The horrible dead look on his face.

What if Dr. Lagerfield had been one of the seers who had

surrounded her father that night? The idea made her sick. She wanted so badly to run right then, take a horse from the stables, and race away, just as she had as a child.

Jolting, Mortibel suddenly cursed, spotting something or someone from across the room. He swallowed the rest of his drink and handed it to Dr. Lagerfield. "Watch her, will you?"

With her eyes, Hazel tried to follow him in the crowd, but he quickly disappeared between gowns and black jackets.

"Seems off today, doesn't he?" Dr. Lagerfield gave her the same innocent smile he had when they had first met. But this time, his dark intentions gleamed through his eyes. "He's nervous about you is all. Tonight is of tremendous importance. Specifically for you, mind."

"How's that?" Did she even want to know?

"Tonight will determine your fate. If we should bestow you the honor of becoming one of us."

"I don't think you have much choice in the matter. And neither do I."

He laughed, sipping his champagne. "I thought there was something different about you. Something about your eyes..." Dr. Lagerfield said. "Yes, there's new wisdom in them, much more now than when we first met. But not too much, I hope."

Hazel smiled, indulging him at his own game. "Didn't Mortibel mention it? I've had some time to grow acquainted with the place. With someone who happens to know the place quite well. Better than anyone, in fact. Likely better than you."

Dr. Lagerfield's smile faded for a brief moment. "I expected you'd be somewhat difficult. I thought that seeing all our members eying you, praising you, might change your mind."

"They're merely gawking at me."

"Not in the least. I think it would please them if we kept you around. But you're wrong—we don't have to. No, not at all." He gripped her bare arm, turning it upright. The ice-cold touch of his fingers made goosebumps form across her skin. He wasn't bluffing.

"There's plenty of antidote in these veins," Dr. Lagerfield said. "Plenty to last us hundreds of visions. By then, we'll have discovered how your father made himself immune. Or perhaps we shall do what Mortibel suggests and have you carry his child, one who shall also inherit your immunity."

Hazel winced, pulling her arm back. "And if I throw myself from a cliff and disappear into the deepest valley? What would happen to the Order then?"

"Are you considering it?" Dr. Lagerfield frowned at her as though she were a child.

"Perhaps."

"We'll have to keep an eye on you, then."

It would be even harder to escape. "The Order has many other tools, you know. Far more fascinating than anything you'd ever find in London. We could do without the antidote. Just as there are people willing to give up their pocket money for our secrets, there are also people willing to die. It would hardly be a first. What do you think the Order did before your father? His family never cared who died to obtain such knowledge."

"Will you be one of them?" Hazel asked, paying no heed to the manipulative words. "One of the men who die for such knowledge?"

The way Dr. Lagerfield looked at her, Hazel knew it to have been true. He had taken the elixir too. Though what he had seen was less clear. She didn't want to know, nor did it matter. She felt a deep sort of satisfaction knowing his life rested in her hands. All she needed to do was escape.

"I say, you don't make for a very gracious host." Dr. Lagerfield blinked away a flash of anger.

"I am nothing of the sort. I signed everything over to Theodore before I left. This house, the land—everything. It's all his. The papers have already been sent to my solicitor."

"You mean the parcel Emmerson was to send?" He laughed. "Pierce will get the honor of dying here. Nothing more."

Then he was close? Her pounding heart stilled. Though Hazel

hoped for it, his presence also meant he wasn't safe—possibly dying, even.

"Where is he?" Hazel demanded.

Dr. Lagerfield grinned. He would never give her a clear answer, no matter how much she begged.

She searched instead for Mortibel. Raising her head over the crowd, she found him at the opposite end of the room, all the way in the corner. With *Lenora*. Though no one else seemed to have noticed, Mortibel had a fierce grip on her wrist and he was muttering something close to her ear. It was likely Lenora wasn't supposed to be here. Though she had certainly dressed the part, she wasn't a member, nor would she ever be.

Her gown, a pale pink with black, muslin ruffles down the bodice, was likely Miss Mortibel's, Hazel thought with a shiver. The color, no doubt uncommon in Miss Mortibel's wardrobe, was gentle even to Hazel's senses. Clearly, Lenora had chosen it in hopes of blending in with the crowd.

Once all this was over, Hazel would mourn Miss Mortibel's death, even if they hadn't been close. The woman had just wanted what was best for her brother. Hazel couldn't blame her for thinking the Order so wicked. Her father and Mortibel had let it become so.

A cloud seemed to pass over Lenora's face now. Had he told her the news? Forced it to sink in that Lenora was destined to die little better than a witch? Perhaps she would get a few crowns out of the deal, but certainly nothing more. And yet, when Mortibel paced back toward Hazel, Lenora didn't leave. She stood there, chest heaving, her cheeks glistening in the candlelight. Hazel finally saw her opportunity. Lenora might know something. She might even be vulnerable enough to disclose it.

"Good, Mortibel is making his way back." Dr. Lagerfield shook her from her thoughts. "He can better keep a leash on you."

Hazel watched Dr. Lagerfield fold into the crowd then, taking solace in the fact that she had incensed him enough to make him leave. If she hadn't spotted the guards at both ends of the hall, their eyes constantly on her, she might have tried to run. As more people entered her home, the crowd seemed to close in. She was trapped, at least for now.

Mortibel swept suddenly alongside her. "You haven't touched your champagne."

"Perhaps it's poisoned."

"Rather, it's delicious." Taking it from her hand, Mortibel drank it down himself. *Let him drink. Let him get drunk,* she thought, especially if it meant she could get away. She almost suggested another glass.

"Was your conversation with Dr. Lagerfield pleasant?"

"He seemed satisfied enough with it."

"Good. I'm about to announce dinner."

He held out an arm. But Hazel already knew what she must do. If she was going to get a word with Lenora, she had to escape.

"Dr. Lagerfield said he will return to collect me. He's requested to escort me into the dining hall."

To Hazel's panic, Mortibel made a face. He searched for Dr. Lagerfield not far within the crowd. A mere nod confirmed the request. "Rather presumptuous, but it must mean he's pleased with you... Very well. I knew Dr. Lagerfield would have little to worry about. You're doing splendidly."

Hazel could have laughed. More than likely, Dr. Lagerfield's nod had meant to acknowledge Mortibel's coming announcement. She was only too glad to take advantage of Mortibel's stupidity.

When Mortibel took to the stairs to make the announcement, Hazel wasted no time. She weaved through the crowd, ignoring stares and smiles. Between bodies, Hazel saw that Lenora stood frozen in the same corner. The tears streamed rapidly now, attracting onlookers.

"What do you want?" She sneered, the smell of liquor on her breath.

"Rather, it's what *you* want." Hazel placed a cautious hand on her shoulder. To her surprise, Lenora didn't shrink away. The witch needed this modicum of comfort now that her dreams had been dashed. If nothing else, they had that in common.

"Doesn't matter what *I* want. I know what *I* want. It's what *he* wants. And that's you."

"He has little chance of that."

Lenora straightened as Mortibel's voice boomed in the distance. Words they both ignored. Soon, the crowd began to shift around them, filtering toward the dining hall.

"I should go."

"No." Hazel caught her arm. Lenora was her only chance, her only hope in this room full of ignorant onlookers.

"Marcus wouldn't allow it, but I knew I should have gotten rid of you," she spit, her face twisted into a sneer.

"Then help me escape." Hazel cast a furtive glance at one of the guards.

"You mean you don't want all of this?" To Lenora, the idea must have seemed utterly ridiculous. But she didn't know the truth of what would happen that night. She'd proven this with what she had said earlier. She hadn't a clue why Mortibel couldn't get rid of her. Not unless she stayed around to see.

"None of it," Hazel said simply—not Mortibel's idea of the Order, anyway. A different Order, the kind Theodore had envisioned over dinner, was still at the back of her mind, growing more alluring by the hour. Until she found Theodore, she absolutely refused to submit to a life amongst the Order or any kind of life, really.

Lenora's face began to brighten. If Hazel succeeded in running away, it would be so much easier to convince Mortibel to accept her, she probably thought. Though in reality, Lenora's chances would still be slim. Her eyes so rosy with love did not see this. Hazel had been counting on it.

"What do you want me to do?"

Hazel hadn't had a plan exactly, not yet. "Surely, you must know things…"

"Everything revolves around you. They want to see first if they can control you."

Hazel looked around her. The crowd was thinning. The roar of voices emanated from a distance. Mortibel would have already noticed she was missing. What then, if they realized they couldn't control her?

"Tell me where Theodore is. Theodore Pierce."

"That man? Dead by now, I should think." She shrugged. "I overheard talk of throwing him in the mausoleum. In this cold, I don't imagine he has long. I told you this winter would be harsh."

"Peculiar too," Hazel reminded her.

In the new quiet, coming footfalls gave Hazel the briefest of warnings. Mortibel twisted her hard against the wall, staring her down.

"You…" He seemed trapped between hitting her and keeping her placated enough to obey.

"Leave at once." He turned to Lenora. Lenora did not hesitate this time. Picking up her great, beautiful skirts she stormed off, shedding even more tears now.

"You must behave… *Please*," he pleaded with her yet again.

Hazel gave no answer as he grabbed her arm and dragged her away. Lenora's words had put her in a sort of daze. Theodore close to dead? Or worse…*dead*? He couldn't have been. It was a possibility she didn't want to entertain. The mere idea drained the blood from her face.

Mortibel had merely been toying with her, wanting her to believe that Theodore had abandoned her. Part of her, she realized, had fallen for it. But with reason to believe he was so close, possibly alive, a new hope filled her, along with a new determination to escape this place.

She just needed to create a distraction. There were enough people here to cause outright panic. The right amount of chaos would allow her enough time to hide. And with enough time to hide, she might even be able to get her cloak.

CHAPTER THIRTY

The Serum

HAZEL TOOK IN her surroundings. She had never seen the great dining hall outfitted like this. Not for years. The furniture had been cleared away. A table a hundred seats long extended down the entirety of the room. The china and glassware had been placed with careful precision, the napkins delicately folded.

"*Smile…*" Mortibel whispered. But Hazel was already breaking apart inside. She didn't care if it showed.

Every face had turned in her direction. Rather than applaud, or cheer, they hemmed and hawed, no doubt surprised to see their hostess of honor in such a state of distress. Hazel turned her gaze to the gleaming, hardwood floor. She didn't know how she could continue to keep up this farce.

She wanted nothing more than to see Theodore's face. She imagined him somewhere amidst all the others. Pistol in hand, he would pull her away and together, they would run out into the hills. That might have been how it happened, if not for the extreme cold that had surrounded the estate for weeks now. Had it been warm, Theodore would have been able to escape anything, handcuffs and all. He was intelligent enough, determined enough. But in this cold…had they thrown him in the mausoleum a few hours ago, he'd have been frozen to the bone and long ago dead.

Hazel ran a hand jaggedly across her face, damning her tears and the staring eyes. She wished they knew the truth of what was to become of her. Of what might have already happened to their rightful leader.

Might, she reminded herself. There was still a chance he was alive. For her, that was enough to keep her going. The goodbye before she'd left in the carriage couldn't be their last. At the time, she still hadn't been completely convinced it had been goodbye at all. She hadn't even told him she loved him. She just wasn't that brave.

"Sit," Mortibel boomed. She felt like a child the way he loomed over her and whispered commands. "Whatever Lenora told you, it's over now. Best you give in."

A servant placed a plate of oysters before them and filled their wineglasses. Hazel could barely look at them. She couldn't erase the image of Theodore's face, his lips blue from cold.

No matter how dismal it seemed, she couldn't give up. Not yet. Not when she knew what Theodore's surroundings must have entailed and the certain death that could soon embrace him. Alongside the tombs of his ancestors, it would have been pitch black, full of dust and grime, cobwebs, and disgusting insects. She couldn't let him endure it alone and she couldn't waste any more time. She needed to leave now. But how?

She let Mortibel make frivolous comments about cuisine and decorations whilst the silver and crystal glittered in his eyes. It was all so extravagant. The dishes' exotic ingredients spanned continents.

Meanwhile, Hazel kept thinking of escape. Theodore had to believe she would save him. His men would be trying too. No matter how impossible it seemed.

Looking around the room, she marked the exits. There was a door at both corners of the room with a guard in the center of each. What seemed more useful were the items on the table: a sharp steak knife and a flickering array of candlesticks. In place of centerpieces, a long, evergreen garland ran down the center of the table dotted with berries the same deep red as her dress.

"Hazel?" Mortibel tried to rouse her. Behind a veil of tears blurring her vision, his face was little more than a swirl of color in the dim candlelight.

The sound of his voice was really starting to grate at her senses. This time, she imagined herself ripping the glass of wine out of his hand and throwing it against the wall. Instead, she dropped her fork so that it clattered on top of her plate.

The sharp sound effectively silenced the room. She didn't care. She watched dazed as the silverware sparked in the candlelight. That was when an idea struck her as clear as the silence. She slid her hand along the table and felt the garland, as dry as tinder.

She went for her glass next but grasped the candelabra instead, tipping it sideways. For a tense moment, the silver wobbled before falling onto the garland. Flames shot up at once then ran down the length of the table. It happened so fast: the women gasping and jumping from their seats, the men struggling to put out the flames with their water glasses. Their efforts made little difference. The deep-black smoke seemed to rise higher, the flames licking at the garland dangling from the chandeliers. Those caught on fire too.

Hazel backed away from the table, momentarily stunned with what she had done. For all she knew, she could have just burned down the estate. But servants were already running amongst them, some with buckets. They dumped water not only on the flames, but all over the remaining courses, effectively knocking over glasses and shattering china.

Hazel froze for a brief moment before coming to her wits. While Mortibel was busy trying to douse the flames, she needed to take off running. There was no longer any hesitating. Even the guards seemed occupied with the commotion.

So, grabbing her skirts, Hazel cut through the smoke and

made a run for it. Every step seemed a miracle that brought her closer to freedom. She didn't get far. She barely made it into the hall when the smoke began to scratch at her throat. She let out a cough. One of the guards noticed her immediately.

"Stop!" he shouted so loud, she almost stilled.

Instead, she picked up her pace. Who knew what they might do to her if she was caught. Mortibel wasn't foolish enough to believe the fire had been an accident. And she would not let them cage her in her room again. She needed to stay on the first floor. It was her best chance of making her way across the lawn to the mausoleum. But she had to lose this guard first. She glimpsed back at him. He was tall and possibly armed.

She couldn't outrun him for long. She certainly couldn't overcome a man three times her size. But if she had the right advantages, she could overcome anyone.

She had the advantages of this home. Almost as well as Theodore, she knew every corner, every crevice. Particularly, the secret priest hole.

Hazel changed directions, making her way toward the library. The guard stumbled a bit but remained on her trail. This had to work. She had to try it. Short of finding some weapon and fighting him, she had no choice.

Steadily, she began to pick up her pace, grasping on to every bit of energy she had left. The distance between them was growing, his footfalls fading into the background as the guard tired. He hadn't the same motivation to match hers. For Hazel, it was life or death.

She could see the doorway, straight down the hall with few obstructions. She hadn't much time. His footfalls were gaining again, louder with each step, the space between them closing fast.

There could be no thought of failure. No fear of the guard's angry bellow that echoed down the hall. Perhaps it was angels who lifted her off the ground and propelled her faster toward the door. Somehow, she made it. Inside the library, she crashed into the bookshelf, applying pressure to the right spot so that it slid aside an inch. The shelf, heavy with books, took every bit of her draining strength to move. With one desperate heave, it opened just enough so she could slip inside and enclose herself in darkness. The gentle click of the shelf resonated, sealing her fate.

The guard entered the room behind her, the dull thud of his footsteps echoing in her head. She had hidden from sight in barely enough time. But had he heard? She struggled to control her panting breaths and a threatening cough.

"I heard that," he confirmed. "Yer in 'ere"

Hazel swallowed, listening intently for the direction of his steps. They came close, then far again. It was too late. He'd never find her.

He cursed and his steps began to fade away. He was sure to come back with more guards. As much as she ached to, she couldn't leave right then through the window. She needed to steal a cloak to last in this cold and an extra one for Theodore too.

The cloakroom was close, at least, but it meant risking the hallways again. At the end of the hall, it was two whole rooms down. At that moment in time, it seemed like miles.

She found the handle and pushed aside the shelf. As of yet, she hadn't heard any footfalls, only the panicked chatter and coughs of the guests. She couldn't wait any longer. Mortibel himself would soon be rushing down the halls in search of her. She could almost hear him shouting at the guards.

Again, she made off in a run, her skirts weighing her down with each step. The distance had somehow grown larger. A faint haze of smoke obscured her vision. Were those her own steps she now heard or those of another? She coughed again, trying to cover the sound with her hand.

Reaching the cloakroom, she swept inside, bracing herself against the wall so she could catch her breath. The footfalls of more guards came closer, headed straight for her. Just how close was difficult to gauge.

It was too late to catch a breath. She needed to work quickly. She took off her slippers first and grabbed boots that seemed close enough to her size. She slipped right into them and pulled the laces tight. Then in the wardrobe, she grabbed two cloaks from among the guests'. She hid her slippers inside as well. She didn't want to leave any clues behind. She wanted it to appear that she was hiding somewhere. The diversion would afford her more time.

Fully dressed, she used her last remaining bits of strength to propel herself forward through the hall. She needed to get to the back door that led to the gardens, a path she had walked a thousand times as a child.

At the door, all she had to do was step out.

CHAPTER THIRTY-ONE
The Tomb

A COLD BLAST of air almost sent Hazel back inside. The snow was another difficulty. Her every step would be visible. Her only hope was that the guards might not think to look for her out here. After all, who would be desperate enough to risk this weather? Only a woman madly in love.

In the distance, great wisps of snow swirled about the courtyard. That was how Hazel knew it was truly cold. The snow was so frozen, there was not the slightest bit of moisture to clump it together. It was a wonder that anything could survive. Imprisoned in ice, the branches of trees ached and cracked at the slightest breeze.

She wrapped one of the cloaks around herself as the snow crunched beneath her boots and pulled at her skirts.

Assuming she found Theodore alive, how many hours would it take to get to the closest neighboring estate that wasn't Mortibel's? Going on foot would be impossible. They'd have to go to the stables to steal horses.

She bundled the spare cloak tighter in her arms and hands, hoping to keep it warm as her feet dug deeper in the snow.

They'd just have to endure. They only had to make it through the night. They could make it. They had to. She squeezed her fists, not allowing herself to consider any other option. A futile effort that didn't last.

This is another fool's errand, just like my desperate escape into the woods, she thought. But if she found nothing more than a body, she would at least know she had tried. She would at least know the truth of what had happened to him.

Otherwise, it would plague her, the knowledge that she might have been able to do something. Curse the Order and their celebration. She simply couldn't live with that.

She couldn't again make the mistake of leaving him. Not when he'd tried to protect her. He hadn't had to do any of it. He needn't have followed her in the carriage. He needn't have tried to fight off Mortibel, not that night, nor the night in the catacombs. She believed in him fully now. Even if it meant killing others, in the end, he had protected not just her, but the sanctity of the Order.

She could trust Theodore's judgment.

The elixir had seemed to be telling her this all along. She despised herself for not realizing it sooner. She had had so little time with him. It wasn't enough. She wanted more. She would fight this unyielding cold, fight fate itself for more.

She lifted her feet higher and moved faster through the snow. The winds tonight were relentless as they whipped her hair out of her braids and raked across her cheeks. At least the stonewalls of the mausoleum might shield Theodore from the wind. But would it make any difference?

By now, she was halfway across the field, her face numbed with cold. Every passing second, Theodore might be closer to death. Every passing second, the guards were figuring out her trail.

Aside from the occasional whoosh of wind, the silence of winter was palpable. Rather than make her uneasy, it encouraged her, reassuring her that she was still alone. Passing the ivy-covered stones, she was getting closer. She could see the circular dome building. Covered in ice and snow, it glistened in the moonlight.

She ran faster along the hard, frozen snow, the cold air burning her lungs with each inhale. The gate, usually locked, had been left open. Hazel stumbled past it. She caught her balance on one of the stone pillars and looked up in silent prayer.

Though the night remained still and quiet, she had a feeling Mortibel and his guards were not far behind. Mortibel was likely mad with anger. There would be no hope of any freedom now. He'd likely chain her up and imprison her forever.

"Miss Hazel?"

She swept around with a gasp. Samuel, the young groom, stepped out from the shadows. "I feared for a moment you were a ghost."

"What are you doing here?" Had he been forced to keep watch? At fifteen or so, the skinny, ashen-haired boy seemed too young for such a horrible task.

"There's someone down there, isn't there?" Hazel asked.

The boy nodded. He was shivering, from fear or cold, she couldn't tell.

"You shouldn't be here."

"But Mr. Mortibel ordered me…"

"I am your master still. Not Mortibel."

The boy chewed his lip. "He said you weren't anymore. That you signed everything over to him."

Hazel stepped closer with some caution. "If you follow him, that will make you an accomplice to murder."

"'*Murder*'?" The boy shrieked. "I don't want to be privy to any crime, miss."

Hazel went to the door then, but chains encircled the door handles. What else did the foolish boy think was going on here?

"It's a terrible thing, dying of cold," Hazel said, trying to listen for any sounds of life inside.

"Then take it." He held out a key, evidently only too relieved to be handing it over. "I won't hang for this, not for a job."

Hazel grasped his hand before he could turn away. "You can't stay here. Take a horse—any of them. Go to Mortibel's stables for the night, then escape first thing in the morning. Leave and don't come back."

"What will happen here?" he asked, shivering in the cold. "There are rumors that—"

"Never mind the rumors. Just get out of here, you hear?"

"What if I get caught?"

"You can say I gave you permission…just do it!" Hazel demanded.

Samuel nodded and ran off in the direction of the stables.

Hazel turned back to the door. She swallowed her breath and with shaky, cold fingers turned the key in the padlock. The chains were another matter. They were so heavy, they required both hands and two hard pulls to fall away. The clanking sounds likely traveled for miles. She definitely didn't have much time now. Whether or not Samuel could really be trusted was questionable too.

She sucked in a breath and tried the icy, metal handles, but the doors wouldn't budge. There was another lock. In the darkness, she could barely make out the keyhole. She breathed out. Samuel had only given her one key and it wouldn't fit, not even remotely. She warmed her aching hands under her arms, wishing she had had time to find gloves.

She attempted the door again, harder this time. The rusted hinges crackled under the pressure. The door was old enough that perhaps… She pulled again with all her strength. She even picked up the chains and, wrapping them through the handles, yanked harder. But nothing. There was only the crackling of rust. And she was running out of time. That worried her worst of all. The cold was getting colder. Her precious body heat, what she hoped might help revive Theodore, seemed all but gone now, carried off by the wind.

Samuel had to have another key. Perhaps he would return with it. But how long Hazel could stand here waiting, she didn't know. How long before she had no choice but to run off on her own? What might she be leaving behind? Despite the silence, perhaps he was still alive, just unconscious. How could she know?

Holding on to the chains, Hazel screamed out. She didn't care who heard her. She couldn't leave. That would be impossible. If the guards or Mortibel were to find her, she would let them. But louder that time, there was a crack, then tugging again, and a splinter. While the hinges still hadn't quite broken, the wood of the door had snapped along the bottom right corner. Hazel kicked at the weak spot, over and over, until finally, it gave way, breaking at the hinges so she could pull away the door completely.

She didn't even allow herself a breath of relief. A part of her hadn't really believed she would make it all the way here. Now she wasn't sure if she could face the truth, if she had the strength to bear the sight of Theodore's lifeless body. She stepped forward, kicking aside the pieces of splintered wood. The silence pressed on, a heavy weight almost worse than the cold.

A staircase disappeared into deep darkness. She forced herself to descend into the stagnant, chilly air, her hands shaking harder than they had those few moments inside the priest hole, her head pounding harder than that night inside the catacombs. Both events paled to this.

"Theodore?" She tucked her hands under her arms.

He could have been in any state, the sight seizing her with either devastation or relief. There would be no in between.

She hadn't thought to bring a lantern or a candle. Stepping down, she tried to let her eyes adjust. The doorway behind her afforded enough moonlight to reveal the shapes of two tombs lined up along the wall. The rest of the place was varying shapes and shadows. But no Theodore. Had Lenora been lying? Had she been smart enough to improvise that quickly? It didn't make sense. Samuel had to have been guarding something.

Hazel approached each shadow, walking along each wall to ensure she hadn't missed anything. Then finally, a groan gave him away. Horribly weak and brief, the sound twisted her heart.

He lay on the floor behind the tomb closest to the wall.

"Theodore?" She fell to her knees and took him into her arms. "I'm sorry," she said over and over. She wasn't entirely sure why she was apologizing. For not coming sooner? For being the reason this had happened to him? For not insisting on staying with him? There seemed so many reasons.

"You can't stay here," he said, his voice soft and weak. "You should leave at once."

She pulled back to stare at the shadow of his face, his expression barely discernible. He didn't know what he was saying. She wrapped the extra cloak over him. Tears swelled around her eyes, freezing on contact with her cheeks.

"Can you walk?"

Theodore coughed. "He left me for dead. And I should be."

"I won't hear it."

Hazel couldn't sense the entirety of his injuries, but she knew she needed to try. She worked her way along his sides, when he gasped.

"My ribs."

Hazel placed a hand over the bare skin, the blood oozing between her fingers at the slightest touch.

"I'll…I'll get a horse. I'll take you to the next estate. We can call a doctor from there."

"No. You best go. I haven't long."

She refused to accept that. "What about the Order? What's left of your family's legacy?"

"It doesn't matter anymore. We failed. All that matters to me now is you."

"You can't just send me away again. I should have never left for London. Not then, not now." She wasn't going anywhere. She wouldn't make that mistake again.

All he needed was hope for his cause.

"Your name doesn't just belong to you, remember?" she pressed. "It belongs to all those past and future. You have to preserve it."

"Perhaps it is a name best forgotten. Even this one or that one." Theodore motioned to the tombs behind him.

"No," Hazel said firmly. "We can still win back the Order. The moment you recover, we'll return. Then we'll dispose of the elixir. Every drop. Just not tonight."

"They'll just make more."

"Then we destroy the lab."

In the weak light, his smile gleamed.

"You would do all that?" Theodore lifted himself up onto an elbow. "You wouldn't leave at once? You hate this place."

"Not anymore." She cupped his face with both hands, hoping to warm him inside and out.

Theodore placed his icy hand atop hers with surprising strength. Her words were finally beginning to rally him. She had been right—he was ambitious just as Mortibel was, but in a different way. A better way. For a cause Hazel could support. That she might even risk her life for. She owed everything to him. Because of him, she had seen the same magic that had lured so many others to the Order. She'd realized it that night amidst the stones. She couldn't just leave them behind. Not after all that she had discovered. Not with all there was they needed to fix. For the sake of both their families, she needed to stay. They both did.

"We belong here," she told him. "We always have. Together."

She wasn't certain of this. She couldn't be. But she could hope.

"You're right." Theodore struggled to his feet, leaning on the stone crypt behind him for support. She shifted the cloak over him so she could button it all the way down. Their journey across the gardens would not be an easy one, but maybe they would find a horse. Their lives depended upon it.

Up the stairwell, she could suddenly hear steps. Perhaps the stableboy had returned with the key, after all.

"Wait here. I'll be back straightaway, I promise." She helped him sit down again and straightened the cloak around his shoulders. He could last here a little while longer, couldn't he?

As Hazel walked up the stairs, the glinting stars and moon seemed to grow bigger and brighter.

"Must you always involve others with your treachery?" At the top of the stairs, Mortibel stepped into view. "Dr. Lagerfield hates betrayers. Can't stand them to live."

Oddly, he didn't seem angry. As much as he tried to hide it, he was hurt. She could see it in his eyes.

"We were so close, you and I. I could have been your perfect match."

But this, he had only decided recently. After he had discovered what lay in her veins.

"If only you could have forgotten about Pierce. Everything would have been perfect." He truly seemed to mourn the idea. "Unfortunately, I have no choice now."

"Nor I," Dr. Lagerfield appeared suddenly behind him, draped in a heavy cloak.

"Take the estate. You can have it lawfully, just let us go." In a desperate plea, Hazel met him face to face at the top of the stairs.

"You know very well that's not enough." Dr. Lagerfield sighed.

Neither Dr. Lagerfield nor Mortibel, it seemed, would afford her the slightest bit of mercy. She considered running, but running from Mortibel would mean running from Theodore too. So she let him grab her arm and pull her forward without protest.

"You prefer it this way, don't you?" Mortibel spit out at her. "You'd prefer to be forced?"

"I'll fight the whole way," Hazel said. "I'll scream…Unless…"

He pulled her closer. "Unless what?"

"You know the things my father keeps in his laboratory. Heal the wounds you inflicted upon Theodore and I shall go willingly. For however long you desire. I'll give you what you want in peace. I'll give you all of me." The Order didn't matter anymore, only survival. If not for both of them, then at least for Theodore.

Mortibel's eyes widened. "You would do that? For *him*?"

"You allow me to administer it, or I'll not move an inch."

Mortibel looked to Dr. Lagerfield.

"The hour is still young," the doctor replied.

"You think we should let him live?"

"In this weather, the fittest man wouldn't make it a mile."

"At least let him try," Hazel begged. She knew well enough he could make it. He had made it to her door in an icy rain storm, hadn't he? He had been injured then too.

"For heaven's sake." Mortibel released her, shoving her into Dr. Lagerfield's arms. "I'll retrieve the healing serum myself."

Hazel watched him walk away, shivering in Dr. Lagerfield's grasp. Was it disappointment that caused Mortibel's shoulders to sag? Was it possible that he had deluded himself into thinking he truly loved her? He certainly hadn't wanted things to end this way. She could sense that.

"You should be proud of your father," Dr. Lagerfield began what Hazel feared would be a long diatribe. "Willingly or unwillingly, he saved the seers and so many others from death. And now so will you."

That was all she was to Dr. Lagerfield: another sacrifice that would allow the Order to continue to prosper. Now that she was to die, Hazel wished she had known more about her father, that she hadn't kept him at such a distance. Even after seeing him that night of the ritual, she could have written, she could have been made to understand what she had seen. She could have helped him, even. It didn't matter that he had created something that would not only bring himself harm, but all his future heirs.

"If anything, my father died filled with regret," Hazel said.

"He might have, had he known."

"Known what?" Hazel stared back into Dr. Lagerfield's horrible pale eyes. Had he decided to have pity on her? Had he decided she finally deserved to know the truth about her father's death?

"He lied to us. He kept the truth about you hidden for years. And it would have stayed hidden if not for Mortibel. He didn't particularly relish the idea of depending on your father like the rest of us. He wanted to be immune too."

"Mortibel consumed the elixir, even though he knew what it would do?"

"On many occasions. He still has you and what remains of your father, doesn't he?"

Hazel shuddered at the thought of her father's remains. "What have you done with my father's body?" The words escaped her throat with a strangled sound. Though Dr. Lagerfield simply smiled, the answer whispered in her mind. Whatever they had done to him, they would sure enough do to her too.

"Aren't you more curious what Mortibel has seen of late? You, moments from now, upon our marble circle." He smiled briefly. "Your father told me once that you were destined to live here among us. If only he knew the manner in which you'd do so. How sad that would have been for him."

There was no stopping it. The truth of it weakened her knees. Dr. Lagerfield's grip was all that kept her upright.

"When your father refused to help Mortibel become immune, he came to me. Your father didn't deserve his place as chair. He was little better than a servant. But his skills in alchemy were godlike, they said. Soon, they didn't care about my bodily experimentations. It was all about the elixir, this antidote. Then the Pierces gave him—an outsider, mind you—the interim chairmanship. And after all my hard work to force the Pierces out. It was not part of the plan."

Recalling Theodore's story, Hazel pieced it together. "You were the man who gave Theodore those incriminating notebooks. The ones that led to blackmail."

"And I ensured the cabbie might find them too." He seemed so proud. "No, your father didn't deserve the position. He betrayed us, didn't he? He kept you a secret. I always suspected as much. In the end, we had no choice. We took it upon ourselves to find out how your father had made himself immune. For days, we searched through his notes. We discovered the truth about you then. But your father interrupted us. Selfish as he is, he ran, hoping to reveal the truth to you so you, too, could run. Naturally, we couldn't have that."

So her father had tried to save her. He had loved her enough for that. All the while, she had hated him for his interests and the unusual life he'd led.

"He hid out in the remote countryside for months before we found him. If he hadn't kept trying to send you letters—all intercepted, of course—we might have never found him."

She had been right. There had been a time when her father had refused to be let, which had led to the deaths of four seers.

"Then you imprisoned him," Hazel finished.

"It was high time for a shift in power. It was only too easy to blame the Pierces for all that had gone wrong since their departure up north. It helped turn many to our cause."

Hazel should have known Mortibel hadn't killed her father alone. No, her father had had two betrayers. The coward Lagerfield was, he preferred a puppet to do his bidding, a puppet that Mortibel would easily become.

"You should know that more than the chairmanship, Mortibel wanted you. He loved you," Lagerfield said almost sweetly.

Hazel shook her head. Mortibel didn't even know what love was.

"Because I suited his plans," she snarled. "From me, he wants nothing more than an antidote that would last him more years than my father would have given him."

"And a son to inherit your ability, don't forget. What are the things that comprise love if not a desire to give you his child?"

But Hazel wasn't listening any longer. All she could think of was her father. She should have never doubted her own flesh and blood. She had thought him a man too obsessed with alchemy to care for her, but he had really been a silent martyr. A truth no one would ever know. A truth that would die with her.

More tears flooded her vision. This time, for both the father she had lost and all she had been unaware. All the regret and guilt she didn't want to bear. She didn't care for a moment what

Mortibel's feelings had once been. They weren't real. They were based on something entirely self-serving. More than her, more than anything, he loved the Order.

No, she'd never loved him. Not to any degree comparable to what she felt for Theodore. A kind of love Mortibel would never know. And all Mortibel wanted to do now was kill it.

"Is the Order to be led by monsters?" Hazel spit. It didn't seem right, not after what Theodore and her father had sacrificed. The Order, their power more real than she had ever imagined, belonged in better hands.

"As I explained to Mortibel, there are many dark deeds necessary on the road to power."

Hazel hated Lagerfield for the pride that seemed to gleam in his eyes, almost more than she hated Mortibel for killing her father. She was surprised by the sudden surge of anger that warmed her face. It had been building, accumulating ever since she'd been forced to return to Whitestone and watch all the lies unravel before her.

Before Hazel could consider violence, Mortibel approached then, the blue vial in his hand and a lantern in the other. He pushed past the both of them, proceeding down the steps faster than Hazel could follow.

Lagerfield let her slip from his grip, following closely behind. With every step back down, the temperature grew colder. In the light of the lantern, Theodore looked far worse than she had imagined. His lips had turned blue and his skin had little color. She pulled up his shirt. The cut on his side was so much worse than it had felt before. She couldn't make out any skin, just pools of blood. He was minutes away from death—seconds, she feared.

"Give it here." Hazel swiped the vial from Mortibel's hands. She was tilting it toward her hand when Lagerfield stopped her.

"It works faster if he drinks," he said.

Hazel looked to Theodore, who with little remaining strength, nodded. On her knees, she pressed the bottle's lip to his. He grasped her hand with surprising strength, pouring nearly all of it into his mouth.

She moved back and waited for the stuff to take effect. Every passing second, her heart squeezed in desperate anticipation.

Hazel opened the vial again to deliver more, but Mortibel stopped her. "It takes a few moments. His wounds are severe."

She honed in on Theodore's waning breaths. Was it just her imagination or were they growing stronger? The serum would heal him, just as it had healed his arm. It had to. She stared at his still body until finally, his arm shifted an inch. She could just barely see the skin joining together.

Hazel breathed out his name, Theodore's eyes twitching in response. After a moment, they popped open.

"We're merely delaying his demise." Mortibel scoffed. He stepped forward, probably to spew meaner words.

Before he could mutter a word, Theodore swung upward, as if by reflex. Oddly, he seemed to embrace Mortibel. But something was off. He was holding something tight to Mortibel's gut. He pulled back a knife glistening with blood and went in again. The sound of breaking flesh was unmistakable.

Hazel screamed, not for Mortibel—in fact, she was surprised at how little she felt for him—but for Theo. Lagerfield was sure to kill him now. She should have known he'd been armed. One of the statues, she noticed now in the weak light, was broken. The sharp end of what should have been a blade was missing.

She shifted forward toward Theodore, desperate to shield him from whatever retaliation was sure to come, but Lagerfield pulled her back. They were only able to lock gazes. For the first and only time, he mouthed, *"I love you."*

Hazel didn't even have a moment to say it back. Lagerfield, who had enough wits to run, was already pulling her with him up the stairs. But Theodore had his strength back. While Lagerfield forced her along, Theodore thudded after them.

At the top of the stairs, Lagerfield pushed Hazel away and whipped around, cloak fluttering out, to face his foe. Suddenly, an explosion sent Theodore backward. A puff of smoke that could only have come from a pistol clouded her vision. Time seemed to still.

"Stupid bastard!" Lagerfield dragged Hazel backward, sending her stumbling into the snow. She wasn't sure if he was talking about Mortibel or Theodore. She didn't care.

Too weak to move, she lay frozen in the snow, her lungs refusing to let her breathe. The loud bang of the gun seemed so final, separating herself and Theodore forever.

Theodore had known what he'd been doing when he'd taken up the knife. He'd known what it would mean for him. He had accepted it, no doubt—only Hazel couldn't. She was crumbling on the inside. She didn't even care to stand, not even to escape the burn of snow as Lagerfield dragged her across it.

CHAPTER THIRTY-TWO

The Circle

H OW COULD HE? Theodore could have lived. She had been willing to give up everything for him. And yet he had squandered her sacrifice away. All for the sake of killing Mortibel. She didn't mourn his death for a moment. In fact, she was glad. But Mortibel's death wasn't worth his.

Hazel struggled once more against her restraints. Tied tightly to an armchair, she barely managed to loosen them. She could hear the voices of guests departing for the last half hour. With a cravat tied around her mouth, she couldn't yell out if she wanted to.

What was worse, in this dark and silent room, she had plenty of time to recount her past mistakes. Theodore's death consumed her, tearing at her insides, not much different than what he had done to Mortibel. She should have known the outcome. She should have known his desire to die a martyr, especially if he couldn't have her. Then neither would Mortibel.

Hazel jolted in the restraints. Footfalls sounded like thunder in the silence. The dark, twisted things they could do flooded her mind. Uselessly, she struggled against the restraints once more. The image of blood running down her father's back ran across her vision, bringing tears of fear to her eyes. All she could do now was beg.

The door swung open. A burst of light momentarily stung her eyes. She made out three slight figures. One of them held a single, flickering candle and was coming straight for her.

"No point in this now." A woman, her face long and pale, ripped away the cravat.

Hazel shifted back. Inches away from her face was Lenora, a smile twisting her face.

"I didn't think you'd get far."

Hazel wanted to spit at the ghost-like woman.

"Why the face?" Lenora asked. "They're going to dress you in jewels."

"That's hardly why I'm here—"

"Yes, I know. Lagerfield told me everything. They're going to do to you what they did to your father. I should have known it was your blood that was so valuable to them. Not your face..."

The woman ran a hand along her cheek. Restrained, all Hazel could do was jolt in anger. "You know they still use his remains. They're so precious, Marcus keeps them hidden away with the woman he trusts the most. In my home, alongside all my other plant specimens."

Hazel ached at the words, at the same time wanting to vomit. She didn't understand how Lagerfield and Mortibel could have done something so sickening in their pursuit of the so-called gift of foresight. Where would he draw the line? It certainly wouldn't be her.

"You will all get your due," Hazel bit out. "Just like Morti-bel...or don't you know? He's dead."

Lenora's smile fell at once. Just as quickly, she rallied. "Lager-field has made me promises too," she said, almost more to herself.

For Lenora, anyone with power would do. Hazel was certain now that the woman had never had any connection to her father. It had been Mortibel and now Lagerfield with whom Lenora had been involved. Her father had only ever been friends with her mother and nothing more.

"My bond with Lagerfield is more potent," Lenora went on. "Not to mention advantageous. He's the one who allowed me a place here. Trusted me enough…unlike Marcus."

"So long as he's alive." Hazel sniffed. Like Mortibel, he would suffer too. She would find a way to avenge Theodore and her father before the night was through, even if she died in the attempt. Of that, she was certain.

"No more speaking. Robe her," Lenora barked in response.

The two other women approached, but in the weak light, their faces were indiscernible. Their black cloaks disappeared into the darkness as they encircled her.

But who were they? New seers to replace the old? It didn't seem right. She could tell by their graceful, nimble movements, they were young. Her age, perhaps. If they were to drain her, she at least deserved to see their faces.

"Stand," Lenora, who seemed a sort of leader, demanded. Not giving her the chance to disobey, the two other women forced her up. Their fingers began pulling her dress down past her hips until it hit the floor. Hazel let out a breath of relief. She had another few moments of life ahead of her. They weren't going to drain her—they had merely been assigned to dress her.

Stripped down to a long chemise and corset, Hazel was grateful for the darkness. She was prepared to be stripped completely naked when they threw a robe over her shoulders. The velvety material caressed her chilled skin with warmth. In the faint haze of the small flame, she could see the brilliant-red color of it. Quite fitting, really, for a person destined for death.

Their fingers pulled at her hair next, freeing the strands from the confines of her already-loose braids. Was there some sort of hairstyle they preferred? Rather, they let her hair drop freely and messily around her shoulders and back.

When they lifted her hood, she was a nameless figure like the rest of them.

Now, it seemed, the ritual could begin. The women stepped

back, all but Lenora. In her hands, a small glass glistened in the darkness. A bright, amber liquid sloshed inside.

"What is that?" Hazel croaked.

By way of answer, Lenora grabbed a handful of Hazel's hair and pulled her head back. Hazel tensed, struggling against the her grip, which was surprisingly strong.

"You may either drink or be injected with it," Lenora barked. With her other hand, she pushed open her lips. Hazel had no choice but to give in.

A hand covered Hazel's mouth until Lenora could be sure she swallowed. The concoction, whatever it was, didn't burn her throat or taste foul, like she had expected. Rather, it was sweet, almost sickly sweet, like too much sugar in her tea.

Perhaps this was the means by which they would kill her: a sweet poison that would be the end of her. Without Mortibel's plans for marriage gone now, would they want her dead? She swallowed hard. She didn't want to think of the other possibility. Desperate to carry on the line, would they want her to carry someone else's child? Maybe even Lagerfield's?

She grit her teeth. Despite what she had promised, she would never surrender, no matter how heavy their chains. She would never let them break her spirit. After what she had done in the dining hall, they had to know that.

Her breaths came more quickly. She prayed it would be a painless death. Though she was doubtful it would be quick. The First Order had certain rituals they needed to perform over her. With Mortibel gone, Lagerfield was sure to be the ringleader. Something told her he would enjoy watching her demise. However many hours it took, she would be dead before morning.

Lenora and the other women stepped back into the far corners of the room, the haze of the light retreating with them. From the open door, a new figure entered the darkness.

"If Mortibel had been any less of a fool, you would have given you that draft from the start."

"What was it?" Hazel gargled out, her throat filling with

saliva.

Lagerfield didn't answer and grasped her arm. For once, she didn't shove it away. There would be no point.

Pulling her to her feet, he led her into the hallway. Lenora and the two other nameless women followed close behind.

"It'll make you more amenable. In fact, you'll feel quite pleased with it all." He must have noticed her distraught look. "It's nothing to fret over," he cooed. "Your father always took it when he was let."

Feeling her hands begin to shake, Hazel dug her nails into the soft velvet of the cloak around her. She didn't feel any different. Not yet.

"Give it a few moments. It takes time, just like the healing serum." Lagerfield was toying with her, knowing the memory of Theodore's limp body would eat away at her. They had healed him, only to kill him again. Now she would never get him back.

Hazel dragged her heels as they continued to venture through the manor. "Where are you taking me?"

"To the stones, of course. Didn't Theodore tell you about them?" The mere mention of his name struck her heart with a thousand tiny needles.

Never had she imagined that the ritual that had scarred her so much as a child would someday become her own. Never had she considered the possibility. She had been right to follow her instincts to get as far away from the estate as she could. In that, she had almost succeeded. A part of her was glad she hadn't. For Theodore, at least. For the days with him she had never wanted to end.

She considered her options. Begging, bribery? None of it seemed fit for a man like Lagerfield. He seemed the type who, like Mortibel, cared only for power. A man like him turned a cheek to everything else.

Given the clear look in his eyes, he hadn't shed a single tear over Mortibel's death. Hazel certainly hadn't. Not even Lenora seemed to mourn for Mortibel. Not when she cared only for money and status.

"Wait, I almost forgot!" He stilled his steps and so did everyone else. "I have something here even you might appreciate."

Lagerfield produced a necklace. Rubies and emeralds weaved together to mimic tiny, intertwining roses. The priceless jewels shimmered, casting shards of light across the room. Whatever power they held, if any, he didn't say.

Still, Hazel could sense there was something significant about them, simply by the way he placed the necklace around her neck, the feel of Lagerfield's pale, almost-translucent skin making her cringe. Something suppressed her urge to push his arm away. She was calmer than she should have been. The draft was already taking effect.

"Very good." He pulled her forward again, continuing their horrible march. "You're going to feed the plants too, you know. Your blood, I mean."

Hazel didn't respond. All she could do was squeeze her fists. In addition to Mortibel, Theodore should have killed Lagerfield too. He would have had he a few more seconds to catch up. If those stairs had had a few more steps, Lagerfield might very well have been dead. While she enjoyed the thought, it didn't erase her present circumstances.

"All has been prepared. Come," Lagerfield said.

Hazel stumbled forward. Lenora and two other women around her, suddenly considerate, helped her gain her balance. The draft was strengthening its hold on her mind. She could both feel and hear the buzzing in her ears. Her face was suddenly quite warm. Her fingers tingled. The sensations were new and unknown to her. What could they mean? Would she lose all control? How much? Perhaps she would die without even knowing it.

Walking down the brightly lit halls, she had to think quickly. But nothing came to mind. In this part of the house, the halls were tight. There was nowhere to run, even if she managed to get far. Lenora, who seemed to hate her most of all, would catch her too quickly. She loathed the idea of being touched by her again. There was something almost Satanic about her that made her fear even the slightest bit of contact. She half-expected it to burn her skin.

Hazel tried to remain calm. Lagerfield was taking her to the back doors that led to the courtyard. Once again, she would have to face the bitter, cold air. The velvet robe seemed too thin for these conditions.

She was right. Outside, the wind swept across her bare skin like knives. Though it stung and burned, she endured it without complaint. The draft had that benefit at least. She tried her best to stay present.

She focused on the branches that crunched beneath her feet—the vines she had once feared would never die away. But they had and now so would she. Oddly, the thought didn't freeze her heart, as it had earlier. The draft continued to dull her senses. She didn't think about what had happened or what could happen. There was only the path to the stone circle ahead.

They passed the open gateway, the scene ahead mesmerizing her for a moment. The landscape was void of color, the sparkling snow in perfect contrast with the black sky above.

Lagerfield barely held on to her now. He didn't need to. With every step into the great hills beyond, she seemed to leave herself behind. What continued forth was merely a shell, absent of life and any will to fight.

Without the strength to resist, her plans for revenge were pointless. It was already becoming more difficult to think. She was sure she only had a few moments of consciousness left.

Hoping to hold on to herself for a minute or two longer, she breathed in the cool, night air. In the open field, the heavy, abrasive winds blew unhindered. They came at her in full force.

She looked ahead as if to stare down her fate. They had pulled away the vines and exposed the crystals. A dozen, much more than she had expected, came together in a circle, perfectly lined up, all roughly the same height with sharp edges and tips that pointed to the sky.

Instead of fearful, she was relieved, almost, praying the pain of the cold would soon go away. For that alone, she would submit to anything.

"We cleared the crystals just for you," Lagerfield said, as if it were some sort of honor.

They weren't cloudy like other quartz crystals she had seen. Rather, they looked like diamonds, like solid columns of ice that had begun to melt just slightly. She remembered how smooth they'd felt that night with Theodore. Not even the draft they had given her could block out that memory. Her feelings that night were simply too strong. She would hold on to them as long as she could.

"Beautiful, aren't they?"

Hazel nodded. She could not deny that. But their power had been twisted into something evil and that was far from pleasing.

Between each of the pillars, Lenora and the two women joined six other seers. They passed around torches, no doubt eager for the ceremony to begin. They blazed brighter as she stepped closer to the center, the flames swirling in a way she had never seen before, in a way that she was sure could only be a hallucination.

The devils wore silver masks and white cloaks, taking her back to the catacombs. This night, however, wouldn't end with Theodore and his men's brazen interruption. Ironic, almost, that she wished for a sudden surge of bullets. For so long, those men had haunted her, when now they'd seem a godsend.

Never should she have doubted him. The elixir had told her all she'd needed to know. Her eyes filling with tears, she clung tighter to this sense of sorrow and regret, emotions the draft had already begun to numb. The cold seemed to dissipate too. Gone, almost as if it were spring.

How many more seconds of free will had she left? Only her running tears indicated she was still herself.

She imagined the draft as some black substance, spreading

across her eyes until there was only darkness there. Perhaps it would be a blessing to forget Theodore and the pain his death brought to her insides. She prayed for a quick end. No matter how unlikely.

Dr. Lagerfield took her hand then, raising it higher into the air as he delivered her to the center of the circle like some medieval gift of sacrifice. The torches crackled, sending shards of light bouncing off her necklace and into her eyes like daggers. Inside the circle, the gems seemed to grow heavier too, pulling her down into the snow by the neck. But still, Lagerfield dragged her forward.

Finally disconnecting from her side, he stepped back. The cloaked seers closed in now. In perfect unison, their cloaked arms joined together in a swoosh of white fabric, effectively locking her inside.

Instead of snow, she stood on a marble circle, strange engravings swirling together. A pentacle and a half moon, their lines vibrating with the violent rhythm of the seers' indiscernible chants.

Low murmurs came first, chants that were too soft to hear against the crackling of the torches. That was when her whole body started to shake. Most of all her legs. She didn't know how much longer she would be able to stand. She had only a few moments longer before she fell to her knees.

The fall might have shattered her bones—she couldn't be sure. But there was no examining them; her knees were rooted to the platform, impossible to move.

As much as she wanted to scream out, she was incapable. Her lips would no longer obey her, nor her limbs. She seemed barely capable of shivering. She couldn't believe that her father had ever done this willingly. Maybe he never had. How long had she sat idle in London when she could have helped him?

Distracting her, somewhere, something burned. The scent, earthy and sharp, bit at her nostrils. A few breaths and she already felt lightheaded—drunk, almost—swaying until she fell to her side. She was moving in and out of consciousness, her eyes opening and closing against the building streams of smoke. She coughed, still tasting the fire from earlier. The air was dirty and heavy again; she couldn't get a single breath of clean air. Instead, her lungs filled with that tainted air. Her throat felt scalded as if she had swallowed boiling water. The smoke was poison—she was sure of that. As hard as she tried not to breathe it in, some impossible instinct had her gulping it in even deeper.

Between the blackness, she caught the shifting robes at her head, pacing round her. At some point, it had started to rain. But over her body, the drops were red in color. In stark contrast against her skin, like the streaks of blood across snow she had seen in a distant dream. The horrible blood fell faster, thousands of tiny droplets that began to pool around her. Soon the blood would be up past her face and she would suffocate in it. Was that how it would end? She'd assumed blood loss would be her demise. Or perhaps they were toying with her, making her suffer for what had happened to Mortibel. They would bring her to the brink of death and revive her just in time for the next torture to begin.

More droplets of blood, impossibly large, fell upon her. But no, it wasn't blood at all. Blood couldn't float like this. Rather, they were petals. Piles and piles of ruby-red rose petals. Hundreds of them covered her body, not blood, thank God. She sucked in the pleasant fragrance, allowing herself a brief moment of calm.

Then something in the air shifted. The temperature was building in the impossible cold of winter. A blast of sudden heat washed over her. With it, the chanting grew into shouting.

"Stop," she managed, her body jerking from side to side against the sudden heat, drops of sweat running down her face. "Please…"

Her eyes went wide, mesmerized by the petals, no longer stationary, but rising up into the air. They levitated and spun around her. She shouted again, begging them to stop, begging them to end her life. She had had enough.

What were they waiting for? Where were their blades, their vials to store her stolen blood and drain her life away?

Something else was taking over now. Her vision began to blur. There was only the constant shift between light and dark. Rapidly, the darkness was winning the battle, closing in on her field of vision.

Before everything turned to complete blackness, a distant shriek jolted her awake.

For a moment at least, the chanting had stilled and so had their white robes and burning torches. Silence had never tasted so sweet. She already began to feel her blood pulse through her veins again, her heart beating in her chest, the cold marble beneath her skin. The spell was wearing away. Every feeling seemed to return, flooding her with sensation.

She even started to shiver against the cold, winter air, a welcome sensation that meant she was alive. But why? She had expected to fall deeper and deeper into the madness of before. One moment, she had been drowning in it; in another, she had been lifted up, breaking the surface of the water that had engulfed her.

The white cloaks were looking about themselves, whispering with long stares of evident concern. She understood. Whatever spell they had cast had been broken, but she still couldn't move. And her skin was growing increasingly cold. Even when calm, the air cut across her cheeks. She didn't know how much longer she could endure it. What would happen when she reached her breaking point?

Through a veil of tears, the circle of white cloaks was breaking apart. With her last remaining bits of strength, she forced herself up onto an elbow. The seers were running across the field too, no longer in the coordinated movements of before, but in utter chaos.

Everyone save for one. By his frame and hunched shoulders, Hazel knew it had to have been Lagerfield. In front of her, he paced back and forth. In his hand at his side, an unsheathed blade was glistening, as if he were to be her guard.

"Vincent," Lenora's voice rang out, muffled behind her mask. She ran up, intoning his name again with sickening intimacy. "We have to get away!" She continued to beg. But he paid her no attention. He kept close to Hazel. Like gold, she was too valuable to abandon.

Men on horses were racing across the field, driving the others farther away. Lagerfield and Lenora didn't have long before the men came for them too. Lenora at least seemed to know this. She called out his name in harsher tones. Lagerfield shifted back and forth, unsure of what to do. No doubt unsure if he was ready to die.

Hazel, who was actively regaining her strength, knew she didn't have much time to act. During his moment of indecision was when she needed to hit him hard. Reaching out with a fist, she struck the hand bearing his knife.

He was shaking so badly, it fell easily from his hands, clattering onto the ground. He didn't even know what was happening until Hazel had the weapon in her hands. She moved up onto her knees, reaching as high as she could before plunging it down into his stomach.

Lagerfield gave out a horrible noise, then, spreading out his arms uselessly, he fell backward. Hazel tried not to let Lenora's screams distract her as she pulled up the knife and shoved it downward again. With Lagerfield, she had to be sure.

She raised the knife up at Lenora.

"Don't tempt me." Hazel's own voice sounded strange to her, like a monster's.

Lenora just held her hands up, clearly unarmed.

"Go then!" Hazel shouted. "Back to the hills."

Lenora didn't so much as give Lagerfield's crumpled body another glance. He wasn't dead yet. But coughing up blood and shaking, he was close. She wanted to be done with all the violence. Perhaps Lagerfield didn't deserve a quick death, either.

All around her, the distant sound of horse hooves was building. Barely visible against the black of night, two men on horses weaved in and out of the pillars impossibly fast. In the far distance, everyone but herself was running like frightened lambs.

Hazel might have too, if only she could. Dressed in black greatcoats, these men looked just as dangerous as the seers. She just didn't know who they were.

She could merely watch as the men came closer and dismounted.

"Easy now," a man approached.

She shrank away. He had an ugly scar across his face and hair long and messy, like a vagrant.

"Would you mind dropping that?"

Dropping what? Then Hazel remembered. She stared at the weapon, then looked at Lagerfield next, his body still now. Had she really done that?

She let the knife fall from her hands in horror. She didn't know where she had gotten the energy, but it seemed to drain from her now. Her whole body went limp, falling hard onto the marble slab.

"Grice?" someone called out.

She tried to find who was speaking, but her vision continued to swim in and out of blackness.

"She's dazed," the man said between breaths. "They've given her something."

"Of course they did, the bastards," said the second voice, his words cut up by screams behind him. The seers hadn't all escaped like she'd thought.

Hazel couldn't turn around if she'd wanted to. She could hear the familiar blasts of the catacombs. There wasn't the spray of pebbles, just explosions of smoke and the thumps of bodies atop snow.

The two strangers picked her up and brought her back into the warmth, onto something impossibly soft…

CHAPTER THIRTY-THREE
Allies

HAZEL COULD HEAR voices. Shadows shifted across her vision. But for a long while, she was too afraid to open her eyes. There was no knowing what kind of danger she might wake up to.

She still didn't understand who precisely had managed to break apart the seers' deadly circle, carrying her to the comfort of a warm bed and the crackling of a fire. Though she strained to hear it, among the voices, she didn't recognize Theodore's.

But of course he wasn't alive. She had witnessed his death herself, had seen his body thrown back through a haze of heavy smoke. She simply didn't want to accept that he had been left to bleed out and die in the cold. That was supposed to have been *her* fate. And yet despite all the odds, she had lived. What were the chances he had too?

She snapped up at the possibility, no matter how unlikely. She had administered the serum on him, after all. What if it was still working its way through his veins? She didn't know how cold it had gotten in the night, but he could still be alive in the mausoleum, couldn't he? But perhaps not for long.

Taking hold of her surroundings, she found she wasn't in a bed at all, but in the library amidst the familiar shelves and books flicking in the light of a raging fire. She was not bound by chains or rope. But at the other side of the door, was there a guard?

She considered her rescuers. Were they merely another faction of the Order interested in her blood too? If so, what would they do with her?

She covered her face with her hands, shaking her head slowly. How could she even think of herself when Theodore was still out there? Empowered by the possibility, she sprang to her feet. Suddenly, the danger became nothing. Through the thin slit between curtains, a sharp line of sunlight cut across the floor. Morning—it had to be. She prayed it wasn't much later than that.

She threw open the curtains, sunshine reflecting off the smooth sheet of snow. The moment was a miracle of sorts. She hadn't thought she'd make it. Had Theodore once thought the same thing? Last night, he had gladly and no doubt knowingly traded his life to take Mortibel's. Just so he could save her from him. Maybe that had been enough, enough to give himself over to death early in the night.

But Hazel still had to be certain. If she had to return to the mausoleum barefoot, she would endure it.

Hazel went to the door. Before opening it, she pressed her ear against the ornate wood and listened for any signs of movement. Nothing. Only the distant sound of some far-off bird, a pleasant reminder that the cold couldn't last forever. With any luck, spring would arrive early.

She cracked the door open an inch and stepped inside. The smell of half-burned garland still lingered. In the great hall, remnants of the night before were scattered everywhere. The servants had left before cleaning up.

Walking beside the table, she could almost hear the screams again. Broken glass and china crunched beneath her feet. But somehow, a five-tier cake with its delicate white-and-gold piping remained intact. Using her finger, Hazel savored some of the sweet frosting. She had her choice of various fruit-covered tart puddings and petit fours as well.

At the sound of footfalls, Hazel swept around. A man's large frame darkened the doorway. He stepped into the light, his face, marked with the scar she recognized, went still. He raised his hands up as if *she* were the one to be feared.

"Who are you?" Hazel demanded.

Two more men followed in behind him. One of them she recognized from the night before. He was cleaned up now, his red hair combed back. He even appeared a gentleman. The third one had a large, imposing build like the others and a beard. Clearly, they had been brought here for a fight, but for what purpose?

"Miss Grey, is it?" The man with the scar came forward.

"Yes." Hazel swallowed her fear and approached him, if only by an inch.

"I'm Nicholas Grice." He looked back to the others. "We're friends of Pierce's."

"Ah, yes." Hazel recalled what felt like a distant dream. "Theodore told me about you."

"We waited eagerly for word and, receiving none, finally set out to Whitestone. When we crossed paths with a wrecked carriage bearing the Pierce emblem, we took to arms. It was already deep into the night when we arrived. The torchlights led us straight to you."

Hazel forced herself to relax. These men were friends. She just didn't know them by their faces. Once hidden behind masks, they were the ones who had attacked the seers in the catacombs. *Rescued* her, rather. Further emphasizing this truth, they had done so again the night before. She should have been thanking them. The right words, however, were lost upon her.

"We can't find the body." Mr. Grice bowed his head. "Pierce—he's dead, isn't he?"

HAZEL RODE HORSEBACK across the snow. The three others followed close behind.

When she had informed the men of the night's events, there had been no hesitation. They bid she show them to the mausoleum straightaway. Hazel was glad to have their company. She knew them all by their names now. Mr. Lawrence was the one with the thick, blond beard and friendly eyes. Mr. Charleston had the red hair. Mr. Grice was the largest and tallest of all three.

Horse hooves broke through the snow at full speed, sending up puffs of powder. Hazel had never seen snow like this. The top layer had frozen, but beneath, the snow was soft and dust-like.

"It rained last night," Mr. Lawrence said as they set out. It gave Hazel a remnant of hope. Rain meant that it had been warm enough that Theodore might still be alive. But this morning, it had frozen again.

No matter how fast Hazel's horse carried her, the mausoleum seemed miles away. She had to be careful weaving in and around the exposed stones, which were almost invisible during the day, but Hazel was convinced it was the quickest way. In the center, a swirl of red rose petals still covered the marble circle. What she'd once believed had been blood. A strange sense of disillusion had gripped her then. Brought on by that draft, she would never forget the feeling.

Already, that horrid night had seemed to change her forever. The stones had filled her with something. Merely racing past them strengthened it, this odd, new sense of resolve. Even the horse she rode on seemed to sense her newfound determination, hastening its strides.

A few more gallops and the domed building appeared between the evergreens. Mr. Lawrence shouted a command to his horse and all three men kicked their horses and bolted ahead. Out of breath and still exhausted from the night before, Hazel could hardly keep up.

Naturally, she was the last to arrive. By the time she'd reached the stone building, the men were already advancing inside.

"Stop!" Hazel shouted before the men could enter. She dismounted and ran up to the entrance. "I'd like to see him first, if you don't mind." She wanted at least a few moments of privacy if she had to say goodbye.

The men looked at each other, silently debating until Mr. Lawrence nodded.

"Thank you." Hazel stepped over the footprints from the night before: a mingling of hers and Lagerfield's. Once more, she didn't know what she might find inside. But she couldn't be afraid. There was no time for hesitation.

"Pierce!" Mr. Grice shouted from behind her. But in return, there were no words or even the slightest ruffle of movement. "Go on now."

"Give her a minute, will ya?" Mr. Charleston spat back. "A few more moments won't make a difference now." As much as Hazel didn't want to admit it, Mr. Charleston was right. Dead or alive, Theodore's fate was already sealed.

She walked past the open, splintered doorway. The air was cooler within, as if the bricks themselves were made of ice.

"Theodore?" She called out his name weakly, her voice echoing down the stairs. But again, no answer came. Surely, if he was alive, he would have heard her in the silence of winter. Hazel paused on the staircase.

She had been filled with too much hope. Now she wasn't sure if she could do this again. What were the chances of her finding him alive twice? No, she was far more likely to find his corpse, pale blue and cold to the touch. She might even trip over it as she descended the stairs. Streaks of hot tears warmed her face. At least she would be the first to say goodbye.

She looked back. The men hovered in the doorframe. Their figures blocked the sunlight, but even a fraction of it still afforded her much more visibility than the night before. The room was illuminated intensely enough that she spotted him quickly. A dark lump of a man huddled at the bottom of the stairs, perfectly still, perfectly dead.

Hazel pieced it together at once. The blast of gunfire had thrown him backward down the stairs. No matter how much the serum healed him, if the bullet hadn't killed him, the fall had at least rendered him unconscious.

She hesitated no longer. She rushed up to his side, feeling his cold, hard skin through the fabric of the cloak she'd given him. It could only have kept him warm for a little while, not the entire night. She couldn't bear to look at his face. On her knees, she could only stare at the cold, tile floor of what had been his prison. One last time, she clenched his hand.

She had expected blood, a whole pool of it. Oddly, there was none. Had Lagerfield's bullet missed him entirely? Was it the cold that had brought on his demise?

She was about to loosen her grip when his fingers moved. It took her a moment to fully believe it. When he coughed her name, there could be no mistake.

It was impossible. Neither of them should have been alive. But they were and Hazel would not waste it, even if she had only a few moments. She checked him for wounds first, running her hands all over him. The feel of him dry and without blood confirmed once more that he had not suffered a bullet wound.

Both grateful and confused by it, Hazel threw her cloak over him and tried to lift him. There was no time to waste with sentiments. "We need to get you out of here."

Hazel turned to shout for help, but reaching out, he stilled her, his hand cupping her face. She didn't care that it was like ice. His glistening eyes so familiar, they brought back a dozen different memories.

"I told Him I wouldn't stay without you, that He had to send you here before you suffered a single moment." His teeth chattered. He was confused; the cold must have done that.

"Come." She pulled him toward the light streaming down the stairs, beckoning them to escape.

With an odd reverence, he grasped a strand of her hair. Like the night before, it still hung loose around her shoulders. A strange and distant look filled his eyes. Almost as if he had been dreaming. "Give us a few moments first, while I still have my earthly wants."

She would have almost laughed, if not for the blue tinge of his lips and the paleness of his cheeks. She understood now what he had mistakenly believed.

"We're not dead," Hazel tried to tell him.

He blinked. "You're wrong."

"Rather, I'm in love with you." She didn't care if he still believed they were dead—she at least needed him to know that much. She had been so desperate to tell him that the night before. In this very spot.

His face brightened. "I'll leave with you this time. Nothing shall stop us."

"Don't you remember? I told you I would stay. I told you I would burn down the lab if I had to. But we need not. We can claim the Order for ourselves."

"Then stay I shall." His eyes fluttered closed.

"No." She shook him, half-laughing. "Not in this cold. We must go now."

His hand shifted to the nape of her neck, pulling her in for a kiss. For a moment, she surrendered, if only to savor the taste of him and warm his icy lips. Losing herself, she pulled him in even closer, pausing only when he winced. She couldn't forget his condition, the frostbite that could be eating away at his toes and limbs as they remained here, wasting precious time.

"Theodore. Please. Can you walk?"

Even if the men came down to help, it would take longer to carry him up the stairs. Perhaps too long.

He nodded.

"Then you have to follow me."

"Anywhere," he mumbled.

With surprising alacrity, he shifted to his knees and then to his feet. "We shall have had a wonderful reign together, you and

I."

Hazel smiled at the idea. What had seemed so impossible weeks ago in London was actually happening. They had been given another chance.

Climbing the stairs, she let him lean on her, not minding when Theodore's icy cheek and hands pressed against her. They had only made it halfway when the men came running.

Despite her firm grip, Hazel allowed them to pull Theodore away, their eyes gleaming with unshed tears. They wouldn't have understood why Theodore shared their tears, mumbling, "You too?"

They rode back to the warmth of the manor, Theodore half-asleep behind Mr. Lawrence. Hazel had refused Mr. Grice's cloak. Somehow, the oppressive cold of winter seemed to have lifted. She no longer minded the silence, either. There was too much of their future to consider. She couldn't tell if Theodore had realized the truth yet. But if he had, she hoped he had meant what he had said about a reign together. She played the words again in her mind. Words she hadn't realized she had been waiting so long to hear.

She didn't mind the Order now. The society had its dark sides—the elixir—but its brighter ones too—the serum. What mattered was how they chose to use these tools. In Theodore's and her hands, and with all the knowledge her father had left for them, the Order could be something entirely different.

For this purpose, it seemed, heaven had spared Theodore. When Mr. Grice, playing doctor, examined him, he found that Theodore hadn't suffered frostbite on any of his limbs or even his toes. Nor had he found a bullet wound. Whether Lagerfield had missed or the serum still coursing through Theodore's veins had healed him, they couldn't be entirely sure. At the very least, it had kept him from dying from cold, Mr. Lawrence had said. More Silver Order magic. Hazel didn't care how scientific her father believed it to be. Theodore's survival was nothing short of a miracle.

CHAPTER THIRTY-FOUR

A Promise

I T TOOK THEO some time to fully understand how he'd gotten here, sitting beside Hazel as they sipped tea next to the fire. It was like he had never been left to die in the mausoleum at all. But he knew the truth now. Hazel had reminded him that he had almost died not once, but twice. He wasn't just *lucky* to be alive—he was *grateful*.

After a few cups of tea, he had completely returned to his senses, the delirium entirely behind him now. The complete reality of what had almost happened slowly began to dawn on him.

It wasn't what he'd had to endure that twisted at his gut, it was what Hazel had. More than that, how it might affect her view of the Order. If he were being honest, how it might have affected her view of *him*. She had seen it all now. Some of the Order's worst, most sadistic rituals, she had stood witness to. No, had been a *victim* to. And he hadn't been there to stop it.

While Theo remained in quiet contemplation, Lawrence filled the silence with talk of their own woes the night before. How their horses had struggled to make it there from London in, at times, three feet of heavy snow. How they had still been tired from their travels when they had heard the chants and discovered

Hazel in the midst of Lagerfield's bloodletting ritual—the very same Theo had accurately guessed Mortibel had meant to perform in the catacombs.

"Lagerfield, he was the catalyst in all of this," Hazel informed them. "He had instructed Mortibel from the start. If Mortibel *had* become chairman, he would have been no more than the other man's puppet."

Theo blinked, in disbelief. In one evening, they had connected so many dots.

"Lagerfield had a hidden animosity toward my family for years, I think," Theo said. It didn't take long to deduce that the same man who had invited his family to stay with him in London had meant for Theo to lose those notebooks. The blackmailer had likely been working for him too. It was all so embarrassing. Even if it had been part of a plot, Theo and his family had been tricked. He couldn't bear to admit it out loud.

After all that had happened, Lagerfield's motives were clearer than the crystals. There was no need to discuss that part of Theo's life any further. He hoped the conversation would end there. Hazel, however, wasn't afraid to face even the harshest truths.

She blew a sprinkling of ash off a raspberry tart and told them more of what Lagerfield had confessed and how her father had tried to tell her the truth.

"After all the horrible things I had come to believe, after ignoring my father for years, in the end, he died trying to save me."

Hazel was not alone in her struggle to keep back tears.

"Did you know him?" Hazel asked of the men.

"Of course, we're all members here," Charleston said.

"Perhaps to an entirely new Order." Lawrence looked to Theo.

He didn't answer. His hands held tightly to his teacup. He was trying not to let the guilt swirling inside take hold. No matter how hard he tried to ignore it, it was there. Theo feared it would always be.

Had his friends not arrived, had they waited another day for a message, what would have happened to them?

Of course it all seemed so obvious now, neatly explained away. But there would have been no way for him to know, no way for him to stop what had almost happened to her. He hated when things swayed so wildly out of his control. He needed to take it back.

"I killed Lagerfield," Hazel said abruptly, though it was no doubt on everyone's minds.

When Theo couldn't find the words, Lawrence cleared his throat.

"For that, we owe you each a debt and so does all of the Order, though they might not yet know it," Lawrence said. "Under Lagerfield, the Order would have become something different, something horrid."

The other men nodded.

"Does it trouble you?" Grice asked. "Sometimes no matter how just a death is, it can still be bothersome."

"Thank you." Hazel smiled weakly. "But, in time, I'm sure I shall come to terms with it all."

At last, the men fell into silence, giving Theo his chance. He'd wanted to be alone with Hazel since the moment she'd woken him in the mausoleum. He took to his feet.

"If none of you mind, I'd like to speak with Hazel alone." He pulled the blanket from his shoulders and threw it over the chair.

The three men got up at once, murmuring awkward words of understanding.

Though he wanted to do so much more than speak, the bastards had left the library door open a crack. It didn't help that he was suddenly nervous. He could barely move from his spot behind the armchair.

He cleared his throat. "You need not stay here out of pity for me, you know. I would understand if you left."

"Left?" She looked at him, blinking.

"After what happened, you must hate the Order now more

than ever before," he said. "I know you must want to get away. I'm not so sure I'd stay myself. The place carries too many painful memories."

"Have you forgotten everything I've told you in the mausoleum? About staying?"

He stumbled slightly when he stepped forward.

"Careful." Hazel stood up and steadied him, her arms gripping him in a half-embrace.

"I can't wait any longer." He pulled her in closer. "Tell me what do you plan to do and I will make my considerations. If it means leaving this place, I will."

For a moment, Hazel just stared, her lips parting. "You would really leave all this?"

"I promised myself I would if you and I survived. You were right. I do deserve a life outside the Order. We both do."

"You've forgotten again." She smiled. "One day, I want to go over everything with you. From start to end, no matter how painful. Maybe even write it all down."

Hazel turned to the window. The stones stole away her attention for a moment. Fully exposed, they sparkled in the sun.

"I felt their power coursing through me last night," she said. Scattered across the snow, their power was evident once more.

"Surely, a life outside the Order would be easier."

"Then why do I struggle to leave all of it behind?"

"You mean..." Did she really want to stay? Gads, that made everything so much easier.

"I told you this. Twice, in fact."

"Then I think..." He closed in on her. There was something else he needed to say too, or rather, ask. He just didn't know precisely how she might react. After the chaos of the last few weeks, would she ask for more time? "We survived last night for a reason."

"Why, pray tell?"

"So we could have a life that was far more than ordinary. Together. I know we haven't gone about things the way we ought to, certainly not the way they might in London. A lapse in judgment on my end, we'll say."

"Theodore. You don't have to apologize."

He thought for a moment to correct her, to tell her to call him "Theo," as he had so often told others who were close to him. But coming from her, he rather liked how his proper name sounded.

"It's quite all right," she went on. "We can just pretend—"

"I'm not going to take it back," he said so fiercely, he felt her shiver. "Everything I did, I meant. I wanted it too much. Hell, I might very well have a second lapse again." He grinned. "You've stirred something inside me, Miss Hazel Grey. In a way I thought only the Order could do."

He grasped her hand. "I won't let it be put off any longer. Nor will I let any other unforeseen event separate us. Marry me," he said rather brusquely.

She looked down at his tight grip and back up at him. He wasn't letting her go for anything. He stood there, transfixed and vulnerable at the same time. She seemed to enjoy it for a moment longer, then she beamed. "Yes."

A new glow of goodness seemed to descend upon the place with Lagerfield and Mortibel gone, a glossy sheen that reflected back at them off the crystalline surface of the stones. Their power was strong, yes. But Hazel and the feel of her newly warmed skin was stronger.

EPILOGUE

HAZEL PEERED THROUGH the black lace of her veil. A crowd much larger than she'd expected was half-immersed in fog. There had to have been at least a hundred or so people surrounding the mausoleum. Some members, some not, they had all come to celebrate her father's memory and, at last, lay him to rest.

With the rising fog, the icy wind of winter had faded away. Though the evening proved dark and overcast, warm, dew-filled air embraced her. The lawn, though damp, was at least green and free from snow.

At her side, Aunt Catherine took a deep breath and let it out in a *whoosh*. Her health improved, Hazel's aunt had been convinced to leave London, temporarily at first. But ever since she had stepped out of the carriage and taken in the fresh, morning air, she had offered Hazel no further argument.

Aunt Catherine had only been here two days and already, Hazel noticed a difference in her breathing. It was less wheezy and sometimes accompanied with a sigh—one of relief, Hazel liked to think. Her once-ashy skin and lips had more color too. As always, she was overdressed. This time, she was wrapped in pearls that had even been worked into her braids.

Aunt Catherine had even smiled when she'd learned of Hazel's engagement to Theodore. There would be no additional Seasons for Hazel, after all. But her aunt didn't seem to mind much. What mattered was that Hazel had found love. Aunt Catherine wouldn't hate it here, not after Hazel explained the truth of her father's "ways." They would have all of tomorrow to discuss that, even Emmerson's horrible betrayal. In the meantime, Aunt Catherine let slip a few more smiles.

Pierce's parents had arrived too, endlessly grateful—thanks to Hazel saving his father's life—and only too happy to have a new daughter to add to the family.

Funeral or not, there seemed so much hope in the air, even if there was still that tiny tinge of danger.

Hazel gripped the crook of Theodore's arm, put at ease with his presence and the ten or so guards he had insisted upon hiring for good measure. Thanks to Hazel's mercy, Lenora was still about, but she had fled from the Malvern Hills. So had Miss Mortibel's former lady's maid.

Alas, there would be no justice for Miss Mortibel. All Hazel could think about was her father. He'd already lost his son to a duel, or so the police had concluded when they'd discovered Mortibel's body on his drive. Theodore may have even been a suspect. But for a man in his position, the police were willing to look the other way.

The elder Mr. Mortibel, however, could never look the other way, especially when it came to his daughter. Eventually, his letters to India would go unanswered. He would never know what became of Miss Mortibel. If he'd known his son and the lengths he would have gone to for the Order, perhaps he might guess. While Hazel wanted to write anonymously and reveal the truth of what had happened, she couldn't risk an investigation.

She had to remind herself that it was Mortibel's fault, really. What they'd found in the days after the solstice would serve as the ultimate reminder.

According to Theodore and his men, Lenora's small cottage had been left ransacked. In her greenhouse, plants had been left to die, all her bottles, books, and remedies gone. In her frenzy to flee, she had forgotten one thing.

Underground in her vacant cellar, Theodore alone had found them. Remains small enough to fill in the marble urn that stood beside them now, no larger than a milk crate—a gory mess that had left little of her father behind. Beyond that, Hazel had refused to learn any more details. Even if she had wanted to identify the body, it would have been impossible, Theodore had said. But *the way* in which it had been found, its purpose had been clear enough.

One day, everyone in the Order would know exactly what her father had done. How he had tried to save her, even though he had failed. Hazel herself would see to it that his story was not just told, but written down.

For now, he would at least have a proper burial. He would be in good company because from this day forward, the mausoleum would house not only Pierces, but any individual who had served the Order with either greatness, sacrifice, or both. Theodore had even had a dedication engraved into the wall: *Though they didn't share the same blood, they shared the same oath.*

When her time came, she, too, would lay beside him—the father she had never known. The man she had promised to spend her time in the afterlife coming to know.

Drops of rain caught on her veil. Heads bowed, the last of the mourners paid their final respects to the urn and, in small groups of black, trailed toward the manor for the banquet that was to follow. Her aunt went ahead, leaving Hazel and Theodore as the last to cross the lawn.

They walked in silence, closer now that they were free from onlookers. His fingers grazed over her wrist with increased intimacy. But for the moment, Hazel's mind was somewhere else. She couldn't help but wonder, besides her blood, how else was she like her father?

Was she willing to die to protect her own too? Or like Theodore, was she willing to die for a name? If the occasion called for it, she hoped so. As they walked across the green expanse between the stones covered again in the emerald vegetation, there was no knowing what acts such secrets might demand.

A sharp wind rolled past, catching wisps of her hair. The power in the air seemed to crackle, reminding her of all the stones could do. A word of caution, perhaps.

THE END

About the Author

Ella Leon writes historical romance with a twist of magic and suspense.

During her 9–5 career, she has delved into many different styles of writing: journalism, public relations and marketing. Fiction, however, is where she finds the most freedom to transform the page. Like the Victorians she writes about, she loves all things gothic and supernatural. Unlike the Victorians, she is a feminist who enjoys exploring the precolonial past.

When she's not writing, you can find her spending time with her family or tending to her rose garden. She lives in the Chicago area.

Links:
Website: ellaleon.weebly.com
Facebook: facebook.com / ella.leon.author
Tiktok: tiktok.com / @ella_leon
Threads: threads.net / @e.k.toth
X: @Stoeverit

9 781965 539736